Other books by Brian Harris

The Surprising Mr Kipling (CreateSpace, 2014)

> An anthology and re-assessment of the poetry of Rudyard Kipling.

> 'A splendid selection... both the material and the introductory discussions are just what we need for a better appreciation of such a massive and many voiced figure.' Dr Rowan Williams.

Tales from the Courtroom (CreateSpace, 2013)

> 'This near 400-page anthology is well served by the elegant prose and dry wit of Mr Harris.'

> 'A fascinating collection'

Passion, Poison and Power (Wildy, Simmonds and Hill, 2010)

> 'A compelling read.'

Intolerance (Wildy, Simmonds and Hill, 2008)

> 'should inspire any number of debates, arguments and disputes, not just among the legal fraternity, but among a much wider readership ...'

Injustice (Sutton Publishing, 2006 now The History Press)

> '... an excellent and ... unique book'

> '... plainly the result of real scholarship'

The Two-Sided Man

A Selection of the Short Stories of Rudyard Kipling

Edited with commentaries and an introductory essay by

BRIAN HARRIS

ISBN: 1508712328
ISBN 13: 9781508712329
Library of Congress Control Number: 2015904310
CreateSpace Independent Publication Platform
North Charleston, South Carolina

CONTENTS

ACKNOWLEDGEMENTS

I am deeply indebted to John Walker M.A., librarian to The Kipling Society for reading an early draft of this anthology and for his wise advice that set my feet in the right direction.

My thanks are also due to my talented grand-daughter, Sarah for her fine sketch of Rudyard Kipling which is incorporated in the cover design.

Much I owe to the Lands that grew-
More to the Lives that fed-
But most to Allah Who gave me two
Separate sides to my head.

('The Two Sided Man')

LIST OF STORIES

The Story of Muhammad Din

('Plain Tales from the Hills')

The unnamed narrator of this story is an Englishman who has a Muslim Khitmatgar, or servant. The infantile games of the servant's child at first annoy, and then amuse the Sahib. Until fate intervenes.

In the House of Suddhoo

('Plain Tales from the Hills')

The narrator describes how he found himself unwittingly caught up in a 'magical' fraud upon an elderly landlord by one of his tenants.

Beyond the Pale

('Plain Tales from the Hills')

A story of the love between a young British civilian and a fifteen year old Indian girl which ends in tragedy when she discovers that he has also been 'attentive to a European lady of his acquaintance'.

The Strange Ride of Morrowbie Jukes

('The Phantom Rickshaw and other Eerie Tales')

Unable to sleep because of a fever, a civil engineer rides out into the desert night to escape the barking of wild dogs. His horse bolts and falls with his rider into a sandy crater that proves to hold horrors undreamed of by the young man.

The Man Who Would be King

('The Phantom Rickshaw and Other Tales')

Two British adventurers enter a remote province of Afghanistan in search of a kingdom. Their success exceeds all expectations - until their luck turns.

At the Pit's Mouth

('Under the Deodars')

A wife ignores her husband's demands that she ends her affair with another. One day they witness a grave being dug.

On the City Wall

('In Black and White')

The beautiful Lalun plies her trade – the oldest one – to a mixed clientele from her house on the city wall. Outside and thirty feet below is the city ditch; inside, a prison harbouring a notorious rebel.

In Flood Time

('In Black and White')

A flooding river gives time for an old ferryman to tell a traveller a tale of long ago when his rival in love inadvertently saved him from drowning.

The Bridge Builders

('The Day's Work')

The conflict between Western technology and 'the old gods' of India is played out against the construction of a mile and three quarter long bridge being built over the holy river Ganges.

They

('Traffics and Discoveries')

More than in most of his stories Kipling pours his own life experience into this tale of a motorist lost in the Sussex countryside who discovers a mansion filled with happy children whom not everyone can see.

Regulus

('A Diversity of Creatures')

'Regulus' cleverly links the teaching of an Horation Ode in a classics class with a discussion between two of the masters concerning the nature and purpose of education.

Mary Postgate

('A Diversity of Creatures')

This, one of Kipling's most enigmatic tales, seemingly depicts the cruelty of a middle aged Englishwoman towards an injured enemy airman. But almost every element of this shocking story is open to more than one interpretation.

Friendly Brook

('A Diversity of Creatures')

Intrigued by a neighbour's decision not to save his hayrick from the flood-ed brook, two Sussex labourers interrupt their work to reflect upon the strange tale of his adopted daughter and a blackmailer.

The Eye of Allah

('Debits and Credits')

'The Eye of Allah' explores what might have happened if a seventeenth century invention had fallen into the hands of a group of scholars in a thirteenth century monastery.

The Gardener

('Debits and Credits')

'Every one in the village knew' that the spinster, Helen Turrell had brought up the son of her dead brother, only to lose him in the war, and it seemed only natural for her to seek to find the boy's grave. To tell more would be a disservice to the reader.

The Wish House

('Debits and Credits')

'The Wish House' takes the form of a conversation between two elderly women who have been friends since childhood. At the heart of it is how one of them resorted to the 'supernatural' in a desperate effort to save her lover.

A Madonna of the Trenches

('Debits and Credits')

Just after the 1914-1918 war the proceedings of a Masonic Lodge are disturbed by the hysterical outburst of a young ex-soldier. After he has been calmed down he reveals a strange story involving the deaths in the trenches of two lovers.

Dayspring Mishandled

('Limits and Renewals')

A man resolves to take his revenge after a friend makes an insulting remark about a woman they had both loved. But all does not work out as planned.

The Church that was at Antioch

('Limits and Renewals')

When a young roman officer is seconded to the city of Antioch in Syria his task is to resolve the complex religious squabbles of the different religious communities. He succeeds, but there is a price to be paid.

KIPLING'S SHORT STORIES
AN INTRODUCTORY ESSAY

In this Essay the titles of stories reproduced in this book
are indicated by an asterisk, and the titles of anthologies,
where they first appear, in bold type.
References to sources are to the volumes listed in
the Select Bibliography at the end unless otherwise stated.

What should we make of someone like Rudyard Kipling who was a publishing sensation in his early twenties and an internationally respected figure in his middle years, but who not long after his death could be said to have 'dropped out of modern literature'?

At the height of his fame Mark Twain described Kipling as 'the only living person not head of a nation, whose voice is heard around the world the moment it drops a remark ...' (Albert Paine. 'Mark Twain. A Biography'). He was so revered that once when his family fell ill in New York bark was spread on the streets to lessen the noise of passing traffic. He was awarded the Nobel Prize for literature and the Gold Medal of the Royal Society of Literature, and he was elected the first Foreign Associate Member of the Académie Française.

But even from the start of his career Kipling had attracted criticism, both for his work and for his opinions. Oscar Wilde famously declared of one of his earlier works that, 'As one turns over [its pages], one feels as if one were seated under a palm-tree, reading life by superb flashes of vulgarity'. ('The True Functions and Value of Criticism.' The Nineteenth Century, September 1891). And the Scottish journalist, Robert Buchanan described his stories as dealing 'almost entirely with the baser aspects of our civilisation, being chiefly devoted to the affairs of idle military men, savage soldiers, frisky wives and widows, and flippant civilians' ('The Voice of the Hooligan', 1899). Kipling's vigorous but ill-judged support for his country's war against the Boers damaged his reputation in the eyes of many. His political views fell out of fashion with the disillusion with established institutions that followed the Great War. And his standing as the unofficial spokesman of empire crumbled with the growth of independence movements around the globe.

Less than two decades after his death Kipling's reputation had fallen so low as to allow the American, Edmund Wilson to conclude that 'The more serious-minded young people do *not* read him; the critics do not take him into account.' Some were positively vitriolic. George Orwell, for example, asserted that 'It is no use pretending that Kipling's view of life, as a whole, can be accepted or even forgiven by any civilized person...' (Horizon. February, 1942.) And Dylan Thomas declared that Kipling 'stands for everything in this cankered world which I would wish were otherwise.' (Letter to Pamela Hansford Johnson, 1943). It is difficult to think of another major English writer who has been so badly mauled.

And yet, at a time when Kipling's reputation was at its lowest, a man of unimpeachable literary credentials stepped forward in his defence. In the introductory essay to his 1942 anthology the Modernist poet, T.S. Eliot undertook a major re-assessment of the writer's poetry that caused a considerable stir. Others lined up to do the same for his prose. Soon, Kipling began to reappear on university syllabi and once again became a subject for dissertations in English departments.

This collection is confined to Kipling's short stories, which were his métier. (He tried his hand at the novel, but save for one glorious exception, without great success.) In 1952 W. Somerset Maugham, himself no mean exponent of the medium, hailed him as 'our greatest short story writer. I can't believe he will ever be equalled. I am sure he will never be excelled'. The poet, Craig Raine agreed, adding that he was 'one whose achievement is more complex and surprising than even his admirers recognize.' (Preface to 'The Wish House and Other Stories'.)

The aim of this book is to introduce to a new generation of readers one of England's greatest writers whose merits have for too long been overlooked. But first I need briefly to sketch in the writer's background and the sources of his inspiration.

In the hush of an April dawning

For a future author Rudyard Kipling chose his parents well.

John Lockwood Kipling has been described as a 'rare, genial soul with happy artistic instincts ... and a generous, cynical sense of humour' (Kay Robinson. M'Clure's Magazine. 1896). He met his future wife, Alice at a picnic on the edge of a reservoir known as Lake Rudyard in Staffordshire. Although she had been engaged more than once before, this time it was love at first sight. Fascinating and flirtatious with a sharp edged wit, Alice came from the lively and talented MacDonald family. Of her three sisters one was to marry a famous painter, another a future president of the Royal Academy, while the third was to become the mother of a prime minister. The family had friends among the Oxford Brotherhood (modelled on the Pre-Raphaelite Brotherhood), which was a good fit with John's job at the Victoria and Albert Museum. Within two years the pair were wed.

But John's prospects in England did not look bright and shortly after his marriage he took a gamble and left with his wife to take up a post in the Jeejeebhoy School of Art in Bombay (now known in India as Mumbai.) He meant to try, in the words of the Dictionary of Literary Biography, 'to preserve, at least in part, and to copy styles of art and architecture which, representing a rich and continuous tradition of thousands of years, were suddenly threatened with extinction.' The couple's first child, the aptly named (Joseph) Rudyard, was born soon thereafter. Known in the family as 'Ruddy', he was to recollect the workshop of his father's School as a 'marvellous place filled with smells of paints and oils and lumps of clay with which I played.' Two years later John secured the chair of architectural sculpture at the School, subsequently becoming its principal. He moved from there to the post of head of the newly created School of Arts in Lahore (now Pakistan's National

College of Arts) in what was then the northernmost part of India. Three years after the birth of Rudyard the Kiplings had another child, christened Alice but known in the family as Trix.

Over the years John Lockwood became a celebrated ceramicist and conservationist, journalist and illustrator. While in charge of the Indian exhibits at the Paris exhibition of 1878 he took his son with him, thus igniting in the boy a lifetime love affair with France and the French. When Ruddy started his writing career his father supplied the illustrations and offered advice on the text that was always gratefully received. Kipling was to recall him as, 'a humorous, tolerant, and expert fellow-craftsman'.

The house of desolation

In his infancy Ruddy had been cosseted by two loving parents, as well as an attentive ayah, or nursemaid, and guarded by a bearer, but all this was to end dramatically before he reached his sixth birthday. After a short period of leave in England his parents returned to India, leaving five year old Ruddy and three year old Trix in the care of paid foster parents in Southsea, then a village outside Portsmouth. The father of the house was an old sea captain whom Ruddy took to immediately; the problem lay in his wife, Mrs Holloway, who ran the house, in Kipling's words,

> 'with the full vigour of the Evangelical as revealed to the Woman. I had never heard of Hell, so I was introduced to it in all its terrors - I and whatever luckless little slavey might be in the house, whom severe rationing had led to steal food. Once I saw the Woman beat such a girl who picked up the kitchen poker and threatened retaliation. Myself I was regularly beaten. The Woman had an only son of twelve or thirteen as religious as she. I was a real joy to him, for when his mother had finished with me for the day he (we slept in the same room) took me on and roasted the other side. I have known a certain amount of bullying, but this was calculated torture - religious as well as scientific. Yet it made me give attention to the lies I soon found

it necessary to tell: and this, I presume, is the foundation of literary effort'

Ruddy was sent to 'a terrible little day-school' where he failed to perform well, for which he was sternly punished. Books formed some sort of escape, but too much reading in bad light led to eyestrain. 'Some sort of nervous breakdown followed, for I imagined I saw shadows and things that were not there...' Trix was not immune from the harsh regime - she was once made to stand on a table in punishment for her 'crimes', but 'the Woman reserved her worst 'punishments and humiliation - above all humiliation' - for himself. His only respite were his visits to his mother's sister, the talented Georgiana Burne-Jones at The Grange, in Fulham, where for a month each year he 'possessed a paradise' of 'love and affection'.

Word finally got back to his mother who returned to England to reclaim him. She told him afterwards that when she first came up to his room to kiss him goodnight, he flung up an arm to guard off the cuff that he had been trained to expect. Some commentators are inclined to play down Kipling's sorrows on the ground that he had was a spoilt brat who had exaggerated his sufferings. They point to the fact he was known as a child to have had a temper and question why, when he was eventually 'rescued' by his mother, she allowed Trix to remain in the care of Mrs Holloway. But, even if Kipling's recollections of Southsea were no more than an over-dramatization of the unsympathetic fostering of a delicately brought up child, it is what he felt that matters. And of that his memoir leaves no doubt.

Sending children 'home' to England for cultural and health reasons at so young an age was common practice among Anglo-Indians at the time. It is nevertheless a mystery why Alice elected to send hers to people chosen from a newspaper advertisement rather than lodging them with any one of her many relatives. Trix was later to reveal another reason for the two children's unhappiness when she wrote: 'the real tragedy of our early days, apart from Aunty's bad temper and unkindness to my brother, sprang from our inability to understand why our parents had deserted us. We had had no preparation or explanation; it was like a double death.' (Quoted by Edmund Wilson.) Kipling never blamed his mother for this betrayal, but it must have rankled.

'Stalky'

At the age of twelve Ruddy was sent to the United Services College at Westward Ho! in Devon, recently founded by a group of army officers as a preparation for Sandhurst. The school was chosen because the head-master, Cormell Price, or 'Crom', was a family friend, and because its fees were low. Nevertheless, Kipling's first year and a half at Westward Ho! was yet another time of grief. In those days boys at British public schools were routinely bullied by staff and pupils alike and he was the only be-spectacled child in the school, mature beyond his years, with bushy eye-brows and an incipient moustache. The chaplain seems to have been the leading tormentor and things improved considerably when he was re-placed, releasing after his second year what he was to call his tide of writ-ing. As it turned out, no fitter institution could have been found for the bookish lad. Unable by reason of his poor sight to take part in most sports, he turned to writing verse. (His mother was to print 23 of them privately without his permission, no great poetry but clear signs of promise.)

He was well prepared for authorship having read most of the contem-porary British writers, from Swinburne to Browning, as well as the best of the contemporary Americans, Emerson, Poe, Longfellow, Whitman, Bret Harte and Mark Twain. The Roman poet, Quintus Horatius Flaccus ('Horace') left a particular mark upon the lad. He was taught 'to loathe [the poet] for two years; to forget him for twenty, and then to love him for the rest of my days and through many sleepless nights.' At the age of 52 he was to 'discover' a 'missing' Fifth Book of Horace, which in fact had been written by himself and a friend.

Towards the end of his time at the school 'Crom' made the boy de facto editor of the school magazine. It was a task he accepted with delight, sub-editing the copy (often his own), correcting proofs and overseeing production at the printers in nearby Bideford. There could have been no finer preparation for a future journalist. In his final term 'Crom' gave

Kipling a supreme gift in the form of unrestricted access to his 'brown bound, tobacco scented library; prohibiting nothing, recommending nothing'. Crom was also a source of tuition, 'sweetened with reminiscences of the men of Crom's youth, and throughout the low, soft drawl and the smoke of his perpetual [cigar] he shed light on the handling of words. Heaven forgive me! I thought these privileges were due to my transcendent personal merits.'

Seven years hard

Upon leaving school Kipling was judged insufficiently bright to gain a scholarship to Oxford and his parents could not afford the fees, so it was arranged that he should return to the land of his birth to pursue a career in journalism. His father had secured for him a post in what was then his home city of Lahore as assistant editor of a small daily newspaper, the Civil and Military Gazette ('the C.M.G.'). It was hard work for a seventeen year old, with long hours and the constant threat of dysentery. He spent much of his time in the Punjab club, but at night would 'wander till dawn in all manner of odd places - liquor-shops, gambling-and opium-dens, which are not a bit mysterious, wayside entertainments such as puppet-shows, native dances; or in and about the narrow gullies under the Mosque of Wazir Khan' ('Something of Myself').

During the stifling summers many of the British, including the Kipling family, withdrew to the cool hill town of Simla (now Shimla) where Rudyard's wit and his skill at dancing, coupled with his sister's charm, were great assets for the family. From a metropolitan point of view Simla might have seemed dull, but its active social life suggests otherwise, as Kipling was to describe in a series of brilliant unsigned articles written for magazines or the Indian Railway's one-rupee paperbacks. Mostly lightweight in nature, they dealt with the life and loves of Anglo-Indian society and launched the fictional career of the formidable Mrs Hauksbee. The author's vivid descriptions of the exotic environment and the fluency and panache of his prose ensured that they were read throughout the sub-continent.

At the age of twenty this private but clubbable man was,

> 'made a Freemason by dispensation (Lodge Hope and
> Perseverance 782 E.C.), being under age, because the Lodge
> hoped for a good Secretary. They did not get him, but I helped,
> and got the Father to advise, in decorating the bare walls of the
> Masonic Hall with hangings after the prescription of Solomon's
> Temple. Here I met Muslims, Hindus, Sikhs, members of the
> Arya and Brahmo Samaj, and a Jew Tyler, who was priest and
> butcher to his little community in the city. So yet another world
> opened to me which I needed.' ('Something of Myself'.)

It may be that he exaggerated the multi-racial composition of his Lodge,
but his poem, 'The Mother Lodge' and many of his stories demonstrate
in the clearest possible way the value he attached to his membership of
an organisation that comprised all manner of men.

The open noon of my pride

After seven years on The Gazette Kipling was transferred to its sister
paper, The Pioneer, in Allahabad a Hindu city some hundreds of miles
south along the river Ganges. (Lahore was an Islamic city) He was to be
editor of a new literary supplement and the paper's special correspondent with a roving commission in the western region of Rajputana. The
experience was to provide invaluable material for his pen.

So well had his magazine stories been received that they were collected
the following year, along with a few more, in a volume entitled, **'Plain
Tales from the Hills'** (the hills being the foothills of the Himalayas and
the word, 'plain' being a pun.) Christopher Hitchens' description of the
British stories as 'unsparing depictions of racial and sexual hypocrisy'
does them less than justice. As well as the British tales the collection
included a number of 'Indian' stories, such as *'Beyond the Pale' and
*'The Story of Muhammed Din'. It is possibly the first time that Indians
had appeared as rounded human beings in Western fiction. Just as with
the English, they are shown as heroes, sufferers and, most difficult of
all to pull off without condescension, villains. Somerset Maugham, who

had travelled extensively in India, wrote that Kipling's stories 'give you the tang of the East, the smell of the bazaars, the torpor of the rains, the heat of the sun scorched earth, the rough life of the barracks in which the occupying troops were quartered, and the other life, so English and yet so alien to the English way.'

Hard on the heels of 'Plain Tales' came another collection, **'Soldiers Three & Other Stories'** (1888) which centred around the adventures, amusing and grim, of three private soldiers, Learoyd, Mulvaney and Ortheris (who had already made an appearance in 'Plain Tales'). Kipling's only direct involvement with the army was when he had enlisted as a private in the 1st Punjab Rifle Corps, but he rapidly lost interest in this pastime, never experienced actual warfare and had to rely upon books to flesh out the military detail in his stories. Further material would have been gathered from the conversations in the clubs and the officers' messes that he frequented, but also from what he called some '8 or 10 boozing chums who belonged to the musket fatigue party' in the barracks near where he worked. His English readers must have been shocked at being brought face to face with the not altogether reputable men on whom the safety of the empire rested.

Included in the same volume as 'Soldiers Three' were two other collections, **'The Story of the Gadsbys'** and **'In Black and White'**, which latter featured among other gems, *'In Flood Time' and *'On the City Wall'. **'Wee Willie Winkie and Other Child Stories'** came out at around the same time. Among the best of these was 'The Drums of the Fore and Aft' which deals with two young drummer boys of ill repute who lose their lives in an act of drink induced bravery which rallies their regiment just as it is about to be defeated by the Afghans.

London Town

It would be difficult to over-estimate the sensation caused by these early tales and the acclaim they brought to their author. In 1889, determined to make the most of his success and spurred on by a disagreement with his employers, the 24 year old journalist handed in his notice, bade farewell to his parents and sailed for 'home', taking in the Far

East and America on the way. He was not to see India again except for a brief visit to his parents in 1891.

When he arrived in London Kipling was feted by the literary set and introduced to the smart clubs, but it was not an unalloyed success. Carrington describes how, 'The new world in which he felt quite alone was as strange to him as a desert island; and its inhabitants offered him no comfort. Though they took notice of him, it was as a rarity, as a curiosity, not as a comrade.' Kipling did make one close friend, however, a young American publisher by the name of Wolcott Balestier. So close was their friendship that the two of them collaborated to write a novel together, 'The Light that Failed'. And Kipling addressed a poem to his friend couched in almost embarrassing terms of affection.

One saving grace of London was the famous music hall within sight and hearing of his lodgings in Villiers Street. It was a form of entertainment of which he was to become very fond, even going so far as to write songs for the stage. But after two years the attractions of the capital began to pall. London's effete intellectuals compared badly in the author's eyes with the dedicated young men and women he had known and admired in India. Some sort of mental breakdown followed and he decided to relax with a world cruise.

The female of the species

While at sea, Kipling was stunned to learn of Wolcott's death from typhoid. Cutting short his trip, he returned to England where in what seemed to his family to be unwonted haste he married his late friend's sister, Caroline. (It seems that they had some sort of prior understanding to marry.) Carrie, as she was known, was three years older than Kipling. Later in life she came under attack for her alleged over-defensiveness of her husband, but this is to under-estimate the difficulty of her role in protecting a world celebrity from his many over-attentive admirers. It is more difficult to judge other criticisms of her character, but it should be remembered that, like her husband, Carrie too suffered from poor health and that she too was to share in the family tragedies ahead. Perhaps we should leave the final judgement to their daughter Elsie who described her mother as:

> 'moody and difficult, often filling those round her with her own tensions: a not unfamiliar type. This attribute sometimes exhausted Kipling, though he never complained. On the other hand, Carrie was intelligent, witty, loyal, kind, and above all brave.' (Quoted by Roger Lancelyn Green.)

There had been other women before Carrie, the most notable of which was Florence Garrard, another boarder at Southsea whom Kipling met while visiting his sister. According to Trix, she had a beautiful ivory face, long hair and large eyes. It was a strong, but on/off infatuation which only foundered years later when Florence discovered her true sexuality. This was a setback, but no disaster for a young man who seems to have enjoyed a vigorous appetite for romantic love.

The last decade of the nineteenth century was perhaps the most fruitful of Kipling's life, with the publication of four further volumes of short stories. **'Life's Handicap'** had been come out in 1891 before his marriage. Among its contents were 'The Courting of Dinah Shadd' and 'On Greenhow Hill'. It was followed within two years by **'Many Inventions'** which introduced in a tale entitled, 'In the Rukh' the character of Mowgli, later to become the protagonist in 'The Jungle Books'. (The author traced the origin of these stories to his early reading at Southsea.) The volume also included 'The Finest Story in the World', a tale of reincarnation, and 'The Record of Badalia Herodsfoot', which is set in the London slums.

Naulakha

Kipling had booked a world tour for his honeymoon, but had to cut it short when he learned that nearly all his savings had been lost in the collapse of the New Oriental Bank Corporation. Carrie's family came to the rescue with the offer of a small cottage in her home state of Vermont. Here in 1892, she was to give birth to their first child, Josephine. By the time their second daughter, Elsie came along four years later Kipling was enjoying a healthy income from his writings and was able to build a house outside the nearby town of Brattleboro that he named 'Naulakha' after his novel. But his perceived standoffishness and visibly high standard of living led to a certain froideur between the Kiplings and their neighbours. A diplomatic tiff between England and his adopted country added to the writer's disillusion with America, but the final straw was an embarrassing dispute with Carrie's surviving brother. It was all too much for Kipling who beat a hasty retreat back to England.

Despite this unpleasantness the Vermont years proved to be most productive from a literary point of view. David Richards has calculated that over a span of two years the author published 78 short stories written over 28 months. He began his novel, 'Kim' there and completed 'Captains Courageous' and 'The Seven Seas'. It was there too that he began the two **'Jungle Books'** that came out in 1894 and 1895 respectively. Drawing heavily on Indian myth, they were written in 'a style that was at once more compelling, more restrained and more formed than the critics anticipated... He [had] reached maturity in a stride'. (Gordon Williams. The Australian Quarterly, June 1936.)

'The Day's Work' (1898) was the first of Kipling's anthologies to demonstrate the author's interest in technology in such tales as *'The Bridge Builders' and 'The Ship that Found Herself'. His 'matching dreams' story, 'The Brushwood Boy', though not without its blemishes, has a mesmeric quality about it that is difficult to forget. The two-part story, 'William the Conqueror' could not be more different. It is a realistic account of the unremitting efforts of two young Englishman and a young woman (a 'new woman' as they were called in those days) to provide famine relief in India. Only two decades before it was written some five million people had died from starvation in Bombay, Madras and Mysore.

Back in England the author changed direction somewhat with the publication of a series of tales based loosely upon his school years. **'Stalky & Co'** (1899) featured the adventures of three characters who shared a study, 'Stalky' (based on Lionel Dunsterville, later to become a Major General), 'M'Turk' (based on G.C. Beresford, later to become a society photographer) and 'Beetle' (based on Kipling himself.) Not without controversy, the theme of this collection is in the late Norman Page's words, 'education in both its narrower and its wider senses.'

The daughter that was all to him

In 1899 after a brief sojourn in South Africa in a house provided for them by Cecil Rhodes the family sailed to America on a journey that was to end in tragedy. On arrival in New York Rudyard and the children became seriously ill, a fact that gave rise to international concern, with even the Kaiser sending a telegram of good wishes. Rudyard recovered with a great deal of support from Carrie, only to learn that his beloved first born, the six-year-old Josephine had died from pneumonia. It was a blow from which he never fully recovered.

The beginnings of a return to stability were signalled in 1902 by publication of the **'Just So Stories'**, which had been written for Josephine. Like the 'Jungle Books', they were and remain a remarkable success.

One spot beloved over all

When the family returned from Vermont it had taken time for them to find their ideal home. First, they tried Torquay (the wrong atmosphere) and then Rottingdean, where their son, John was born in 1897. In time that too proved unacceptable on account of the gawping trippers who came to see the celebrity. It was not until 1902 that Rudyard chanced upon a Jacobean house called Bateman's outside the quiet Sussex village of Burwash. It was built for an ironmaster in 1634 and the facilities were less than those judged normal in the early twentieth century, but it suited them ideally. The grounds, the surrounding countryside and its peoples were to fuel the author's inspiration for years to come.

Kipling's first serious venture into international affairs turned out to be disastrous. When the Boers in Transvaal resumed their armed struggle for independence (as we would call it today) Britain sent a modern army to put down the uppity farmers – only for it to encounter a far more skilled and determined enemy than they expected. British generalship in the field was less than competent and its weapons not always superior. British conduct towards the civil population was no better, with thousands being thrown into concentration camps, where large numbers of them died from neglect. Kipling, who had vigorously supported the war, could not plead ignorance for he had been there in person as a correspondent for a British soldiers' newspaper. He was to acknowledge his nation's misjudgement in verse ('We have had no end of a lesson: it will do us no end of good.') But the damage to his reputation had been done, particularly in places like Holland, Germany and in the Dutch and German settled parts of America.

The next collection, **'Traffics and Discoveries'** came out in 1904. It marked the beginning of the author's later period and included the controversial, 'Mrs Bathurst', as well as *'They', which recounted a man's magical encounter with his dead daughter. For the first time the stories were accompanied by poems. 'Traffics and Discoveries' was followed by **'Puck of Pook's Hill'** and **'Rewards and Fairies'**, two volumes of historical fantasy based on episodes in English history. Written ostensibly for children but appealing to a wider readership, they were inspired by a play that Kipling had staged for his own children in a fairy ring beside the brook at Bateman's. The central characters, 'Dan' and 'Una' were based respectively on John and Elsie. His next collection of adult tales, **'Actions and Reactions'** (1909) betokened a somewhat gentler, more reflective mood, which was in harmony with its time.

Kipling was one of the first to recognize and warn against the threat of war in Europe, but his record on South Africa meant that his warnings did not receive the attention they deserved, at least until 1914, by which time they had ceased to be relevant. Early in the conflict the Kiplings were only two among the multitude of parents who were to lose a child on the battlefields of Flanders. A curious myth has grown up that Ruddy pushed his son into uniform: the facts are otherwise. The seventeen-year-old John had been desperate to serve, but had twice been rejected on the ground of poor eyesight. It was only after he threatened to join as a gentleman ranker that his father pulled strings and got him into the Irish Guards as a subaltern. He was killed on his first day of fighting.

When his father learnt the news he was said to have cried a 'curse like the cry of a dying man'.

Most of the stories in Kipling's first post-war collection, **'A Diversity of Creatures'** (1917) were written before the war began, but *'Mary Postgate', one of the bleakest and most powerful of all, was an explicit product of the conflict. Like England itself, Kipling was never the same after the war. Lack of public support for his imperialist views led to an increasing isolation which, coupled with his ill health, made him appear to some as a sad figure. The mood is reflected in his poem, 'The Support':

> *Heart may fail, and strength outwear and Purpose turn to Loathing*
> *But the everyday affair of business, meals and clothing,*
> *Builds a bulkhead 'twixt Despair and the Edge of Nothing.*

One event however seems to have given him some comfort, and for the best of reasons. In 1922 he had accepted the Rectorship of St Andrew's university where he was rapturously received by the students who had elected him. Somehow, 'the frost at his heart' was broken by these enthusiastic youngsters, which prompted him to contemplate 'The passing of Time and the passion/Of Youth over all!' ('A Rector's Memory')

But all this was to change: Kipling had gone through a world war and two family tragedies; he was no longer the youth who had written the brash tales of Simla or even the light fables of Puck and Mowgli, and this was reflected in his next collection, **'Debits and Credits'** (1926). It was a mixed bunch, containing a number of his less successful pieces, but also some of his best work on one of his profoundest themes, the relationship between love and pain. Fame still weighed heavily on this most private of men. When a society was set up devoted to him and his works – a society that still flourishes today – Kipling strongly disapproved.

His last collection, **'Limits and Renewals'** came out in 1932. Carrington judged it to be 'the book of a tired and aging invalid', but that judgement is difficult to justify in relation to a volume containing such fine tales as *'Dayspring Mishandled' and *'The Church that was at Antioch'.

As with many men, age brought a cooling of old friendships and a nostalgia for things as they were, but despite Carrie's ill health and his own Kipling never became a recluse, enjoying Noel Coward's comedy, 'Hay Fever' and the company of old friends like Rider Haggard, as well as new ones like the 'charming' P.G. Wodehouse.

Kipling died of a perforated duodenal ulcer on 18 January 1936; it was the anniversary of his marriage. His ashes were buried in Poets' Corner in Westminster Abbey, next to those of Charles Dickens and Thomas Hardy.

Man dies too soon his work half planned

Kipling believed passionately in the ideal of service, to the family, the nation and the empire. He was 'honorary literary adviser' to the Imperial War Graves Commission and after his son's death undertook to write a history of his regiment, the Irish Guards. It was a long and gruelling task that kept him occupied during his time of grief. He would not take any payment for 'Recessional', or for any other of what he called his 'serious' poems. He did this work while refusing most forms of public recognition, including the Laureateship, a Knighthood and the Order of Merit. But no one could claim that he was a man of unblemished character.

The Kipling scholar, Thomas Pinney has drawn attention to Kipling's tendency to make cruel comments about people of whom he disapproved and his preference to see conspiracy or active malice at work when things went wrong. It is difficult to know the extent to which such frailties can be attributed as many do, to the traumas of his youth, and how much - was just Kipling. Those wishing to explore this murky area might wish to consult his own remarkable account of the delirium he experienced while seriously ill in New York. (It can be found in Appendix A to Birkenhead's biography).

Practically every critic of Kipling has pointed to the contradictions that are all too easy to see in his life and work: his belief in England's civilizing mission and his disdain for his country's parochialism, his fascination with the spiritual and his lack of interest in dogma, his admiration of the working man and his abhorrence of the unions. It goes on and on. In fact, it is only the ideologically inclined and the young who are prepared to believe that human beings can ever be without their contradictions. Paradox is inherent in most of what we believe and what we do, and our lives are spent in fruitless attempts to resolve it.

***

Before turning to Kipling the writer I would like to examine a few issues with which his name is ineluctably linked.

Dominion over palm and pine

George Orwell in his famous essay of 1942 called Kipling 'a jingo imperialist' who did not realize that 'an empire is primarily a money-making concern'. Kipling would have rejected the description 'jingoist' with anger, though he would have happily embraced the term, 'imperialist', which had a meaning for him entirely different from Orwell's. '[My] concept of empire', Kipling once wrote, 'was that which I saw around me – men devoted to burdensome tasks under difficult conditions without much assistance or any immediate hope of reward, working for impersonal ends.' (Letter to Andre Chevrillon. 6 October 1919).

The British Empire, like most empires, was won with blood and the sword. Men who went out to administer it did so for all the usual motives, public service, ambition, wealth and adventure. But motives are irrelevant: it is consequences that matter. For his part Kipling had no doubt what they were. In his poem, 'The Widow's Party' an ordinary soldier, asked what he has he been up to, answers:

> *We broke a King and we built a road –*
> *A courthouse stands where the reg'ment goed.*
> *And the river's clean where the raw blood flowed*
> *When the Widow gives the party.*

'The Widow', of course, being Queen Victoria. Closely similar claims may be heard from today's Squaddie in Afghanistan.

Kipling was fond of making parallels between the British and the Roman empires. See for example *'Regulus' and *'The Church that was at Antioch'. There are limits to this comparison, but at least it cannot be said of the British, as Tacitus said of his fellow Romans, that, 'To ravage, to slaughter, to usurp under false titles, they call empire; and where they make a desert, they call it peace'.

The English like to think that with the passage of time they are in a position to make a balanced judgement on the effects of their empire: it had its faults, they concede, but they were less grievous than those of some other nations. Perhaps. Ultimately however, it is only the inhabitants of the former colonial territories who are entitled to make that judgement.

Kipling was quite uninterested in political theory – a benefit from his lack of a university education, perhaps? - but he was a Tory who was happy to speak and canvass on behalf of the party. The only service he would not perform was to stand for Parliament. 'Politics,' he once said, 'was a dog's life without a dog's decencies.' But what sort of conservatism did he espouse? Evelyn Waugh summed it up well when he suggested that he:

> '... was a Conservative in the sense that he believed civilization to be something laboriously achieved which was only precariously defended. He wanted to see the defences fully manned and he hated the liberals because he thought them gullible and feeble, believing in the easy perfectibility of man and ready to abandon the work of centuries for sentimental qualms.' (The Sunday Times, 22 March 1964).

It would be natural for someone with such views to conclude that a failure to maintain peace and order can give rise to disaster, and that is exactly what had happened seven years before Kipling was born.

There had been discontent among the soldiers of the East India Company which then ruled India under a royal charter at the introduction of a new type of cartridge widely believed to be greased with animal fat. The problem was that in order to be fired from a musket the cartridge had to be bitten, but Muslims were forbidden to eat pig fat and Hindus cow fat. On 29 February 1857 a Sepoy of the 34th Bengal Native Infantry, attacked two European officers and called on his comrades to rebel. He was hanged and his regiment disbanded. But nothing could stop the mutiny, which spread like fire, first to Delhi, Agra, Cawnpore and, then, Lucknow. Both the uprising and its repression were marked with great cruelty on both sides. When it was over the East India Company, which had long ruled large parts of India, was gone and replaced by direct rule from the London government. But the appalling events of that year left a dark shadow at the back of every Anglo-Indian's mind. Despite the fact that it was over before he was born Rudyard Kipling must have shared this apprehension, so why did he write so very little about it and that obliquely? (Two such exceptions are a few passages in Kim and the reference in *'The Bridge Builders', below to the incorporation into civil construction of defences against insurrection.)

The law...

I would venture the suggestion that, instead of tackling the Mutiny head on, Kipling translated its horrors into a concept that appears in much of his writing as 'the law'. It was a term that he used to include the law as administered in the courts. (Just consider his wonderful lines, still cited by jurists, 'Ancient Right unnoticed as the breath we draw—/ Leave to live by no man's leave, underneath the Law.' 'The Old Issue'). But Kipling's 'law' was much wider than lawyers' law. According to the Indian academic, Shamsul Islam in his book, 'Kipling's Law: A Study of his Philosophy' (1975) it consisted of 'such universal values as discipline, devotion to work, positive action, suffering and love'. Richard Jaffa lends support to this analysis in his book, 'Man and Mason – Rudyard Kipling' (2011). Jaffa also makes the interesting point that all of these concepts can be found within the obligations, charges and addresses made to a candidate during the course of the three craft ceremonies of a Mason such as Rudyard Kipling.

No one can write about Kipling today without confronting his oft-expressed opposition to self-rule for India. (His candid but erroneous views on this subject can be found in *'On the City Wall' below.) Time, fortunately, has proved him wrong, but even in 1947 not all the English supporters of independence were confident that it could be successfully achieved and some were to feel confirmed in that belief by the horrifying inter-communal violence of 1947. At least Kipling's was an error based on an understanding of and sympathy for the Indian peoples more profound than most. How proud he would have been of his connection with what is now the longest lasting democracy in Asia.

... and the prophet

If he got the independence issue wrong there is no doubt that at certain critical times in his life Kipling saw more clearly than most certain dangers that threatened his country. He mentioned two of them in 'Something for Myself', but they were nothing compared with what was to follow. Prior to the 1914/1918 war he had condemned for their lack of preparedness the 'flannelled fools at the wicket and the muddied oafs at the goals' ('The Islanders', 1902) And he was proved tragically correct on the bloody fields of Flanders. Later, in the inter-war years when the great mass of his fellow countrymen wanted only to be left in peace he drew attention to the dangers of further conflict ahead. At the very end of his life he warned of Nazism and Communism alike as 'State-controlled murder and torture, open and secret, within and outside the borders of a State; State-engineered famine, starvation and slavery as requisite.' (Speech to the Royal Society of St George in 1935.)

Kipling's warnings proved right so often that T.S. Eliot in his 1942 essay seriously advanced the view that the writer had 'a queer gift of second sight, of transmitting messages from elsewhere, a gift so disconcerting when we are made aware of it that thenceforth we are never sure when it is not present.' Kipling dismissed the notion summarily:

> ... I am in no way 'psychic.' Dealing as I have done with large, superficial areas of incident and occasion, one is bound to make

a few lucky hits or happy deductions. But there is no need to drag in the 'clairvoyance,' or the rest of the modern jargon. I have seen too much evil and sorrow and wreck of good minds on the road to Endor to take one step along that perilous track.' ('Something of Myself').

***

There are three strands that go throughout so much of Kipling's writing as to demand separate recognition; his belief in the equal importance of every human being, his obsession with pain and suffering and his quest to understand the ineffable.

Neither East nor West, Border, nor Breed, nor Birth

It is as well to begin by conceding that Kipling was as susceptible to contemporary prejudices and assumptions as the next man. His short story, 'The Head of the District' depicts a well-educated Bengali who replaces a white District Officer but fails signally at his task at a moment of crisis. Attempts to explain such pre-conceptions in non-racist terms are unconvincing. But such gaffes should be seen for what they were, sentiments that were widespread among Western people at the time. The same could be said of the low level British prejudice against the Jews and the Irish. (I leave aside Kipling's virulent hatred of the Germans that arose at a time when he might have felt his views amply justified.) We should remember that he lived in a society whose view of the world was unimaginably different from today's. Throughout his formative years England was the sole super-power of its day enjoying the fruits of the industrial revolution it had launched. There is a social theory – the just world theory, it is called - that successful people tend to attribute their superior station to their intrinsic superiority; and in those days no country was more successful than Britain. (There is a striking comparison here with present day Americans' belief in their nation's 'exceptionalism'. Both countries were economically dominant; both were forced by their wealth and military reach to be the world's policeman and both were tempted by the same illusions.) Many of the attitudes and assumptions of Victorian Britain now appear antipathetic, even distasteful to our eyes: it is a reaction that our descendants will recognize with a wry smile when they come to judge our own shortcomings.

What is plain is that Kipling had no time for those who would judge a man by his birth or position in life, by his colour, creed or sex; for him, character and conduct were all. As he wrote of the fictional battalion water carrier, Gunga Din, 'for all 'is dirty 'ide, 'E was white, pure white inside.' Most comment to the contrary can be traced to misunderstandings, misreadings or simple prejudice, as I sought to show in my book, 'The *Surprising* Mr Kipling'.

The British working class are invariably treated sympathetically in Kipling's stories. *'The Wish House', for example, takes the form of an extended conversation between two elderly Sussex women recounted with great realism but not a hint of condescension. Similar sensitivity and respect are displayed in 'On Greenhow Hill', a tale of love rivalry that moves in time from India to the lead mines of the Yorkshire Dales and back again.

In Victorian England the 'other ranks' of the British army were regularly barred from places of public entertainment. Kipling set about rectifying this with his bitter poem, 'Tommy' and stories such as 'In the Matter of a Private' and 'The Drums of the Fore and Aft'. And his compassion extended well beyond his own people, even to his country's enemies, as for example in his poems, 'The American Rebellion', 'Fuzzy Wuzzy' and 'The Settler'.

Kipling's interest in and understanding of peoples of different races, religions and backgrounds probably stemmed from his infancy in Bombay in the charge of his Portuguese, Roman Catholic ayah and his Hindu bearer whose language was the first he came to know. It was an intimate introduction to the diversity of the great sub-continent. Later, as a journalist he was brought face to face with the poverty, disease and flood that were the bane of the Indian peasant; and never forgot it.

Dread mother of Forgetfulness

In Victorian times cancer was the archetypal bogeyman of all classes, and Kipling was as fearful of it as everyone, even insisting on an exploratory operation to discover whether he had contracted it. (He hadn't.) The disease crops up menacingly in a number of his stories, such as *'The Wish House' and 'The Children of the Zodiac'. But it was not cancer that got him in the end, but a duodenal ulcer. He experienced the first pangs of 'gastritis', as it was then believed to be, at the time of his son's death and the symptoms were to dog him throughout the rest of his life, once becoming so bad that he had all his teeth removed in pursuit of a fashionable 'cure'.

Worse even than his physical ailments were Kipling's frequent descents into what he described in his poem, 'Rahere' as 'the Great Darkness' - clinical depression, as we would call it. In 'Something of Myself' he wrote of having 'broken down twice in India'. I have already touched upon his trauma at Southsea. At Torquay he suffered a 'growing depression that enveloped - a gathering blackness of mind and sorrow of the heart'. And after Elsie had declared her intent to leave home, he was 'quite hopeless with depression, depression and nerves.' Like most creative people Kipling put his suffering to artistic use. 'The House Surgeon' concerns a 'haunted house' which gives its inhabitants a sense of 'swift striding gloom ... despair upon despair, misery upon misery, fear after fear...'. In 'His Brother's Keeper' and in 'Thrown Away' he explored the theme of men driven to extremes by depression. And shell shock, as posttraumatic stress disorder was then known, features in *'A Madonna of the Trenches'.

The complex relationship between love and pain is one of the author's constant themes.

The last of Kipling's interests to which I would draw special attention is his attitude towards the spiritual.

God of our fathers

Kipling's childhood left him attached to no religion and to all. His parents, both from lapsed Methodist backgrounds, seem to have studiously ignored the subject, something that could not be said of the two other influential people of his infancy:

> 'Our ayah was a Portuguese Roman Catholic who would pray - I beside her - at a wayside Cross. Meeta, my Hindu bearer, would sometimes go into little Hindu temples where, being below the age of caste, I held his hand and looked at the dimly-seen, friendly Gods.' ('Something of Myself'.)

Anyone coming from such a background could never suppose that wisdom resided solely in an established church, or, indeed, in any single faith. At a time when 'pagans' were looked down upon he wrote his beautifully respectful poem, 'Buddha at Kamakura'. As a Mason he was committed to a belief in a supreme ruler of the universe and he liked to play with the idea of a deity as a trope. It was a conceit that he was still toying with in his seventieth year when in 'Something of Myself' he ascribed 'all good fortune to Allah the Dispenser of Events'. Yet, for all his admiration of Islam Kipling was no Muslim, so what did he actually believe in?

Once in his callow youth Kipling had attempted to set out his attitude to religion in a letter to a girl friend, 'Chiefly I believe in the existence of a personal God to whom we are personally responsible for wrong doing.... I disbelieve directly in eternal punishment... I disbelieve in an eternal reward' (Letter to Miss Caroline Taylor. 9 December 1889). The present writer finds this a less convincing credo than his 1908 description of himself as a 'God-fearing Christian atheist'. (Letter to Lady Edward Cecil. 1 December 1908.) In an article entitled 'Egypt of the Magicians' (1913) he observed cryptically, 'All sensible men are of the same religion, but no sensible man ever tells.'

His writings, I am convinced, reveal someone who respected Christian values, but who had little time for church or dogma (see his poems, 'The Pilgrim's Way' and 'The Dawn Wind'). It is summed up, I believe, in the last lines of another poem, 'The Prayer', which contrasts the diversity, and relative unimportance, of belief with the universality and centrality of the human condition:

My brother kneels, so saith Kabir,
To stone and brass in heathen wise,
But in my brother's voice I hear
My own unanswered agonies.
His God is as his fates assign,
His prayer is all the world's - and mine.

Whatever Kipling may have felt about religion he had a very real interest in the spiritual. Like many of us, he struggled to understand the powerful impulses, emotions and feelings that religion has traditionally grappled with, but for which science has as yet no full explanation. To take merely a few examples, *"The Church That was at Antioch" beautifully affirms the virtue of forgiveness, *"The Gardener' does the same for compassion, and *'The Wish House' for self-sacrifice. Because of its numinous nature the spiritual can sometimes be better expressed in verse than in prose, a fact of which Kipling took full advantage in his poem, 'By the Hoof of the Wild Goat', a mysterious piece seemingly about predestination, a notion to which he returned more than once.

Perhaps the closest Kipling got to expressing his own view are the words of the eponymous hero of his masterwork, 'Kim' who asks himself, 'Who is Kim? ... What am I? Mussalman, Hindu, Jain, or Buddhist?', only to conclude, 'I am Kim. I am Kim. And what is Kim?'

***

There are nine and sixty ways of constructing tribal lays

The recent discovery of Kipling's advice on the writing of short stories, which he had addressed to his wife's younger sister, raised expectations among enthusiasts (see The Kipling Journal of July, 2014), but few of his precepts proved to rise above the workaday; which only goes to show that even the greatest of writers can be a poor judge of his own talents. This is not the place for an exposition of Kipling's style, even if the present editor were qualified for the task, but our author was such an exceptionally gifted writer that it would be perverse to ignore the subject altogether. Before going further we should recognize how much he enjoyed the discipline of writing. As he wrote to the American author, C.E. Norton, 'I love the fun and the riot of writing ... and there are times when it is just a comfort and a delight to let out with the pen and ink - as long as it doesn't do anyone any moral harm.' (Letter, 3 December 1896. Quoted in Carrington.)

We are fortunate in having Kipling's own description of how he set about his task:

> 'I made my own experiments in the weights, colours, perfumes, and attributes of words in relation to other words, either as read aloud so that they may hold the ear, or, scattered over the page, draw the eye. There is no line of my verse or prose which has not been mouthed till the tongue has made all smooth, and memory, after many recitals, has mechanically skipped the grosser superfluities.'

He went on to describe a habit he employed to an increasing degree as time went on,

> [The stories] were originally much longer than when they ap-peared, but the shortening of them first to my own fancy after rapturous re-readings, and next to the space available, taught me that a tale from which pieces have been raked out is like a fire that has been poked. One does not know that the operation has been performed, but every one feels the effect. ('Something of Myself').

Kipling shared the not entirely unique conceit that his writing was guided by what he called his 'Daemon'. 'Most men,' he wrote,

> 'and some most unlikely keep [their Daemon] under an alias which varies with their literary or scientific attainments. Mine came to me early when I sat bewildered among other notions, and said; 'Take this and no other.' I obeyed, and was rewarded... My Daemon was with me in the Jungle Books, Kim, and both Puck books, and good care I took to walk delicately, lest he

should withdraw. I know that he did not, because when those books were finished they said so themselves with, almost, the water-hammer click of a tap turned off. One of the clauses in our contract was that I should never follow up 'a success,' for by this sin fell Napoleon and a few others. Note here. When your Daemon is in charge, do not try to think consciously. Drift, wait, and obey.' ('Something of Myself').

Kipling's talents were nourished by his reading at school, to which must be added the Bible and the Prayer Book he was forced to study at Southsea. Later came the discipline of journalism that is apparent in the compression and brevity of his prose. He also acquired an extraordinarily wide vocabulary, including recycled archaisms and the terminology of countless trades and professions, as well as words and phrases culled from all parts of the world and the English regions. 'Who else,' wrote George Moore, 'except Whitman, has written with the whole language since the Elizabethans?' (Moore. 'Avowals', 1910). T.S. Eliot referred to his 'immense gift for using words, ... amazing curiosity and power of observation with his mind and with all his senses, the mask of the entertainer...'

I am not aware of any of Kipling's contemporaries who could seriously challenge his mastery of descriptive prose. In 'The Finest Story in the World', for example, the central character paints this unforgettable picture of a galley slave:

> 'With an iron band round his waist fixed to the bench he sits on, and a sort of handcuff on his left wrist chaining him to the oar. He's on the lower deck where the worst men are sent, and the only light comes from the hatchways and through the oar-holes. Can't you imagine the sunlight just squeezing through between the handle and the hole and wobbling about as the ship moves?'

Rayner has pointed out how in his story, 'Wireless' the author describes a chemist's shop as though it were a setting worthy of Scheherazade:

> 'Across the street, blank shutters flung back the gaslight in cold smears; the dried pavement seemed to rough up in goose-flesh

under the scouring of the savage wind, and we could hear, long ere he passed, the policeman flapping his arms to keep himself warm. Within, the flavours of cardamoms and chloric-ether disputed those of the pastilles and a score of drugs and perfume and soap scents. Our electric lights, set down low in the windows before the tun-bellied Rosamond jars, flung inward three monstrous daubs of red, blue, and green, that broke into kaleidoscopic lights on the faceted knobs of the drug-drawers, the cut-glass scent flagons, and the bulbs of the sparklet bottles. They flushed the white-tiled floor in gorgeous patches; splashed along the nickel-silver counter-rails, and turned the mahogany counter-panels to the likeness of intricate grained marbles — slabs of porphyry and malachite.'

And a murder scene has seldom been laid out for the reader in as throat-gripping a way as in the opening paragraph of 'Love o' Women':

'The horror, the confusion, and the separation of the murderer from his comrades were all over before I came. There remained only on the barrack-square the blood of man calling from the ground. The hot sun had dried it to a dusky goldbeater-skin film, cracked lozenge-wise by the heat; and as the wind rose, each lozenge, rising a little, curled up at the edges as if it were a dumb tongue. Then a heavier gust blew all away down wind in grains of dark coloured dust. It was too hot to stand in the sunshine before breakfast. The men were in barracks talking the matter over. A knot of soldiers' wives stood by one of the entrances to the married quarters, while inside a woman shrieked and raved with wicked filthy words.'

Anyone coming to Kipling for the first time should be alive to two technical features of his craft. Who, he should ask himself, is actually telling the story, and within what frame is it being displayed?

Sometimes the narrator is the author himself, or someone very like him. See for example, *'The Man Who Would be King' and *'On the City Wall'. Sometimes he can be an impersonal third party, perhaps

even a character in the story, as in *'In Flood Time', where the narrator is a ferryman. Occasionally, Kipling wrote in the role of what commentators like to call an 'imperfectly informed narrator', a device that
allowed him to distance himself from such deliberate ironies as the
notorious opening of *'Beyond the Pale' concerning the supposed un-
desirability of inter-racial marriage. (The ill conceived attribution of
such sentiments to the author himself is very much as if Shakespeare
were to be damned for Iago's lies, or Dickens for the crimes of Bill
Sykes.)

Kipling would often resort to a literary device as old as The Arabian
Nights, namely a 'frame story' into which the core narrative is embed-
ded. The frame could reinforce or be in contrast to that of the central
story. 'The Phantom Rickshaw' and *'The Strange Ride of Morrowbie
Jukes' are only two examples of this. The Danish academic, the late
Carl Adolf Bodelsen pointed out how sophisticated this device could
be:

> 'the frame is used to throw a new light on the events of the story,
> which sometimes could hardly be fully understood without it,
> and it contains clues that help to explain symbolic passages in
> the narrative. This is in some cases done by making the frame
> play through themes that, on closer examination, prove to be
> echoes of themes in the narrative itself, but transposed in the
> same way as a composer plays variations on a musical motif, or
> as an overture gives a foretaste of the leitmotifs of an opera.'

Kipling was the first major writer to have his characters speak in the ac-
cents of the British regions. His attempts at this in the 'Soldiers Three'
stories were not universally applauded, but by the time of *'Friendly
Brook', the Sussex dialect of the farm workers is impeccable. For the
speech of his Indian characters he evolved, in the words of his biographer, Harry Ricketts, 'an elaborately ornate English intended to convey
the richly allusive, ritualistic texture of the vernacular.'

Kipling's early style, though compelling, was not without its blemishes,
as the novelist, Andrew Lang pointed out:

'There is a false air of hardness (quite in contradiction to the sentiment in his tales of childish life); there is a knowing air; there are mannerisms, such as "But that is another story"; there is a display of slang; there is the too obtrusive knocking of the nail on the head. Everybody can mark these errors; a few cannot overcome their antipathy, and so lose a great deal of pleasure.' (Essays in Little, 1912.)

To which the late Professor Norman Page added:

'Kipling's narrative technique does not woo or buttonhole the reader: it takes him by storm. His narrator is often a man of self-confidence, even audacity, as well as being possessed or much worldly wisdom – not the fatigued, bored and cynical worldli-ness of Somerset Maugham's tales, but a brisk, energetic, take-it-or leave-it variety ...'

Another flaw in the early Kipling was his fascination with bullying. It probably came from his experience at Southsea and his first few terms at Westward Ho! In his stories it sometimes take the form of tragedy, as in 'The Man who Was' and 'The Mark of the Beast', or as the payback for cruelty, as in 'The Moral Reformers', it is even dressed up as farce, as in 'His Wedded Wife'. Usually the revenge is taken at the hand of the wronged, but occasionally fate takes a hand, as in *'Friendly Brook'. It is heartening to note that the finest of his 'revenge' stories, *'Dayspring Mishandled', turned out in the end to be a case of revenge withheld. Written towards the end of his life, it seems finally to have expelled this particular devil from his psyche.

But all this disappeared as the writer grew in maturity and skill. As Philip Mason observed, 'Not all of [his] late stories are wise or kind, but compassion and understanding grow more frequent; personal revenge is slowly transmuted into impersonal retribution.' His biographer, Lord Birkenhead observed of the late stories: 'A close study shows that they are composed of layer upon layer of meaning, close packed like the skin of an onion.' Bodelsen expanded upon this when he described, 'a highly organized and almost incredibly complex pattern of parallelisms, cross-references, and interconnections, where straightforward narrative alternates with indirect communication; where passages are sometimes meant to be taken literally, sometimes symbolically, and sometimes both; where words and phrases are brought into prominence by various means so as to indicate the importance of the messages they convey, and where one must expect practically every word and sentence to be as indispensable for the whole as a sequence of bars in a Beethoven quartet, though their full import may elude one after several readings.'

To hurry after shadows

Kipling's range of subject matter is probably unequalled throughout English literature. The Kipling Society lists some 100 topics on which he wrote, although classification is very much a matter of judgement. His friend and admirer, Henry James once jokingly suggested that he had abandoned humans for horses, dogs, locomotives and parts of ships. Merely to take a few examples, he was equally adept at love stories ('The Record of Badalia Herodsfoot'), war ('The Taking of Lungtungpen'), mystery ('Mrs Bathurst'), satire ('The Limitations of Pambé Serang'), revenge (*'Dayspring Mishandled') and anthropomorphism ('The Ship that Found Itself'). It has been pointed out that he sometimes concealed the real topic of his writing. 'He writes ostensibly about big howitzers, and it is really a lover's tribute to Jane Austen. He writes a story apparently about wireless, and it means nothing save to a student of Keats.' (Christopher Morley. 'Saturday Review of Literature', 2 October 1926).

Tales of horror and the supernatural were all the fashion when Kipling began his career, and he was not slow to indulge the popular taste. 'The Phantom Rickshaw' and 'The Mark of the Beast' (which shocks by describing how two Englishmen torture an Indian.) compare favourably with the best of Edgar Allen Poe. But the supernatural was never an all-consuming interest, and he was quite capable of throwing cold water on the notion, for example in 'My Own True Ghost Story' and 'The Rout of the White Hussars'. His most successful ventures into the supernatural leave it to the reader to decide whether the events recounted are of temporal or paranormal origin. (See *'The Wish House' and *'A Madonna of the Trenches'.)

What Kipling could not abide was spiritualism, or the supposed art of communicating with the dead, which had cast such blight over the life of his mentally fragile sister, Trix. His contempt for this quackery can be seen in 'The Sending of Dana Da' and in *'In the House of Suddhoo'.

Some may be surprised to learn of Kipling's interest in technology and science fiction. 'Wireless' (1902) is a story about the enthusiasm of men for the potentialities of a new medium. ('There's nothing we shan't be able to do in ten years. I want to live - my God, how I want to live, and see it develop!') 'With the Night Mail: A Story of 2000 AD' (1905) purports to be a journalist's description of an Atlantic mail service by airship. 'As Easy as ABC' (1912) concerns a new world order governed by aviators. (Was it from here that H.G. Wells' picked up the idea of a world government of aviators which appears in his screenplay for the film, 'Things to Come', 1936?) So successful was he in this genre that the late Poul Anderson, a leading figure of the science fiction world, described Kipling's influence as 'pervad(ing) modern science fiction and fantasy writing.' ('All One Universe', 1997.)

As the son of a craftsman and himself a Freemason Kipling was disposed to admire the practitioners of all crafts and professions. He was also the first English writer to truly comprehend and express the central place of work in men's lives. The story entitled '.007', for example, deals with the world of the railways, while *'The Bridge Builders' is a mystical examination of the construction of a modern river bridge. I cannot agree with Somerset Maugham who wrote of tales like these that 'You would have to be respectively an engine driver and a ship builder to read these stories with comprehension': I am neither, yet they gripped me from the first reading.

Man dies too soon, beside his work half planned

So why should we read Kipling today?

Kipling should be read for the same reasons we turn to any great writer, for the beauty, lucidity and force of his prose and for his perspicacity and insights. Here is someone who paid the respect that is due, but not always accorded even now, to the alien, the poor and the oppressed. As the unofficial spokesman of the greatest empire in the history of the world he described accurately and sympathetically the lives of the peoples living under its jurisdiction. Though no orthodox believer, he prized and in his writings illustrated the great Christian virtues of charity, compassion and forgiveness, as well as the more modest British virtue of toleration. Nor is it possible to read his stories without being surprised by the light they so often throw on the eternal mysteries of love, pain and loss.

Ultimately, however, we read him, as our fathers have done before us, for sheer enjoyment.

***

The anthology

How, then, did I make my selection from among what the historian, Prof. Hugh Brogan has called Kipling's 'incomparable procession of short stories'?

Opinions are divided on the respective merits of the early and the later stories, some praising the 'vigour' of the former, while others prefer the obliquity and challenge of the latter. As it seems to me, Kipling produced amazing work at every stage of his life and no story has been included or rejected simply because of its date of composition. Instead, I have worked on one simple principle, to include only stories that have consistently stimulated, intrigued or moved me over a good many years. So personal an approach will inevitably leave out many excellent tales, each of which is girded round by its valiant defenders, so let me begin by confessing my own prejudices.

For many today, Kipling is known mostly for the excellent stories he wrote for children, particularly those in 'The Jungle Books', the 'Just So Stories' and the 'Puck' tales, of which last I am an unashamed worshipper. Solely on grounds of space, however, I decided to confine my selection to stories written *for* adults. Perhaps someone else should put together an anthology of the children's tales?

Like other writers of his day Kipling very occasionally crossed the line between sentiment and sentimentality, which is, I concede, very much a matter of taste. I personally am not attracted to many of his stories about children or dogs, though *'The Story of Muhammad Din' is a beautifully written exception that cried out to be included. Similarly, like other enthusiasts, I am sometimes disappointed in Kipling's 'practical joke' tales and revenge stories. On the other hand, I do enjoy a good enigma: which compels me to explain why I have not included the much admired 'Mrs Bathurst'.

I concede at once that no one who has read 'Mrs Bathurst' can ever forget it. Consider, for example the description of the corpses of the two tramps,

> 'One of 'em was standin' up by the dead-end of the siding and the other was squattin' down lookin' up at 'im... There'd been a bit of a thunderstorm in the teak, you see, and they were both stone dead and as black as charcoal. That's what they really were, you see - charcoal. They fell to bits when we tried to shift 'em. The man who was standin' up had the false teeth. I saw 'em shinin' against the black. Fell to bits he did too, like his mate squatting down an' watchin' him, both of 'em all wet in the rain. Both burned to charcoal, you see.'

Despite the story's undoubted merits, I share P.G. Wodehouse's view of its plot: 'Listen, Bill,' he wrote, 'something really must be done about Kip's "Mrs Bathurst". I read it years ago and didn't understand a word of it. I thought to myself, "Ah, youthful ignorance!" A week ago I re-read it. Result: precisely the same.' (Letter published in 'Performing Flea', 1953.)

I decided to leave out the justly admired 'soldiers three' yarns for an entirely different reason. I have no philological objections to Kipling's attempts at regional dialects, indeed, they seem fairly accurate to me, but I find that negotiating them on the page can be an obstacle course that I would rather avoid. For those wishing to dip their toes into this particular pool I recommend starting gently with the admirable, 'On Greenhow Hill'.

I was in two minds over the 'Stalky & Co' canon. I agree with the pseudonymous Ian Hay when he wrote of the portraits in these tales that they might be 'cruel, biased, not sufficiently representative', but went on to add, 'but how they live!' (Hay. 'The Lighter Side of School Life'. 1914.) Wonderful as I once found these fictionalized dramatizations of the author's schooldays, like me, they do not all age well. Fears that I might have to ignore them entirely were allayed when I remembered the splendid, *'Regulus', a 'Stalky' tale that was written some years after the rest. Strange to think that the debate on the purpose of education, which it rehearses so well, is still being played out in today's headlines.

To the army of fellow enthusiasts frustrated at the exclusion of their favourite story I offer my heartfelt apologies. If you care to let me know which you would most wish to have seen included I undertake to re-read it in light of your comments in the hope of achieving the enlightenment for which Kim's Lama yearned.

Dating individual stories is a minefield better navigated by scholars than a mere anthologist, so I have arranged my selection in order of publication of the volumes in which the stories were first collected. At the foot of each story I offer some thoughts on its significance, on its more cryptic aspects and on a few of the finer points of its language. And because anthologies are intended to be dipped into I have added short 'teasers' to the list of contents, taking care not to reveal too much of the plots.

My time will have been well spent if the few jewels that I have collected here move the reader to explore further the amazing treasure chest that is Kipling's prose.

Brian Harris

April 2015

THE ANTHOLOGY

THE STORY OF MUHAMMAD DIN

Who is the happy man? He that sees in his own house at home, little children crowned with dust, leaping and falling and crying.—Munichandra, translated by Professor Peterson.

The polo-ball was an old one, scarred, chipped, and dinted. It stood on the mantelpiece among the pipe-stems which Imam Din, *khitmatgar*, was cleaning for me.

'Does the Heaven-born want this ball?' said Imam Din deferentially.

The Heaven-born set no particular store by it; but of what use was a polo-ball to a *khitmatgar* ?

'By Your Honour's favour, I have a little son. He has seen this ball, and desires it to play with. I do not want it for myself.'

No one would for an instant accuse portly old Imam Din of wanting to play with polo-balls. He carried out the battered thing into the verandah; and there followed a hurricane of joyful squeaks, a patter of small feet, and the *thud-thud-thud* of the ball rolling along the ground. Evidently the little son had been waiting outside the door to secure his treasure. But how had he managed to see that polo-ball ?

Next day, coming back from office half an hour earlier than usual, I was aware of a small figure in the dining-room' a tiny, plump figure in a ridiculously inadequate shirt which came, perhaps, halfway down the tubby

3

stomach. It wandered round the room, thumb in mouth, crooning to itself as it took stock of the pictures. Undoubtedly this was the 'little son.'

He had no business in my room, of course; but was so deeply absorbed in his discoveries that he never noticed me in the doorway. I stepped into the room and startled him nearly into a fit. He sat down on the ground with a gasp. His eyes opened, and his mouth followed suit. I knew what was coming, and fled, followed by a long, dry howl which reached the servants' quarters far more quickly than any command of mine had ever done. In ten seconds Imam Din was in the dining-room. Then despairing sobs arose, and I returned to find Imam Din admonishing the small sinner who was using most of his shirt as a handkerchief.

'This boy,' said Imam Din judicially, 'is a *budmash*—a big *budmash*. He will, without doubt, go to the *jail-khana* for his behaviour.' Renewed yells from the penitent, and an elaborate apology to myself from Imam Din.

'Tell the baby,' said I, 'that the *Sahib* is not angry, and take him away.' Imam Din conveyed my forgiveness to the offender, who had now gathered all his shirt round his neck, stringwise, and the yell subsided into a sob. The two set off for the door. 'His name,' said Imam Din, as though the name were part of the crime, 'is Muhammad Din, and he is a *budmash*.' Freed from present danger, Muhammad Din turned round in his father's arms, and said gravely, 'It is true that my name is Muhammad Din, *Tahib*, but I am not a *budmash*. I am a *man*!'

From that day dated my acquaintance with Muhammad Din. Never again did he come into my dining-room, but on the neutral ground of the garden we greeted each other with much state, though our conversation was confined to '*Talaam, Tahib*' from his side, and '*Salaam, Muhammad Din*' from mine. Daily on my return from office, the little white shirt and the fat little body used to rise from the shade of the creeper-covered trellis where they had been hid; and daily I checked my horse here, that my salutation might not be slurred over or given unseemly.

Muhammad Din never had any companions. He used to trot about the compound, in and out of the castor-oil bushes, on mysterious errands of

4

his own. One day I stumbled upon some of his handiwork far down the grounds. He had half buried the polo-ball in dust, and stuck six shrivelled old marigold flowers in a circle round it. Outside that circle again was a rude square, traced out in bits of red brick alternating with fragments of broken china; the whole bounded by a little bank of dust. The water-man from the well-curb put in a plea for the small architect, saying that it was only the play of a baby and did not much disfigure my garden.

Heaven knows that I had no intention of touching the child's work then or later; but, that evening, a stroll through the garden brought me unawares full on it; so that I trampled, before I knew, marigold-heads, dustbank, and fragments of broken soap-dish into confusion past all hope of mending. Next morning, I came upon Muhammad Din crying softly to himself over the ruin I had wrought. Some one had cruelly told him that the *Sahib* was very angry with him for spoiling the garden, and had scattered his rubbish, using bad language the while. Muhammad Din laboured for an hour at effacing every trace of the dustbank and pottery fragments, and it was with a tearful and apologetic face that he said, '*Talaam Tahib,*' when I came home from office. A hasty inquiry resulted in Imam Din informing Muhammad Din that, by my singular favour, he was permitted to disport himself as he pleased. Whereat the child took heart and fell to tracing the ground-plan of an edifice which was to eclipse the marigold-poloball creation.

For some months the chubby little eccentricity revolved in his humble orbit among the castor-oil bushes and in the dust; always fashioning magnificent palaces from stale flowers thrown away by the bearer, smooth water-worn pebbles, bits of broken glass, and feathers pulled, I fancy, from my fowls—always alone, and always crooning to himself.

A gaily-spotted sea-shell was dropped one day close to the last of his little buildings; and I looked that Muhammad Din should build something more than ordinarily splendid on the strength of it. Nor was I disappointed. He meditated for the better part of an hour, and his crooning rose to a jubilant song. Then he began tracing in the dust. It would certainly be a wondrous palace, this one, for it was two yards long and a yard broad in ground-plan. But the palace was never completed.

Next day there was no Muhammad Din at the head of the carriage-drive, and no '*Talaam, Tahib*' to welcome my return. I had grown accustomed to the greeting, and its omission troubled me. Next day Imam Din told me that the child was suffering slightly from fever and needed quinine. He got the medicine, and an English Doctor.

'They have no stamina, these brats,' said the Doctor, as he left Imam Din's quarters.

A week later, though I would have given much to have avoided it, I met on the road to the Mussulman burying-ground Imam Din, accompanied by one other friend, carrying in his arms, wrapped in a white cloth, all that was left of little Muhammad Din.

Thoughts on The Story of Muhammad Din

'The Story of Muhammad Din' is a masterpiece of condensed story-telling written by a young man who had barely reached his majority. It is a parable about the value of life and how differently it may appear, according to the viewer's perspective.

The late Joyce Tompkins, that supreme interpreter of Kipling drew attention to, 'The sentences that tell the end of the child, Muhammad Din [which] are like pebbles dropped into a little pool; the rings spread and are stopped by the margin, and the small disturbance is over.'

IN THE HOUSE OF SUDDHOO

A stone's throw out on either hand
From that well-ordered road we tread,
And all the world is wild and strange:
Churel and ghoul and Djinn and sprite
Shall bear us company to-night,
For we have reached the Oldest Land
Wherein the Powers of Darkness range.
From the Dusk to the Dawn

The house of Suddhoo, near the Taksali Gate, is two-storied, with four carved windows of old brown wood, and a flat roof. You may recognise it by five red hand-prints arranged like the Five of Diamonds on the whitewash between the upper windows. Bhagwan Dass the grocer and a man who says he gets his living by seal-cutting live in the lower story with a troop of wives, servants, friends, and retainers. The two upper rooms used to be occupied by Janoo and Azizun, and a little black-and-tan terrier that was stolen from an Englishman's house and given to Janoo by a soldier. Today, only Janoo lives in the upper rooms. Suddhoo sleeps on the roof generally, except when he sleeps in the street. He used to go to Peshawar in the cold weather to visit his son who sells curiosities near the Edwardes' Gate, and then he slept under a real mud roof. Suddhoo is a great friend of mine, because his cousin had a son who secured, thanks to my recommendation, the post of head-messenger to a big firm in the Station. Suddhoo says that God will make me a Lieutenant-Governor one of these days. I daresay his prophecy will come true. He is very, very old, with white hair and no teeth worth showing, and he has outlived his wits—outlived nearly everything except his fondness for his son at Peshawar. Janoo and Azizun are Kashmiris, Ladies of the City, and theirs was an ancient and more or less honourable profession; but Azizun has since married a medical student from the North-West and has settled down to a most respectable life somewhere near Bareilly. Bhagwan Dass is an extortioner and an adulterator. He is very rich. The man who is supposed to get his living by seal-cutting pretends to be very poor. This lets you know as much as is necessary of the four principal tenants in the house of Suddhoo. Then there is Me of course; but I am only the chorus that comes in at the end to explain things. So I do not count.

Suddhoo was not clever. The man who pretended to cut seals was the cleverest of them all—Bhagwan Dass only knew how to lie—except Janoo. She was also beautiful, but that was her own affair.

Suddhoo's son at Peshawar was attacked by pleurisy, and old Suddhoo was troubled. The seal-cutter man heard of Suddhoo's anxiety and made capital out of it. He was abreast of the times. He got a friend in Peshawar to telegraph daily accounts of the son's health. And here the story begins.

Suddhoo's cousin's son told me, one evening, that Suddhoo wanted to see me; that he was too old and feeble to come personally, and that I should be conferring an everlasting honour on the House of Suddhoo if I went to him. I went; but I think, seeing how well off Suddhoo was then, that he might have sent something better than an *ekka*, which jolted fearfully, to haul out a future Lieutenant-Governor to the City on a muggy April evening. The *ekka* did not run quickly. It was full dark when we pulled up opposite the door of Ranjit Singh's Tomb near the main gate of the Fort. Here was Suddhoo, and he said that by reason of my condescension, it was absolutely certain that I should become a Lieutenant-Governor while my hair was yet black. Then we talked about the weather and the state of my health, and the wheat crops, for fifteen minutes, in the Huzuri Bagh, under the stars.

Suddhoo came to the point at last. He said that Janoo had told him that there was an order of the *Sirkar* against magic, because it was feared that magic might one day kill the Empress of India. I didn't know anything about the state of the law; but I fancied that something interesting was going to happen. I said that so far from magic being discouraged by the Government it was highly commended. The greatest officials of the State practised it themselves. (If the Financial Statement isn't magic, I don't know what is.) Then, to encourage him further, I said that, if there was any *jadoo* afoot, I had not the least objection to giving it my countenance and sanction, and to seeing that it was clean *jadoo*—white magic, as distinguished from the unclean *jadoo* which kills folk. It took a long time before Suddhoo admitted that this was just what he had asked me to come for. Then he told me, in jerks and quavers, that the man who said he cut seals was a sorcerer of the cleanest kind; that every day he gave Suddhoo news of the sick son in Peshawar more quickly than the lightning could fly, and that this news was always corroborated by the letters. Further, that he had told Suddhoo how a great danger was threatening his son, which could be removed by clean *jadoo*; and, of course, heavy payment. I began to see exactly how the land lay, and told Suddhoo that I also understood a little *jadoo* in the Western line, and would go to his house to see that everything was done decently and in order. We set off together; and on the way Suddhoo told me that he had paid the seal-cutter between one hundred and two hundred rupees already; and the *jadoo* of that night would cost two hundred more. Which was cheap, he said, considering the greatness of his son's danger; but I do not think he meant it.

The lights were all cloaked in the front of the house when we arrived. I could hear awful noises from behind the seal-cutter's shop-front, as if some one were groaning his soul out. Suddhoo shook all over, and while we groped our way upstairs told me that the *jadoo* had begun. Janoo and Azizun met us at the stair-head, and told us that the *jadoo*-work was coming off in their rooms, because there was more space there. Janoo is a lady of a free-thinking turn of mind. She whispered that the *jadoo* was an invention to get money out of Suddhoo, and that the seal-cutter would go to a hot place when he died. Suddhoo was nearly crying with fear and old age. He kept walking up and down the room in the half-light, repeating his son's name over and over again, and asking Azizun if the seal-cutter ought not to make a reduction in the case of his own landlord. Janoo pulled me over to the shadow in the recess of the carved bow-windows.

The boards were up, and the rooms were only lit by one tiny oillamp. There was no chance of my being seen if I stayed still.

Presently, the groans below ceased, and we heard steps on the staircase. That was the seal-cutter. He stopped outside the door as the terrier barked and Azizun fumbled at the chain, and he told Suddhoo to blow out the lamp. This left the place in jet darkness, except for the red glow from the two huqas that belonged to Janoo and Azizun. The seal-cutter came in, and I heard Suddhoo throw himself down on the floor and groan. Azizun caught her breath, and Janoo backed on to one of the beds with a shudder. There was a clink of something metallic, and then shot up a pale bluegreen flame near the ground. The light was just enough to show Azizun, pressed against one corner of the room with the terrier between her knees; Janoo, with her hands clasped, leaning forward as she sat on the bed; Suddhoo, face down, quivering, and the seal-cutter.

I hope I may never see another man like that seal-cutter. He was stripped to the waist, with a wreath of white jasmine as thick as my wrist round his forehead, a salmon coloured loin-cloth round his middle, and a steel bangle on each ankle. This was not awe-inspiring. It was the face of the man that turned me cold. It was blue-gray in the first place. In the second, the eyes were rolled back till you could only see the whites of them; and, in the third, the face was the face of a demon— a ghoul—anything you please except of the sleek, oily old ruffian who sat in the daytime over his turning-lathe downstairs. He was lying on his stomach with his arms turned and crossed behind him, as if he had been thrown down pinioned. His head and neck were the only parts of him off the floor. They were nearly at right angles to the body, like the head of a cobra at spring. It was ghastly. In the centre of the room, on the bare earth floor, stood a big, deep, brass basin, with a pale bluegreen light floating in the centre like a night-light. Round that basin the man on the floor wriggled himself three times. How he did it I do not know. I could see the muscles ripple along his spine and fall smooth again; but I could not see any other motion. The head seemed the only thing alive about him, except that slow curl and uncurl of the labouring backmuscles. Janoo from the bed was breathing seventy to the minute;

Azizun held her hands before her eyes; and old Suddhoo, fingering at the dirt that had got into his white beard, was crying to himself. The horror of it was that the creeping, crawly thing made no sound—only crawled! And, remember, this lasted for ten minutes, while the terrier whined, and Azizun shuddered, and Janoo gasped, and Suddhoo cried.

I felt the hair lift at the back of my head, and my heart thump like a thermantidote paddle. Luckily, the seal-cutter betrayed himself by his most impressive trick and made me calm again. After he had finished that unspeakable triple crawl, he stretched his head away from the floor as high as he could, and sent out a jet of fire from his nostrils. Now I knew how fire-spouting is done—I can do it myself—so I felt at ease. The business was a fraud. If he had only kept to that crawl without trying to raise the effect, goodness knows what I might not have thought. Both the girls shrieked at the jet of fire and the head dropped, chin-down on the floor, with a thud; the whole body lying there like a corpse with its arms trussed. There was a pause of five full minutes after this, and the blue-green flame died down. Janoo stooped to settle one of her anklets, while Azizun turned her face to the wall and took the terrier in her arms. Suddhoo put out an arm mechanically to Janoo's *huqa*, and she slid it across the floor with her foot. Directly above the body and on the wall were a couple of flaming portraits, in stamped-paper frames, of the Queen and the Prince of Wales. They looked down on the performance, and to my thinking, seemed to heighten the grotesqueness of it all.

Just when the silence was getting unendurable, the body turned over and rolled away from the basin to the side of the room, where it lay stomach-up. There was a faint 'plop' from the basin—exactly like the noise a fish makes when it takes a fly—and the green light in the centre revived.

I looked at the basin, and saw, bobbing in the water, the dried, shrivelled, black head of a native baby—open eyes, open mouth, and shaved scalp. It was worse, being so very sudden, than the crawling exhibition. We had no time to say anything before it began to speak.

Read Poe's account of the voice that came from the mesmerised dying man, and you will realise less than one-half of the horror of that head's voice.

There was an interval of a second or two between each word, and a sort of 'ring, ring, ring,' in the note of the voice, like the timbre of a bell. It pealed slowly, as if talking to itself, for several minutes before I got rid of my cold sweat. Then the blessed solution struck me. I looked at the body lying near the doorway, and saw, just where the hollow of the throat joins on the shoulders, a muscle that had nothing to do with any man's regular breathing twitching away steadily. The whole thing was a careful reproduction of the Egyptian teraphim that one reads about sometimes; and the voice was as clever and as appalling a piece of ventriloquism as one could wish to hear. All this time the head was 'lip-lip-lapping' against the side of the basin, and speaking. It told Suddhoo, on his face again whining, of his son's illness and of the state of the illness up to the evening of that very night. I always shall respect the seal-cutter for keeping so faithfully to the time of the Peshawar telegrams. It went on to say that skilled doctors were night and day watching over the man's life; and that he would eventually recover if the fee to the potent sorcerer, whose servant was the head in the basin, were doubled.

Here the mistake from the artistic point of view came in. To ask for twice your stipulated fee in a voice that Lazarus might have used when he rose from the dead, is absurd. Janoo, who is really a woman of masculine intellect, saw this as quickly as I did. I heard her say 'Asli nahin! Fareib!' scornfully under her breath; and just as she said so the light in the basin died out, the head stopped talking, and we heard the room door creak on its hinges. Then Janoo struck a match, lit the lamp, and we saw that head, basin, and seal-cutter were gone. Suddhoo was wringing his hands, and explaining to any one who cared to listen, that, if his chances of eternal salvation depended on it, he could not raise another two hundred rupees. Azizun was nearly in hysterics in the corner; while Janoo sat down composedly on one of the beds to discuss the probabilities of the whole thing being a *bunao*, or 'makeup.'

I explained as much as I knew of the seal cutter's way of *jadoo*; but her argument was much more simple—'The magic that is always demanding gifts is no true magic,' said she. 'My mother told me that the only potent love-spells are those which are told you for love. This seal-cutter man is a liar and a devil. I dare not tell, do anything, or get anything done, because I am in debt to Bhagwan Dass the bunnia for two gold rings and a heavy anklet. I must get my food from his shop. The seal-cutter is the friend of Bhagwan Dass, and he would poison my food. A fool's *jadoo* has been going on for ten days, and has cost Suddhoo many rupees each night. The seal-cutter used black hens and lemons and *mantras* before. He never showed us anything like this till to-night. Azizun is a fool, and will be a *purdahnashin* soon. Suddhoo has lost his strength and his wits. See now! I had hoped to get from Suddhoo many rupees while he lived, and many more after his death; and behold, he is spending everything on that offspring of a devil and a she-ass, the seal-cutter!'

Here I said, 'But what induced Suddhoo to drag me into the business? Of course I can speak to the seal-cutter, and he shall refund. The whole thing is child's talk—shame—and senseless.'

'Suddhoo is an old child,' said Janoo. 'He has lived on the roofs these seventy years and is as senseless as a milch-goat. He brought you here to assure himself that he was not breaking any law of the *Sirkar*, whose salt he ate many years ago. He worships the dust off the feet of the seal-cutter, and that cow-devourer has forbidden him to go and see his son. What does Suddhoo know of your laws or the lightning-post? I have to watch his money going day by day to that lying beast below.'

Janoo stamped her foot on the floor and nearly cried with vexation; while Suddhoo was whimpering under a blanket in the corner, and Azizun was trying to guide the pipe-stem to his foolish old mouth.

***

Now, the case stands thus. Unthinkingly, I have laid myself open to the charge of aiding and abetting the seal-cutter in obtaining money under false pretences, which is forbidden by Section 420 of the Indian Penal Code. I am helpless in the matter for these reasons. I cannot inform the Police. What witnesses would support my statements? Janoo refuses flatly, and Azizun is a veiled woman somewhere near Bareilly - lost in this big India of ours. I dare not again take the law into my own hands, and speak to the seal-cutter; for certain am I that, not only would Suddhoo disbelieve me, but this step would end in the poisoning of Janoo, who is bound hand and foot by her debt to the *bunnia*. Suddhoo is an old dotard; and whenever we meet mumbles my idiotic joke that the *Sirkar* rather patronises the Black Art than otherwise. His son is well now; but Suddhoo is completely under the influence of the seal-cutter, by whose advice he regulates the affairs of his life. Janoo watches daily the money that she hoped to wheedle out of Suddhoo taken by the seal-cutter, and becomes daily more furious and sullen.

She will never tell, because she dare not; but, unless something happens to prevent her, I am afraid that the seal-cutter will die of cholera—the white arsenic kind—about the middle of May. And thus I shall be privy to a murder in the House of Suddhoo.

Thoughts on In the House of Suddhoo

The narrator tells this tale of fraud with a light mocking touch until he realizes how he has been robbed of the detachment he needs.

He cannot intervene to stop the fraud on the lodging house keeper because of his support of 'white magic' ('The greatest officials of the State practised it themselves'.) Nor can he directly attack the grocer who pretends to be a 'seal cutter' out of fear that he will be poisoned by the prostitute, Janoo. She in turn deplores the fraud on Suddhoo because it has robbed her of her hopes of profiting from her landlord. As Louis Cornell wrote, 'On one level Western technology ... has been perverted to the uses of fraud and superstition. On another, Western judicial institutions ... have been made impotent by a conspiracy of custom, ignorance, and malice.' ('Kipling in India'. 1966).

Despite our knowledge of its fakery the description of the magician's eerie 'magic' is genuinely unsettling.

A thermantidote was a window fitted hand operated fan.

BEYOND THE PALE

"Love heeds not caste nor sleep a broken bed.
I went in search of
love and lost myself."
                                                        Hindu Proverb.

A man should, whatever happens, keep to his own caste, race and breed. Let the White go to the White and the Black to the Black. Then, whatever trouble falls is in the ordinary course of things—neither sudden, alien, nor unexpected.

This is the story of a man who willfully stepped beyond the safe limits of decent every-day society, and paid for it heavily.

He knew too much in the first instance; and he saw too much in the second. He took too deep an interest in native life; but he will never do so again.

Deep away in the heart of the City, behind Jitha Megji's bustee, lies Amir Nath's Gully, which ends in a dead-wall pierced by one grated window. At the head of the Gully is a big cow-byre, and the walls on either side of the Gully are without windows. Neither Suchet Singh nor Gaur Chand approved of their women-folk looking into the world. If Durga Charan had been of their opinion, he would have been a happier man to-day, and little Biessa would have been able to knead her own bread. Her room looked out through the grated window into the narrow dark Gully where the sun never came and where the buffaloes wallowed in the blue slime. She was a widow, about fifteen years old, and she prayed the Gods, day and night, to send her a lover; for she did not approve of living alone.

One day the man - Trejago his name was - came into Amir Nath's Gully on an aimless wandering; and, after he had passed the buffaloes, stumbled over a big heap of cattle food.

Then he saw that the Gully ended in a trap, and heard a little laugh from behind the grated window. It was a pretty little laugh, and Trejago, knowing that, for all practical purposes, the old Arabian Nights are good guides, went forward to the window, and whispered that verse of "The Love Song of Har Dyal" which begins:

> *Can a man stand upright in the face of the naked Sun;*
> *or a Lover in the Presence of his Beloved?*
> *If my feet fail me, O Heart of my Heart, am I to blame,*
> *being blinded by the glimpse of your beauty?*

There came the faint tchinks of a woman's bracelets from behind the grating, and a little voice went on with the song at the fifth verse:

> *Alas! alas! Can the Moon tell the Lotus of her love when the*
> *Gate of Heaven is shut and the clouds gather for the rains?*
> *They have taken my Beloved, and driven her with the pack-horses*
> *to the North.*
> *There are iron chains on the feet that were set on my heart.*
> *Call to the bowman to make ready—*

The voice stopped suddenly, and Trejago walked out of Amir Nath's Gully, wondering who in the world could have capped "The Love Song of Har Dyal" so neatly.

Next morning, as he was driving to the office, an old woman threw a packet into his dog-cart. In the packet was the half of a broken glass bangle, one flower of the blood red dhak, a pinch of bhusa or cattle-food, and eleven cardamoms. That packet was a letter—not a clumsy compromising letter, but an innocent, unintelligible lover's epistle.

Trejago knew far too much about these things, as I have said. No Englishman should be able to translate object-letters. But Trejago spread all the trifles on the lid of his office-box and began to puzzle them out.

A broken glass-bangle stands for a Hindu widow all India over; because, when her husband dies a woman's bracelets are broken on her wrists. Trejago saw the meaning of the little bit of the glass. The flower of the dhak means diversely "desire," "come," "write," or "danger," according to the other things with it. One cardamom means "jealousy;" but when any article is duplicated in an object-letter, it loses its symbolic meaning and stands merely for one of a number indicating time, or, if incense, curds, or saffron be sent also, place. The message ran then:—"A widow dhak flower and bhusa—at eleven o'clock." The pinch of bhusa enlightened Trejago. He saw—this kind of letter leaves much to instinctive knowledge—that the bhusa referred to the big heap of cattle-food over which he had fallen in Amir Nath's Gully, and that the message must come from the person behind the grating; she being a widow. So the message ran then:—"A widow, in the Gully in which is the heap of bhusa, desires you to come at eleven o'clock."

Trejago threw all the rubbish into the fireplace and laughed. He knew that men in the East do not make love under windows at eleven in the forenoon, nor do women fix appointments a week in advance. So he went, that very night at eleven, into Amir Nath's Gully, clad in a boorka, which cloaks a man as well as a woman. Directly the gongs in the City made the hour, the little voice behind the grating took up "The Love Song of Har Dyal" at the verse where the Panthan girl calls upon Har Dyal to return. The song is really pretty in the Vernacular. In English you miss the wail of it. It runs something like this:

> *Alone upon the housetops, to the North*
> *I turn and watch the lightning in the sky,—*
> *The glamour of thy footsteps in the North,*
> *Come back to me, Beloved, or I die!*
>
> *Below my feet the still bazar is laid*
> *Far, far below the weary camels lie,—*

The camels and the captives of thy raid,
Come back to me, Beloved, or I die!

My father's wife is old and harsh with years,
And drudge of all my father's house am I.—
My bread is sorrow and my drink is tears,
Come back to me, Beloved, or I die!

As the song stopped, Trejago stepped up under the grating and whispered:—"I am here."

Bisesa was good to look upon.

That night was the beginning of many strange things, and of a double life so wild that Trejago to-day sometimes wonders if it were not all a dream. Bisesa or her old handmaiden who had thrown the object-letter had detached the heavy grating from the brick-work of the wall; so that the window slid inside, leaving only a square of raw masonry, into which an active man might climb.

In the day-time, Trejago drove through his routine of office-work, or put on his calling-clothes and called on the ladies of the Station; wondering how long they would know him if they knew of poor little Bisesa. At night, when all the City was still, came the walk under the evil-smelling boorka, the patrol through Jitha Megji's bustee, the quick turn into Amir Nath's Gully between the sleeping cattle and the dead walls, and then, last of all, Bisesa, and the deep, even breathing of the old woman who slept outside the door of the bare little room that Durga Charan allotted to his sister's daughter. Who or what Durga Charan was, Trejago never inquired; and why in the world he was not discovered and knifed never occurred to him till his madness was over, and Bisesa... But this comes later.

Bisesa was an endless delight to Trejago. She was as ignorant as a bird; and her distorted versions of the rumors from the outside world that had reached her in her room, amused Trejago almost as much as her lisping attempts to pronounce his name—"Christopher." The first syllable was always more than she could manage, and she made funny little

22

gestures with her rose-leaf hands, as one throwing the name away, and then, kneeling before Trejago, asked him, exactly as an Englishwoman would do, if he were sure he loved her. Trejago swore that he loved her more than any one else in the world. Which was true.

After a month of this folly, the exigencies of his other life compelled Trejago to be especially attentive to a lady of his acquaintance. You may take it for a fact that anything of this kind is not only noticed and discussed by a man's own race, but by some hundred and fifty natives as well. Trejago had to walk with this lady and talk to her at the Band-stand, and once or twice to drive with her; never for an instant dreaming that this would affect his dearer out-of-the-way life. But the news flew, in the usual mysterious fashion, from mouth to mouth, till Bisesa's duenna heard of it and told Bisesa. The child was so troubled that she did the household work evilly, and was beaten by Durga Charan's wife in consequence.

A week later, Bisesa taxed Trejago with the flirtation. She understood no gradations and spoke openly. Trejago laughed and Bisesa stamped her little feet—little feet, light as marigold flowers, that could lie in the palm of a man's one hand.

Much that is written about "Oriental passion and impulsiveness" is exaggerated and compiled at second-hand, but a little of it is true; and when an Englishman finds that little, it is quite as startling as any passion in his own proper life. Bisesa raged and stormed, and finally threatened to kill herself if Trejago did not at once drop the alien Memsahib who had come between them. Trejago tried to explain, and to show her that she did not understand these things from a Western standpoint. Bisesa drew herself up, and said simply:

"I do not. I know only this—it is not good that I should have made you dearer than my own heart to me, Sahib. You are an Englishman. I am only a black girl"—she was fairer than bar-gold in the Mint—"and the widow of a black man."

Then she sobbed and said: "But on my soul and my Mother's soul, I love you. There shall no harm come to you, whatever happens to me."

23

Trejago argued with the child, and tried to soothe her, but she seemed quite unreasonably disturbed. Nothing would satisfy her save that all relations between them should end. He was to go away at once. And he went. As he dropped out at the window, she kissed his forehead twice, and he walked away wondering.

A week, and then three weeks, passed without a sign from Bisesa. Trejago, thinking that the rupture had lasted quite long enough, went down to Amir Nath's Gully for the fifth time in the three weeks, hoping that his rap at the sill of the shifting grating would be answered. He was not disappointed.

There was a young moon, and one stream of light fell down into Amir Nath's Gully, and struck the grating, which was drawn away as he knocked. From the black dark, Bisesa held out her arms into the moonlight. Both hands had been cut off at the wrists, and the stumps were nearly healed.

Then, as Bisesa bowed her head between her arms and sobbed, some one in the room grunted like a wild beast, and something sharp—knife, sword or spear—thrust at Trejago in his boorka. The stroke missed his body, but cut into one of the muscles of the groin, and he limped slightly from the wound for the rest of his days.

The grating went into its place. There was no sign whatever from inside the house—nothing but the moonlight strip on the high wall, and the blackness of Amir Nath's Gully behind.

The next thing Trejago remembers, after raging and shouting like a madman between those pitiless walls, is that he found himself near the river as the dawn was breaking, threw away his boorka and went home bareheaded.

What the tragedy was—whether Bisesa had, in a fit of causeless despair, told everything, or the intrigue had been discovered and she tortured to tell, whether Durga Charan knew his name, and what became of Bisesa—Trejago does not know to this day. Something horrible had happened, and the thought of what it must have been comes upon Trejago in the night now and again, and keeps him company till the morning. One special feature of the case is that he does not know where lies the front of Durga Charan's house. It may open on to a courtyard common to two or more houses, or it may lie behind any one of the gates of Jitha Megji's bustee. Trejago cannot tell. He cannot get Bisesa—poor little Bisesa—back again. He has lost her in the City, where each man's house is as guarded and as unknowable as the grave; and the grating that opens into Amir Nath's Gully has been walled up.

But Trejago pays his calls regularly, and is reckoned a very decent sort of man.

There is nothing peculiar about him, except a slight stiffness, caused by a riding-strain, in the right leg.

Thoughts on Beyond the Pale

For the background of this simple tale the author drew inspiration from his own life as a young journalist in Lahore. Like Trejago, he had wandered the crowded streets and alleyways of the great metropolis at night, occasionally sampling its delights, licit or otherwise. Like Trejago, it was a period in his life when he formed ready liaisons with young women, their only memorial a few lines of verse.

Bisesa entered into the Trejago affair with her uncle's implied consent. When her lover's betrayal became clear it seems that the uncle was affronted, not so much by the Sahib's interest in other women, but by the fact that his niece had allowed the affair to become common knowledge among his community. His primitive code of 'honour' allowed him to justify his horrific assault on his niece, but Trejago's moral code was little better for it failed to prevent his own lack of fidelity. The Grand Guignol *climax hits the reader like a slap. It was a tragedy for the girl but a minor inconvenience for the man.*

Strange to say, some have read the first lines of this story ('A man should, whatever happens, keep to his own caste, race and breed') as representing the author's own view. They miss the point entirely: 'Beyond the Pale' is a lesson in what can happen to thoughtless expatriates happy to take sex where they find it, but who reserve love for 'their own kind'. This should be obvious from the way in which the narrator consciously tells the story from a condescending Western viewpoint wholly alien to Kipling's own.

I understand why some prefer another of Kipling's tales on a similar theme, 'Without Benefit of Clergy', to 'Beyond the Pale', yet in its almost Shakespearean horror the latter surely has the edge.

A 'Pale' was a fence, metaphorical or otherwise, that delimited part of a territory under the control of an occupying power. (The most famous was Dublin's.) In this story it also serves as a trope for social rejection.

Trejago asserts that 'The Love Song of Har Dyal' is 'really pretty in the Vernacular'. In fact the lines were almost certainly of the author's own devising.

THE STRANGE RIDE
OF MORROWBIE JUKES

Alive or dead—there is no other way.
—*Native Proverb.*

There is, as the conjurers say, no deception about this tale. Jukes by accident stumbled upon a village that is well known to exist, though he is the only Englishman who has been there. A somewhat similar institution used to flourish on the outskirts of Calcutta, and there is a story that if you go into the heart of Bikanir, which is in the heart of the Great Indian Desert, you shall come across not a village but a town where the Dead who did not die but may not live have established their headquarters. And, since it is perfectly true that in the same Desert is a wonderful city where all the rich money lenders retreat after they have made their fortunes (fortunes so vast that the owners cannot trust even the strong hand of the Government to protect them, but take refuge in the waterless sands), and drive sumptuous C-spring barouches, and buy beautiful girls and decorate their palaces with gold and ivory and Minton tiles and mother-n'-pearl, I do not see why Jukes's tale should not be true. He is a Civil Engineer, with a head for plans and distances and things of that kind, and he certainly would not take the trouble to invent imaginary traps. He could earn more by doing his legitimate work. He never varies the tale in the telling, and grows very hot and indignant when he thinks of the disrespectful treatment he received. He wrote this quite straightforwardly at first, but he has since touched it up in places and introduced Moral Reflections, thus:—

In the beginning it all arose from a slight attack of fever. My work necessitated my being in camp for some months between Pakpattan and Muharakpur—a desolate sandy stretch of country as every one who has had the misfortune to go there may know. My coolies were neither more nor less exasperating than other gangs, and my work demanded sufficient attention to keep me from moping, had I been inclined to so unmanly a weakness.

On the 23d December, 1884, I felt a little feverish. There was a full moon at the time, and, in consequence, every dog near my tent was baying it. The brutes assembled in twos and threes and drove me frantic. A few days previously I had shot one loud-mouthed singer and suspended his carcass *in terrorem* about fifty yards from my tent-door. But his friends fell upon, fought for, and ultimately devoured the body; and, as it seemed to me, sang their hymns of thanksgiving afterward with renewed energy.

The light-heartedness which accompanies fever acts differently on different men. My irritation gave way, after a short time, to a fixed determination to slaughter one huge black and white beast who had been foremost in song and first in flight throughout the evening. Thanks to a shaking hand and a giddy head I had already missed him twice with both barrels of my shot-gun, when it struck me that my best plan would be to ride him down in the open and finish him off with a hog-spear. This, of course, was merely the semi-delirious notion of a fever patient; but I remember that it struck me at the time as being eminently practical and feasible.

I therefore ordered my groom to saddle Pornic and bring him round quietly to the rear of my tent. When the pony was ready, I stood at his head prepared to mount and dash out as soon as the dog should again lift up his voice. Pornic, by the way, had not been out of his pickets for a couple of days; the night air was crisp and chilly; and I was armed with a specially long and sharp pair of persuaders with which I had been rousing a sluggish cob that afternoon. You will easily believe, then, that when he was let go he went quickly. In one moment, for the brute bolted as straight as a die, the tent was left far behind, and we were flying over the smooth sandy soil at racing speed. In another we had passed the wretched dog, and I had almost forgotten why it was that I had taken the horse and hog-spear.

The delirium of fever and the excitement of rapid motion through the air must have taken away the remnant of my senses. I have a faint recollection of standing upright in my stirrups, and of brandishing my hog-spear at the great white Moon that looked down so calmly on my mad gallop; and of shout-log challenges to the camel-thorn bushes as they whizzed past. Once or twice I believe, I swayed forward on Pornic's neck, and literally hung on by my spurs—as the marks next morning showed.

The wretched beast went forward like a thing possessed, over what seemed to be a limitless expanse of moonlit sand. Next, I remember, the ground rose suddenly in front of us, and as we topped the ascent I saw the waters of the Sutlej shining like a silver bar below. Then Pornic blundered heavily on his nose, and we rolled together down some unseen slope.

I must have lost consciousness, for when I recovered I was lying on my stomach in a heap of soft white sand, and the dawn was beginning to break dimly over the edge of the slope down which I had fallen. As the light grew stronger I saw that I was at the bottom of a horse-shoe shaped crater of sand, opening on one side directly on to the shoals of the Sutlej. My fever had altogether left me, and, with the exception of a slight dizziness in the head, I felt no had effects from the fall over night.

Pornic, who was standing a few yards away, was naturally a good deal exhausted, but had not hurt himself in the least. His saddle, a favorite polo one was much knocked about, and had been twisted under his belly. It took me some time to put him to rights, and in the meantime I had ample opportunities of observing the spot into which I had so foolishly dropped.

At the risk of being considered tedious, I must describe it at length: inasmuch as an accurate mental picture of its peculiarities will be of material assistance in enabling the reader to understand what follows.

Imagine then, as I have said before, a horseshoe-shaped crater of sand with steeply graded sand walls about thirty-five feet high. (The slope, I fancy, must have been about 65°.) This crater enclosed a level piece of ground about fifty yards long by thirty at its broadest part, with a crude well in the centre. Round the bottom of the crater, about three feet from the level of the ground proper, ran a series of eighty-three semi-circular ovoid, square, and multilateral holes, all about three feet at the mouth. Each hole on inspection showed that it was carefully shored internally with drift-wood and bamboos, and over the mouth a wooden drip-board projected, like the peak of a jockey's cap, for two feet. No sign of life was visible in these tunnels, but a most sickening stench pervaded the entire amphitheatre—a stench fouler than any which my wanderings in Indian villages have introduced me to.

Having remounted Pornic, who was as anxious as I to get back to camp, I rode round the base of the horseshoe to find some place whence an exit would be practicable. The inhabitants, whoever they might be, had not thought fit to put in an appearance, so I was left to my own devices. My first attempt to "rush" Pornic up the steep sand-banks showed me that I had fallen into a trap exactly on the same model as that which the ant-lion sets for its prey. At each step the shifting sand poured down from above in tons, and rattled on the drip-boards of the holes like small shot. A couple of ineffectual charges sent us both rolling down to the bottom, half choked with the torrents of sand; and I was constrained to turn my attention to the river-bank.

Here everything seemed easy enough. The sand hills ran down to the river edge, it is true, but there were plenty of shoals and shallows across which I could gallop Pornic, and find my way back to *terra firma* by turning sharply to the right or left. As I led Pornic over the sands I was startled by the faint pop of a rifle across the river; and at the same moment a bullet dropped with a sharp *"whit"* close to Pornic's head.

There was no mistaking the nature of the missile—a regulation Martini-Henry "picket." About five hundred yards away a country-boat was anchored in midstream; and a jet of smoke drifting away from its bows in the still morning air showed me whence the delicate attention had come. Was ever a respectable gentleman in such an *impasse*? The treacherous sand slope allowed no escape from a spot which I had visited most involuntarily, and a promenade on the river frontage was the signal for a bombardment from some insane native in a boat. I'm afraid that I lost my temper very much indeed.

Another bullet reminded me that I had better save my breath to cool my porridge; and I retreated hastily up the sands and back to the horseshoe, where I saw that the noise of the rifle had drawn sixty-five human beings from the badger-holes which I had up till that point supposed to be untenanted. I found myself in the midst of a crowd of spectators—about forty men, twenty women, and one child who could not have been more than five years old. They were all scantily clothed in that salmon-colored cloth which one associates with Hindu mendicants, and, at first sight, gave me the impression of a band of loathsome *fakirs*. The filth and repulsiveness of the assembly were beyond all description, and I shuddered to think what their life in the badger-holes must be.

Even in these days, when local self government has destroyed the greater part of a native's respect for a Sahib, I have been accustomed to a certain amount of civility from my inferiors, and on approaching the crowd naturally expected that there would be some recognition of my presence. As a matter of fact there was; but it was by no means what I had looked for.

The ragged crew actually laughed at me—such laughter I hope I may never hear again. They cackled, yelled, whistled, and howled as I walked into their midst; some of them literally throwing themselves down on the ground in convulsions of unholy mirth. In a moment I had let go Pornic's head, and. irritated beyond expression at the morning's adventure, commenced cuffing those nearest to me with all the force I could. The wretches dropped under my blows like nine-pins, and the laughter gave place to wails for mercy; while those yet untouched clasped me round the knees, imploring me in all sorts of uncouth tongues to spare them.

In the tumult, and just when I was feeling very much ashamed of myself for having thus easily given way to my temper, a thin, high voice murmured in English from behind my shoulder:—"Sahib! Sahib! Do you not know me? Sahib, it is Gunga Dass, the telegraph-master."

I spun round quickly and faced the speaker.

Gunga Dass, (I have, of course, no hesitation in mentioning the man's real name) I had known four years before as a Deccanee Brahmin loaned by the Pun-jab Government to one of the Khalsia States. He was in charge of a branch telegraph-office there, and when I had last met him was a jovial, full-stomached, portly Government servant with a marvelous capacity for making had puns in English—a peculiarity which made me remember him long after I had forgotten his services to me in his official capacity. It is seldom that a Hindu makes English puns.

Now, however, the man was changed beyond all recognition. Caste-mark, stomach, slate-colored continuations, and unctuous speech were all gone. I looked at a withered skeleton, turban-less and almost naked, with long matted hair and deep-set codfish-eyes. But for a crescent-shaped scar on the left cheek—the result of an accident for which I was responsible—I should never have known him. But it was indubitably Gunga Dass, and—for this I was thank-full—an English-speaking native who might at least tell me the meaning of all that I had gone through that day.

The crowd retreated to some distance as I turned toward the miserable figure, and ordered him to show me some method of escaping from the crate?. He held a freshly plucked crow in his hand, and in reply to my question climbed slowly on a platform of sand which ran in front of the holes, and commenced lighting a fire there in silence. Dried bents, sand-poppies, and driftwood burn quickly; and I derived much consolation from the fact that he lit them with an ordinary sulphur-match. When they were in a bright glow, and the crow was nearly spitted in front thereof, Gunga Dass began without a word of preamble:

"There are only two kinds of men, Sar—the alive and the dead. When you are dead you are dead, but when you are alive you live." (Here the crow demanded his attention for an instant as it twirled before the fire in danger of being burned to a cinder.) "If you die at home and do not die when you come to the ghat to be burned you come here."

The nature of the reeking village was made plain now, and all that I had known or read of the grotesque and the horrible paled before the fact just communicated by the ex-Brabmin. Sixteen years ago, when I first landed in Bombay, I had been told by a wandering Armenian of the existence, somewhere in India, of a place to which such Hindus as had the misfortune to recover from trance or catalepsy were conveyed and kept, and I recollect laughing heartily at what I was then pleased to consider a traveler's tale.

Sitting at the bottom of the sand-trap, the memory of Watson's Hotel, with its swinging punkahs, white-robed attendants, and the sallow-faced Armenian, rose up in my mind as vividly as a photograph, and I burst into a loud fit of laughter. The contrast was too absurd!

Gunga Dass, as he bent over the unclean bird, watched me curiously. Hindus seldom laugh, and his surroundings were not such as to move Gunga Dass to any undue excess of hilarity. He removed the crow solemnly from the wooden spit and as solemnly devoured it. Then he continued his story, which I give in his own words:—

"In epidemics of the cholera you are carried to be burned almost before you are dead. When you come to the riverside the cold air, perhaps, makes you alive, and then, if you are only little alive, mud is put on your nose and mouth and you die conclusively. If you are rather more alive, more mud is put; but if you are too lively they let you go and take you away. I was too lively, and made protestation with anger against the indignities that they endeavored to press upon me. In those days I was Brahmin and proud man. Now I am dead man and eat"—here he eyed the well-gnawed breast bone with the first sign of emotion that I had seen in him since we met—"crows, and other things. They took me from my sheets when they saw that I was too lively and gave me medicines for one week, and I survived successfully. Then they sent me by rail from my place to Okara Station, with a man to take care of me; and at Okara Station we met two other men, and they conducted we three on camels, in the night, from Okara Station to this place, and they propelled me from the top to the bottom, and the other two succeeded, and I have been here ever since two and a half years. Once I was Brahmin and proud man, and now I eat crows."

"There is no way of getting out?"

"None of what kind at all. When I first came I made experiments frequently and all the others also, but we have always succumbed to the sand which is precipitated upon our heads."

"But surely," I broke in at this point, "the river-front is open, and it is worth while dodging the bullets; while at night——"

I had already matured a rough plan of escape which a natural instinct of selfishness forbade me sharing with Gunga Dass. He, however, divined my unspoken thought almost as soon as it was formed; and, to my intense astonishment, gave vent to a long low chuckle of derision—the laughter, be it understood, of a superior or at least of an equal.

"You will not"—he had dropped the 'Sir' completely after his opening sentence—"make any escape that way. But you can try. I have tried. Once only."

The sensation of nameless terror and abject fear which I had in vain attempted to strive against overmastered me completely. My long fast—it was now close upon ten o'clock, and I had eaten nothing since tiffin on the previous day—combined with the violent and unnatural agitation of the ride had exhausted me, and I verily believe that, for a few minutes, I acted as one mad. I hurled myself against the pitiless sand-slope I ran round the base of the crater, blaspheming and praying by turns. I crawled out among the sedges of the river-front, only to be driven back each time in an agony of nervous dread by the rifle-bullets which cut up the sand round me—for I dared not face the death of a mad dog among that hideous crowd—and finally fell, spent and raving, at the curb of the well. No one bad taken the slightest notion of an exhibition which makes me blush hotly even when I think of it now.

Two or three men trod on my panting body as they drew water, but they were evidently used to this sort of thing, and had no time to waste upon me. The situation was humiliating. Gunga Dass, indeed, when he had banked the embers of his fire with sand, was at some pains to throw half a cupful of fetid water over my head, an attention for which I could have fallen on my knees and thanked him, but he was laughing all the while in the same mirthless, wheezy key that greeted me on my first attempt to force the shoals. And so, in a semi-comatose condition, I lay till noon.

Then, being only a man after all, I felt hungry, and intimated as much to Gunga Dass, whom I had begun to regard as my natural protector. Following the impulse of the outer world when dealing with natives, I put my hand into my pocket and drew out four annas. The absurdity of the gift struck me at once, and I was about to replace the money.

Gunga Dass, however, was of a different opinion. "Give me the money," said he; "all you have, or I will get help, and we will kill you!" All this as if it were the most natural thing in the world!

A Briton's first impulse, I believe, is to guard the contents of his pockets; but a moment's reflection convinced me of the futility of differing with the one man who had it in his power to make me comfortable; and with whose help it was possible that I might eventually escape from the crater. I gave him all the money in my possession, Rs. 9-8-5—nine rupees eight annas and five pice—for I always keep small change as *bakshish* when I am in camp. Gunga Dass clutched the coins, and hid them at once in his ragged loin cloth, his expression changing to something diabolical as he looked round to assure himself that no one had observed us.

"*Now* I will give you something to eat," said he.

What pleasure the possession of my money could have afforded him I am unable to say; but inasmuch as it did give him evident delight I was not sorry that I had parted with it so readily, for I had no doubt that he would have had me killed if I had refused. One does not protest against the vagaries of a den of wild beasts; and my companions were lower than any beasts. While I devoured what Gunga Dass had provided, a coarse *chapatti* and a cupful of the foul well-water, the people showed not the faintest sign of curiosity—that curiosity which is so rampant, as a rule, in an Indian village.

I could even fancy that they despised me. At all events they treated me with the most chilling indifference, and Gunga Dass was nearly as bad. I plied him with questions about the terrible village, and received extremely unsatisfactory answers. So far as I could gather, it had been in existence from time immemorial—whence I concluded that it was at least a century old—and during that time no one had ever been known to escape from it. (I had to control myself here with both hands, lest the blind terror should lay hold of me a second time and drive me raving round the crater.) Gunga Dass took a malicious pleasure in emphasizing this point and in watching me wince. Nothing that I could do would induce him to tell me who the mysterious "They" were.

"It is so ordered," he would reply, "and I do not yet know any one who has disobeyed the orders."

"Only wait till my servants find that I am missing," I retorted, "and I promise you that this place shall be cleared off the face of the earth, and I'll give you a lesson in civility, too, my friend."

"Your servants would be torn in pieces before they came near this place; and, besides, you are dead, my dear friend. It is not your fault, of course, but none the less you are dead *and* buried."

At irregular intervals supplies of food, I was told, were dropped down from the land side into the amphitheatre, and the inhabitants fought for them like wild beasts. When a man felt his death coming on he retreated to his lair and died there. The body was sometimes dragged out of the hole and thrown on to the sand, or allowed to rot where it lay

The phrase "thrown on to the sand" caught my attention, and I asked Gunga Dass whether this sort of thing was not likely to breed a pestilence.

"That." said he. with another of his wheezy chuckles, "you may see for yourself subsequently. You will have much time to make observations."

Whereat, to his great delight, I winced once more and hastily continued the conversation:—"And how do you live here from day to day? What do you do?" The question elicited exactly the same answer as before—coupled with the information that "this place is like your European heaven; there is neither marrying nor giving in marriage."

Gunga Dass had been educated at a Mission School, and, as he himself admitted, had he only changed his religion "like a wise man," might have avoided the living grave which was now his portion. But as long as I was with him I fancy he was happy.

Here was a Sahib, a representative of the dominant race, helpless as a child and completely at the mercy of his native neighbors. In a deliberate lazy way he set himself to torture me as a schoolboy would devote a rapturous half-hour to watching the agonies of an impaled beetle, or as a ferret in a blind burrow might glue himself comfortably to the neck of a rabbit. The burden of his conversation was that there was no escape "of no kind whatever," and that I should stay here till I died and was "thrown on to the sand." If it were possible to forejudge the conversation of the Damned on the advent of a new soul in their abode, I should say that they would speak as Gunga Dass did to me throughout that long afternoon. I was powerless to protest or answer; all my energies being devoted to a struggle against the inexplicable terror that threatened to overwhelm me again and again. I can compare the feeling to nothing except the struggles of a man against the overpowering nausea of the Channel passage—only my agony was of the spirit and infinitely more terrible.

As the day wore on, the inhabitants began to appear in full strength to catch the rays of the afternoon sun, which were now sloping in at the mouth of the crater. They assembled in little knots, and talked among themselves without even throwing a glance in my direction. About four o'clock, as far as I could judge Gunga Dass rose and dived into his lair for a moment, emerging with a live crow in his hands. The wretched bird was in a most draggled and deplorable condition, but seemed to be in no way afraid of its master, Advancing cautiously to the river front, Gunga Dass stepped from tussock to tussock until he had reached a smooth patch of sand directly in the line of the boat's fire. The occupants of the boat took no notice. Here he stopped, and, with a couple of dexterous turns of the wrist, pegged the bird on its back with outstretched wings. As was only natural, the crow began to shriek at once and beat the air with its claws. In a few seconds the clamor had attracted the attention of a bevy of wild crows on a shoal a few hundred yards away, where they were discussing something that looked like a corpse. Half a dozen crows flew over at once to see what was going on, and also, as it proved, to attack the pinioned bird. Gunga Dass, who had lain down on a tussock, motioned to me to be quiet, though I fancy this was needless precaution. In a moment, and before I could see how it happened, a wild crow, who had grappled with the shrieking and helpless bird, was entangled in the latter's claws, swiftly disengaged by Gunga Dass, and pegged down beside its companion in adversity. Curiosity, it seemed, overpowered the rest of the flock, and almost before Gunga Dass and I had time to withdraw to the tussock, two more captives were struggling in the upturned claws of the decoys. So the chase—if I can give it so dignified a name—continued until Gunga Dass had captured seven crows. Five of them he throttled at once, reserving two for further operations another day. I was a good deal impressed by this, to me, novel method of securing food, and complimented Gunga Dass on his skill.

"It is nothing to do," said he. "Tomorrow you must do it for me. You are stronger than I am."

This calm assumption of superiority upset me not a little, and I answered peremptorily;—"Indeed, you old ruffian! What do you think I have given you money for?"

"Very well," was the unmoved reply. "Perhaps not to-morrow, nor the day after, nor subsequently; but in the end, and for many years, you will catch crows and eat crows, and you will thank your European God that you have crows to catch and eat."

I could have cheerfully strangled him for this; but judged it best under the circumstances to smother my resentment. An hour later I was eating one of the crows; and, as Gunga Dass had said, thanking my God that I had a crow to eat. Never as long as I live shall I forget that evening meal. The whole population were squatting on the hard sand platform opposite their dens, huddled over tiny fires of refuse and dried rushes. Death, having once laid his hand upon these men and forborne to strike, seemed to stand aloof from them now; for most of our company were old men, bent and worn and twisted with years, and women aged to all appearance as the Fates themselves. They sat together in knots and talked—God only knows what they found to discuss—in low equable tones, curiously in contrast to the strident babble with which natives are accustomed to make day hideous. Now and then an access of that sudden fury which had possessed me in the morning would lay hold on a man or woman; and with yells and imprecations the sufferer would attack the steep slope until, baffled and bleeding, he fell back on the platform incapable of moving a limb. The others would never even raise their eyes when this happened, as men too well aware of the futility of their fellows' attempts and wearied with their useless repetition. I saw four such outbursts in the course of the evening.

Gunga Dass took an eminently business-like view of my situation, and while we were dining—I can afford to laugh at the recollection now, but it was painful enough at the time—propounded the terms on which he would consent to "do" for me. My nine rupees eight annas, he argued, at the rate of three annas a day, would provide me with food for fifty-one days, or about seven weeks; that is to say, he would be willing to cater for me for that length of time. At the end of it I was to look after myself. For a further consideration—*videlicet* my boots—he would be willing to allow me to occupy the den next to his own, and would supply me with as much dried grass for bedding as he could spare.

"Very well, Gunga Dass," I replied; "to the first terms I cheerfully agree, but, as there is nothing on earth to prevent my killing you as you sit here and taking everything that you have" (I thought of the two invaluable crows at the time), "I flatly refuse to give you my boots and shall take whichever den I please."

The stroke was a bold one, and I was glad when I saw that it had succeeded. Gunga Dass changed his tone immediately, and disavowed all intention of asking for my boots. At the time it did not strike me as at all strange that I, a Civil Engineer, a man of thirteen years' standing in the Service, and, I trust, an average Englishman, should thus calmly threaten murder and violence against the man who had, for a consideration it is true, taken me under his wing. I had left the world, it seemed, for centuries. I was as certain then as I am now of my own existence, that in the accursed settlement there was no law save that of the strongest; that the living dead men had thrown behind them every canon of the world which had cast them out; and that I had to depend for my own life on my strength and vigilance alone. The crew of the ill-fated *Mignonette* are the only men who would understand my frame of mind. "At present," I argued to myself, "I am strong and a match for six of these wretches. It is imperatively necessary that I should, for my own sake, keep both health and strength until the hour of my release comes—if it ever does."

Fortified with these resolutions, I ate and drank as much as I could, and made Gunga Dass understand that I intended to be his master, and that the least sign of insubordination on his part would be visited with the only punishment I had it in my power to inflict—sudden and violent death. Shortly after this I went to bed. That is to say, Gunga Dass gave me a double armful of dried bents which I thrust down the mouth of the lair to the right of his, and followed myself, feet foremost; the hole running about nine feet into the sand with a slight downward inclination, and being neatly shored with timbers. From my den, which faced the river-front, I was able to watch the waters of the Sutlej flowing past under the light of a young moon and compose myself to sleep as best I might.

The horrors of that night I shall never forget. My den was nearly as narrow as a coffin, and the sides had been worn smooth and greasy by the contact of innumerable naked bodies, added to which it smelled abominably. Sleep was altogether out of question to one in my excited frame of mind. As the night wore on, it seemed that the entire amphitheatre was filled with legions of unclean devils that, trooping up from the shoals below, mocked the unfortunates in their lairs.

Personally I am not of an imaginative temperament,—very few Engineers are,—but on that occasion I was as completely prostrated with nervous terror as any woman. After half an hour or so, however, I was able once more to calmly review my chances of escape. Any exit by the steep sand walls was, of course, impracticable. I had been thoroughly convinced of this some time before. It was possible, just possible, that I might, in the uncertain moonlight, safely run the gauntlet of the rifle shots. The place was so full of terror for me that I was prepared to undergo any risk in leaving it. Imagine my delight, then, when after creeping stealthily to the river-front I found that the infernal boat was not there. My freedom lay before me in the next few steps!

By walking out to the first shallow pool that lay at the foot of the projecting left horn of the horseshoe, I could wade across, turn the flank of the crater, and make my way inland. Without a moment's hesitation I marched briskly past the tussocks where Gunga Dass had snared the crows, and out in the direction of the smooth white sand beyond. My first step from the tufts of dried grass showed me how utterly futile was any hope of escape; for, as I put my foot down, I felt an indescribable drawing, sucking motion of the sand below. Another moment and my leg was swallowed up nearly to the knee. In the moonlight the whole surface of the sand seemed to be shaken with devilish delight at my disappointment. I struggled clear, sweating with terror and exertion, back to the tussocks behind me and fell on my face.

My only means of escape from the semicircle was protected with a quicksand!

How long I lay I have not the faintest idea; but I was roused at last by the malevolent chuckle of Gunga Dass at my ear "I would advise you, Protector of the Poor" (the ruffian was speaking English) "to return to your house. It is unhealthy to lie down here. Moreover, when the boat returns, you will most certainly be rifled at." He stood over me in the dim light of the dawn, chuckling and laughing to himself. Suppressing my first impulse to catch the man by the neck and throw him on to the quicksand, I rose sullenly and followed him to the platform below the burrows.

Suddenly, and futilley as I thought while I spoke, I asked—"Gunga Dass, what is the good of the boat if I can't get out *anyhow*?" I recollect that even in my deepest trouble I had been speculating vaguely on the waste of ammunition in guarding an already well protected foreshore.

Gunga Dass laughed again and made answer:—"They have the boat only in daytime. It is for the reason that *there is a way*. I hope we shall have the pleasure of your company for much longer time. It is a pleasant spot when you have been here some years and eaten roast crow long enough."

I staggered, numbed and helpless, toward the fetid burrow allotted to me, and fell asleep. An hour or so later I was awakened by a piercing scream—the shrill, high-pitched scream of a horse in pain. Those who have once heard that will never forget the sound. I found some little dif-ficulty in scrambling out of the burrow. When I was in the open, I saw Pornic, my poor old Pornic, lying dead on the sandy soil. How they had killed him I cannot guess. Gunga Dass explained that horse was better than crow, and "greatest good of greatest number is political maxim. We are now Republic, Mister Jukes, and you are entitled to a fair share of the beast. If you like, we will pass a vote of thanks. Shall I propose?"

Yes, we were a Republic indeed! A Republic of wild beasts penned at the bottom of a pit, to eat and fight and sleep till we died. I attempted no protest of any kind, but sat down and stared at the hideous sight in front of me. In less time almost than it takes me to write this, Pornic's body was divided, in some unclear way or other; the men and women had dragged the fragments on to the platform and were preparing their normal meal. Gunga Dass cooked mine. The almost irresistible impulse to fly at the sand walls until I was wearied laid hold of me afresh, and I had to struggle against it with all my might. Gunga Dass was offensively jocular till I told him that if he addressed another remark of any kind whatever to me I should strangle him where he sat. This silenced him till silence became insupportable, and I bade him say something.

"You will live here till you die like the other Feringhi," he said, coolly, watching me over the fragment of gristle that he was gnawing.

"What other Sahib, you swine? Speak at once, and don't stop to tell me a lie."

"He is over there," answered Gunga Dass, pointing to a burrow-mouth about four doors ta the left of my own. "You can see for yourself. He died in the burrow as you will die, and I will die, and as all these men and women and the one child will also die."

"For pity's sake tell me all you know about him. Who was he? When did he come, and when did he die?"

This appeal was a weak step on my part. Gunga Dass only leered and replied:—"I will not—unless you give me something first."

Then I recollected where I was, and struck the man between the eyes, partially stunning him. He stepped down from the platform at once, and, cringing and fawning and weeping and attempting to embrace my feet, led me round to the burrow which he had indicated.

"I know nothing whatever about the gentleman. Your God be my witness that I do not. He was as anxious to escape as you were, and he was shot from the boat, though we all did all things te prevent him from attempting. He was shot here." Gunga Dass laid his hand on his lean stomach and bowed to the earth.

"Well, and what then? Go on!"

"And then—and then, Your Honor, we carried him in to his house and gave him water, and put wet cloths on the wound, and he laid down in his house and gave up the ghost."

"In how long? In how long?"

"About half an hour, after he received his wound. I call Vishnu to witness," yelled the wretched man, "that I did everything for him. Everything which was possible, that I did!"

He threw himself down on the ground and clasped my ankles. But I had my doubts about Gunga Dass's benevolence, and kicked him off as he lay protesting.

"I believe you robbed him of everything he had. But I can find out in a minute or two. How long was the Sahib here?"

"Nearly a year and a half. I think he must have gone mad. But hear me swear Protector of the Poor! Won't Your Honor hear me swear that I never touched an article that belonged to him? What is Your Worship going to do?"

I had taken Gunga Dass by the waist and had hauled him on to the platform opposite the deserted burrow. As I did so I thought of my wretched fellow-prisoner's unspeakable misery among all these horrors for eighteen months, and the final agony of dying like a rat in a hole, with a bullet-wound in the stomach. Gunga Dass fancied I was going to kill him and howled pitifully. The rest of the population, in the plethora that follows a full flesh meal, watched us without stirring.

"Go inside, Gunga Dass," said I, "and fetch it out."

I was feeling sick and faint with horror now. Gunga Dass nearly rolled off the platform and howled aloud.

"But I am Brahmin, Sahib—a high-caste Brahmin. By your soul, by your father's soul, do not make me do this thing!"

"Brahmin or no Brahmin, by my soul and my father's soul, in you go!" I said, and, seizing him by the shoulders, I crammed his head into the mouth of the burrow, kicked the rest of him in, and, sitting down, covered my face with my hands.

At the end of a few minutes I heard a rustle and a creak; then Gunga Dass in a sobbing, choking whisper speaking to himself; then a soft thud—and I uncovered my eyes.

The dry sand had turned the corpse entrusted to its keeping into a yellow-brown mummy. I told Gunga Dass to stand off while I examined it. The body—clad in an olive-green hunting-suit much stained and worn, with leather pads on the shoulders—was that of a man between thirty and forty, above middle height, with light, sandy hair, long mustache, and a rough unkempt beard. The left canine of the upper jaw was missing, and a portion of the lobe of the right ear was gone. On the second finger of the left hand was a ring—a shield-shaped bloodstone set in gold, with a monogram that might have been either "B.K." or "B.L." On the third finger of the right hand was a silver ring in the shape of a coiled cobra, much worn and tarnished. Gunga Dass deposited a handful of trifles he had picked out of the burrow at my feet, and, covering the face of the body with my handkerchief, I turned to examine these. I give the full list in the hope that it may lead to the identification of the unfortunate man:—

1. Bowl of a briarwood pipe, serrated at the edge; much worn and blackened; bound with string at the crew.

2. Two patent-lever keys; wards of both broken.

3. Tortoise-shell-handled penknife, silver or nickel. name-plate, marked with monogram "B.K."

4. Envelope, postmark undecipherable, bearing a Victorian stamp, addressed to "Miss Mon—" (rest illegible)—"ham"—"nt."

5. Imitation crocodile-skin notebook with pencil. First forty-five pages blank; four and a half illegible; fifteen others filled with private

memoranda relating chiefly to three persons—a Mrs.L. Singleton, abbreviated several times to "Lot Single," "Mrs. S. May," and "Garmison," referred to in places as "Jerry" or "Jack."

6.Handle of small-sized hunting-knife. Blade snapped short. Buck's horn, diamond cut, with swivel and ring on the butt; fragment of cotton cord attached.

It must not be supposed that I inventoried all these things on the spot as fully as I have here written them down. The notebook first attracted my attention, and I put it in my pocket with a view of studying it later on. The rest of the articles I conveyed to my burrow for safety's sake, and there being a methodical man, I inventoried them. I then returned to the corpse and ordered Gunga Dass to help me to carry it out to the river-front. While we were engaged in this, the exploded shell of an old brown cartridge dropped out of one of the pockets and rolled at my feet. Gunga Dass had not seen it; and I fell to thinking that a man does not carry exploded cartridge-cases, especially "browns," which will not bear loading twice, about with him when shooting. In other words, that cartridge-case had been fired inside the crater. Consequently there must be a gun somewhere. I was on the verge of asking Gunga Dass, but checked myself, knowing that he would lie. We laid the body down on the edge of the quicksand by the tussocks. It was my intention to push it out and let it be swallowed up—the only possible mode of burial that I could think of. I ordered Gunga Dass to go away.

Then I gingerly put the corpse. out on the quicksand. In doing so—it was lying face downward—I tore the frail and rotten khaki shooting-coat open, disclosing a hideous cavity in the back. I have already told you that the dry sand had, as it were, mummified the body. A moment's glance showed that the gaping hole had been caused by a gun-shot wound; the gun must have been fired with the muzzle almost touching the back. The shooting-coat, being intact, had been drawn over the body after death, which must have been instantaneous. The secret of the poor wretch's death was plain to me in a flash. Some one of the crater, presumably Gunga Dass, must have shot him with his own gun—the gun that fitted the brown cartridges. He had never attempted to escape in the face of the rifle-fire from the boat.

I pushed the corpse out hastily, and saw it sink from sight literally in a few seconds. I shuddered as I watched. In a dazed, half-conscious way I turned to peruse the notebook. A stained and discolored slip of paper bad been inserted between the binding and the back, and dropped out as I opened the pages. This is what it contained:—*"Four out from crow-clump: three left; nine out; two right; three back; two left; fourteen out; two left; seven out; one left; nine back; two right; six back; four right; seven back."* The paper had been burned and charred at the edges. What it meant I could not understand. I sat down on the dried bents turning it over and over between my fingers, until I was aware of Gunga Dass standing immediately behind me with glowing eyes and outstretched hands.

"Have you got it?" he panted. "Will you not let me look at it also? I swear that I will return it."

"Got what? Return what?" asked.

"That which you have in your hands. It will help us both." He stretched out his long, bird-like talons, trembling with eagerness.

"I could never find it," he continued. "He had secreted it about his person. Therefore I shot him, but nevertheless I was unable to obtain it."

Gunga Dass had quite forgotten his little fiction about the rifle-bullet. I received the information perfectly calmly. Morality is blunted by consorting with the Dead who are alive.

"What on earth are you raving about? What is it you want me to give you?"

"The piece of paper in the notebook. It will help us both. Oh, you fool! You fool! Can you not see what it will do for us? We shall escape!"

His voice rose almost to a scream, and he danced with excitement before me. I own I was moved at the chance of my getting away.

"Don't skip! Explain yourself. Do you mean to say that this slip of paper will help us? What does it mean?"

"Read it aloud! Read it aloud! I beg and I pray you to read it aloud."

I did so. Gunga Dass listened delightedly, and drew an irregular line in the sand with his fingers.

"See now! It was the length of his gun-barrels without the stock. I have those barrels. Four gun-barrels out from the place where I caught crows Straight out; do you follow me? Then three left-Ah! how well I remember when that man worked it out night after night Then nine out, and so on. Out is always straight before you across the quicksand. He told me so before I killed him."

"But if you knew all this why didn't you get out before?"

"I did *not* know it. He told me that he was working it out a year and a half ago, and how he was working it out night after night when the boat bad gone away, and he could get out near the quicksand safely. Then he said that we would get away together. But I was afraid that he would leave me behind one night when he had worked it all out, and so I shot him. Besides, it is not advisable that the men who once get in here should escape. Only I, and *I* am a Brahmin."

The prospect of escape had brought Gunga Dass's caste back to him. He stood up, walked about and gesticulated violently. Eventually I managed to make him talk soberly, and he told me how this Englishman had spent six months night after night in exploring, inch by inch, the passage across the quicksand; how he had declared it to be simplicity itself up to within about twenty yards of the river bank after turning the flank of the left horn of the horseshoe. This much he had evidently not completed when Gunga Dass shot him with his own gun.

In my frenzy of delight at the possibilities of escape I recollect shaking hands effusively with Gunga Dass, after we had decided that we were to make an attempt to get away that very night. It was weary work waiting throughout the afternoon.

About ten o'clock, as far as I could judge, when the Moon had just risen above the lip of the crater, Gunga Dass made a move for his burrow to bring out the gun-barrels whereby to measure our path. All the other wretched inhabitants had retired to their lairs long ago. The guardian boat drifted downstream some hours before, and we were utterly alone by the crow-clump. Gunga Dass, while carrying the gun-barrels, let slip the piece of paper which was to be our guide. I stooped down hastily to recover it, and, as I did so, I was aware that the diabolical Brahmin was aiming a violent blow at the back of my head with the gun-barrels. It was too late to turn round. I must have received the blow somewhere on the nape of my neck. A hundred thousand fiery stars danced before my eyes, and I fell forwards senseless at the edge of the quicksand.

When I recovered consciousness, the Moon was going down, and I was sensible of intolerable pain in the back of my head. Gunga Dass had disappeared and my mouth was full of blood. I lay down again and prayed that I might die without more ado. Then the unreasoning fury which I had before mentioned, laid hold upon me, and I staggered inland toward the walls of the crater. It seemed that some one was calling to me in a whisper—"Sahib! Sahib! Sahib!" exactly as my bearer used to call me in the morning I fancied that I was delirious until a handful of sand fell at my feet. Then I looked up and saw a head peering down into the amphitheatre—the head of Dunnoo, my dog-boy, who attended to my collies. As soon as he had attracted my attention, he held up his hand and showed a rope. I motioned. staggering to and fro for the while, that he should throw it down. It was a couple of leather punkah-ropes knotted together, with a loop at one end. I slipped the loop over my head and under my arms; heard Dunnoo urge something forward; was conscious that I was being dragged, face downward, up the steep sand slope, and the next instant found myself choked and half fainting on the sand hills overlooking the crater.

Dunnoo, with his face ashy grey in the moonlight, implored me not to stay but to get back to my tent at once.

It seems that he had tracked Pornic's footprints fourteen miles across the sands to the crater; had returned and told my servants, who flatly refused to meddle with any one, white or black, once fallen into the hideous Village of the Dead; whereupon Dunnoo had taken one of my ponies and a couple of punkah-ropes, returned to the crater, and hauled me out as I have described.

To cut a long story short, Dunnoo is now my personal servant on a gold mohur a month—a sum which I still think far too little for the services he has rendered. Nothing on earth will induce me to go near that devilish spot again, or to reveal its whereabouts more clearly than I have done. Of Gunga Dass I have never found a trace, nor do I wish to do. My sole motive in giving this to be published is the hope that some one may possibly identify, from the details and the inventory which I have given above, the corpse of the man in the olive-green hunting-suit.

Thoughts on The Strange Ride of Morrowbie Jukes

'The Strange Ride of Morrowbie Jukes' is widely seen as an allegory of empire overthrown, and it certainly contains plenty of details unflattering to the British, but the role reversals are not all one way, as witness the vicissitudes of Gunga Dass.

Dass, whom Jukes in his former life had known as 'a jovial, full-stomached, portly Government servant', assumes in the crater the wholly different persona of a treacherous, self-serving blackmailer. 'We are now Republic, Mister Jukes.' But the bravado disappears when Jukes stands up for himself. Caste mark and turban gone, he wails: 'Once I was Brahmin and proud man, and now I eat crows.' ('Eating crow' is an American idiom first recorded at about the time this story was written.)

Jukes has to accommodate himself to the new reality. When Dass admits to having shot a white man who had been there for a year and a half he merely observes that 'Morality is blunted by consorting with the Dead who are alive.'

The story ends happily for Jukes, his escape being effected, not by the use of his skills as an engineer, but with the aid of a former servant whom he later rewards with a generous salary.

No one has been able to trace in Hindu practice a model for the community in the crater. The author's representation of it as merely one example of a widespread custom was probably no more than an attempt to lend a degree of realism to an otherwise other-worldly tale.

Some have suggested that Jukes' condition could have been the result of heat stroke upon an insomniac. And perhaps that's how we should think of it, as a horror story of a type that the nineteen year old author enjoyed writing, involving an imaginary locale where the accepted normalities of life were stood upon their heads, where friends became foes and conventional assumptions could no longer be relied upon.

Kipling later told the students at McGill university that he, like many other young men, had once experienced the 'horror of desolation, abandonment and realized worthlessness'. Could this story have come out of such an occasion?

THE MAN WHO WOULD BE KING

Brother to a Prince and fellow to a beggar if he be found worthy
- Native Proverb

The law, as quoted, lays down a fair conduct of life, and one not easy to follow. I have been fellow to a beggar again and again under circumstances which prevented either of us finding out whether the other was worthy. I have still to be brother to a Prince, though I once came near to kinship with what might have been a veritable King, and was promised the reversion of a Kingdom—army, law-courts, revenue, and policy all complete. But, today, I greatly fear that my King is dead, and if I want a crown I must go hunt it for myself.

The beginning of everything was in a railway train upon the road to Mhow from Ajmir. There had been a Deficit in the Budget, which necessitated travelling, not Second-class, which is only half as dear as First-class, but by Intermediate, which is very awful indeed. There are no cushions in the Intermediate class, and the population are either Intermediate, which is Eurasian, or native, which for a long night journey is nasty, or Loafer, which is amusing though intoxicated. Intermediates do not buy from refreshment-rooms. They carry their food in bundles and pots, and buy sweets from the native sweetmeat-sellers, and drink the road-side water. That is why in the hot weather Intermediates are taken out of the carriages dead, and in all weathers are most properly looked down upon.

My particular Intermediate happened to be empty till I reached Nasirabad, when a big black-browed gentleman in shirt-sleeves entered, and, following the custom of Intermediates, passed the time of day. He was a wanderer and a vagabond like myself, but with an edu-cated taste for whisky. He told tales of things he had seen and done, of out-of-the-way corners of the Empire into which he had penetrated, and of adventures in which he risked his life for a few days' food.

'If India was filled with men like you and me, not knowing more than the crows where they'd get their next day's rations, it isn't seventy millions of revenue the land would be paying—it's seven hundred millions,' said he; and as I looked at his mouth and chin I was disposed to agree with him.

We talked politics—the politics of Loaferdom, that see things from the underside where the lath and plaster is not smoothed off—and we talked postal arrangements because my friend wanted to send a telegram back from the next station to Ajmir, the turning-off place from the Bombay to the Mhow line as you travel westward. My friend had no money be-yond eight annas, which he wanted for dinner, and I had no money at all, owing to the hitch in the Budget before mentioned. Further, I was going into a wilderness where, though I should resume touch with the Treasury, there were no telegraph offices. I was, therefore, unable to help him in any way.

'We might threaten a Station-master, and make him send a wire on tick,' said my friend, 'but that'd mean inquiries for you and for me, and I've got my hands full these days. Did you say you are travelling back along this line within any days?'

'Within ten,' I said.

'Can't you make it eight?' said he. 'Mine is rather urgent business.'

'I can send you telegram within ten days if that will serve you,' I said.

'I couldn't trust the wire to fetch him now I think of it. It's this way. He leaves Delhi on the 23rd for Bombay. That means he'll be running through Ajmir about the night of the 23rd.'

'But I'm going into the Indian Desert,' I explained.

'Well *and* good,' said he. 'You'll be changing at Marwar Junction to get into Jodhpore territory—you must do that—and he'll be coming through Marwar Junction in the early morning of the 24th by the Bombay Mail. Can you be at Marwar Junction on that time? 'Twon't be inconveniencing you because I know that there's precious few pickings to be got out of these Central Indian States—even though you pretend to be correspondent of the *Backwoodsman*.'

'Have you ever tried that trick?' I asked.

'Again and again, but the Residents find you out, and then you get escorted to the Border before you've time to get your knife into them. But about my friend here. I *must* give him a word o' mouth to tell him what's come to me or else he won't know where to go. I would take it more than kind of you if you was to come out of Central India in time to catch him at Marwar Junction, and say to him: "He has gone South for the week." He'll know what that means. He's a big man with a red beard, and a great swell he is. You'll find him sleeping like a gentleman with all his luggage round him in a Second-class compartment. But don't you be afraid. Slip down the window, and say: "He has gone South for the week," and he'll tumble. It's only cutting your time of stay in those parts by two days. I ask you as a stranger—going to the West.' He said with emphasis.

'Where have *you* come from?' said I.

'From the East,' said he, 'and I am hoping that you will give him the message on the Square—for the sake of my Mother as well as your own.'

Englishmen are not usually softened by appeals to the memory of their mothers, but for certain reasons, which will be fully apparent, I saw fit to agree.

'It's more than a little matter,' said he, 'and that's why I asked you to do it—and now I know that I can depend on you doing it. A Second-class carriage at Marwar Junction, and a red-haired man asleep in it. You'll be sure to remember. I get out at the next station, and I must hold on there till he comes or sends me what I want.'

'I'll give the message if I catch him,' I said, 'and for the sake of your Mother as well as mine I'll give you a word of advice. Don't try to run the Central Indian States just now as the correspondent of the *Backwoodsman.* There's a real one knocking about here, and it might lead to trouble.'

'Thank you,' said he simply, 'and when will the swine be gone? I can't starve because he's ruining my work. I wanted to get hold of the Degumber Rajah down here about his father's widow, and give him a jump.'

'What did you do to his father's widow, then?'

'Filled her up with red pepper and slippered her to death as she hung from a beam. I found that out myself, and I'm the only man that would dare going into the State to get hush-money for it. They'll try to poison me, same as they did in Chortumna when I went on the loot there. But you'll give the man at Marwar Junction my message?'

He got out at a little roadside station, and I reflected. I had heard, more than once, of men personating correspondents of newspapers and bleeding small Native States with threats of exposure, but I had never met any of the caste before. They led a hard life, and generally die with great suddenness. The Native States have a wholesome horror of English newspapers which may throw light on their peculiar methods of government, and do their best to choke correspondents with champagne, or drive them out of their mind with four-in-hand barouches. They do not understand that nobody cares a straw for the internal administration of Native States so long as oppression and crime are kept within decent limits, and the ruler is not drugged, drunk, or diseased from one end of the year to the other. They are the dark places of the earth, full of unimaginable cruelty, touching the Railway and the Telegraph on one side, and, on the other, the days of Harun-al-Raschid. When I left the train I did business with divers Kings, and in eight days passed through many changes of life. Sometimes I wore dress-clothes and consorted with Princes and Politicals, drinking from crystal and eating from silver. Sometimes I lay out upon the ground and devoured what I could get, from a plate made of leaves, and drank the running water, and slept under the same rug as my servant. It was all in the day's work.

Then I headed for the Great Indian Desert upon the proper date, as I had promised, and the night Mail set me down at Marwar Junction, where a funny, little, happy-go-lucky, native-managed railway runs to Jodhpore. The Bombay Mail from Delhi makes a short halt at Marwar. She arrived as I got in, and I had just time to hurry to her platform and go down the carriages. There was only one Second-class on the train. I slipped the window and looked down upon a flaming red beard, half covered by a railway rug. That was my man, fast asleep, and I dug him gently in the ribs. He woke with a grunt, and I saw his face in the light of the lamps. It was a great and shining face.

'Tickets again?' said he.

'No,' said I. 'I am to tell you that he is gone South for the week. He has gone South for the week!'

The train had begun to move out. The red man rubbed his eyes. 'He has gone South for the week,' he repeated. 'Now that's just like his impidence. Did he say that I was to give you anything? 'Cause I won't.'

'He didn't,' I said, and dropped away, and watched the red lights die out in the dark. It was horribly cold because the wind was blowing off the sands. I climbed into my own train—not an Intermediate Carriage this time—and went to sleep.

If the man with the beard had given me a rupee I should have kept it as a memento of a rather curious affair. But the consciousness of having done my duty was my only reward.

Later on I reflected that two gentlemen like my friends could not do any good if they forgathered and personated correspondents of newspapers, and might, if they black-mailed one of the little rat-trap states of Central India or Southern Rajputana, get themselves into serious difficulties. I therefore took some trouble to describe them as accurately as I could remember to people who would be interested in deporting them; and succeeded, so I was later informed, in having them headed back from the Degumber borders.

Then I became respectable, and returned to an Office where there were no Kings and no incidents outside the daily manufacture of a newspaper. A newspaper office seems to attract every conceivable sort of person, to the prejudice of discipline. Zenana-mission ladies arrive, and beg that the Editor will instantly abandon all his duties to describe a Christian prize-giving in a back-slum of a perfectly inaccessible village; Colonels who have been overpassed for command sit down and sketch the outline of a series of ten, twelve, or twenty-four leading articles on Seniority *versus* Selection; Missionaries wish to know why they have not been permitted to escape from their regular vehicles of abuse and swear at a brother-missionary under special patronage of the editorial We; stranded theatrical companies troop up to explain that they cannot pay for their advertisements, but on their return from New Zealand or Tahiti will do so with interest; inventors of patent punkah-pulling machines, carriage couplings, and unbreakable swords and axle-trees, call with specifications in their pockets and hours at their disposal; tea-companies enter and elaborate their prospectuses with the office pens; secretaries of ball-committees clamour to have the glories of their last dance more fully described; strange ladies rustle in and say, 'I want a hundred lady's cards printed *at once*, please,' which is manifestly part of an Editor's duty; and every dissolute ruffian that ever tramped the Grand Trunk Road makes it his business to ask for employment as a proof-reader. And, all the time, the telephone-bell is ringing madly, and Kings are being killed on the Continent, and Empires are saying, 'You're another,' and Mister Gladstone is calling down brimstone upon the British Dominions, and the little black copy-boys are whining, 'kaa-pi chay-ha-yeg' tired bees, and most of the paper is as blank as Modred's shield.

But that is the amusing part of the year. There are six other months when none ever comes to call, and the thermometer walks inch by inch up to the top of the glass, and the office is darkened to just above reading-light, and the press-machines are red-hot of touch, and nobody writes anything but accounts of amusements in the Hill-stations or obituary notices. Then the telephone becomes a tinkling terror, because it tells you of the sudden deaths of men and women that you knew intimately, and the prickly-heat covers you with a garment, and you sit down and write: 'A slight increase of sickness is reported from the Khuda Janta Khan District. The outbreak is purely sporadic in its nature, and, thanks to the energetic efforts of the District authorities, is now almost at an end. It is, however, with deep regret we record the death, etc.'

Then the sickness really breaks out, and the less recording and reporting the better for the peace of the subscribers. But the Empires and the Kings continue to divert themselves as selfishly as before, and the Foreman thinks that a daily paper really ought to come out once in twenty-four hours, and all the people at the Hill-stations in the middle of their amusements say: 'Good gracious! Why can't the paper be sparkling? I'm sure there's plenty going on up here.'

That is the dark half of the moon, and, as the advertisements say, 'must be experienced to be appreciated'.

It was in that season, and a remarkably evil season, that the paper began running the last issue of the week on Saturday night, which is to say Sunday morning, after the custom of a London paper. This was a great convenience, for immediately after the paper was put to bed, the dawn would lower the thermometer from 96° to almost 84° for half an hour, and in that chill—you have no idea how cold is 84° on the grass until you begin to pray for it—a very tired man could get off to sleep ere the heat roused him.

One Saturday night it was my pleasant duty to put the paper to bed alone. A King or courtier or a courtesan or a Community was going to die or get a new Constitution, or do something that was important on the other side of the world, and the paper was to be held open till the latest possible minute in order to catch the telegram.

It was a pitchy black night, as stifling as a June night can be, and the *loo,* the red-hot wind from the westward, was booming among the tinder-dry trees and pretending that the rain was on its heels. Now and again a spot of almost boiling water would fall on the dust with the flop of a frog, but all our weary world knew that was only pretence. It was a shade cooler in the press-room than the office, so I sat there, while the type ticked and clicked, and the night-jars hooted at the windows, and the all but naked compositors wiped the sweat from their foreheads, and called for water. The thing that was keeping us back, whatever it was, would not come off, though the *loo* dropped and the last type was set, and the whole round earth stood still in the choking heat, with its finger on its lip, to wait the event. I drowsed, and wondered whether the telegraph was a blessing, and whether this dying man, or struggling people, might be aware of the inconvenience the delay was causing. There was no special reason beyond the heat and worry to make tension, but, as the clock-hands crept up to three o'clock, and the machines spun their fly-wheels two or three times to see that all was in order before I said the word that would set them off, I could have shrieked aloud.

Then the roar and rattle of the wheels shivered the quiet into little bits. I rose to go away, but two men in white clothes stood in front of me. The first one said: 'It's him!' The second said: 'So it is!' And they both laughed almost as loudly as the machinery roared, and mopped their foreheads. 'We seed there was a light burning across the road, and we were sleeping in that ditch there for coolness, and I said to my friend here, The office is open. Let's come along and speak to him as turned us back from the Degumber State,' said the smaller of the two. He was the man I had met in the Mhow train, and his fellow was the red-bearded man of Marwar Junction. There was no mistaking the eyebrows of the one or the beard of the other.

I was not pleased, because I wished to go to sleep, not to squabble with loafers. 'What do you want?' I asked.

'Half an hour's talk with you, cool and comfortable, in the office,' said the red-bearded man. 'We'd *like* some drink—the Contrack doesn't begin yet, Peachey, so you needn't look—but what we really want is advice.

We don't want money. We ask you as a favour, because we found out you did us a bad turn about Degumber State.'

I led from the press-room to the stifling office with the maps on the walls, and the red-haired man rubbed his hands. 'That's something like,' said he. 'This was the proper shop to come to. Now, Sir, let me introduce to you Brother Peachey Carnehan, that's him, and Brother Daniel Dravot, that is *me,* and the less said about our professions the better, for we have been most things in our time. Soldier, sailor, compositor, photographer, proof-reader, street-preacher, and correspondents of the *Backwoodsman* when we thought the paper wanted one. Carnehan is sober, and so am I. Look at us first, and see that's sure. It will save you cutting into my talk. We'll take one of your cigars apiece, and you shall see us light up.'

I watched the test. The men were absolutely sober, so I gave them each a tepid whisky and soda.

'Well *and* good,' said Carnehan of the eyebrows, wiping the froth from his moustache. 'Let me talk now, Dan. We have been all over India, mostly on foot. We have been boiler-fitters, engine-drivers, petty contractors, and all that, and we have decided that Indian isn't big enough for such as us.'

They certainly were too big for the office. Dravot's beard seemed to fill half the room and Carnehan's shoulders the other half, as they sat on the big table. Carnehan continued: 'The country isn't half worked out because they that governs it won't let you touch it. They spend all their blessed time in governing it, and you can't lift a spade, nor chip a rock, nor look for oil, nor anything like that, without all the Government saying, "Leave it alone, and let us govern." Therefore, such *as* it is, we will let it alone, and go away to some other place where a man isn't crowded and can come to his own. We are not little men, and there is nothing that we are afraid of except Drink, and we have signed a Contrack on that. *Therefore,* we are going away to be Kings.'

'Kings in our own right,' muttered Dravot.

'Yes, of course,' I said. 'You've been tramping in the sun, and it's a very warm night, and hadn't you better sleep over the notion? Come tomorrow.'

'Neither drunk nor sunstruck,' said Dravot. 'We have slept over the notion half a year, and require to see Books and Atlases, and we have decided that there is only one place now in the world that two strong men can Sar-a-*whack*. They call it Kafiristan. By my reckoning it's the top right-hand corner of Afghanistan, not more than three hundred miles from Peshawar. They have two-and-thirty heathen idols there, and we'll be the thirty-third and thirty-fourth. It's a mountainous country, and the women of those parts are very beautiful.'

'But that is provided against in the Contrack,' said Carnehan. 'Neither Woman nor Liqu-or, Daniel.'

'And that's all we know, except that no one has gone there, and they fight, and in any place where they fight a man who knows how to drill men can always be a King. We shall go to those parts and say to any King we find—"D'you want to vanquish your foes?" and we will show him how to drill men; for that we know better than anything else. Then we will subvert that King and seize his Throne and establish a Dy-nasty.'

'You'll be cut to pieces before you're fifty miles across the Border,' I said. 'You have to travel through Afghanistan to get to that country. It's one mass of mountains and peaks and glaciers, and no Englishman has been through it. The people are utter brutes, and even if you reached them you couldn't do anything.'

'That's more like,' said Carnehan. 'If you could think us a little more mad we would be more pleased. We have come to you to know about this country, to read a book about it, and to be shown maps. We want you to tell us that we are fools and to show us your books.' He turned to the bookcases.

'Are you at all in earnest?' I said.

'A little,' said Dravot sweetly. 'As big a map as you have got, even if it's all blank where Kafiristan is, and any books you've got. We can read, though we aren't very educated.'

I uncased the big thirty-two-miles-to-the-inch map of India, and two smaller Frontier maps, hauled down volume INF-KAN of the *Encyclopædia Britannica,* and the men consulted them.

'See here!' said Dravot, his thumb on the map. 'Up to Jagdallak, Peachey and me know the road. We was there with Roberts' Army. We'll have to turn off to the right at Jagdallak through Laghmann territory. Then we get among the hills—fourteen thousand feet—fifteen thousand—it will be cold work there, but it don't look very far on the map.'

I handed him wood on the *Sources of the Oxus.* Carnehan was deep in the *Encyclopædia.*

'They're a mixed lot,' said Dravot reflectively; 'and it won't help us to know the names of their tribes. The more tribes the more they'll fight, and the better for us. From Jagdallak to Ashang H'mm!'

'But all the information about the country is as sketchy and inaccurate as can be,' I protested. 'No one knows anything about it really. Here's the file of *United Services' Institute.* Read what Bellew says.'

'Blow Bellew,!' said Carnehan. 'Dan, they're a stinkin' lot of heathens, but this book here says they think they're related to us English.'

I smoked while the men poured over Raverty, Wood, the maps, and the *Encyclopædia.*

'There is no use your waiting,' said Dravot politely. 'It's about four o'clock now. We'll go before six o'clock if you want to sleep, and we won't steal any of the papers. Don't you sit up. We're two harmless lunatics, and if you come tomorrow evening down to the Serai, we'll say good-bye to you.'

'You *are* two fools,' I answered. 'You'll be turned back at the Frontier or cut up the minute you set foot in Afghanistan. Do you want any money or a recommendation down-country? I can help you to the chance of work next week.'

'Next week we shall be hard at work ourselves, thank you,' said Dravot. 'It isn't so easy being a King as it looks. When we've got our Kingdom in going order we'll let you know, and you can come up and help us to govern it.'

"Would two lunatics make a contrack like that?" said Carnehan, with subdued pride, showing me a greasy half-sheet of notepaper on which was written the following. I copied it, then and there, as a curiosity—

This Contract between me and you persuing witnesseth in the name of God—Amen and so forth.

(One) That me and you will settle this matter together; i.e. to be Kings of Kafiristan.

(Two) That you and me will not, while this matter is being settled, look at any Liquor, nor any Woman black, white, or brown, so as to get mixed up with one or the other harmful.

(Three) That we conduct ourselves with Dignity and Discretion, and if one of us gets into trouble the other will stay by him.

Signed by you and me this day,

Peachey Taliaferro Carnehan

Daniel Dravot

Both Gentlemen at Large

'There was no need for the last article,' said Carnehan, blushing modestly; 'but it looks regular. Now you know the sort of men that loafers are—we *are* loafers, Dan, until we get out of India—and *do* you think that we would sign a Contrack like that unless we was in earnest? We have kept away from the two things that make life worth having.'

'You won't enjoy your lives much longer if you are going to try this idiotic adventure. Don't set the office on fire,' I said, 'and go away before nine o'clock.

I left them still poring over the maps and making notes on the back of the 'Contrack'. 'Be sure to come down to the Serai tomorrow,' were their parting words.

The Kumharsen Serai is the great four-square sink of humanity where the strings of camels and horses from the North load and unload. All the nationalities of Central Asia may be found there, and most of the folk of India proper. Balkh and Bokhara there meet Bengal and Bombay, and try to draw eye-teeth. You can buy ponies, turquoises, Persian pussy-cats, saddle-bags, fat-tailed sheep and musk in the Kumharsen Serai, and get many strange things for nothing. In the afternoon I went down to see whether my friends intended to keep their word or were lying there drunk.

A priest attired in fragments of ribbons and rags stalked up to me, gravely twisting a child's paper whirligig. Behind him was his servant bending under a load of a crate of mud toys. The two were loading up two camels, and the inhabitants of the Serai watched them with shrieks of laughter.

'The priest is mad,' said a horse-dealer to me. 'He is going up to Kabul to sell toys to the Amir. He will either be raised to honor or have his head cut off. He came in here this morning and has been behaving madly ever since.'

'The witless are under the protection of God,' stammered a flat-cheeked Usbeg in broken Hindi. 'They foretell future events.'

'Would they could have foretold that my caravan would have been cut up by the Shinwaris almost within shadow of the Pass!' grunted the Eusufzai agent of a Rajputana trading-house whose goods had been diverted into the hands of other robbers just across the Border, and whose misfortunes were the laughing-stock of the basar. 'Ohé, priest, whence come you and whither do you go?'

'From Roum have I come,' shouted the priest, waving his whirligig; 'from Roum, blown by the breath of a hundred devils across the sea! O thieves, robbers, liars, the blessing of Pir Khan on pigs, dogs, and per-jurers! Who will take the Protected of God to the North to sell charms that are never still to the Amir? The camels shall not gall, the sons shall not fall sick, and the wives shall remain faithful while they are away, of the men who give me place in their caravan. Who will assist me to slip-per the King of the Roos with a golden slipper with a silver heel? The protection of Pir Khan be upon his labours!' He spread out the skirts of his gaberdine and pirouetted between the lines of tethered horses.

'There starts a caravan from Peshawar to Kabul in twenty days, *Huzrut,*' said the Eusufzai trader. 'My camels go therewith. Do thou also go and bring us good luck.'

'I will go even now!' shouted the priest. 'I will depart upon my winged camels, and be at Peshawar in a day! Ho! Hazar Mir Khan,' he yelled to his servant, 'drive out the camels, but let me first mount my own.'

He leaped on the back of his beast as it knelt, and, turning round to me, cried: 'Come thou also, Sahib, a little along the road, and I will sell thee a charm—an amulet that shall make thee King of Kafiristan.'

Then the light broke upon me, and I followed the two camels out of the Serai till we reached open road and the priest halted.

'What d'you think o' that?' said he in English. 'Carnehan can't talk their patter, so I've made him my servant. He makes a handsome serv-ant. 'Tisn't for nothing that I've been knocking about the country for fourteen years. Didn't I do that talk neat? We'll hitch on to a caravan at

Peshawar till we get to Jagdallak, and then we'll see if we can get donkeys for our camels, and strike into Kafiristan. Whirligigs for the Amir, O Lor! Put your hand under the camel-bags and tell me what you feel.'

I felt the butt of a Martini, and another and another.

'Twenty of 'em,' said Dravot placidly. 'Twenty of 'em and ammunition to correspond, under the whirligigs and the mud dolls.'

'Heaven help you if you are caught with those things!' I said. 'A Martini is worth her weight in silver among the Pathans.'

'Fifteen hundred rupees of capital—every rupee we could beg, borrow, or steal—are invested on these two camels,' said Dravot. 'We won't get caught. We're going through the Khaiber with a regular caravan. Who'd touch a poor mad priest?'

'Have you got everything you want?' I asked, overcome with astonishment.

'Not yet, but we shall soon. Give us a memento of your kindness, *Brother*. You did me a service, yesterday, and that time in Marwar. Half my Kingdom shall you have, as the saying is.' I slipped a small charm compass from my watch-chain and handed it up to the priest.

'Good-bye,' said Dravot, giving me hand cautiously. 'It's the last time we'll shake hands with an Englishman these many days. Shake hands with him, Carnehan,' he cried, as the second camel passed me.

Carnehan leaned down and shook hands. Then the camels passed away along the dusty road, and I was left alone to wonder. My eye could detect no failure in disguises. The scene in the Serai proved that they were complete to the native mind. There was just the chance, therefore, that Carnehan and Dravot would be able to wander through Afghanistan without detection. But, beyond, they would find death—certain and awful death.

Ten days later a native correspondent giving me the news of the day from Peshawar, wound up his letter with: 'There has been much laughter here on account of a certain mad priest who is going in his estimation to sell petty gauds and insignificant trinkets which he ascribes as great charms to H.H. the Amir of Bukhara. He passed through Peshawar and associated himself to the Second Summer caravan that goes to Kabul. The merchants are pleased because through superstition they imagine that such mad fellows bring good fortune.'

The two, then, were beyond the Border. I would have prayed for them, but, that night, a real King died in Europe, and demanded an obituary notice.

***

The wheel of the world swings through the same phases again and again. Summer passed and winter thereafter, and came and passed again. The daily paper continued and I with it, and upon the third summer there fell a hot night, a night-issue, and a strained waiting for something to be telegraphed from the other side of the world, exactly as had happened before. A few great men had died in the past two years, the machines worked with more clatter, and some of the trees in the office garden were a few feet taller. But that was all the difference.

I passed over to the press-room, and went through just such a scene as I have already described. The nervous tension was stronger than it had been two years before, and I felt the heat more acutely. At three o'clock I cried, 'Print off,' and turned to go when there crept to my chair what was left of a man. He was bent into a circle, his head was sunk between his shoulders, and he moved his feet one over the other like a bar. I could hardly see whether he walked or crawled—this rag-wrapped, whining cripple who addressed me by name, crying that he was come back. 'Can you give me a drink?' he whimpered. 'For the Lord's sake give me a drink!'

I went back to the office, the man following with groans of pain, and I turned on the lamp.

'Don't you know me?' he gasped, dropping into a chair, and he turned his drawn face, surmounted by a shock of grey hair, to the light.

68

I looked at him intently. Once before had I seen eyebrows that met over the nose in an inch-broad black band, but for the life of me I could not tell where.

'I don't know you,' I said, handing him the whisky. 'What can I do for you?'

He took a gulp of the spirit raw, and shivered in spite of the suffocating heat.

'I've come back,' he repeated; 'and I was the King of Kafiristan—me and Dravot—crowned Kings we was! In this office we settled it—you setting there and giving us the books. I am Peachey—Peachey Taliaferro Carnehan, and you've been setting here ever since—O Lord!'

I was more than a little astonished, and expressed my feelings accordingly.

'It's true,' said Carnehan, with a dry cackle, nursing his feet, which were wrapped in rags. 'True as gospel. Kings we were, with crowns upon our heads—me and Dravot—poor Dan—oh, poor, poor Dan, that would never take advice, not though I begged of him!'

'Take the whisky,' I said, 'and take your own time. Tell me all you can recollect of everything from beginning to end. You got across the Border on your camels, Dravot dressed as a mad priest and you his servant. Do you remember that?'

'I ain't mad—yet, but I shall be that way soon. Of course I remember. Keep looking at me, or maybe my words will go all to pieces. Keep looking at me in my eyes and don't say anything.'

I leaned forward and looked into his face as steadily as I could. He dropped one hand upon the table and I grasped it by the wrist. It was twisted like a bird's claw, and upon the back was a ragged red diamond-shaped scar.

'No, don't look there. Look at *me*,' said Carnehan. 'That comes afterwards, but for the Lord's sake don't distrack me. We left with that caravan, me and Dravot playing all sorts of antics to amuse the people we were with. Dravot used to make us laugh in the evenings when all the people was cooking their dinners—cooking their dinners, and . . . what did they do then? They lit little fires with sparks that went into Dravot's beard, and we all laughed—fit to die. Little red fires they was, going into Dravot's big red beard—so funny.' His eyes left mine and he smiled foolishly.

'You went as far as Jagdallak with that caravan,' I said at a venture, 'after you had lit those fires. To Jagdallak, where you turned off to try to get into Kafiristan.'

'No, we didn't neither. What are you talking about? We turned off before Jagdallak, because we heard the roads was good. But they wasn't good enough for our two camels—mine and Dravot's. When we left the caravan, Dravot took off all his clothes and mine too, and said we would be heathen, because the Kafirs didn't allow Mohammedans to talk to them. So we dressed betwixt and between, and such a sight as Daniel Dravot I never saw yet nor expect to see again. He burned half his beard, and slung a sheep-skin over his shoulder, and shaved his head into patters. He shaved mine, too, and made me wear outrageous things to look like a heathen. That was in a most mountaineous country, and our camels couldn't go along any more because of the mountains. They were tall and black, and coming home I saw them fight like wild goats— there are lots of goats in Kafiristan. And these mountains, they never keep still, no more than the goats. Always fighting they are, and don't let you sleep at night.'

'Take some more whisky,' I said very slowly. 'What did you and Daniel Dravot do when the camels could go no farther because of the rough roads that led into Kafiristan?'

'What did which do? There was a party called Peachey Taliaferro Carnehan that was with Dravot. Shall I tell you about him? He died out there in the cold. Slap from the bridge fell old Peachy, turning and twisting in the air like a penny whirligig that you can sell to the Amir— No; they was two for three ha'pence, those whirligigs, or I am much mistaken and woful sore . . . And then these camels were no use, and Peachey said to Dravot— "For the Lord's sake let's get out of this before our heads are chopped off," and with that they killed the camels all among the mountains, not having anything in particular to teat, but first they took off the boxes with the guns and the ammunition, till two men came along driving four mules. Dravot up and dances in front of them, singing— "Sell me four mules." Says the first man— "If you are rich enough to buy, you are rich enough to rob"; but before ever he could put his hand to his knife, Dravot breaks his neck over his knee, and the other party runs away. So Carnehan loaded the mules with the rifles that was taken off the camels, and together we starts forward into those bitter cold mountaineous parts, and never a road broader than the back of your hand.'

He paused for a moment, while I asked him if he could remember the nature of the country through which he had journeyed.

'I am telling you as straight as I can, but my head isn't as good as it might be. They drove nails through it to make me hear better how Dravot died. The country was mountaineous and the mules were most contrary, and the inhabitants was dispersed and solitary. They went up and up, and down and down, and that other party, Carnehan, was imploring of Dravot not to sing and whistle so loud, for fear of bringing down the tremenjus avalanches. But Dravot says that if a King couldn't sing it wasn't worth being King, and whacked the mules over the rump, and never took no heed for ten cold days. We came to a big level valley all among the mountains, and the mules were near dead, so we killed them, not having anything in special for them or us to eat. We sat upon the boxes, and played odd and even with the cartridges that was jolted out.

'Then ten men with bows and arrows ran down that valley, chasing twenty men with bows and arrows, and the row was tremenjus. They was fair men—fairer than you or me—with yellow hair and remarkable well built. Says Dravot, unpacking the guns— "This is the beginning of the business. We'll fight for the ten men," and with that he first two rifles at the twenty men, and drops one of them at two hundred yards from the rock where he was sitting. The other men began to run, but

Carnehan and Dravot sits on the boxes picking them off at all ranges, up and down the valley. Then we goes up to the ten men that had run across the snow too, and they fires a footy little arrow at us. Dravot he shoots above their heads and they all falls down flat. Then he walks over them and kicks them, and then he lifts them up and shakes hands all round to make them friendly like. He calls them and gives them the boxes to carry, and waves his hand for all the world as though he was King already. They takes the boxes and him across the valley and up the hill into a pine wood on the top, where there was half-a-dozen big stone idols. Dravot he goes to the biggest—a fellow they call Imbra— and lays a rifle and a cartridge at his feet, rubbing his nose respectful with his own nose, patting him on the head, and saluting in front of it. He turns round to the men and nods his head, and says— "That's all right. I'm in the know too, and all these old jim-jams are my friends." Then he opens his mouth and points down it, and when the first man brings him food, he says— "No"; and when the second man brings him food, he says— "No"; but when one of the old priests and the boss of the village brings him food, he says— "Yes," very haughty, and eats it slow. That was how we came to our first village, without any trouble, just as though we had tumbled from the skies. But we tumbled from one of those damned rope-bridges, you see, and—you couldn't expect a man to laugh much after that?'

'Take some more whisky and go on,' I said. 'That was the first village you came into. How did you get to be King?'

'I wasn't King,' said Carnehan. 'Dravot he was the King, and a handsome man he looked with the gold crown on his head and all. Him and the other party stayed in that village, and every morning Dravot sat by the side of old Imbra, and the people came and worshipped. That was Dravot's order. Then a lot of men came into the valley, and Carnehan and Dravot picks them off with the rifles before they knew where they was, and runs down into the valley and up again the other side and finds another village, same as the first one, and the people all falls down flat on their faces, and Dravot says— "Now what is the trouble between you two villages?" and the people points to a woman, as fair as you or me, that was carried off, and Dravot takes her back to the first village and counts up the dead—eight there was. For each dead man Dravot pours a little milk on the ground and waves his arms like a whirligig, and "That's all right," says he. Then he and Carnehan takes the big boss of each village by the arm and walks them down into the valley, and shows them how to scratch a line with a spear right down the valley, and gives each a sod of turf form both sides of the line. Then all the people comes down and shouts like the devil and all, and Dravot says— "Go and dig the land, and be fruitful and multiply," which they did, though they didn't understand. Then we asks the names of things in their lingo—bread and water and fire and idols and such, and Dravot leads the priest of each village up to the idol, and says he must sit there and judge the people, and if anything goes wrong he is to be shot.

'Next week they was all turning up the land in the village as quiet as bees and much prettier, and the priests heard all the complaints and told Dravot in dumb show what it was about. "That's just the beginning," says Dravot. "They think we're Gods." He and Carnehan picks out twenty good men and shows them how to click off a rifle, and form fours, and advance in line, and they was very pleased to do so, and clever to see the hang of it. Then he takes out his pipe and is baccy-pouch and leaves one at one village, and one at the other, and off we two goes to see what was to be done in the next valley. That was all rock, and there was a little village there, and Carnehan says— "Send 'em to the old valley to plant," and takes 'em there, and gives 'em some land that wasn't took before. They were a poor lot, and we blooded 'em with a kid before letting 'em into the new Kingdom. That was to impress the people, and then they settled down quiet, and Carnehan went back to Dravot who had got into another valley, all snow and ice and most mountaineous. There was no people there and the Army got afraid, so Dravot shoots one of them, and goes on till he finds some people in a village, and the Army explains that unless the people wants to be killed they had better not shoot their little matchlocks; for they had matchlocks. We makes friends with the priest, and I stays there alone with two of the Army, teaching the men how to drill, and a thundering big Chief comes across the snow with kettle-drums and horns twanging, because he heard there was a new God kicking about. Carnehan sights for the brown of the men half a mile across the snow and wings one of them. Then he sends a message to the Chief that, unless he wished to be killed, he must come and shake hands with me and leave his arms behind. The Chief comes alone first, and Carnehan shakes hands with him and whirls his arms about, same as Dravot used, and very much surprised that Chief was, and strokes my eyebrows. Then Carnehan goes alone to the Chief, and asks him in dumb show if he had an enemy he hated. "I have," says the Chief. So Carnehan weeds out the pick of his men, and sets the two of the Army to show them drill, and at the end of two weeks the men can manoeuvre about as well as Volunteers. So he marches with the Chief to a great big plain on the top of a mountain, and the Chief's men rushes into a village and takes it, we three Martinis firing into the brown of the enemy. So we took that village too, and I gives the Chief a rag from my coat and says, "Occupy till I come"; which was scriptural. By way of a reminder, when me and the Army was eighteen hundred yards away, I drops a bullet near him standing on the snow, and all the people falls flat on their faces. Then I sends a letter to Dravot wherever he be by land or by sea.'

At the risk of throwing the creature out of train I interrupted— 'How could you write a letter up yonder?'

'The letter?—Oh!—The letter! Keep looking at me between the eyes, please. It was a string-talk letter, that we'd learned the way of it from a blind beggar in the Punjab.'

I remember that there had once come to the office a blind man with a knotted twig and a piece of string which he wound round the twig according to some cipher of his own. He could, after the lapse of days or hours, repeat the sentence which he had reeled up. He had reduced the alphabet to eleven primitive sounds, and tried to teach me the method, but I could not understand.

'I sent that letter to Dravot,' said Carnehan; 'and told him to come back because this Kingdom was growing too big for me to handle, and then I struck for the first valley, to see how the priests were working. They called the village we took along with the Chief, Bashkai, and the first village we took, Er-Heb. The priests at Er-Heb was doing all right, but they had a lot of pending cases about land to show me, and some men from another village had been firing arrows at night. I went out and looked for that village, and fired four rounds at it from a thousand yards. That used all the cartridges I cared to spend, and I waited for Dravot, who had been away two or three months, and I kept my people quiet.

'One morning I heard the devil's own noise of drums and horns, and Dan Dravot marches down the hill with his Army and a tail of hundreds of men, and, which was the most amazing, a great gold crown on his head. "My Gord, Carnehan," says Daniel, "this is a tremenjus business, and we've got the whole country as far as it's worth having. I am the son of Alexander by Queen Semiramis, and you're my younger brother and a God too! It's the biggest thing we've ever seen. I've been marching and fighting for six weeks with the Army, and every footy little village for fifty miles has come in rejoiceful; and more than that, I've got the key of the whole show, as you'll see, and I've got a crown for you! I told 'em to make two of 'em at a place called Shu, where the gold lies in the rock like suet in mutton. Gold I've seen, and turquoise I've kicked out of the cliffs, and there's garnets in the sands of the river, and here's a chunk of amber that a man brought me. Call up all he priests and, here, take your crown."

'One of the men opens a black hair bag, and I slips the crown on It was too small and too heavy, but I wore it for the glory. Hammered gold it was—five pound weight, like a hoop of a barrel.

'"Peachey," says Dravot, "we don't want to fight no more. The Craft's the trick, so help me!" and he brings forward that same Chief that I left at Bashkai—Billy Fish we called him afterwards, because he was so like Billy Fish that drove the big tank-engine at Mach on the Bolan in the old days. "Shake hands with him," says Dravot, and I shook hands and nearly dropped, for Billy Fish gave me the Grip. I said nothing, but tried him with the Fellow Craft Grip. He answers all right, and I tried the Master's Grip, but that was a slip. "A Fellow Craft he is!" I says to Dan, "Does he know the word? — "He does," says Dan, "and all the priests know. It's a miracle! The Chiefs and the priests can work a Fellow Craft Lodge in a way that's very like ours, and they've cut the marks on the rocks, but they don't know the Third Degree, and they've come to find out. It's Gord's Truth. I've known these long years that the Afghans knew up to the Fellow Craft Degree, but this is a miracle. A God and a Grand-Master of the Craft am I, and a Lodge in the Third Degree I will open, and we'll raise the head priests and the Chiefs of the Village."

"'It's against all the law," says I, "holding a Lodge without warrant from any one; and you know we never held office in any Lodge."

"'It's a master-stroke o' policy," says Dravot. "It means running the country as easy as a four-wheeled bogie on a down grade. We can't stop to inquire now, or they'll turn against us. I've forty Chiefs at my heel, and passed and raised according to their merit they shall be. Billet these men on the villages, and see that we run up a Lodge of some kind. The temple of Imbra will do for the Lodge-room. The women must make aprons as you show them. I'll hold a levee of Chiefs tonight and Lodge tomorrow."

'I was fair run off my legs, but I wasn't such a fool as not to see what a pull this Craft business gave us. I showed the priests' families how to make aprons of the degrees, but for Dravot's apron the blue border and marks was made of turquoise lumps on white hide, not cloth. We took a great square stone in the temple for the Master's chair, and little stones for the officers' chairs, and painted the black pavement with white squares, and did what we could to make things regular.

'At the levee which was held that night on the hillside with big bonfires, Dravot gives out that him and me were Gods and sons of Alexander, and Past Grand-Masters in the Craft, and was come to make Kafiristan a country where every man should eat in peace and drink in quiet, and especially obey us. Then the Chiefs come round to shake hands, and they were so hairy and white and fair it was just shaking hands with old friends. We gave them names according as they was like men we had known in India—Billy Fish, Holly Dilworth, Pikky Kergan, that was Bazar-master when I was at Mhow, and so on, and so on.

'*The* most amazing miracles was at Lodge next night. One of the old priests was watching us continuous, and I felt uneasy, for I knew we'd have to fudge the Ritual, and I didn't know what the man knew. The old priest was a stranger come in from beyond the village of Bashkai. The minute Dravot puts on that Master's apron that the girls had made for him, the priest fetches a whoop and a howl, and tries to overturn the stone that Dravot was sitting on. "It's all up now," I says. "That comes of meddling with the Craft without warrant!" Dravot never winked an eye, not when ten priests took and tilted over the Grand-Master's chair—which was to say the stone of Imbra. The priests begins rubbing the bottom end of it to clear away the black dirt, and presently he shows all the other priests the Master's Mark, same as was on Dravot's apron, cut into the stone. Not even the priests of the temple of Imbra knew it was there. The old chap falls flat on his face at Dravot's feet and kisses 'em. "Luck again," says Dravot, across the Lodge to me; "they say it's the Missing Mark that no one could understand the why of. We're more than safe now." Then he bangs the butt of his gun for a gavel and says: "By virtue of the authority vested in me by my own right hand and the help of Peachey, I declare myself Grand-Master of all Freemasonry in Kafiristan in this the Mother Lodge o' the country, and King of Kafiristan equally with Peachey!" At that he puts on his crown and I puts on mine—I was doing Senior Warden—and we opens the Lodge in most ample form. It was an amazing miracle! The priests moved in Lodge through the first two degrees almost without telling, as if the memory was coming back to them. After than, Peachey and Dravot raised such as was worthy—high priests and Chiefs of far-off villages. Billy Fish was the first, and I can tell you we scared the soul out of him. It was not in any way according to Ritual, but it served our turn. We didn't raise more than ten of the biggest men, because we didn't want to make the Degree common. And they was clamouring to be raised.

"'In another six months," says Dravot, "we'll hold another Communication, and see how you are working." Then he asks them about their villages, and learns that they was fighting one against the other, and were sick and tired of it. And when they weren't doing that they was fighting with the Mohammedans. "You can fight those when they come into our country," says Dravot. "Tell off every tenth man of your tribes for a Frontier guard, and send two hundred at a time to this valley to be drilled. Nobody is going to be shot or speared any more so long as he does well, and I know that you won't cheat me, because you're white people—sons of Alexander—and not like common, black Mohammedans. You are *my* people, and by God," says he, running off into English at the end— "I'll make a damned fine Nation of you, or I'll die in the making!"

'I can't tell all we did for the next six months, because Dravot did a lot I couldn't see the hang of, and he learned their lingo in a way I never could. My work was to help the people plough, and now and again go out with some of the Army and see what the other villages were doing, and make 'em throw rope-bridges across the ravines which cut up the country horrid. Dravot was very kind to me, but when he walked up and down in the pine wood pulling that bloody red beard of his with both fists I knew he was thinking plans I would not advise about, and I just waited for orders.

'But Dravot never showed me disrespect before the people. They were afraid of me and the Army, but they loved Dan. He was the best of friends with the priests and the Chiefs; but anyone could come across the hills with a complaint, and Dravot would hear him out fair, and call four priests together and say what was to be done. He used to call in Billy Fish from Bashkai, and Pikky Kergan from Shu, and an old Chief we called Kafuzelum—it was like enough to his real name—and hold councils with 'em when there was any fighting to be done in small villages. That was his Council of War, and the four preists of Bashkai, Shu, Khawak, and Madora was his Privy Council. Between the lot of 'em they sent me, with forty men and twenty rifles and sixty men carrying turquoises, into the Ghorband country to buy those hand-made Martini rifles, that come out of the Amir's workshops at Kabul, from one of the Amir's Herati regiments that would have sold the very teeth out of their mouths for turquoises.

'I stayed in Ghorband a month, and gave the Governor there the pick of my baskets for hush-money, and bribed the Colonel of the regiment some more, and, between the two and the tribespeople, we got more than a hundred hand-made Martinis, a hundred good Kohat Jezails that'll throw to six hundred yards, and forty man-loads of very bad ammunition for the rifles. I came back with what I had, and distributed 'em among the men that the Chiefs sent in to me to drill. Dravot was too busy to attend to those things, but the old Army that we first made helped me, and we turned out five hundred men that could drill, and two hundred that knew how to hold arms pretty straight. Even those cork-screwed, hand-made guns was a miracle to them. Dravot talked big about powder-shops and factories, walking up and down in the pine wood when the winter was coming on.

"'I won't make a Nation," says he. "I'll make an Empire! These men aren't niggers; they're English! Look at their eyes—look at their mouths. Look at the way they stand up. They sit on chairs in their own houses. They're the Lost Tribes, or something like it, and they've grown to be English. I'll take a census in the spring if the priests don't get frightened. There must be a fair two million of 'em in these hills. The villages are full o' little children. Two million people—two hundred and fifty thousand fighting men—and all English! They only want the rifles and a little drilling. Two hundred and fifty thousand men, ready to cut in on Russia's right flank when she tries for India! Peachey, man," he says, chewing his bard in great hunks, "we shall be Emperors—Emperors of the Earth! Rajah Brooke will be a suckling to us. I'll treat with the Viceroy on equal terms. I'll ask him to send me twelve picked English—to help us govern a bit. There's Mackray, Sergeant-pensioner at Segowli—many's the good dinner he's given me, and his wife a pair of trousers. There's Donkin, the Warder of Tounghoo Jail; there's hundreds that I could lay my hands on if I was in India. The Viceroy shall do it for me. I'll send a man through in the spring for those men, and I'll write for a dispensation from the Grand Lodge for what I've done as Grand-Master. That—and all the Sniders that'll be thrown out when the native troops in India take up the Martini. They'll be worn smooth, but they'll do for fighting in these hills. Twelve English, a hundred thousand Sniders run through the Amir's country in driblets—I'd be content with twenty thousand in one year—and we'd be an Empire. When everything was shipshape I'd hand over the crown—this crown that I'm wearing now—to Queen Victoria on my knees, and she'd say: 'Rise up, Sir Daniel Dravot.' Oh, it's big! It's big, I tell you! But there's so much to be done in every place—Bashkai, Khawak, Shu, and everywhere else."

79

"'What is it?" I says. "There are no more men coming in to be drilled this autumn. Look at those fat, black clouds. They're bringing the snow."

"'It isn't that," says Daniel, putting his hand very hard on my shoulder; "and I don't wish to say anything that's against you, for no other living man would have followed me and made me what I am as you have done. You're a first-class Commander-in-Chief, and the people know you, but—it's a big country, and somehow you can't help me, Peachey, in the way I want to be helped."

"'Go to your blasted priests, then!" I said, and I was sorry when I made that remark, but it did hurt me sore to find Daniel talking so superior when I'd drilled all the men, and done all he told me.

"'Don't let's quarrel, Peachey," says Daniel without cursing. "You're a King too, and the half of this Kingdom is yours; but can't you see, Peachey, we want cleverer men than us now—three or four of 'em, that we can scatter about for our Deputies. It's a hugeous great State, and I can't always tell the right thing to do, and I haven't time for all I want to do, and here's the winter coming on and all." He put half his beard into his mouth, all red like the gold of his crown.

"'I'm sorry, Daniel," says I. "I've done all I could. I've drilled the men and shown the people how to stack their oats better; and I've brought in those tinware rifles from Ghorband—but I know what you're driving at. I take it Kings always feel oppressed that way."

"'There's another thing too," says Dravot, walking up and down. "The winter's coming and these people won't be giving much trouble, and if they do we can't move about. I want a wife."

"'For God's sake leave the women alone!" I says. "We've both got all the work we can, though I *am* a fool. Remember the Contrack, and keep clear o' women."

"'The Contrack only lasted till such time as we was Kings; and Kings we have been these months past," says Dravot, weighting his crown in his hand. "You go get a wife too, Peachey—a nice, strappin', plump girl that'll keep you warm in the winter. They're prettier than English girls, and we can take the pick of 'em. Boil 'em once or twice in hot water and they'll come out like chicken and ham."

"'Don't tempt me!' I says. "I will not have any dealings with a woman not till we are a dam' side more settled than we are now. I've been doing the work o' two men, and you've been doing the work o' three. Let's lie off a bit, and see if we can get some better tobacco from Afghan country and run in some good liquor; but no women."

"'Who's talking o' *women?*" says Dravot. "I said *wife*—a Queen to breed a King's son for the King. A Queen out of the strongest tribe, that'll make them your blood-brothers, and that'll lie by your side and tell you all the people thinks about you and their own affairs. That's what I mena."

"'Do you remember that Bengali woman I kept at Mogul Serai when I was a plate-layer?" says I. "A fat lot o' good she was to me. She taught me the lingo and one or two other things; but what happened? She ran away with the Station-master's servant and half my month's pay. Then she turned up at Dadur Junction in tow of a half-caste, and had the impidence to say I was her husband—all among the drivers in the running-shed too!"

"'We've done with that," says Dravot; "these women are whiter than you or me, and a Queen I will have for the winter months."

"'For the last time o' asking, Dan, do *not*," I says. "It'll only bring us harm. The Bible says that Kings ain't to waste their strength on women, 'specially when they've got a new raw Kingdom to work over."

"'For the last time of answering I will," said Dravot, and he went away through the pine-trees looking like a big red devil, the sun being on his crown and beard and all.

'But getting a wife was not as easy as Dan thought. He put it before the Council, and there was no answer till Billy Fish said that he'd better ask the girls. Dravot damned them all around. "What's wrong with me?" he shouts, standing by the idol Imbra. "Am I a dog or am I not enough of a man for your wenches? Haven't I put the shadow of my hand over this country? Who stopped the last Afghan raid?" It was me really, but Dravot was too angry to remember. "Who bought your guns? Who repaired the bridges? Who's the Grand-Master of the sign cut in the stone?" says he, and he thumped his hand on the block that he used to sit on in Lodge, and at Council, which opened like Lodge always. Billy Fish said nothing and no more did the others. "Keep your hair on, Dan," said I; "and ask the girls. That's how it's done at Home, and these people are quite English."

"'The marriage of the King is a matter of State," says Dan, in a white-hot rage, for he could feel, I hope, that he was going against his better mind. He walked out of the Council-room, and the others sat still, looking at the ground.

"'Billy Fish," says I to the Chief of Bashkai, "what's the difficulty here? A straight answer to a true friend."

"'You know," says Billy Fish. "How should a man tell you who knows everything? How can daughters of men marry Gods or Devils? It's not proper."

'I remembered something like that in the Bible; but if, after seeing us as long as they had, they still believed we were Gods, it wasn't for me to undeceive them.

"'A God can do anything," says I. "If the King is fond of a girl he'll not let her die." — "She'll have to," said Billy Fish. "There are all sorts of Gods and Devils in these mountains, and now and again a girl marries one of them and isn't seen any more. Besides, you two know the Mark cut in the stone. Only the Gods know that. We thought you were men till you showed the sign of the Master."

'I wished then that we had explained about the loss of the genuine secrets of a Master-Mason at the first go-off; but I said nothing. All that night there was a blowing of horns in a little dark temple half-way down the hill, and I heard a girl crying fit to die. One of the priests told us that she was being prepared to marry the King.

"'I'll have no nonsense of that kind," says Dan. "I don't want to interfere with your customs, but I'll take my own wife." — "The girl's a bit afraid," says the priest. "She thinks she's going to die, and they are a-heartening of her up down in the temple."

"'Hearten her very tender, then," says Dravot, "or I'll hearten you with the butt of a gun so you'll never want to be heartened again." He licked his lips, did Dan, and stayed up walking about more than half the night, thinking of the wife that he was going to get in the morning. I wasn't any means comfortable, for I knew that dealings with a woman in foreign parts, though you was a crowned King twenty times over, could not but be risky. I got up very early in the morning while Dravot was asleep, and I saw the priests talking together in whispers, and the Chiefs talking together too, and they looked at me out of the corners of their eyes.

"'What is up, Fish?" I say to the Bashkai man, who was wrapped up in his furs and looking splendid to behold.

"'I can't rightly say," says he, "but if you can make the King drop all this nonsense about marriage, you'll be doing him and me and yourself a great service."

"'That I do believe," says I. "But sure, you know, Billy, as well as me, having fought against and for us, that the King and me are nothing more than two of the finest men that God Almighty ever made. Nothing more, I do assure you."

"'That may be," says Billy Fish, "and yet I should be sorry if it was." He sinks his head upon his great fur cloak for a minute and thinks. "King," says he, "be you man or God or Devil, I'll stick by you today. I have twenty of my men with me, and they will follow me. We'll go to Bashkai until the storm blows over."

'A little snow had fallen in the night, and everything was white except the greasy fat clouds that blew down and down from the north. Dravot came out with his crown on his head, swinging his arms and stamping his feet, and looking more pleased than Punch.

'"For the last time, drop it, Dan," says I in a whisper, "Billy Fish here says that there will be a row."

'"A row amongst my people!" says Dravot. "Not much, Peachey, you're a fool not to get a wife too. Where's the girl?" says he with a voice as loud as the braying of a jackass. "Call up all the Chiefs and priests, and let the Emperor see if his wife suits him."

'There was no need to call anyone. They were all there leaning on their guns and spears round the clearing in the centre of the pine wood. A lot of priests went down to the little temple to bring up the girl, and the horns blew fit to wake the dead. Billy Fish saunters round and gets as close to Daniel as he could, and behind him stood his twenty men with matchlocks. Not a man of them under six feet. I was next to Dravot, and behind me was twenty men of the regular Army. Up comes the girl, and a strapping wench she was, covered with silver and turquoises, but white as death, and looking back every minute at the priests.

'"She'll do," said Dan, looking her over. "What's to be afraid of, lass? Come and kiss me." He puts his arm round her. She shuts her eyes, gives a bit of a squeak, and down goes her face in the side of Dan's flaming red beard.

'"The slut's bitten me!" says he, clapping his hand to his neck, and, sure enough, his hand was red with blood. Billy Fish and two of his match-lock-men catches hold of Dan by the shoulders and drags him into the Bashkai lot, while the priests howls in their lingo— "Neither God nor Devil but a man!" I was all taken aback, for a priest cut at me in front, and the Army behind began firing into the Bashkai men.

'"God A'mighty!" says Dan. "What is the meaning o' this?"

"'Come back! Come away!" says Billy Fish. "Ruin and Mutiny is the matter. We'll break for Bashkai if we can."

'I tried to give some sort of orders to my men—the men of the Regular Army—but it was no use, so I fired into the brown of 'em with an English Martini and drilled three beggars in a line. The valley was full of shouting, howling creatures, and every soul was shrieking, "Not a God or a Devil but only a man!" The Bashkai troops stuck to Billy Fish for all they were worth, but their matchlocks wasn't half as good as the Kabul breech-loaders, and four of them dropped. Dan was bellowing like a bull, for he was very wrathy; and Billy Fish had a hard job to prevent him running out at the crowd.

"'We can't stand," says Billy Fish. "Make a run for it down the valley! The whole place is against us." The matchlock-men ran, and we went down the valley in spite of Dravot. He was swearing horribly and crying out he was King. The priests rolled great stones on us, and the regular Army fired hard, and there wasn't more than six men, not counting Dan, Billy Fish, and Me, that came down to the bottom of the valley alive.

'Then they stopped firing and the horns in the temple blew again. "Come away—for God's sake come away!" says Billy Fish. "They'll send runners out to all the villages before ever we get to Bashkai. I can protect you there, but I can't do anything now."

'My own notion is that Dan began to go mad in his head from that hour. He stared up and down like a stuck pig. Then he was all for walking back alone and killing the priests with his bare hands; which he could have done. "An Emperor am I," says Daniel, "and next year I shall be a Knight of the Queen."

"'All right, Dan," says I, "but come along now while there's time."

"'It's your fault," says he, "for not looking after your Army better. There was mutiny in the midst, and you didn't know—you damned engine-driving, plate-laying, missionary's-pass-hunting hound!" He sat upon a rock and called me every foul name he could lay tongue to. I was too heart-sick to care, though it was all his foolishness that brought the smash.

"'I'm sorry, Dan,' says I, "but there's no accounting for natives. This business is our Fifty-Seven. Maybe we'll make something out of it yet, when we've got to Bashkai."

"'Let's get to Bashkai, then,' says Dan, "and, by God, when I come back here again I'll sweep the valley so there isn't a bug in a blanket left!"

'We walked all that day, and all that night Dan was stumping up and down on the snow, chewing his beard and muttering to himself.

"'There's no hope o' getting clear,' said Billy Fish. "The priests will have sent runners to the villages to say that you are only men. Why didn't you stick on as Gods till things was more settled? I'm a dead man," says Billy Fish, and he throws himself down on the snow and begins to pray to his Gods.

'Next morning we was in a cruel bad country—all up and down, no level ground at all, and no food either. The six Bashkai men looked at Billy Fish hungry-way as if they wanted to ask something, but they said never a word. At noon we came to the top of a flat mountain all covered with snow, and when we climbed up into it, behold, there was an Army in position waiting in the middle!

"'The runners have been very quick,' says Billy Fish, with a little bit of a laugh. "They are waiting for us."

'Three or four men began to fire from the enemy's side, and a chance shot took Daniel in the calf of the leg. That brought him to his senses. He looks across the snow at the Army, and sees the rifles that we had brought into the country.

"'We're done for,' says he. "They are Englishmen, these people—and it's by blasted nonsense that has brought you to this. Get back, Billy Fish, and take your men away; you've done what you could, and now cut for it. Carnehan," says he, "shake hands with me and go along with Billy. Maybe they won't kill you. I'll go and meet 'em alone. It's me that did it. Me, the King!"

"Go!" says I. "Go to Hell, Dan! I'm with you here. Billy Fish, you clear out, and we two will meet these folk."

"'I'm a Chief," says Billy Fish, quite quiet. "I stay with you. My men can go."

'The Bashkai fellows didn't wait for a second word, but ran off, and Dan and Me and Billy Fish walked across to where the drums were drumming and the horns were horning. It was cold—awful cold. I've got that cold in the back of my head now. There's a lump of it there.'

The punkah-coolies had gone to sleep. Two kerosene lamps were blazing in the office, and the perspiration poured down my face and splashed on the blotter as I leaned forward. Carnehan was shivering, and I feared that his mind might go. I wiped my face, took a fresh grip of the piteously mangled hands, and said: 'What happened after that?'

The momentary shift of my eyes had broken the clear current.

'What was you pleased to say?' whined Carnehan. 'They took them without any sound. Not a little whisper all along the snow, not though the King knocked down the first man that set hand on him—not though old Peachey fired his last cartridge into the brown of 'em. Not a single solitary sound did those swines make. They just closed up tight, and I tell you their furs stunk. There was a man called Billy Fish, a good friend of us all, and they cut his throat, Sir, then and there, like a pig; and the King kicks up the bloody snow and says: "We've had a dashed fine run for our money. What's coming next?" But Peachey, Peachey Taliaferro, I tell you, Sir, in confidence as betwixt two friends, he lost his head, Sir. No, he didn't neither. The King lost his head, so he did, all along o' one of those cunning rope-bridges. Kindly let me have the paper-cutter, Sir. It tilted this way. They marched him a mile across that snow to a rope-bridge over a ravine with a river at the bottom. You may have seen such.

They prodded him behind like an ox. "Damn your eyes!" says the King. "D'you suppose I can't die like a gentleman?" He turns to Peachey— Peachey that was crying like a child. "I've brought you to this, Peachey," says he. "Brought you out of your happy life to be killed in Kafiristan, where you was late Commander-in-Chief of the Emperor's forces. Say you forgive me, Peachey." — "I do," says Peachey. "Fully and freely do I forgive you, Dan." — "Shake hands, Peachey," says he. "I'm going now." Out he goes, looking neither right nor left, and when he was plumb in the middle of those dizzy looking ropes— "Cut, you beggars," he shouts; and they cut, and old Dan fell, turning round and round and round, twenty thousand miles, for he took half an hour to fall till he struck the water, and I could see his body caught on a rock with the gold crown close beside.

'But do you know what they did to Peachey between two pine-trees? They crucified him, Sir, as Peachey's hand will show. They used wooden pegs for his hands and his feet; and he didn't die. He hung there and screamed, and they took him down next day, and said it was a miracle that he wasn't dead. They took him down—poor old Peachey that hadn't done them any harm—that hadn't done them any—'

He rocked to and fro and wept bitterly, wiping his eyes with the back of his scarred hands and moaning like a child for some ten minutes.

'They was cruel enough to feed him up in the temple, because they said he was more of a God than old Daniel that was a man. Then they turned him out on the snow, and told him to go home, and Peachey came home in about a year, begging along the roads quite safe; for Daniel Dravot he walked before and said, "Come along, Peachey. It's a big thing we're doing." The mountains they danced at night, and the mountains they tried to fall on Peachey's head, but Dan he held up his hand, and Peachey came along bent double. He never let go of Dan's hand, and he never let go of Dan's head. They gave it to him as a present in the temple, to remind him not to come again, and though the crown was pure gold, and Peachey was starving, never would Peachey sell the same. You knew Dravot, Sir! You knew Right Worshipful Brother Dravot! Look at him now!'

He fumbled in the mass of rags round his bent waist; brought out a black horsehair bag embroidered with silver thread, and shook therefrom on to my table—the dried withered head of Daniel Dravot! The morning sun that had long been paling the lamps struck the red beard and blind sunken eyes; struck, too, a heavy circlet of gold studded with raw turquoises, that Carnehan placed tenderly on the battered temples.

'You be'old now,' said Carnehan, 'the Emperor in his 'abit as he lived—the King of Kafiristan with his crown upon his head. Poor old Daniel that was a monarch once!'

I shuddered, for, in spite of defacements manifold, I recognized the head of the man of Marwar Junction. Carnehan rose to go. I attempted to stop him. He was not fit to walk abroad. 'Let me take away the whisky, and give me a little money,' he gasped. 'I was a King once. I'll go to the Deputy Commissioner and ask to be set in the Poorhouse till I get my health. No, thank you, I can't wait till you get a carriage for me. I've urgent private affairs—in the south—at Marwar.'

He shambled out of the office and departed in the direction of the Deputy Commissioner's house. That day at noon I had occasion to go down the blinding hot Mall, and I saw a crooked man crawling along the white dust of the roadside, his hat in his hand, quavering dolorously after the fashion of street-singers at Home. There was not a soul in sight, and he was out of all possible earshot of houses. And he sang through his nose, turning his head from right to left:

'The Son of Man goes forth to war,

A golden crown to gain;

His blood-red banner streams afar—

Who follows in his train?'

I waited to hear no more, but put the poor wretch into my carriage and drove him off to the nearest missionary for eventual transfer to the

Asylum. He repeated the hymn twice while he was with me whom he did not in the least recognize, and I left him singing it to the missionary.

Two days later I inquired after his welfare of the Superintendent of the Asylum.

'He was admitted suffering from sunstroke. He died early yesterday morning,' said the Superintendent. 'Is it true that he was half an hour bare-headed in the sun at mid-day?'

'Yes,' said I, 'but do you happen to know if he had anything upon him by any chance when he died?'

'Not to my knowledge,' said the Superintendent.

And there the matter rests.

Thoughts on The Man Who Would be King

When a great director like John Huston made a movie out of this story it was bound to be a success, but it left an indelible image on the cinema-goer that is in many ways different from and less than that of the printed page. It is now nearly four decades since the film was first released and a new generation has grown up which can approach the tale otherwise than through the distorting lens of a different medium.

Daniel Dravot and Peachy Carnehan, like the subject of Kipling's poem, 'Sestina of the Tramp Royal', found India too small for them, too bureaucratic, and burned to go beyond the known and seize whatever good fortune they could. It is difficult not to admire their audacity, their good humour, and their determination in the form of the 'contrack' they submitted themselves to. Nevertheless, a story that begins as the broadest of comedies ends as the blackest of tragedies.

The writing contains many of the author's brilliant touches. The child's paper whirligig held by the gun-running priest, for example, is paralleled by the image of Peachey falling from the bridge 'turning and twisting in the air like a penny whirligig that you can sell to the Amir'.

Almost all serious critics have judged 'The Man Who Would be King' to be one of Kipling's finest stories. Just as with 'Morrowbie Jukes', a case may be made for it as an allegory of empire, but that is not the only possible metaphor. Christianity figures prominently in the story: Peachey's crucifixion evokes Christ's sufferings on the cross, the beheading of Dravot suggests the end of John the Baptist, and so on. And of course the narrative is shot through with images of Freemasonry. (The Kipling Society point out that the 'native proverb' at the head of the story, 'Brother to a Prince and fellow to a beggar if he be found worthy' is in fact an echo of a Masonic verse.) I prefer to see the story's dominant motif as the hubris of over-vaulting ambition.

Kafiristan (the land of the Kaffirs, or non-Muslims) was the name of an area of Afghanistan south of the Hindu Kush that Kipling came to know during his time as a journalist on The Pioneer. The plot may have been inspired by the life of the American Quaker and adventurer, Josiah Harlan, who in the 1830s became the Prince of Ghor 'in perpetuity', only to be rudely evicted from office by the British. It has been suggested that Dan's decapitation was based on the fate of the German botanist and explorer, Adolf Schlagintweit.

J. M. Barrie described this story as "the most audacious thing in fiction, and yet reads as true as Robinson Crusoe.'

The term, 'our fifty-seven' refers to the Indian Mutiny of 1857.

AT THE PIT'S MOUTH

Men say it was a stolen tide—
The Lord that sent it He knows all,
But in mine ear will aye abide
The message that the bells let fall—
And awesome bells they were to me,
That in the dark rang,
'Enderby.'

Jean Ingelow

Once upon a time there was a Man and his Wife and a Tertium Quid.

All three were unwise, but the Wife was the unwisest. The Man should have looked after his Wife, who should have avoided the Tertium Quid, who, again, should have married a wife of his own, after clean and open flirtations, to which nobody can possibly object, round Jakko or Observatory Hill. When you see a young man with his pony in a white lather and his hat on the back of his head, flying downhill at fifteen miles an hour to meet a girl who will be properly surprised to meet him, you naturally approve of that young man, and wish him Staff appointments, and take an interest in his welfare, and, as the proper time comes, give them sugar-tongs or side-saddles according to your means and generosity.

The Tertium Quid flew downhill on horseback, but it was to meet the Man's Wife; and when he flew uphill it was for the same end. The Man was in the Plains, earning money for his Wife to spend on dresses and four-hundred-rupee bracelets, and inexpensive luxuries of that kind. He worked very hard, and sent her a letter or a post-card daily. She also wrote to him daily, and said that she was longing for him to come up to Simla. The Tertium Quid used to lean over her shoulder and laugh as she wrote the notes. Then the two would ride to the Post-office together.

Now, Simla is a strange place and its customs are peculiar; nor is any man who has not spent at least ten seasons there qualified to pass judgment on circumstantial evidence, which is the most un-trustworthy in the Courts. For these reasons, and for others which need not appear, I decline to state positively whether there was any-thing irretrievably wrong in the relations between the Man's Wife and the Tertium Quid. If there was, and hereon you must form your own opinion, it was the Man's Wife's fault. She was kittenish in her manners, wearing generally an air of soft and fluffy innocence. But she was deadlily learned and evil-instructed; and, now and again, when the mask dropped, men saw this, shuddered and—almost drew back. Men are occasionally particular, and the least particular men are always the most exacting.

Simla is eccentric in its fashion of treating friendships. Certain attach-ments which have set and crystallised through half-a-dozen seasons ac-quire almost the sanctity of the marriage bond, and are revered as such. Again, certain attachments equally old, and, to all appearance, equally venerable, never seem to win any recognised official status; while a chance-sprung acquaintance, not two months born, steps into the place which by right belongs to the senior. There is no law reducible to print which regulates these affairs.

Some people have a gift which secures them infinite toleration, and others have not. The Man's Wife had not. If she looked over the gar-den wall, for instance, women taxed her with stealing their husbands. She complained pathetically that she was not allowed to choose her own friends. When she put up her big white muff to her lips, and gazed over it and under her eyebrows at you as she said this thing, you felt that she had been infamously misjudged, and that all the other wom-en's instincts were all wrong; which was absurd. She was not allowed to own the Tertium Quid in peace; and was so strangely constructed that she would not have enjoyed peace had she been so permitted. She preferred some semblance of intrigue to cloak even her most common-place actions.

After two months of riding, first round Jakko, then Elysium, then Summer Hill, then Observatory Hill, then under Jutogh, and lastly up and down the Cart Road as far as the Tara Devi gap in the dusk, she said to the Tertium Quid, 'Frank, people say we are too much together, and people are so horrid.'

The Tertium Quid pulled his moustache, and replied that horrid people were unworthy of the consideration of nice people.

'But they have done more than talk—they have written—written to my hubby—I'm sure of it,' said the Man's Wife, and she pulled a letter from her husband out of her saddle-pocket and gave it to the Tertium Quid.

It was an honest letter, written by an honest man, then stewing in the Plains on two hundred rupees a month (for he allowed his wife eight hundred and fifty), and in a silk banian and cotton trousers. It said that, perhaps, she had not thought of the unwisdom of allowing her name to be so generally coupled with the Tertium Quid's; that she was too much of a child to understand the dangers of that sort of thing; that he, her husband, was the last man in the world to interfere jealously with her little amusements and interests, but that it would be better were she to drop the Tertium Quid quietly and for her husband's sake. The letter was sweetened with many pretty little pet names, and it amused the Tertium Quid considerably. He and She laughed over it, so that you, fifty yards away, could see their shoulders shaking while the horses slouched along side by side.

Their conversation was not worth reporting. The upshot of it was that, next day, no one saw the Man's Wife and the Tertium Quid together. They had both gone down to the Cemetery, which, as a rule, is only vis-ited officially by the inhabitants of Simla.

A Simla funeral with the clergyman riding, the mourners riding, and the coffin creaking as it swings between the bearers, is one of the most depressing things on this earth, particularly when the procession passes under the wet, dank dip beneath the Rockcliffe Hotel, where the sun is shut out, and all the hill streams are wailing and weeping together as they go down the valleys.

Occasionally folk tend the graves, but we in India shift and are transferred so often that, at the end of the second year, the Dead have no friends—only acquaintances who are far too busy amusing themselves up the hill to attend to old partners. The idea of using a Cemetery as a rendezvous is distinctly a feminine one. A man would have said simply, 'Let people talk. We'll go down the Mall.' A woman is made differently, especially if she be such a woman as the Man's Wife. She and the Tertium Quid enjoyed each other's society among the graves of men and women whom they had known and danced with aforetime.

They used to take a big horse-blanket and sit on the grass a little to the left of the lower end, where there is a dip in the ground, and where the occupied graves stop short and the ready-made ones are not ready. Each well-regulated Indian Cemetery keeps half-a-dozen graves permanently open for contingencies and incidental wear and tear. In the Hills these are more usually baby's size, because children who come up weakened and sick from the Plains often succumb to the effects of the Rains in the Hills or get pneumonia from their *ayahs* taking them through damp pine-woods after the sun has set. In Cantonments, of course, the man's size is more in request; these arrangements varying with the climate and population.

One day when the Man's Wife and the Tertium Quid had just arrived in the Cemetery, they saw some coolies breaking ground. They had marked out a full-size grave, and the Tertium Quid asked them whether any Sahib was sick. They said that they did not know; but it was an order that they should dig a Sahib's grave.

'Work away,' said the Tertium Quid, 'and let's see how it's done.'

The coolies worked away, and the Man's Wife and the Tertium Quid watched and talked for a couple of hours while the grave was being

96

deepened. Then a coolie, taking the earth in baskets as it was thrown up, jumped over the grave.

'That's queer,' said the Tertium Quid. 'Where's my ulster?'

'What's queer?' said the Man's Wife.

'I have got a chill down my back—just as if a goose had walked over my grave.'

'Why do you look at the thing, then?' said the Man's Wife. 'Let us go.'

The Tertium Quid stood at the head of the grave, and stared without answering for a space. Then he said, dropping a pebble down, 'It is nasty— and cold: horribly cold. I don't think I shall come to the Cemetery any more. I don't think grave-digging is cheerful.'

The two talked and agreed that the Cemetery was depressing. They also arranged for a ride next day out from the Cemetery through the Mashobra Tunnel up to Fagoo and back, because all the world was going to a garden-party at Viceregal Lodge, and all the people of Mashobra would go too.

Coming up the Cemetery road, the Tertium Quid's horse tried to bolt uphill, being tired with standing so long, and managed to strain a back sinew.

'I shall have to take the mare to-morrow,' said the Tertium Quid, 'and she will stand nothing heavier than a snaffle.'

They made their arrangements to meet in the Cemetery, after allowing all the Mashobra people time to pass into Simla. That night it rained heavily, and, next day, when the Tertium Quid came to the trysting-place, he saw that the new grave had a foot of water in it, the ground being a tough and sour clay.

''Jove! That looks beastly,' said the Tertium Quid. 'Fancy being boarded up and dropped into that well!'

They then started off to Fagoo, the mare playing with the snaffle and picking her way as though she were shod with satin, and the sun shining divinely. The road below Mashobra to Fagoo is officially styled the Himalayan-Thibet road; but in spite of its name it is not much more than six feet wide in most places, and the drop into the valley below may be anything between one and two thousand feet.

'Now we're going to Thibet,' said the Man's Wife merrily, as the horses drew near to Fagoo. She was riding on the cliff-side.

'Into Thibet,' said the Tertium Quid, 'ever so far from people who say horrid things, and hubbies who write stupid letters. With you to the end of the world!'

A coolie carrying a log of wood came round a corner, and the mare went wide to avoid him—forefeet in and haunches out, as a sensible mare should go.

'To the world's end,' said the Man's Wife, and looked unspeakable things over her near shoulder at the Tertium Quid.

He was smiling, but, while she looked, the smile froze stiff as it were on his face, and changed to a nervous grin—the sort of grin men wear when they are not quite easy in their saddles. The mare seemed to be sinking by the stern, and her nostrils cracked while she was trying to realise what was happening. The rain of the night before had rotted the drop-side of the Himalayan-Thibet Road, and it was giving way under her. 'What are you doing?' said the Man's Wife. The Tertium Quid gave no answer. He grinned nervously and set his spurs into the mare, who rapped with her forefeet on the road, and the struggle began. The Man's Wife screamed, 'Oh, Frank, get off!'

But the Tertium Quid was glued to the saddle—his face blue and white—and he looked into the Man's Wife's eyes. Then the Man's Wife clutched at the mare's head and caught her by the nose instead of the bridle. The brute threw up her head and went down with a scream, the Tertium Quid upon her, and the nervous grin still set on his face.

The Man's Wife heard the tinkle-tinkle of little stones and loose earth falling off the roadway, and the sliding roar of the man and horse going down. Then everything was quiet, and she called on Frank to leave his mare and walk up. But Frank did not answer. He was underneath the mare, nine hundred feet below, spoiling a patch of Indian corn.

As the revellers came back from Viceregal Lodge in the mists of the evening, they met a temporarily insane woman, on a temporarily mad horse, swinging round the corners, with her eyes and her mouth open, and her head like the head of a Medusa. She was stopped by a man at the risk of his life, and taken out of the saddle, a limp heap, and put on the bank to explain herself. This wasted twenty minutes, and then she was sent home in a lady's 'rickshaw, still with her mouth open and her hands picking at her riding-gloves.

She was in bed through the following three days, which were rainy; so she missed attending the funeral of the Tertium Quid, who was lowered into eighteen inches of water, instead of the twelve to which he had first objected.

Thoughts on At the Pit's Mouth

Among the many burdens of the British in India was the summer heat of the Plains. So hard was it for white skinned northerners to bear that those in a position to do so migrated yearly to the cooler airs of the foothills of the Himalayas. Strange as is may seem, from mid March to mid October each year the government of the vast sub-continent was largely directed from the small town of Simla, where civil servants, soldiers and their families lived side by side in some four hundred European style houses built along the main street, or 'Mall'.

Notwithstanding its mild climate Simla could be an emotional hothouse which formed the basis for many of the author's early tales. Husbands separated by their duties from wives had to seek the company of their own sex or accept social isolation. A few, however, chose to explore the third option, often with tragic results for all concerned. As the narrator put it, 'we in India shift and are transferred so often that, at the end of the second year, the Dead have no friends only acquaintances who are far too busy amusing themselves up the hill to attend to old partners'.

There is perhaps no description in the whole of the Kipling canon more skilled and vivid than that of the riding accident, in particular the expression on the face of the Tertium Quid as he and his horse slide slowly and inexorably to their deaths. No one who reads it can forget the last words spoken immediately beforehand by 'The Wife'. Any twenty three year old who could write like that deserves a front seat in the pantheon of literature.

Although the unlovable lovers' tryst takes place in a graveyard and contains mild hints of the supernatural, these seem to be no more than mood music to a plot, however simple, of real horror.

Kipling chose the epigraphs to his stories with care. At the Pit's Mouth begins with an extract from a poem entitled 'High Tide on the Coast of Lincolnshire 1571' by the once popular poet, Jean Ingelow. Mavis Enderby is a hamlet in the Lincolnshire Wolds. A 'stolen tide' is an unexpected inundation.

ON THE CITY WALL

Then she let them down by a cord through the window; for her house was upon the town wall, and she dwelt upon the wall.—Joshua ii. 15.

Lalun is a member of the most ancient profession in the world. Lilith was her very-great-grandmamma, and that was before the days of Eve, as every one knows. In the West, people say rude things about Lalun's profession, and write lectures about it, and distribute the lectures to young persons in order that Morality may be preserved. In the East, where the profession is hereditary, descending from mother to daughter, nobody writes lectures or takes any notice; and that is a distinct proof of the inability of the East to manage its own affairs.

Lalun's real husband, for even ladies of Lalun's profession in the East must have husbands, was a big jujube-tree. Her Mamma, who had married a fig-tree, spent ten thousand rupees on Lalun's wedding, which was blessed by forty-seven clergymen of Mamma's Church, and distributed five thousand rupees in charity to the poor. And that was the custom of the land. The advantages of having a jujube-tree for a husband are obvious. You cannot hurt his feelings, and he looks imposing.

Lalun's husband stood on the plain outside the City walls, and Lalun's house was upon the east wall facing the river. If you fell from the broad window-seat you dropped thirty feet sheer into the City Ditch. But if you stayed where you should and looked forth, you saw all the cattle of the City being driven down to water, the students of the Government College playing cricket, the high grass and trees that fringed the river-bank, the great sand-bars that ribbed the river, the red tombs of dead

Emperors beyond the river, and very far away through the blue heat-haze a glint of the snows of the Himalayas.

Wali Dad used to lie in the window-seat for hours at a time watching this view. He was a young Mohammedan who was suffering acutely from education of the English variety and knew it. His father had sent him to a Mission-school to get wisdom, and Wali Dad had absorbed more than ever his father or the Missionaries intended he should. When his father died, Wali Dad was independent and spent two years experimenting with the creeds of the Earth and reading books that are of no use to anybody.

After he had made an unsuccessful attempt to enter the Roman Catholic Church and the Presbyterian fold at the same time (the Missionaries found him out and called him names; but they did not understand his trouble), he discovered Lalun on the City wall and became the most constant of her few admirers. He possessed a head that English artists at home would rave over and paint amid impossible surroundings—a face that female novelists would use with delight through nine hundred pages. In reality he was only a clean-bred young Mohammedan, with pencilled eyebrows, small-cut nostrils, little feet and hands, and a very tired look in his eyes. By virtue of his twenty-two years he had grown a neat black beard which he stroked with pride and kept delicately scented. His life seemed to be divided between borrowing books from me and making love to Lalun in the window-seat. He composed songs about her, and some of the songs are sung to this day in the City from the Street of the Mutton-Butchers to the Copper-Smiths' ward.

One song, the prettiest of all, says that the beauty of Lalun was so great that it troubled the hearts of the British Government and caused them to lose their peace of mind. That is the way the song is sung in the streets; but, if you examine it carefully and know the key to the explanation, you will find that there are three puns in it—on 'beauty,' 'heart,' and 'peace of mind,'—so that it runs: 'By the subtlety of Lalun the administration of the Government was troubled and it lost such-and-such a man.' When Wali Dad sings that song his eyes glow like hot coals, and Lalun leans back among the cushions and throws bunches of jasmine-buds at Wali Dad.

But first it is necessary to explain something about the Supreme Government which is above all and below all and behind all. Gentlemen come from England, spend a few weeks in India, walk round this great Sphinx of the Plains, and write books upon its ways and its works, denouncing or praising it as their own ignorance prompts. Consequently all the world knows how the Supreme Government conducts itself. But no one, not even the Supreme Government, knows everything about the administration of the Empire. Year by year England sends out fresh drafts for the first fighting-line, which is officially called the Indian Civil Service. These die, or kill themselves by overwork, or are worried to death, or broken in health and hope in order that the land may be protected from death and sickness, famine and war, and may eventually become capable of standing alone. It will never stand alone, but the idea is a pretty one, and men are willing to die for it, and yearly the work of pushing and coaxing and scolding and petting the country into good living goes forward. If an advance be made all credit is given to the native, while the Englishmen stand back and wipe their foreheads. If a failure occurs the Englishmen step forward and take the blame. Overmuch tenderness of this kind has bred a strong belief among many natives that the native is capable of administering the country, and many devout Englishmen believe this also, because the theory is stated in beautiful English with all the latest political colours.

There are other men who, though uneducated, see visions and dream dreams, and they, too, hope to administer the country in their own way—that is to say, with a garnish of Red Sauce. Such men must exist among two hundred million people, and, if they are not attended to, may cause trouble and even break the great idol called *Pax Britannica*, which, as the newspapers say, lives between Peshawur and Cape Comorin. Were the Day of Doom to dawn to-morrow, you would find the Supreme Government 'taking measures to allay popular excitement,' and putting guards upon the graveyards that the Dead might troop forth orderly. The youngest Civilian would arrest Gabriel on his own responsibility if the Archangel could not produce a Deputy-Commissioner's permission to 'make music or other noises' as the licence says.

Whence it is easy to see that mere men of the flesh who would create a tumult must fare badly at the hands of the Supreme Government. And they do. There is no outward sign of excitement; there is no confusion; there is no knowledge. When due and sufficient reasons have been given, weighed and approved, the machinery moves forward, and the dreamer of dreams and the seer of visions is gone from his friends and following. He enjoys the hospitality of Government; there is no restriction upon his movements within certain limits; but he must not confer any more with his brother dreamers. Once in every six months the Supreme Government assures itself that he is well and takes formal acknowledgment of his existence. No one protests against his detention, because the few people who know about it are in deadly fear of seeming to know him; and never a single newspaper 'takes up his case' or organises demonstrations on his behalf, because the newspapers of India have got behind that lying proverb which says the Pen is mightier than the Sword, and can walk delicately.

So now you know as much as you ought about Wali Dad, the educational mixture, and the Supreme Government.

Lalun has not yet been described. She would need, so Wali Dad says, a thousand pens of gold, and ink scented with musk. She has been variously compared to the Moon, the Dil Sagar Lake, a spotted quail, a gazelle, the Sun on the Desert of Kutch, the Dawn, the Stars, and the young bamboo. These comparisons imply that she is beautiful exceedingly according to the native standards, which are practically the same as those of the West. Her eyes are black and her hair is black, and her eyebrows are black as leeches; her mouth is tiny and says witty things; her hands are tiny and have saved much money; her feet are tiny and have trodden on the naked hearts of many men. But, as Wali Dad sings: 'Lalun *is* Lalun, and when you have said that, you have only come to the Beginnings of Knowledge.'

The little house on the City wall was just big enough to hold Lalun, and her maid, and a pussycat with a silver collar. A big pink-and-blue cut-glass chandelier hung from the ceiling of the reception room. A petty Nawab had given Lalun the horror, and she kept it for politeness' sake. The floor of the room was of polished chunam, white as curds. A latticed window of carved wood was set in one wall; there was a profusion of squabby pluffy cushions and fat carpets everywhere, and Lalun's silver hookah, studded with turquoises, had a special little carpet all to its shining self. Wali Dad was nearly as permanent a fixture as the chandelier. As I have said, he lay in the window-seat and meditated on Life and Death and Lalun—'specially Lalun. The feet of the young men of the City tended to her doorways and then—retired, for Lalun was a particular maiden, slow of speech, reserved of mind, and not in the least inclined to orgies which were nearly certain to end in strife. 'If I am of no value, I am unworthy of this honour,' said Lalun. 'If I am of value, they are unworthy of Me.' And that was a crooked sentence.

In the long hot nights of latter April and May all the City seemed to assemble in Lalun's little white room to smoke and to talk. Shiahs of the grimmest and most uncompromising persuasion; Sufis who had lost all belief in the Prophet and retained but little in God; wandering Hindu priests passing southward on their way to the Central India fairs and other affairs; Pundits in black gowns, with spectacles on their noses and undigested wisdom in their insides; bearded headmen of the wards; Sikhs with all the details of the latest ecclesiastical scandal in the Golden Temple; red-eyed priests from beyond the Border, looking like trapped wolves and talking like ravens; M.A.'s of the University, very superior and very voluble—all these people and more also you might find in the white room. Wali Dad lay in the window-seat and listened to the talk.

'It is Lalun's *salon*,' said Wali Dad to me, 'and it is electic—is not that the word? Outside of a Freemasons' Lodge I have never seen such gatherings. *There* I dined once with a Jew—a Yahoudi!' He spat into the City Ditch with apologies for allowing national feelings to overcome him. 'Though I have lost every belief in the world,' said he, 'and try to be proud of my losing, I cannot help hating a Jew. Lalun admits no Jews here.'

'But what in the world do all these men do? 'I asked.

'The curse of our country,' said Wali Dad. 'They talk. It is like the Athenians—always hearing and telling some new thing. Ask the Pearl and she will show you how much she knows of the news of the City and the Province. Lalun knows everything.'

'Lalun,' I said at random—she was talking to a gentleman of the Kurd persuasion who had come in from God-knows-where—'when does the 175th Regiment go to Agra?'

'It does not go at all,' said Lalun, without turning her head. 'They have ordered the 118th to go in its stead. That Regiment goes to Lucknow in three months, unless they give a fresh order.'

'That is so,' said Wali Dad, without a shade of doubt. 'Can you, with your telegrams and your newspapers, do better? Always hearing and telling some new thing,' he went on. 'My friend, has your God ever smitten a European nation for gossiping in the bazars? India has gossiped for centuries—always standing in the bazars until the soldiers go by. Therefore—you are here to-day instead of starving in your own country, and I am not a Mohammedan—I am a Product—a Demnition Product. *That* also I owe to you and yours: that I cannot make an end to my sentence without quoting from your authors.' He pulled at the hookah and mourned, half feelingly, half in earnest, for the shattered hopes of his youth. Wali Dad was always mourning over something or other—the country of which he despaired, or the creed in which he had lost faith, or the life of the English which he could by no means understand.

Lalun never mourned. She played little songs on the *sitar*, and to hear her sing, 'O Peacock, cry again,' was always a fresh pleasure. She knew all the songs that have ever been sung, from the war-songs of the South, that make the old men angry with the young men and the young men angry with the State, to the love-songs of the North, where the swords whinny-whicker like angry kites in the pauses between the kisses, and the Passes fill with armed men, and the Lover is torn from his Beloved and cries *Ai! Ai! Ai!* evermore. She knew how to make up tobacco for the pipe so that it smelt like the Gates of Paradise and wafted you gently through them. She could embroider strange things in gold and silver, and dance softly with the moonlight when it came in at the window. Also she knew the hearts of men, and the heart of the City, and whose wives were faithful and whose untrue, and more of the secrets of the Government Offices than are good to be set down in this place. Nasiban, her maid, said that her jewelry was worth ten thousand pounds, and that, some night, a thief would enter and murder her for its possession; but Lalun said that all the City would tear that thief limb from limb, and that he, whoever he was, knew it.

So she took her *sitar* and sat in the window-seat, and sang a song of old days that had been sung by a girl of her profession in an armed camp on the eve of a great battle—the day before the Fords of the Jumna ran red and Sivaji fled fifty miles to Delhi with a Toorkh stallion at his horse's tail and another Lalun on his saddle-bow. It was what men call a Mahratta *laonee*, and it said:—

Their warrior forces Chimnajee
    Before the Peishwa led,
The Children of the Sun and Fire
    Behind him turned and fled.

        And the chorus said:

With them there fought who rides so free
    With sword and turban red,
The warrior-youth who earns his fee
    At peril of his head.

'At peril of his head,' said Wali Dad in English to me. 'Thanks to your Government, all our heads are protected, and with the educational facilities at my command'—his eyes twinkled wickedly—'I might be a distinguished member of the local administration. Perhaps, in time, I might even be a member of a Legislative Council.'

'Don't speak English,' said Lalun, bending over her *sitar* afresh. The chorus went out from the City wall to the blackened wall of Fort Amara which dominates the City. No man knows the precise extent of Fort Amara. Three kings built it hundreds of years ago, and they say that there are miles of underground rooms beneath its walls. It is peopled with many ghosts, a detachment of Garrison Artillery, and a Company of Infantry. In its prime it held ten thousand men and filled its ditches with corpses.

'At peril of his head,' sang Lalun again and again.

A head moved on one of the ramparts—the grey head of an old man—and a voice, rough as shark-skin on a sword-hilt, sent back the last line of the chorus and broke into a song that I could not understand, though Lalun and Wali Dad listened intently.

'What is it?' I asked. 'Who is it?'

'A consistent man,' said Wali Dad. 'He fought you in '46, when he was a warrior-youth; refought you in '57, and he tried to fight you in '71, but you had learned the trick of blowing men from guns too well. Now he is old; but he would still fight if he could.'

'Is he a Wahabi, then? Why should he answer to a Mahratta *laonee* if he be Wahabi—or Sikh?' said I.

'I do not know,' said Wali Dad. 'He has lost, perhaps, his religion. Perhaps he wishes to be a King. Perhaps he *is* a King. I do not know his name.'

'That is a lie, Wali Dad. If you know his career you must know his name.'

'That is quite true. I belong to a nation of liars. I would rather not tell you his name. Think for yourself.'

Lalun finished her song, pointed to the Fort, and said simply: 'Khem Singh.'

'Hm,' said Wali Dad. 'If the Pearl chooses to tell you, the Pearl is a fool.'

I translated to Lalun, who laughed. 'I choose to tell what I choose to tell. They kept Khem Singh in Burma,' said she. 'They kept him there for many years until his mind was changed in him. So great was the kindness of the Government. Finding this, they sent him back to his own country that he might look upon it before he died. He is an old man, but when he looks upon this his country his memory will come. Moreover, there be many who remember him.'

'He is an Interesting Survival,' said Wali Dad, pulling at the pipe. 'He returns to a country now full of educational and political reform, but, as the Pearl says, there are many who remember him. He was once a great man. There will never be any more great men in India. They will all, when they are boys, go whoring after strange gods, and they will become citizens—"fellow-citizens"—"illustrious fellow-citizens." What is it that the native papers call them?'

Wali Dad seemed to be in a very bad temper. Lalun looked out of the window and smiled into the dust-haze. I went away thinking about Khem Singh, who had once made history with a thousand followers, and would have been a princeling but for the power of the Supreme Government aforesaid.

The Senior Captain Commanding Fort Amara was away on leave, but the Subaltern, his Deputy, had drifted down to the Club, where I found him and inquired of him whether it was really true that a political prisoner had been added to the attractions of the Fort. The Subaltern explained at great length, for this was the first time that he had held command of the Fort, and his glory lay heavy upon him.

'Yes,' said he, 'a man was sent in to me about a week ago from down the line—a thorough gentleman, whoever he is. Of course I did all I could for him. He had his two servants and some silver cooking-pots, and he looked for all the world like a native officer. I called him Subadar Sahib. Just as well to be on the safe side, y'know. "Look here, Subadar Sahib," I said, "you're handed over to my authority, and I'm supposed to guard you. Now I don't want to make your life hard, but you must make things easy for me. All the Fort is at your disposal, from the flagstaff to the dry Ditch, and I shall be happy to entertain you in any way I can, but you mustn't take advantage of it. Give me your word that you won't try to escape, Subadar Sahib, and I'll give you my word that you shall have no heavy guard put over you." I thought the best way of getting at him was by going at him straight, y'know; and it was, by Jove! The old man gave me his word, and moved about the Fort as contented as a sick crow. He's a rummy chap—always asking to be told where he is and what the buildings about him are. I had to sign a slip of blue paper when he turned up, acknowledging receipt of his body and all that, and I'm responsible, y'know, that he doesn't get away. Queer thing, though, looking after a Johnnie old enough to be your grandfather, isn't it? Come to the Fort one of these days and see him.'

For reasons which will appear, I never went to the Fort while Khem Singh was then within its walls. I knew him only as a grey head seen from Lalun's window—a grey head and a harsh voice. But natives told me that, day by day, as he looked upon the fair lands round Amara, his memory came back to him and, with it, the old hatred against the Government that had been nearly effaced in far-off Burma. So he raged up and down the West face of the Fort from morning till noon and from evening till the night, devising vain things in his heart, and croaking war-songs when Lalun sang on the City wall. As he grew more acquainted with the Subaltern he unburdened his old heart of some of the passions that had withered it. 'Sahib,' he used to say, tapping his stick against the parapet, 'when I was a young man I was one of twenty thousand horsemen who came out of the City and rode round the plain here. Sahib, I was the leader of a hundred, then of a thousand, then of five thousand, and now!'—he pointed to his two servants. 'But from the beginning to to-day I would cut the throats of all the Sahibs in the land if I could. Hold me fast, Sahib, lest I get away and return to those who would follow me. I forgot them when I was in Burma, but now that I am in my own country again, I remember everything.'

'Do you remember that you have given me your Honour not to make your tendance a hard matter? ' said the Subaltern.

'Yes, to you, only to you, Sahib,' said Khem Singh. 'To you because you are of a pleasant countenance. If my turn comes again, Sahib, I will not hang you nor cut your throat.'

'Thank you,' said the Subaltern gravely, as he looked along the line of guns that could pound the City to powder in half an hour. 'Let us go into our own quarters, Khem Singh. Come and talk with me after dinner.'

Khem Singh would sit on his own cushion at the Subaltern's feet, drinking heavy, scented aniseed brandy in great gulps, and telling strange stories of Fort Amara, which had been a palace in the old days, of Begums and Ranees tortured to death—in the very vaulted chamber that now served as a mess-room; would tell stories of Sobraon that made the Subaltern's cheeks flush and tingle with pride of race, and of the Kuka rising from which so much was expected and the fore-knowledge of which was shared by a hundred thousand souls. But he never told tales of '57 because, as he said, he was the Subaltern's guest, and '57 is a year that no man, Black or White, cares to speak of. Once only, when the aniseed brandy had slightly affected his head, he said 'Sahib, speaking now of a matter which lay between Sobraon and the affair of the Kukas, it was ever a wonder to us that you stayed your hand at all, and that, having stayed it, you did not make the land one prison. Now I hear from without that you do great honour to all men of our country and by your own hands are destroying the Terror of your Name which is your strong rock and defence. This is a foolish thing. Will oil and water mix? Now in '57——'

'I was not born then, Subadar Sahib,' said the Subaltern, and Khem Singh reeled to his quarters.

The Subaltern would tell me of these conversations at the Club, and my desire to see Khem Singh increased. But Wali Dad, sitting in the window-seat of the house on the City wall, said that it would be a cruel thing to do, and Lalun pretended that I preferred the society of a grizzled old Sikh to hers.

'Here is tobacco, here is talk, here are many friends and all the news of the City, and, above all, here is myself. I will tell you stories and sing you songs, and Wali Dad will talk his English nonsense in your ears. Is that worse than watching the caged animal yonder? Go to-morrow then, if you must, but to-day such-and-such an one will be here, and he will speak of wonderful things.'

It happened that To-morrow never came, and the warm heat of the latter Rains gave place to the chill of early October almost before I was aware of the flight of the year. The Captain Commanding the Fort returned from leave and took over charge of Khem Singh according to the laws of seniority. The Captain was not a nice man. He called all natives 'niggers,' which, besides being extreme bad form, shows gross ignorance.

'What's the use of telling off two Tommies to watch that old nigger?' said he.

'I fancy it soothes his vanity,' said the Subaltern. 'The men are ordered to keep well out of his way, but he takes them as a tribute to his importance, poor old chap.'

'I won't have Line men taken off regular guards in this way. Put on a couple of Native Infantry.'

'Sikhs?' said the Subaltern, lifting his eyebrows.

'Sikhs, Pathans, Dogras—they're all alike, these black people,' and the Captain talked to Khem Singh in a manner which hurt that old gentleman's feelings. Fifteen years before, when he had been caught for the second time, every one looked upon him as a sort of tiger. He liked being regarded in this light. But he forgot that the world goes forward in fifteen years, and many Subalterns are promoted to Captaincies.

'The Captain-pig is in charge of the Fort?' said Khem Singh to his native guard every morning. And the native guard said: 'Yes, Subadar Sahib,' in deference to his age and his air of distinction; but they did not know who he was.

In those days the gathering in Lalun's little white room was always large and talked more than before.

'The Greeks,' said Wali Dad, who had been borrowing my books, 'the inhabitants of the city of Athens, where they were always hearing and telling some new thing, rigorously secluded their women—who were fools. Hence the glorious institution of the heterodox women—is it not?—who were amusing and not fools. All the Greek philosophers delighted in their company. Tell me, my friend, how it goes now in Greece and the other places upon the Continent of Europe. Are your women-folk also fools?'

'Wali Dad,' I said, 'you never speak to us about your women-folk and we never speak about ours to you. That is the bar between us.'

'Yes,' said Wali Dad, 'it is curious to think that our common meeting-place should be here, in the house of a common—how do you call *her*?' He pointed with the pipe-mouth to Lalun.

'Lalun is nothing but Lalun,' I said, and that was perfectly true. 'But if you took your place in the world, Wali Dad, and gave up dreaming dreams—'

'I might wear an English coat and trousers. I might be a leading Mohammedan pleader. I might be received even at the Commissioner's tennis-parties where the English stand on one side and the natives on the other, in order to promote social intercourse throughout the Empire. Heart's Heart,' said he to Lalun quickly, 'the Sahib says that I ought to quit you.'

'The Sahib is always talking stupid talk,' returned Lalun with a laugh. 'In this house I am a Queen and thou art a King. The Sahib' she put her arms above her head and thought for a moment—'the Sahib shall be our Vizier—thine and mine, Wali Dad—because he has said that thou shouldst leave me.'

Wali Dad laughed immoderately, and I laughed too. 'Be it so,' said he. 'My friend, are you willing to take this lucrative Government appointment? Lalun, what shall his pay be?'

But Lalun began to sing, and for the rest of the time there was no hope of getting a sensible answer from her or Wali Dad. When the one stopped, the other began to quote Persian poetry with a triple pun in every other line. Some of it was not strictly proper, but it was all very funny, and it only came to an end when a fat person in black, with gold pince-nez, sent up his name to Lalun, and Wali Dad dragged me into the twinkling night to walk in a big rose-garden and talk heresies about Religion and Governments and a man's career in life.

The Mohurrum, the great mourning-festival of the Mohammedans, was close at hand, and the things that Wali Dad said about religious fanaticism would have secured his expulsion from the loosest-thinking Muslim sect. There were the rose-bushes round us, the stars above us, and from every quarter of the City came the boom of the big Mohurrum drums. You must know that the City is divided in fairly equal proportions between the Hindus and the Mussulmans, and where both creeds belong to the fighting races, a big religious festival gives ample chance for trouble. When they can—that is to say, when the authorities are weak enough to allow it—the Hindus do their best to arrange some minor feast-day of their own in time to clash with the period of general mourning for the martyrs Hasan and Hussain, the heroes of the Mohurrum. Gilt and painted paper representations of their tombs are borne with shouting and wailing, music, torches, and yells, through the principal thoroughfares of the City; which fakements are called *tazias*. Their passage is rigorously laid down beforehand by the Police, and detachments of Police accompany each *tazia*, lest the Hindus should throw bricks at it and the peace of the Queen and the heads of Her loyal subjects should thereby be broken. Mohurrum time in a 'fighting' town means anxiety to all the officials, because, if a riot breaks out, the officials and not the rioters are held responsible. The former must foresee everything, and while not making their precautions ridiculously elaborate, must see that they are at least adequate.

'Listen to the drums!' said Wali Dad. 'That is the heart of the people—empty and making much noise. How, think you, will the Mohurrum go this year? I think that there will be trouble.'

He turned down a side-street and left me alone with the stars and a sleepy Police patrol. Then I went to bed and dreamed that Wali Dad had sacked the City and I was made Vizier, with Lalun's silver pipe for mark of office.

All day the Mohurrum drums beat in the City, and all day deputations of tearful Hindu gentlemen besieged the Deputy-Commissioner with assurances that they would be murdered ere next dawning by the Mohammedans. 'Which,' said the Deputy-Commissioner, in confidence to the Head of Police, 'is a pretty fair indication that the Hindus are going to make 'emselves unpleasant. I think we can arrange a little surprise for them. I have given the heads of both Creeds fair warning. If they choose to disregard it, so much the worse for them.'

There was a large gathering in Lalun's house that night, but of men that I had never seen before, if I except the fat gentleman in black with the gold pince-nez. Wali Dad lay in the window-seat, more bitterly scornful of his Faith and its manifestations than I had ever known him. Lalun's maid was very busy cutting up and mixing tobacco for the guests. We could hear the thunder of the drums as the processions accompanying each *tazia* marched to the central gathering-place in the plain outside the City, preparatory to their triumphant re-entry and circuit within the walls. All the streets seemed ablaze with torches, and only Fort Amara was black and silent.

When the noise of the drums ceased, no one in the white room spoke for a time. 'The first *tazia* has moved off,' said Wali Dad, looking to the plain.

'That is very early,' said the man with the pince-nez. 'It is only half-past eight.' The company rose and departed.

'Some of them were men from Ladakh,' said Lalun, when the last had gone. 'They brought me brick-tea such as the Russians sell, and a tea-urn from Peshawur. Show me, now, how the English Memsahibs make tea.'

The brick-tea was abominable. When it was finished Wali Dad suggested going into the streets. 'I am nearly sure that there will be trouble to-night,' he said. 'All the City thinks so, and *Vox Populi* is *Vox Dei*, as the

Babus say. Now I tell you that at the corner of the Padshahi Gate you will find my horse all this night if you want to go about and to see things. It is a most disgraceful exhibition. Where is the pleasure of saying "*Ya Hasan! a Hussain!*" twenty thousand times in a night?'

All the processions—there were two-and-twenty of them—were now well within the City walls. The drums were beating afresh, the crowd were howling '*Ya Hasan! a Hussain!*' and beating their breasts, the brass bands were playing their loudest, and at every corner where space allowed, Mohammedan preachers were telling the lamentable story of the death of the Martyrs. It was impossible to move except with the crowd, for the streets were not more than twenty feet wide. In the Hindu quarters the shutters of all the shops were up and cross-barred. As the first *tazia*, a gorgeous erection, ten feet high, was borne aloft on the shoulders of a score of stout men into the semi-darkness of the Gully of the Horsemen, a brickbat crashed through its talc and tinsel sides.

'Into thy hands, O Lord!' murmured Wali Dad profanely, as a yell went up from behind, and a native officer of Police jammed his horse through the crowd. Another brickbat followed, and the *tazia* staggered and swayed where it had stopped.

'Go on! In the name of the Sirkar, go forward!' shouted the Policeman, but there was an ugly cracking and splintering of shutters, and the crowd halted, with oaths and growlings, before the house whence the brickbat had been thrown.

Then, without any warning, broke the storm—not only in the Gully of the Horsemen, but in half-a-dozen other places. The *tazias* rocked like ships at sea, the long pole-torches dipped and rose round them while the men shouted: 'The Hindus are dishonouring the *tazias*! Strike! strike! Into their temples for the Faith!' The six or eight Policemen with each *tazia* drew their batons, and struck as long as they could in the hope of forcing the mob forward, but they were overpowered, and as contingents of Hindus poured into the streets, the fight became general. Half a mile away where the *tazias* were yet untouched the drums and the shrieks of

'*Ya Hasan! Ya Hussain!*' continued, but not for long. The priests at the corners of the streets knocked the legs from the bedsteads that supported their pulpits and smote for the Faith, while stones fell from the silent houses upon friend and foe, and the packed streets bellowed: '*Din! Din! Din!*' A *tazia* caught fire, and was dropped for a flaming barrier between Hindu and Mussulman at the corner of the Gully. Then the crowd surged forward, and Wali Dad drew me close to the stone pillar of a well.

'It was intended from the beginning!' he shouted in my ear, with more heat than blank unbelief should be guilty of. 'The bricks were carried up to the houses beforehand. These swine of Hindus! We shall be killing kine in their temples to-night!'

Tazia after *tazia*, some burning, others torn to pieces, hurried past us and the mob with them, howling, shrieking, and striking at the house doors in their flight. At last we saw the reason of the rush. Hugonin, the Assistant District Superintendent of Police, a boy of twenty, had got together thirty constables and was forcing the crowd through the streets. His old grey Policehorse showed no sign of uneasiness as it was spurred breast—on into the crowd, and the long dog-whip with which he had armed himself was never still.

'They know we haven't enough Police to hold 'em,' he cried as he passed me, mopping a cut on his face. 'They *know* we haven't! Aren't any of the men from the Club coming down to help? Get on, you sons of burnt fathers!' The dog-whip cracked across the writhing backs, and the constables smote afresh with baton and gun-butt. With these passed the lights and the shouting, and Wali Dad began to swear under his breath. From Fort Amara shot up a single rocket; then two side by side. It was the signal for troops.

Petitt, the Deputy-Commissioner, covered with dust and sweat, but calm and gently smiling, cantered up the clean-swept street in rear of the main body of the rioters. 'No one killed yet,' he shouted. 'I'll keep 'em on the run till dawn! Don't let 'em halt, Hugonin! Trot 'em about till the troops come.'

The science of the defence lay solely in keeping the mob on the move. If they had breathing-space they would halt and fire a house, and then the work of restoring order would be more difficult, to say the least of it. Flames have the same effect on a crowd as blood has on a wild beast.

Word had reached the Club, and men in evening-dress were beginning to show themselves and lend a hand in heading off and breaking up the shouting masses with stirrup-leathers, whips, or chance-found staves. They were not very often attacked, for the rioters had sense enough to know that the death of a European would not mean one hanging but many, and possibly the appearance of the thrice-dreaded Artillery. The clamour in the City redoubled. The Hindus had descended into the streets in real earnest and ere long the mob returned. It was a strange sight. There were no *tazias*—only their riven platforms—and there were no Police. Here and there a City dignitary, Hindu or Mohammedan, was vainly imploring his co-religionists to keep quiet and behave them-selves—advice for which his white beard was pulled. Then a native officer of Police, unhorsed but still using his spurs with effect, would be borne along, warning all the crowd of the danger of insulting the Government. Everywhere men struck aimlessly with sticks, grasping each other by the throat, howling and foaming with rage, or beat with their bare hands on the doors of the houses.

'It is a lucky thing that they are fighting with natural weapons,' I said to Wali Dad, 'else we should have half the City killed.'

I turned as I spoke and looked at his face. His nostrils were distended, his eyes were fixed, and he was smiting himself softly on the breast. The crowd poured by with renewed riot—a gang of Mussulmans hard pressed by some hundred Hindu fanatics. Wali Dad left my side with an oath, and shouting: '*Ya Hasan! Ya Hussain!*' plunged into the thick of the fight, where I lost sight of him.

I fled by a side alley to the Padshahi Gate, where I found Wali Dad's horse, and thence rode to the Fort. Once outside the City wall, the tu-mult sank to a dull roar, very impressive under the stars and reflect-ing great credit on the fifty thousand angry able-bodied men who were making it. The troops who, at the Deputy-Commissioner's instance, had been ordered to rendezvous quietly near the Fort, showed no signs of being impressed. Two companies of Native Infantry, a squadron of Native Cavalry, and a company of British Infantry were kicking their heels in the shadow of the East face, waiting for orders to march in. I am sorry to say that they were all pleased, unholily pleased, at the chance of what they called 'a little fun.' The senior officers, to be sure, grumbled at having been kept out of bed, and the English troops pretended to be sulky, but there was joy in the hearts of all the subalterns, and whispers ran up and down the line: 'No ball-cartridge—what a beastly shame!' 'D'you think the beggars will really stand up to us?' 'Hope I shall meet my money-lender there. I owe him more than I can afford.' 'Oh, they won't let us even unsheath swords.' 'Hurrah! Up goes the fourth rocket. Fall in, there!'

The Garrison Artillery, who to the last cherished a wild hope that they might be allowed to bombard the City at a hundred yards' range, lined the parapet above the East gateway and cheered themselves hoarse as the British Infantry doubled along the road to the Main Gate of the City. The Cavalry cantered on to the Padshahi Gate, and the Native Infantry marched slowly to the Gate of the Butchers. The surprise was intended to be of a distinctly unpleasant nature, and to come on top of the defeat of the Police, who had been just able to keep the Mohammedans from firing the houses of a few leading Hindus. The bulk of the riot lay in the north and north-west wards. The east and south-east were by this time dark and silent, and I rode hastily to Lalun's house, for I wished to tell her to send some one in search of Wali Dad. The house was un-lighted, but the door was open, and I climbed upstairs in the darkness. One small lamp in the white room showed Lalun and her maid leaning half out of the window, breathing heavily and evidently pulling at some-thing that refused to come.

'Thou art late—very late,' gasped Lalun without turning her head. 'Help us now, O Fool, if thou hast not spent thy strength howling among the *tazias*. Pull! Nasiban and I can do no more! O Sahib, is it you? The Hindus have been hunting an old Mohammedan round the Ditch with clubs. If they find him again they will kill him. Help us to pull him up.'

I put my hands to the long red silk waist-cloth that was hanging out of the window, and we three pulled and pulled with all the strength at our command. There was something very heavy at the end, and it swore in an unknown tongue as it kicked against the City wall.

'Pull, oh, pull!' said Lalun at the last. A pair of brown hands grasped the window-sill and a venerable Mohammedan tumbled upon the floor, very much out of breath. His jaws were tied up, his turban had fallen over one eye, and he was dusty and angry.

Lalun hid her face in her hands for an instant and said something about Wali Dad that I could not catch.

Then, to my extreme gratification, she threw her arms round my neck and murmured pretty things. I was in no haste to stop her; and Nasiban, being a handmaiden of tact, turned to the big jewel-chest that stands in the corner of the white room and rummaged among the contents. The Mohammedan sat on the floor and glared.

'One service more, Sahib, since thou hast come so opportunely,' said Lalun. 'Wilt thou'—it is very nice to be thou-ed by Lalun—'take this old man across the City—the troops are everywhere, and they might hurt him, for he is old—to the Kumharsen Gate? There I think he may find a carriage to take him to his house. He is a friend of mine, and thou art—more than a friend—therefore I ask this.'

Nasiban bent over the old man, tucked something into his belt, and I raised him up and led him into the streets. In crossing from the east to the west of the City there was no chance of avoiding the troops and the crowd. Long before I reached the Gully of the Horsemen I heard the shouts of the British Infantry crying cheerily '*Hutt*, ye beggars! *Hutt*, ye devils! Get along Go forward, there!' Then followed the ringing of rifle-butts and shrieks of pain. The troops were banging the bare toes of the mob with their gun-butts—for not a bayonet had been fixed. My companion mumbled and jabbered as we walked on until we were carried back by the crowd and had to force our way to the troops. I caught him by the wrist and felt a bangle there—the iron bangle of the Sikhs—but I had no suspicions, for Lalun had only ten minutes before put her arms round me. Thrice we were carried back by the crowd, and when we made our way past the British Infantry it was to meet the Sikh Cavalry driving another mob before them with the butts of their lances.

'What are these dogs?' said the old man.

'Sikhs of the Cavalry, Father,' I said, and we edged our way up the line of horses two abreast and found the Deputy-Commissioner, his helmet smashed on his head, surrounded by a knot of men who had come down from the Club as amateur constables and had helped the Police mightily.

'We'll keep 'em on the run till dawn,' said Petitt. 'Who's your villainous friend? '

I had only time to say: 'The Protection of the Sirkar!' when a fresh crowd flying before the Native Infantry carried us a hundred yards nearer to the Kumharsen Gate, and Petitt was swept away like a shadow.

'I do not know—I cannot see—this is all new to me!' moaned my companion. 'How many troops are there in the City?'

'Perhaps five hundred,' I said.

'A lakh of men beaten by five hundred—and Sikhs among them! Surely, surely, I am an old man, but—the Kumharsen Gate is new. Who pulled down the stone lions? Where is the conduit? Sahib, I am a very old man, and, alas, I—I cannot stand.' He dropped in the shadow of the Kumharsen Gate where there was no disturbance. A fat gentleman wearing gold pince-nez came out of the darkness.

'You are most kind to bring my old friend,' he said suavely. ' He is a landholder of Akala. He should not be in a big City when there is religious excitement. But I have a carriage here. You are quite truly kind. Will you help me to put him into the carriage? It is very late.'

We bundled the old man into a hired victoria that stood close to the gate, and I turned back to the house on the City wall. The troops were driving the people to and fro, while the Police shouted, 'To your houses! Get to your houses! ' and the dog-whip of the Assistant District Superintendent cracked remorselessly. Terror-stricken *bunnias* clung to the stirrups of the Cavalry, crying that their houses had been robbed (which was a lie), and the burly Sikh horsemen patted them on the shoulder and bade them return to those houses lest a worse thing should happen. Parties of five or six British soldiers, joining arms, swept down the side-gullies, their rifles on their backs, stamping, with shouting and song, upon the toes of Hindu and Mussulman. Never was religious enthusiasm more systematically squashed; and never were poor breakers of the peace more utterly weary and footsore. They were routed out of holes and corners, from behind well-pillars and byres, and bidden to go to their houses. If they had no houses to go to, so much the worse for their toes.

On returning to Lalun's door I stumbled over a man at the threshold. He was sobbing hysterically and his arms flapped like the wings of a goose. It was Wali Dad, Agnostic and Unbeliever, shoeless, turbanless, and frothing at the mouth, the flesh on his chest bruised and bleeding from the vehemence with which he had smitten himself. A broken torch-handle lay by his side, and his quivering lips murmured, '*Ya Hasan! Ya Hussain!*' as I stooped over him. I pushed him a few steps up the staircase, threw a pebble at Lalun's City window and hurried home.

Most of the streets were very still, and the cold wind that comes before the dawn whistled down them. In the centre of the Square of the Mosque a man was bending over a corpse. The skull had been smashed in by gun-butt or bamboo-stave.

'It is expedient that one man should die for the people,' said Petitt grimly, raising the shape less head. 'These brutes were beginning to show their teeth too much.'

And from afar we could hear the soldiers singing 'Two Lovely Black Eyes' as they drove the remnant of the rioters within doors.

***

Of course you can guess what happened? I was not so clever. When the news went abroad that Khem Singh had escaped from the Fort, I did not, since I was then living this story, not writing it, connect myself, or Lalun, or the fat gentleman of the gold pince-nez, with his disappearance. Nor did it strike me that Wali Dad was the man who should have convoyed him across the City, or that Lalun's arms round my neck were put there to hide the money that Nasiban gave to Khem Singh, and that Lalun had used me and my white face as even a better safeguard than Wali Dad who proved himself so untrustworthy. All that I knew at the time was that, when Fort Amara was taken up with the riots, Khem Singh profited by the confusion to get away, and that his two Sikh guards also escaped.

But later on I received full enlightenment; and so did Khem Singh. He fled to those who knew him in the old days, but many of them were dead and more were changed, and all knew something of the Wrath of the Government. He went to the young men, but the glamour of his name had passed away, and they were entering native regiments or Government offices, and Khem Singh could give them neither pension, decorations, nor influence—nothing but a glorious death with their back to the mouth of a gun. He wrote letters and made promises, and the letters fell into bad hands, and a wholly insignificant subordinate officer of Police tracked them down and gained promotion thereby. Moreover, Khem Singh was old, and aniseed brandy was scarce, and he had left his silver cooking-pots in Fort Amara with his nice warm bedding, and the gentleman with the gold pince-nez was told by Those who had employed him that Khem Singh as a popular leader was not worth the money paid.

'Great is the mercy of these fools of English!' said Khem Singh when the situation was put before him. 'I will go back to Fort Amara of my own free will and gain honour. Give me good clothes to return in.'

So, at his own time, Khem Singh knocked at the wicket-gate of the Fort and walked to the Captain and the Subaltern, who were nearly grey-headed on account of correspondence that daily arrived from Simla marked 'Private.'

'I have come back, Captain Sahib,' said Khem Singh. 'Put no more guards over me. It is no good out yonder.'

A week later I saw him for the first time to my knowledge, and he made as though there were an understanding between us.

'It was well done, Sahib,' said he, 'and greatly I admired your astuteness in thus boldly facing the troops when I, whom they would have doubtless torn to pieces, was with you. Now there is a man in Fort Ooltagarh whom a bold man could with ease help to escape. This is the position of the Fort as I draw it on the sand—'

But I was thinking how I had become Lalun's Vizier after all.

Thoughts on At the City Wall

The narrator of this remarkable tale is a young British Subaltern of the type Kipling wrote about so often in his early years. He stands as a symbol of a race confident of its ability to deliver what they saw as a civilizing mission. The story contrasts him, not with 'the natives', but with the brutish, Indian-hating Captain who falls far short of these ideals.

Nevertheless. the central character is Lalun, a dancing woman, or courtesan, whose salon on the city wall is the haunt of a diverse crowd of intellectuals of all races and religions. She is exceptional in that few of her sex and race were at that time literate, even fewer of her occupation. She has bravely overcome her background and fashioned a life acceptable to herself.

Prominent among Lalun's regular patrons is the young Muhammadan (sic), Wali Dad who passes his days 'making love to', that is flirting with, Lalun in the window-seat. When violence breaks out in the town he is shown as reverting to what the narrator calls the 'natural' behaviour of his people. This comment has attracted complaints of racial prejudice. In fact, the story makes plain that the young man's defects are personal to himself and, perhaps, the Methodist missionaries who brought him up.

For background to this tale, Kipling probably drew on his explorations of Lahore as a young journalist, where his conduct seems to have belied his later stuffy image. (See Charles Allen.)

The story is one of triple disillusionment, of the rebel, Khem Singh when he discovers what little time his young compatriots have for an old hero, of Lalun when she discovers that her efforts to save someone she admired have proved fruitless, and of the narrator who was told by Lalun that he would be her vizier, only to find himself her pawn.

'On the City Wall' is one of the most impressive of Kipling's early works. The writer and historian, Matthew Lyons has suggested on his blog that the story's source is the book of Joshua and the tale of his capture of Jericho thanks to the harlot, Rahab, whose house was also on the city wall.

More tellingly he has observed that, 'It is a fair prospectus of Kipling's art: comprehending the mute, forgotten peoples of the world; listening for the distant halting rhythm of another story, for the approach of the Daemon: waiting patiently, as Lalun's vizier must wait on the city wall, and as Bagheera waits, too, dark and still and deadly amid the shadows and shapes of things that are and are not there, ready to make his kill that death might buy another life.'

Fort Amara is based upon Fort Lahore which also features in Kipling's story, 'With the Main Guard'.

IN FLOOD TIME

Tweed said tae Till:
'What gars ye rin sae still?
Till said tae Tweed
'Though ye rin wi' speed
An' I rin slaw—
Yet where ye droon ae man
I droon twa.'

There is no getting over the river to-night, Sahib. They say that a bullock-cart has been washed down already, and the *ekka* that went over a half-hour before you came has not yet reached the far side. Is the Sahib in haste? I will drive the ford-elephant in to show him. Ohé, mahout there in the shed! Bring out Ram Pershad, and if he will face the current, good. An elephant never lies, Sahib, and Ram Pershad is separated from his friend Kala Nag. He, too, wishes to cross to the far side. Well done! Well done! my King Go half-way across, *mahoutji*, and see what the river says. Well done, Ram Pershad! Pearl among elephants, go into the river! Hit him on the head, fool! Was the goad made only to scratch thine own fat back with, bastard? Strike strike! What are the boulders to thee, Ram Pershad, my Rustum, my mountain of strength? Go in! Go in!

No, Sahib! It is useless. You can hear him trumpet. He is telling Kala Nag that he cannot come over. See! He has swung round and is shaking his head. He is no fool. He knows what the Barhwi means when it is angry. Aha! Indeed, thou art no fool, my child! Salaam, Ram Pershad, Bahadur! Take him under the trees, mahout, and see that he gets his spices. Well done, thou chiefest among tuskers! Salaam to the Sirkar and go to sleep.

What is to be done? The Sahib must wait till the river goes down. It will shrink to-morrow morning, if God pleases, or the day after at the latest! Now why does the Sahib get so angry? I am his servant. Before God, *I* did not create this stream! What can I do? My hut and all that is therein is at the service of the Sahib, and it is beginning to rain. Come away, my Lord. How will the river go down for your throwing abuse at it? In the old days the English people were not thus. The fire-carriage has made them soft. In the old days, when they drave behind horses by day or by night, they said naught if a river barred the way, or a carriage sat down in the mud. It was the will of God—not like a fire-carriage which goes and goes and goes, and would go though all the devils in the land hung on to its tail. The fire-carriage hath spoiled the English people. After all, what is a day lost, or, for that matter, what are two days? Is the Sahib going to his own wedding, that he is so mad with haste? Ho! ho! ho! I am an old man and see few Sahibs. Forgive me if I have forgotten the respect that is due to them. The Sahib is not angry?

His own wedding! Ho! ho! ho! The mind of an old man is like the *numah*-tree. Fruit, bud, blossom, and the dead leaves of all the years of the past flourish together. Old and new and that which is gone out of remembrance, all three are there! Sit on the bedstead, Sahib, and drink milk. Or—would the Sahib in truth care to drink my tobacco? It is good. It is the tobacco of Nuklao. My son, who is in service there, sends it to me. Drink, then, Sahib, if you know how to handle the tube. The Sahib takes it like a Mussulman. Wah! Wah! Where did he learn that? His own wedding! Ho! ho! ho! The Sahib says that there is no wedding in the matter at all. Now *is* it likely that the Sahib would speak true talk to me who am only a black man? Small wonder, then, that he is in haste. Thirty years have I beaten the gong at this ford, but never have I seen a Sahib in such haste. Thirty years, Sahib! That is a very long time. Thirty years ago this ford was on the track of the *bunjaras*, and I have seen two thousand pack-bullocks cross in one night. Now the rail has come, and the fire-carriage says *buz-buz-buz*, and a hundred lakhs of maunds slide across that big bridge. It is very wonderful; but the ford is lonely now that there are no *bunjaras* to camp under the trees.

Nay, do not trouble to look at the sky without.

It will rain till the dawn. Listen! The boulders are talking to-night in the bed of the river. Hear them! They would be husking your bones, Sahib, had you tried to cross. See, I will shut the door and no rain can enter. *Wahi! Ahi! Ugh!* Thirty years on the banks of the ford. An old man am I and—where is the oil for the lamp?

***

Your pardon, but, because of my years, I sleep no sounder than a dog; and you moved to the door. Look then, Sahib. Look and listen. A full half *koss* from bank to bank is the stream now—you can see it under the stars—and there are ten feet of water therein. It will not shrink because of the anger in your eyes, and it will not be quiet on account of your curses. Which is louder, Sahib—your voice or the voice of the river? Call to it—perhaps it will be ashamed. Lie down and sleep afresh, Sahib. I know the anger of the Barhwi when there has fallen rain in the foot-hills. I swam the flood, once, on a night tenfold worse than this, and by the Favour of God I was released from Death when I had come to the very gates thereof.

May I tell the tale? Very good talk. I will fill the pipe anew.

Thirty years ago it was, when I was a young man and had but newly come to the ford. I was strong then, and the *bunjaras* had no doubt when I said: 'This ford is clear.' I have toiled all night up to my shoulder-blades in running water amid a hundred bullocks mad with fear, and have brought them across losing not a hoof. When all was done I fetched the shivering men, and they gave me for reward the pick of their cattle—the bell-bullock of the drove. So great was the honour in which I was held! But to-day, when the rain falls and the river rises, I creep into my hut and whimper like a dog. My strength is gone from me. I am an old man and the fire-carriage has made the ford desolate. They were wont to call me the Strong One of the Barhwi.

Behold my face, Sahib—it is the face of a monkey. And my arm—it is the arm of an old woman. I swear to you, Sahib, that a woman has loved this face and has rested in the hollow of this arm. Twenty years ago, Sahib. Believe me, this was true talk—twenty years ago.

129

Come to the door and look across. Can you see a thin fire very far away down the stream? That is the temple-fire, in the shrine of Hanuman, of the village of Pateera. North, under the big star, is the village itself, but it is hidden by a bend of the river. Is that far to swim, Sahib? Would you take off your clothes and adventure? Yet I swam to Pateera—not once, but many times; and there are *muggers* in the river too.

Love knows no caste; else why should I, a Mussulman and the son of a Mussulman, have sought a Hindu woman—a widow of the Hindus—the sister of the headman of Pateera? But it was even so. They of the headman's household came on a pilgrimage to Muttra when She was but newly a bride. Silver tyres were upon the wheels of the bullock-cart, and silken curtains hid the woman. Sahib, I made no haste in their conveyance, for the wind parted the curtains and I saw Her. When they returned from pilgrimage the boy that was Her husband had died, and I saw Her again in the bullock-cart. By God, these Hindus are fools! What was it to me whether She was Hindu or Jain—scavenger, leper, or whole? I would have married Her and made Her a home by the ford. The Seventh of the Nine Bars says that a man may not marry one of the idolaters? Is that truth? Both Shiahs and Sunnis say that a Mussulman may not marry one of the idolaters? Is the Sahib a priest, then, that he knows so much? I will tell him something that he does not know. There is neither Shiah nor Sunni, forbidden nor idolater, in Love; and the Nine Bars are but nine little faggots that the flame of Love utterly burns away. In truth, I would have taken Her; but what could I do? The headman would have sent his men to break my head with staves. I am not—I was not—afraid of any five men; but against half a village who can prevail?

Therefore it was my custom, these things having been arranged between us twain, to go by night to the village of Pateera, and there we met among the crops, no man knowing aught of the matter. Behold, now! I was wont to cross here, skirting the jungle to the river bend where the railway bridge is, and thence across the elbow of land to Pateera. The light of the shrine was my guide when the nights were dark. That jungle near the river is very full of snakes—little *karaits* that sleep on the sand—and moreover, Her brothers would have slain me had they found me in the crops. But none knew—none knew save She and I; and the blown sand of the river-bed covered the track of my feet. In the hot months it was an easy thing to pass from the ford to Pateera, and in the first Rains, when the river rose slowly, it was an easy thing also. I set the strength of my body against the strength of the stream, and nightly I ate in my hut here and drank at Pateera yonder. She had said that one Hirnam Singh, a thief, had sought Her, and he was of a village up the river but on the same bank. All Sikhs are dogs, and they have refused in their folly that good gift of God—tobacco. I was ready to destroy Hirnam Singh that ever he had come nigh Her; and the more because he had sworn to Her that She had a lover, and that he would lie in wait and give the name to the headman unless She went away with him. What curs are these Sikhs!

After that news I swam always with a little sharp knife in my belt, and evil would it have been for a man had he stayed me. I knew not the face of Hirnam Singh, but I would have killed any who came between me and Her.

Upon a night in the beginning of the Rains I was minded to go across to Pateera, albeit the river was angry. Now the nature of the Barhwi is this, Sahib. In twenty breaths it comes down from the Hills a wall three feet high, and I have seen it, between the lighting of a fire and the cooking of a cake, grow from a runnel to a sister of the Jumna.

When I left this bank there was a shoal a half-mile down, and I made shift to fetch it and draw breath there ere going forward; for I felt the hands of the river heavy upon my heels. Yet what will a young man not do for Love's sake? There was but little light from the stars, and midway to the shoal a branch of the stinking deodar tree brushed my mouth as I swam. That was a sign of heavy rain in the foot-hills and beyond, for the deodar is a strong tree, not easily shaken from the hillsides. I made haste, the river aiding me, but ere I had touched the shoal, the pulse of the stream beat, as it were, within me and around, and, behold, the shoal was gone and I rode high on the crest of a wave that ran from bank to bank. Has the Sahib ever been cast into much water that fights and will not let a man use his limbs? To me, my head upon the water, it seemed as though there were naught but water to the world's end, and the river drave me with its driftwood. A man is a very little thing in the belly of a flood. And *this* flood, though I knew it not, was the Great Flood about which men talk still. My liver was dissolved and I lay like a log upon my back in the fear of Death. There were living things in the water, crying and howling grievously—beasts of the forest and cattle, and once the voice of a man asking for help. But the rain came and lashed the water white, and I heard no more save the roar of the boulders below and the roar of the rain above. Thus I was whirled downstream, wrestling for the breath in me. It is very hard to die when one is young. Can the Sahib, standing here, see the railway bridge? Look, there are the lights of the mail-train going to Peshawur! The bridge is now twenty feet above the river, but upon that night the water was roaring against the lattice-work, and against the lattice came I feet first. But much driftwood was piled there and upon the piers, and I took no great hurt. Only the river pressed me as a strong man presses a weaker. Scarcely could I take hold of the lattice-work and crawl to the upper boom. Sahib, the water was foaming across the rails a foot deep! Judge therefore what manner of flood it must have been. I could not hear. I could not see. I could but lie on the boom and pant for breath.

After a while the rain ceased and there came out in the sky certain new-washed stars, and by their light I saw that there was no end to the black water as far as the eye could travel, and the water had risen upon the rails. There were dead beasts in the driftwood on the piers, and others caught by the neck in the lattice-work, and others not yet drowned who strove to find a foothold on the lattice-work-buffaloes and kine, and wild pig, and deer one or two, and snakes and jackals past all counting. Their bodies were black upon the left side of the bridge, but the smaller of them were forced through the lattice-work and whirled down-stream.

Thereafter the stars died and the rain came down afresh and the river rose yet more, and I felt the bridge begin to stir under me as a man stirs in his sleep ere he wakes. But I was not afraid, Sahib. I swear to you that I was not afraid, though I had no power in my limbs. I knew that I should not die till I had seen Her once more. But I was very cold, and I felt that the bridge must go.

There was a trembling in the water, such a trembling as goes before the coming of a great wave, and the bridge lifted its flank to the rush of that coming so that the right lattice dipped under water and the left rose clear. On my beard, Sahib, I am speaking God's truth! As a Mirzapore stone-boat careens to the wind, so the Barhwi Bridge turned. Thus and in no other manner.

I slid from the boom into deep water, and behind me came the wave of the wrath of the river. I heard its voice and the scream of the middle part of the bridge as it moved from the piers and sank, and I knew no more till I rose in the middle of the great flood. I put forth my hand to swim, and lo! it fell upon the knotted hair of the head of a man. He was dead, for no one but I, the Strong One of Barhwi, could have lived in that race. He had been dead full two days, for he rode high, wallowing, and was an aid to me. I laughed then, knowing for a surety that I should yet see Her and take no harm; and I twisted my fingers in the hair of the man, for I was far spent, and together we went down the stream—he the dead and I the living. Lacking that help I should have sunk: the cold was in my marrow, and my flesh was ribbed and sodden on my bones. But *he* had no fear who had known the uttermost of the power of the river; and I let him go where he chose. At last we came into the power of a side-current that set to the right bank, and I strove with my feet to draw with it. But the dead man swung heavily in the whirl, and I feared that some branch had struck him and that he would sink. The tops of the tamarisks brushed my knees, so I knew we were come into flood-water above the crops, and, after, I let down my legs and felt bottom— the ridge of a field—and, after, the dead man stayed upon a knoll under a fig-tree, and I drew my body from the water rejoicing.

Does the Sahib know whither the backwash of the flood had borne me? To the knoll which is the eastern boundary-mark of the village of Pateera! No other place. I drew the dead man up on the grass for the service that he had done me, and also because I knew not whether I should need him again. Then I went, crying thrice like a jackal, to the appointed place, which was near the byre of the headman's house. But my Love was already there, weeping. She feared that the flood had swept my hut at the Barhwi Ford. When I came softly through the ankle-deep water, She thought it was a ghost and would have fled, but I put my arms round Her, and—I was no ghost in those days, though I am an old man now. Ho! ho! Dried corn, in truth. Maize without juice. Ho! ho!1

I told Her the story of the breaking of the Barhwi Bridge, and She said that I was greater than mortal man, for none may cross the Barhwi in full flood, and I had seen what never man had seen before. Hand in hand we went to the knoll where the dead lay, and I showed Her by what help I had made the ford. She looked also upon the body under the stars, for the latter end of the night was clear, and hid Her face in Her hands, crying: 'It is the body of Hirnam Singh! ' I said: 'The swine is of more use dead than living, my Beloved,' and She said: 'Surely, for he has saved the dearest life in the world to my love. None the less, he cannot stay here, for that would bring shame upon me.' The body was not a gunshot from Her door.

Then said I, rolling the body with my hands 'God hath judged between us, Hirnam Singh, that thy blood might not be upon my head. Now, whether I have done thee a wrong in keeping thee from the burning-ghat, do thou and the crows settle together.' So I cast him adrift into the flood-water, and he was drawn out to the open, ever wagging his thick black beard like a priest under the pulpit-board. And I saw no more of Hirnam Singh.

Before the breaking of the day we two parted, and I moved towards such of the jungle as was not flooded. With the full light I saw what I had done in the darkness, and the bones of my body were loosened in my flesh, for there ran two *koss* of raging water between the village of Pateera and the trees of the far bank, and, in the middle, the piers of the Barhwi Bridge showed like broken teeth in the jaw of an old man. Nor was there any life upon the waters—neither birds nor boats, but only an army of drowned things—bullocks and horses and men—and the river was redder than blood from the clay of the foot-hills. Never had I seen such a flood—never since that year have I seen the like—and, O Sahib, no man living had done what I had done. There was no return for me that day. Not for all the lands of the headman would I venture a second time without the shield of darkness that cloaks danger. I went a *koss* up the river to the house of a blacksmith, saying that the flood had swept me from my hut, and they gave me food. Seven days I stayed with the blacksmith, till a boat came and I returned to my house. There was no trace of wall, or roof, or floor—naught but a patch of slimy mud. Judge, therefore, Sahib, how far the river must have risen.

It was written that I should not die either in my house, or in the heart of the Barhwi, or under the wreck of the Barhwi Bridge, for God sent down Hirnam Singh two days dead, though I know not how the man died, to be my buoy and support. Hirnam Singh has been in Hell these twenty years, and the thought of that night must be the flower of his torment.

Listen, Sahib! The river has changed its voice. It is going to sleep before the dawn, to which there is yet one hour. With the light it will come down afresh. How do I know? Have I been here thirty years without knowing the voice of the river as a father knows the voice of his son? Every moment it is talking less angrily. I swear that ere will be no danger for one hour or, perhaps, two. I cannot answer for the morning. Be quick, Sahib! I will call Ram Pershad, and he will not turn back this time. Is the paulin tightly corded upon all the baggage? Ohé, mahout with a mud head, the elephant for the Sahib, and tell them on the far side that there will be no crossing after daylight.

Money? Nay, Sahib. I am not of that kind. No, not even to give sweetmeats to the baby-folk. My house, look you, is empty, and I am an old man.

Dutt, Ram Pershad! *Dutt! Dutt! Dutt!* Good luck go with you, Sahib.

1. I grieve to say that the Warden of the Barhwi Ford is responsible here for two very bad puns in the vernacular.—*R.K.*

Thoughts on In Flood Time

Various literary precedents have been suggested for 'In Flood Time' (Hero and Leander, The Ancient Mariner and so on), but in essence it is a tale of desperate love set against the drama of a swollen river. The description of the force of the river and the detritus it carries with it has surely never been bettered. Nevertheless, the story's strength lies in the empathy which the reader is made to feel for the narrator, who on this occasion is the central character.

Curiously, after the two lovers finally part we hear nothing more of the woman, who seems to float away as silent and unremarked as the body of the dead man 'wagging his thick black beard like a priest under the pulpit-board'. The story's dramatic force lies in the life changing encounter between the narrator and the body of the man who would have killed him.

It should be noted that Kipling used the same trope of water in spate in 'Friendly Brook'.

The epigraph is an old Border poem which takes the form of a dialogue between two rivers.

THE BRIDGE-BUILDERS

The least that Findlayson, of the Public Works Department, expected was a C.I.E.; he dreamed of a C.S.I.. Indeed, his friends told him that he deserved more. For three years he had endured heat and cold, disappointment, discomfort, danger, and disease, with responsibility almost to top-heavy for one pair of shoulders; and day by day, through that time, the great Kashi Bridge over the Ganges had grown under his charge. Now, in less than three months, if all went well, his Excellency the Viceroy would open the bridge in state, an archbishop would bless it, and the first trainload of soldiers would come over it, and there would be speeches.

Findlayson, C. E., sat in his trolley on a construction line that ran along one of the main revetments—the huge stone-faced banks that flared away north and south for three miles on either side of the river and permitted himself to think of the end. With its approaches, his work was one mile and three-quarters in length; a lattice-girder bridge, trussed with the Findlayson truss standing on seven-and-twenty brick piers. Each one of those piers was twenty-four feet in diameter, capped with red Agra stone and sunk eighty feet below the shifting sand of the Ganges' bed. Above them was a railway-line fifteen feet broad; above that, again, a cart-road of eighteen feet, flanked with footpaths. At either end rose towers, of red brick, loopholed for musketry and pierced for big guns, and the ramp of the road was being pushed forward to their haunches. The raw earth-ends were crawling and alive with hundreds upon hundreds of tiny asses climbing out of the yawning borrow-pit below with sackfuls of stuff; and the hot afternoon air was filled with the noise of hooves, the rattle of the drivers' sticks, and the swish and roll-down of the dirt. The river was very low, and on the dazzling white sand between the three centre piers stood squat cribs of railway-sleepers, filled within and daubed without with mud, to support the last of the girders as those were riveted up. In the little deep water left by the drought, an overhead crane travelled to and fro along its spile-pier, jerking sections of iron into place, snorting and backing and grunting as an elephant grunts in the timberyard. Riveters by the hundred swarmed about the lattice side-work and the iron roof of the railway line hung from invisible staging under the bellies of the girders, clustered round the throats of the piers, and rode on the overhang of the footpath-stanchions; their fire-pots and the spurts of flame that answered each hammer-stroke showing no more than pale yellow in the sun's glare. East and west and north and south the construction-trains rattled and shrieked up and down the embankments, the piled trucks of brown and white stone banging behind them till the side-boards were unpinned, and with a roar and a grumble a few thousand tons' more material were flung out to hold the river in place.

Findlayson, C. E., turned on his trolley and looked over the face of the country that he had changed for seven miles around. Looked back on the humming village of five thousand work-men; up stream and down, along the vista of spurs and sand; across the river to the far piers, lessening in the haze; overhead to the guard-towers—and only he knew how strong those were—and with a sigh of contentment saw that his work was good. There stood his bridge before him in the sunlight, lacking only a few weeks' work on the girders of the three middle piers—his bridge, raw and ugly as original sin, but *pukka*—permanent—to endure when all memory of the builder, yea, even of the splendid Findlayson truss, has perished. Practically, the thing was done.

Hitchcock, his assistant, cantered along the line on a little switch-tailed Kabuli pony who through long practice could have trotted securely over trestle, and nodded to his chief.

"All but," said he, with a smile.

"I've been thinking about it," the senior answered. "Not half a bad job for two men, is it?"

"One—and a half. 'Gad, what a Cooper's Hill cub I was when I came on the works!" Hitchcock felt very old in the crowded experiences of the past three years, that had taught him power and responsibility.

"You *were* rather a colt," said Findlayson. "I wonder how you'll like going back to office-work when this job's over."

"I shall hate it!" said the young man, and as he went on his eye followed Findlayson's, and he muttered, "Isn't it damned good?"

"I think we'll go up the service together," Findlayson said to himself. "You're too good a youngster to waste on another man. Cub thou wast; assistant thou art. Personal assistant, and at Simla, thou shalt be, if any credit comes to me out of the business!"

Indeed, the burden of the work had fallen altogether on Findlayson and his assistant, the young man whom he had chosen because of his rawness to break to his own needs. There were labour contractors by the half-hundred—fitters and riveters, European, borrowed from the railway workshops, with, perhaps, twenty white and half-caste subordinates to direct, under direction, the bevies of workmen—but none knew better than these two, who trusted each other, how the underlings were not to be trusted. They had been tried many times in sudden crises—by slipping of booms, by breaking of tackle, failure of cranes, and the wrath of the river—but no stress had brought to light any man among men whom Findlayson and Hitchcock would have honoured by working as remorselessly as they worked them-selves. Findlayson thought it over from the beginning: the months of office-work destroyed at a blow when the Government of India, at the last moment, added two feet to the width of the bridge, under the impression that bridges were cut out of paper, and so brought to ruin at least half an acre of calculations—and Hitchcock, new to disappointment, buried his head in his arms and wept; the heart-breaking delays over the filling of the contracts in England; the futile correspondences hinting at great wealth of commissions if one, only one, rather doubtful consignment were passed; the war that followed the refusal; the careful, polite obstruction at the other end that followed the war, till young Hitchcock, putting one month's leave to another month, and borrowing ten days from Findlayson, spent his poor little savings of a year in a wild dash to London, and there, as his own tongue asserted and the later consignments proved, put the fear of God into a man so great that he feared only Parliament and said so till Hitchcock wrought with him across his own dinner table, and—he feared the Kashi Bridge and all who spoke in its name. Then there was the cholera that came in the night to the village by the bridge works; and after the cholera smote the small-pox. The fever they had always with them. Hitchcock had been appointed a magistrate of the third class with whipping powers, for the better government of the community, and Findlayson watched him wield his powers temperately, learning what to overlook and what to look after. It was a long, long reverie, and it covered storm, sudden freshets, death in every manner and shape, violent and awful rage against red tape half frenzying a mind that knows it should be busy on other things; drought, sanitation, finance; birth, wedding, burial, and riot in the village of twenty warring castes; argument, expostulation, persuasion, and the blank despair that a man goes to bed upon, thankful that his rifle is all in pieces in the guncase. Behind everything rose the black frame of the Kashi Bridge—plate by plate, girder by girder, span by span—and each pier of it recalled Hitchcock, the all-round man, who had stood by his chief without failing from the very first to this last.

So the bridge was two men's work—unless one counted Peroo, as Peroo certainly counted himself. He was a Lascar, a Kharva from Bulsar, familiar with every port between Rockhampton and London, who had risen to the rank of serang on the British India boats, but wearying of routine musters and clean clothes, had thrown up the service and gone inland, where men of his calibre were sure of employment. For his knowledge of tackle and the handling of heavy weights, Peroo was worth almost any price he might have chosen to put upon his services; but custom decreed the wage of the overhead-men, and Peroo was not within many silver pieces of his proper value. Neither running water nor extreme heights made him afraid; and, as an ex-serang, he knew how to hold authority. No piece of iron was so big or so badly placed that Peroo could not devise a tackle to lift it—a loose-ended, sagging arrangement, rigged with a scandalous amount of talking, but perfectly equal to the work in hand. It was Peroo who had saved the girder of Number Seven pier from destruction when the new wire-rope jammed in the eye of the crane, and the huge plate tilted in its slings, threatening to slide out sideways. Then the native workmen lost their heads with great shoutings, and Hitchcock's right arm was broken by a falling T-plate, and he buttoned it up in his coat and swooned, and came to and directed for four hours till Peroo, from the top of the crane, reported "All's well," and the plate swung home. There was no one like Peroo, serang, to lash, and guy, and hold, to control the donkey-engines, to hoist a fallen locomotive craftily out of the borrow-pit into which it had tumbled; to strip, and dive, if need be, to see how the concrete blocks round the piers stood the scouring of Mother Gunga, or to adventure upstream on a monsoon night and report on the state of the embankment-facings. He would interrupt the field-councils of Findlayson and Hitchcock without fear, till his wonderful English, or his still more wonderful *lingua franca*, half Portuguese and half Malay, ran out and he was forced to take string and show the knots that he would recommend. He controlled his own gang of tackle men—mysterious relatives from Kutch Mandvi gathered month by month and tried to the uttermost. No consideration of family or kin allowed Peroo to keep weak hands or a giddy head on the pay-roll. "My honour is the honour of this bridge," he would say to the about-to-be-dismissed. "What do I care for your honour? Go and work on a steamer. That is all you are fit for."

The little cluster of huts where he and his gang lived centred round the tattered dwelling of a sea-priest—one who had never set foot on black water, but had been chosen as ghostly counsellor by two generations of sea-rovers all unaffected by port missions or those creeds which are thrust upon sailors by agencies along Thames bank. The priest of the Lascars had nothing to do with their caste, or indeed with anything at all. He ate the offerings of his church, and slept and smoked, and slept again, "for," said Peroo, who had haled him a thousand miles inland, "he is a very holy man. He never cares what you eat so long as you do not eat beef, and that is good, because on land we worship Shiva, we Kharvas; but at sea on the Kumpani's boats we attend strictly to the orders of the Burra Malum [the first mate], and on this bridge we observe what Finlinson Sahib says."

141

Finlinson Sahib had that day given orders to clear the scaffolding from the guard-tower on the right bank, and Peroo with his mates was casting loose and lowering down the bamboo poles and planks as swiftly as ever they had whipped the cargo out of a coaster.

From his trolley he could hear the whistle of the serang's silver pipe and the creek and clatter of the pulleys. Peroo was standing on the top-most coping of the tower, clad in the blue dungaree of his abandoned service, and as Findlayson motioned to him to be careful, for his was no life to throw away, he gripped the last pole, and, shading his eyes ship-fashion, answered with the long-drawn wail of the fo'c'sle lookout: "*Ham dekhta hai*" ("I am looking out"). Findlayson laughed and then sighed. It was years since he had seen a steamer, and he was sick for home. As his trolley passed under the tower, Peroo descended by a rope, ape-fashion, and cried: "It looks well now, Sahib. Our bridge is all but done. What think you Mother Gunga will say when the rail runs over?"

"She has said little so far. It was never Mother Gunga that delayed us."

"There is always time for her; and none the less there has been delay. Has the Sahib forgotten last autumn's flood, when the stone-boats were sunk without warning—or only a half-day's warning?"

"Yes, but nothing save a big flood could hurt us now. The spurs are holding well on the West Bank."

"Mother Gunga eats great allowances. There is always room for more stone on the revetments. I tell this to the Chota Sahib"—he meant Hitchcock—"and he laughs."

"No matter, Peroo. Another year thou wilt be able to build a bridge in thine own fashion."

The Lascar grinned. "Then it will not be in this way—with stonework sunk under water, as the *Qyetta* was sunk. I like sus-sus-pen-sheen bridges that fly from bank to bank. with one big step, like a gang-plank.

142

Then no water can hurt. When does the Lord Sahib come to open the bridge?"

"In three months, when the weather is cooler."

"Ho! ho! He is like the Burra Malum. He sleeps below while the work is being done. Then he comes upon the quarter-deck and touches with his finger, and says: 'This is not clean! Dam jibboonwallah!'"

"But the Lord Sahib does not call me a dam jibboonwallah, Peroo."

"No, Sahib; but he does not come on deck till the work is all finished. Even the Burra Malum of the *Nerbudda* said once at Tuticorin——"

"Bah! Go! I am busy."

"I, also!" said Peroo, with an unshaken countenance. "May I take the light dinghy now and row along the spurs?"

"To hold them with thy hands? They are, I think, sufficiently heavy."

"Nay, Sahib. It is thus. At sea, on the Black Water, we have room to be blown up and down without care. Here we have no room at all. Look you, we have put the river into a dock, and run her between stone sills."

Findlayson smiled at the "we."

"We have bitted and bridled her. She is not like the sea, that can beat against a soft beach. She is Mother Gunga—in irons." His voice fell a little.

"Peroo, thou hast been up and down the world more even than I. Speak true talk, now. How much dost thou in thy heart believe of Mother Gunga?"

"All that our priest says. London is London, Sahib. Sydney is Sydney, and Port Darwin is Port Darwin. Also Mother Gunga is Mother Gunga, and when I come back to her banks I know this and worship. In London I did poojah to the big temple by the river for the sake of the God within. . . . Yes, I will not take the cushions in the dinghy."

Findlayson mounted his horse and trotted to the shed of a bungalow that he shared with his assistant. The place had become home to him in the last three years. He had grilled in the heat, sweated in the rains, and shivered with fever under the rude thatch roof; the lime-wash beside the door was covered with rough drawings and formulae, and the sentry-path trodden in the matting of the verandah showed where he had walked alone. There is no eight-hour limit to an engineer's work, and the evening meal with Hitchcock was eaten booted and spurred: over their cigars they listened to the hum of the village as the gangs came up from the river-bed and the lights began to twinkle.

"Peroo has gone up the spurs in your dinghy. He's taken a couple of nephews with him, and he's lolling in the stern like a commodore," said Hitchcock.

"That's all right. He's got something on his mind. You'd think that ten years in the British India boats would have knocked most of his religion out of him."

"So it has," said Hitchcock, chuckling. "I overheard him the other day in the middle of a most atheistical talk with that fat old *guru* of theirs. Peroo denied the efficacy of prayer; and wanted the *guru* to go to sea and watch a gale out with him, and see if he could stop a monsoon."

"All the same, if you carried off his *guru* he'd leave us like a shot. He was yarning away to me about praying to the dome of St. Paul's when he was in London."

"He told me that the first time he went into the engine-room of a steamer, when he was a boy, he prayed to the low-pressure cylinder."

"Not half a bad thing to pray to, either. He's propitiating his own Gods now, and he wants to know what Mother Gunga will think of a bridge being run across her. Who's there?" A shadow darkened the doorway, and a telegram was put into Hitchcock's hand.

"She ought to be pretty well used to it by this time. Only a *tar*. It ought to be Ralli's answer about the new rivets.... Great Heavens!" Hitchcock jumped to his feet.

"What is it?" said the senior, and took the form. *"That's* what Mother Gunga thinks, is it," he said, reading. "Keep cool, young 'un. We've got all our work cut out for us. Let's see. Muir wired half an hour ago: *'Floods on the Ramgunga. Look out.'* Well, that gives us—one, two—nine and a half for the flood to reach Melipur Ghaut and seven's sixteen and a half to Lataoli—say fifteen hours before it comes down to us."

"Curse that hill-fed sewer of a Ramgunga! Findlayson, this is two months before anything could have been expected, and the left bank is littered up with stuff still. Two full months before the time!"

"That's why it comes. I've only known Indian rivers for five-and-twenty years, and I don't pretend to understand. Here comes another *tar*." Findlayson opened the telegram. "Cockran, this time, from the Ganges Canal: *'Heavy rains here. Bad.'* He might have saved the last word. Well, we don't want to know any more. We've got to work the gangs all night and clean up the riverbed. You'll take the east bank and work out to meet me in the middle. Get everything that floats below the bridge: we shall have quite enough river-craft coming down adrift anyhow, without letting the stone-boats ram the piers. What have you got on the east bank that needs looking after?

"Pontoon—one big pontoon with the overhead crane on it. T'other overhead crane on the mended pontoon, with the cart-road rivets from Twenty to Twenty-three piers—two construction lines, and a turning-spur. The pilework must take its chance," said Hitchcock.

"All right. Roll up everything you can lay hands on. We'll give the gang fifteen minutes more to eat their grub."

Close to the verandah stood a big night-gong, never used except for flood, or fire in the village. Hitchcock had called for a fresh horse, and was off to his side of the bridge when Findlayson took the cloth-bound stick and smote with the rubbing stroke that brings out the full thunder of the metal.

Long before the last rumble ceased every night-gong in the village had taken up the warning. To these were added the hoarse screaming of conches in the little temples; the throbbing of drums and tom-toms; and, from the European quarters, where the riveters lived, Mc'Cartney's bugle, a weapon of offence on Sundays and festivals, brayed desperately, calling to "Stables." Engine after engine toiling home along the spurs at the end of her day's work whistled in answer till the whistles were answered from the far bank. Then the big gong thundered thrice for a sign that it was flood and not fire; conch, drum, and whistle echoed the call, and the village quivered to the sound of bare feet running upon soft earth. The order in all cases was to stand by the day's work and wait instructions. The gangs poured by in the dusk; men stopping to knot a loin-cloth or fasten a sandal; gang-foremen shouting to their subordinates as they ran or paused by the tool-issue sheds for bars and mattocks; locomotives creeping down their tracks wheel-deep in the crowd; till the brown torrent disappeared into the dusk of the river-bed, raced over the pilework, swarmed along the lattices, clustered by the cranes, and stood still—each man in his place.

Then the troubled beating of the gong carried the order to take up everything and bear it beyond high-water mark, and the flare-lamps broke out by the hundred between the webs of dull iron as the riveters began a night's work, racing against the flood that was to come. The girders of the three centre piers—those that stood on the cribs—were all but in position. They needed just as many rivets as could be driven into them, for the flood would assuredly wash out their supports, and the ironwork would settle down on the caps of stone if they were not blocked at the ends. A hundred crowbars strained at the sleepers of the temporary line that fed the unfinished piers. It was heaved up in lengths, loaded into trucks, and backed up the bank beyond flood-level by the groaning locomotives. The tool-sheds on the sands melted away before the attack of shouting armies, and with them went the stacked ranks of Government stores, iron-hound boxes of rivets, pliers, cutters, duplicate parts of the riveting-machines, spare pumps and chains. The big crane would be the last to be shifted, for she was hoisting all the heavy stuff up to the main structure of the bridge. The concrete blocks on the fleet of stone-boats were dropped overside, where there was any depth of water, to guard the piers, and the empty boats themselves were poled under the bridge down-stream. It was here that Peroo's pipe shrilled loudest, for the first stroke of the big gong had brought the dinghy back at racing speed, and Peroo and his people were stripped to the waist, working for the honour and credit which are better than life.

"I knew she would speak," he cried. "I knew, but the telegraph gives us good warning. O sons of unthinkable begetting—children of unspeakable shame—are we here for the look of the thing?" It was two feet of wire-rope frayed at the ends, and it did wonders as Peroo leaped from gunnel to gunnel, shouting the language of the sea.

Findlayson was more troubled for the stone boats than anything else. Mc'Cartney, with his gangs, was blocking up the ends of the three doubtful spans. But boats adrift, if the flood chanced to be a high one, might endanger the girders; and there was a very fleet in the shrunken channel.

"Get them behind the swell of the guard tower," he shouted down to Peroo. "It will be dead-water there. Get them below the bridge."

"*Achcha!* [Very good.] *I* know; we are mooring them with wire-rope," was the answer. "Heh! Listen to the Chota Sahib. He is working hard."

From across the river came an almost continuous whistling of locomotives, backed by the rumble of stone. Hitchcock at the last minute was spending a few hundred more trucks of Tarakee stone in reinforcing his spurs and embankments.

"The bridge challenges Mother Gunga," said Peroo, with a laugh. "But when *she* talks I know whose voice will be the loudest."

For hours the naked men worked, screaming and shouting under the lights. It was a hot, moonless night; the end of it was darkened by clouds and a sudden squall that made Findlayson very grave.

"She moves!" said Peroo, just before the dawn. "Mother Gunga is awake! Hear!" He dipped his hand over the side of a boat and the current mumbled on it. A little wave hit the side of a pier with a crisp slap.

"Six hours before her time," said Findlayson, mopping his forehead savagely. "Now we can't depend on anything. We'd better clear all hands out of the riverbed."

Again the big gong beat, and a second time there was the rushing of naked feet on earth and ringing iron; the clatter of tools ceased. In the silence, men heard the dry yawn of water crawling over thirsty sand.

Foreman after foreman shouted to Findlayson, who had posted himself by the guard-tower, that his section of the river-bed had been cleaned out, and when the last voice dropped Findlayson hurried over the bridge till the iron plating of the permanent way gave place to the temporary plank-walk over the three centre piers, and there he met Hitchcock.

"'All clear your side?" said Findlayson. The whisper rang in the box of lattice work.

"Yes, and the east channel's filling now. We're utterly out of our reckoning. When is this thing down on us?"

"There's no saying. She's filling as fast as she can. Look!" Findlayson pointed to the planks below his feet, where the sand, burned and defiled by months of work, was beginning to whisper and fizz.

"What orders?" said Hitchcock.

"Call the roll—count stores—sit on your hunkers—and pray for the bridge. That's all I can think of. Good night. Don't risk your life trying to fish out anything that may go downstream."

"Oh, I'll be as prudent as you are! 'Night. Heavens, how she's filling! Here's the rain in earnest."

Findlayson picked his way back to his bank, sweeping the last of Mc'Cartney's riveters before him. The gangs had spread themselves along the embankments, regardless of the cold rain of the dawn, and there they waited for the flood. Only Peroo kept his men together behind the swell of the guard-tower, where the stone-boats lay tied fore and aft with hawsers, wire-rope, and chains.

A shrill wail ran along the line, growing to a yell, half fear and half wonder: the face of the river whitened from bank to hank between the stone facings, and the far-away spurs went out in spouts of foam. Mother Gunga had come bank-high in haste, and a wall of chocolate-coloured water was her messenger. There was a shriek above the roar of the water, the complaint of the spans coming down on their blocks as the cribs were whirled out from under their bellies. The stone-boats groaned and ground each other in the eddy that swung round the abutment, and their clumsy masts rose higher and higher against the dim sky-line.

"Before she was shut between these walls we knew what she would do. Now she is thus cramped God only knows what she will do!" said Peroo, watching the furious turmoil round the guard-tower. "Ohé! Fight, then! Fight hard, for it is thus that a woman wears herself out."

But Mother Gunga would not fight as Peroo desired. After the first down-stream plunge there came no more walls of water, but the river lifted herself bodily, as a snake when she drinks in midsummer, plucking and fingering along the revetments, and banking up behind the piers till even Findlayson began to recalculate the strength of his work.

When day came the village gasped. "Only last night," men said, turning to each other, "it was as a town in the river-bed! Look now!"

And they looked and wondered afresh at the deep water, the racing water that licked the throat of the piers. The farther bank was veiled by rain, into which the bridge ran out and vanished; the spurs up-stream were marked by no more than eddies and spoutings, and down-stream the pent river, once freed of her guide-lines, had spread like a sea to the horizon. Then hurried by, rolling in the water, dead men and oxen together, with here and there a patch of thatched roof that melted when it touched a pier.

"Big flood," said Peroo, and Findlayson nodded. It was as big a flood as he had any wish to watch. His bridge would stand what was upon her now, but not very much more, and if by any of a thousand chances there happened to be a weakness in the embankments, Mother Gunga would carry his honour to the sea with the other raffle. Worst of all, there was nothing to do except to sit still; and Findlayson sat still under his macintosh till his helmet became pulp on his head, and his boots were over-ankle in mire. He took no count of time, for the river was marking the hours, inch by inch and foot by foot, along the embankment, and he listened, numb and hungry, to the straining of the stone-boats, the hollow thunder under the piers, and the hundred noises that make the full note of a flood. Once a dripping servant brought him food, but he could not eat; and once he thought that he heard a faint toot from a locomotive across the river, and then he smiled. The bridge's failure would hurt his assistant not a little, hut Hitchcock was a young man with his big work yet to do. For himself the crash meant everything—everything that made a hard life worth the living. They would say, the men of his own profession— he remembered the half-pitying things that he himself had said when Lockhart's new waterworks burst and broke down in brick-heaps and sludge, and Lockhart's spirit broke in him and he died. He remembered what he himself had said when the Sumao Bridge went out in the big cyclone by the sea; and most he remembered poor Hartopp's face three weeks later, when the shame had marked it. His bridge was twice the size of Hartopp's, and it carried the Findlayson truss as well as the new pier-shoe—the Findlayson bolted shoe. There were no excuses in his service. Government might listen, perhaps, but his own kind would judge him by his bridge, as that stood or fell. He went over it in his head, plate by plate, span by span, brick by brick, pier by pier, remembering, comparing, estimating, and recalculating, lest there should be any mistake; and through the long hours and through the flights of formulae that danced and wheeled before him a cold fear would come to pinch his heart. His side of the sum was beyond question; but what man knew Mother Gunga's arithmetic? Even as he was making all sure by the multiplication table, the river might be scooping a pot-hole to the very bottom of any one of those eighty-foot piers that carried his reputation. Again a servant came to him with food, but his mouth was dry, and he could only drink and return to the decimals in his brain. And the river was still rising. Peroo, in a mat shelter coat, crouched at his feet, watching now his face and now the face of the river, but saying nothing.

At last the Lascar rose and floundered through the mud towards the village, but he was careful to leave an ally to watch the boats.

Presently he returned, most irreverently driving before him the priest of his creed—a fat old man, with a grey beard that whipped the wind with the wet cloth that blew over his shoulder. Never was seen so lamentable a *guru*.

"What good are offerings and little kerosene lamps and dry grain," shouted Peroo, "if squatting in the mud is all that thou canst do? Thou hast dealt long with the Gods when they were contented and well-wishing. Now they are angry. Speak to them!"

"What is a man against the wrath of Gods?" whined the priest, cowering as the wind took him. "Let me go to the temple, and I will pray there."

"Son of a pig, pray *here*! Is there no return for salt fish and curry powder and dried onions? Call aloud! Tell Mother Gunga we have had enough. Bid her be still for the night. I cannot pray, but I have been serving in the Kumpani's boats, and when men did not obey my orders I——" A flourish of the wire-rope colt rounded the sentence, and the priest, breaking free from his disciple, fled to the village.

"Fat pig!" said Peroo. "After all that we have done for him! When the flood is down I will see to it that we get a new *guru*. Finlinson Sahib, it darkens for night now, and since yesterday nothing has been eaten. Be wise, Sahib. No man can endure watching and great thinking on an empty belly. Lie down, Sahib. The river will do what the river will do."

"The bridge is mine; I cannot leave it."

"Wilt thou hold it up with thy hands, then?" said Peroo, laughing. "I was troubled for my boats and sheers *before* the flood came. Now we are in the hands of the Gods. The Sahib will not eat and lie down? Take these, then. They are meat and good toddy together, and they kill all weariness, besides the fever that follows the rain. I have eaten nothing else today at all."

He took a small tin tobacco-box from his sodden waist-belt and thrust it into Findlayson's hand, saying: "Nay, do not be afraid. It is no more than opium—clean Malwa opium."

Findlayson shook two or three of the dark-brown pellets into his hand, and hardly knowing what he did, swallowed them. The stuff was at least a good guard against fever—the fever that was creeping upon him out of the wet mud—and he had seen what Peroo could do in the stewing mists of autumn on the strength of a dose from the tin box.

Peroo nodded with bright eyes. "In a little—in a little the Sahib will find that he thinks well again. I too will——" He dived into his treasure-box, resettled the rain-coat over his head, and squatted down to watch the boats. It was too dark now to see beyond the first pier, and the night seemed to have given the river new strength. Findlayson stood with his chin on his chest, thinking. There was one point about one of the piers—the seventh—that he had not fully settled in his mind. The figures would not shape themselves to the eye except one by one and at enormous intervals of time. There was a sound rich and mellow in his ears like the deepest note of a double-bass—an entrancing sound upon which he pondered for several hours, as it seemed. Then Peroo was at his elbow, shouting that a wire hawser had snapped and the stone-boats were loose. Findlayson saw the fleet open and swing out fanwise to a long-drawn shriek of wire straining across gunnels.

"A tree hit them. They will all go," cried Peroo. "The main hawser has parted. What does the Sahib do?"

An immensely complex plan had suddenly flashed into Findlayson's mind. He saw the ropes running from boat to boat in straight lines and angles—each rope a line of white fire. But there was one rope which was the master rope. He could see that rope. If he could pull it once, it was absolutely and mathematically certain that the disordered fleet would reassemble itself in the backwater behind the guard-tower. But why, he wondered, was Peroo clinging so desperately to his waist as he hastened down the bank? It was necessary to put the Lascar aside, gently and slowly, because it was necessary to save the boats, and, further, to demonstrate the extreme ease of the problem that looked so difficult. And then—but it was of no conceivable importance— a wire-rope raced through his hand, burning it, the high bank disappeared, and with it all the slowly dispersing factors of the problem. He was sitting in the rainy darkness—sitting in a boat that spun like a top, and Peroo was standing over him.

"I had forgotten," said the Lascar, slowly, "that to those fasting and unused, the opium is worse than any wine. Those who die in Gunga go to the Gods. Still, I have no desire to present myself before such great ones. Can the Sahib swim?"

"What need? He can fly—fly as swiftly as the wind," was the thick answer.

"He is mad!" muttered Peroo, under his breath. "And he threw me aside like a bundle of dung-cakes. Well, he will not know his death. The boat cannot live an hour here even if she strike nothing. It is not good to look at death with a clear eye."

He refreshed himself again from the tin box, squatted down in the bows of the reeling, pegged, and stitched craft, staring through the mist at the nothing that was there. A warm drowsiness crept over Findlayson, the Chief Engineer, whose duty was with his bridge. The heavy raindrops struck him with a thousand tingling little thrills, and the weight of all time since time was made hung heavy on his eyelids. He thought and perceived that he was perfectly secure, for the water was so solid that a man could surely step out upon it, and, standing still with his legs apart to keep his balance—this was the most important point—would be borne with great and easy speed to the shore. But yet a better plan came to him. It needed only an exertion of will for the soul to hurl the body ashore as wind drives paper, to waft it kite-fashion to the bank. Thereafter—the boat spun dizzily—suppose the high wind got under the freed body? Would it tower up like a kite and pitch headlong on the far-away sands, or would it duck about, beyond control, through all eternity? Findlayson gripped the gunnel to anchor himself, for it seemed that he was on the edge of taking the flight before he had settled all his plans. Opium has more effect on the white man than the black. Peroo was only comfortably indifferent to accidents. "She cannot live," he grunted. "Her seams open already. If she were even a dinghy with oars we could have ridden it out; but a box with holes is no good. Finlinson Sahib, she fills."

"*Achcha!* I am going away. Come thou also." In his mind, Findlayson had already escaped from the boat, and was circling high in air to find a rest for the sole of his foot. His body—he was really sorry for its gross helplessness—lay in the stern, the water rushing about its knees.

"How very ridiculous!" he said to himself from his eyrie -" that—is Findlayson— chief of the Kashi Bridge. The poor beast is going to be drowned, too. Drowned when it's close to shore. I'm—I'm on shore already. Why doesn't it come along?"

To his intense disgust, he found his soul back in his body again, and that body spluttering and choking in deep water. The pain of the reunion was atrocious, but it was necessary, also, to fight for the body. He was conscious of grasping wildly at wet sand, and striding prodigiously, as one strides in a dream, to keep foothold in the swirling water, till at last he hauled himself clear of the hold of the river, and dropped, panting, on wet earth.

"Not this night," said Peroo, in his ear. "The Gods have protected us." The Lascar moved his feet cautiously, and they rustled among dried stumps. "This is some island of last year's indigo-crop," he went on. "We shall find no men here; but have great care, Sahib; all the snakes of a hundred miles have been flooded out. Here comes the lightning, on the heels of the wind. Now we shall be able to look; but walk carefully."

Findlayson was far and far beyond any fear of snakes, or indeed any merely human emotion. He saw, after he had rubbed the water from his eyes, with an immense clearness, and trod, so it seemed to himself with world-encompassing strides. Somewhere in the night of time he had built a bridge—a bridge that spanned illimitable levels of shining seas; but the Deluge had swept it away, leaving this one island under heaven for Findlayson and his companion, sole survivors of the breed of Man.

An incessant lightning, forked and blue, showed all that there was to be seen on the little patch in the flood—a clump of thorn, a clump of swaying creaking bamboos, and a grey gnarled peepul overshadowing a Hindoo shrine, from whose dome floated a tattered red flag. The holy man whose summer resting-place it was had long since abandoned it, and the weather had broken the red-daubed image of his god. The two men stumbled, heavy-limbed and heavy-eyed, over the ashes of a brick-set cooking-place, and dropped down under the shelter of the branches, while the rain and river roared together.

The stumps of the indigo crackled, and there was a smell of cattle, as a huge and dripping Brahminee bull shouldered his way under the tree. The flashes revealed the trident mark of Shiva on his flank, the insolence of head and hump, the luminous stag-like eyes, the brow crowned with a wreath of sodden marigold blooms, and the silky dewlap that almost swept the ground. There was a noise behind him of other beasts coming up from the flood-line through the thicket, a sound of heavy feet and deep breathing.

"Here be more beside ourselves," said Findlayson, his head against the tree pole, looking through half-shut eyes, wholly at ease.

"Truly," said Peroo, thickly, "and no small ones."

"What are they, then? I do not see clearly."

"The Gods. Who else? Look!"

"Ah, true! The Gods surely—the Gods." Findlayson smiled as his head fell forward on his chest. Peroo was eminently right. After the Flood, who should be alive in the land except the Gods that made it—the Gods to whom his village prayed nightly—the Gods who were in all men's mouths and about all men's ways. He could not raise his head or stir a finger for the trance that held him, and Peroo was smiling vacantly at the lightning.

The Bull paused by the shrine, his head lowered to the damp earth. A green Parrot in the branches preened his wet wings and screamed against the thunder as the circle under the tree filled with the shifting shadows of beasts. There was a black Buck at the Bull's heels—such a Buck as Findlayson in his far-away life upon earth might have seen in dreams—a Buck with a royal head, ebon back, silver belly, and gleaming straight horns. Beside him, her head bowed to the ground, the green eyes burning under the heavy brows, with restless tail switching the dead grass, paced a Tigress, full-bellied and deep-jowled.

The Bull crouched beside the shrine, and there leaped from the darkness a monstrous grey Ape, who seated himself man-wise in the place of the fallen image, and the rain spilled like jewels from the hair of his neck and shoulders.Other shadows came and went behind the circle, among them a drunken Man flourishing staff and drinking-bottle. Then a hoarse bellow broke out from near the ground. "The flood lessens even now," it cried. "Hour by hour the water falls, and their bridge still stands!"

"My bridge," said Findlayson to himself, "That must be very old work now. What have the Gods to do with my bridge?"

His eyes rolled in the darkness following the roar. A Mugger—the blunt-nosed, ford-haunting Mugger of the Ganges—draggled herself before the beasts, lashing furiously to right and left with her tail.

"They have made it too strong for me. In all this night I have only torn away a handful of planks. The walls stand. The towers stand. They have chained my flood, and the river is not free any more. Heavenly Ones, take this yoke away! Give me clear water between bank and bank! It is I, Mother Gunga, that speak. The Justice of the Gods! Deal me the Justice of the Gods!"

"What said I?" whispered Peroo. "This is in truth a Punchayet of the Gods. Now we know that all the world is dead, save you and I, Sahib."

The Parrot screamed and fluttered again, and the Tigress, her ears flat to her head, snarled wickedly.

Somewhere in the shadow, a great trunk and gleaming tusks swayed to and fro, and a low gurgle broke the silence that followed on the snarl.

"We be here," said a deep voice, "the Great Ones. One only and very many. Shiv, my father, is here, with Indra. Kali has spoken already. Hanuman listens also."

"Kashi is without her Kotwal tonight," shouted the Man with the drinking-bottle, flinging his staff to the ground, while the island rang to the baying of hounds. "Give her the Justice of the Gods."

"Ye were still when they polluted my waters," the great Crocodile bellowed. "Ye made no sign when my river was trapped between the walls. I had no help save my own strength, and that failed—the strength of Mother Gunga failed—before their guard-towers. What could I do? I have done everything. Finish now, Heavenly Ones!"

"I brought the death; I rode the spotted sickness from hut to hut of their workmen, and yet they would not cease." A nose-slitten, hide-worn Ass, lame, scissor-legged, and galled, limped forward. "I cast the death at them out of my nostrils, but they would not cease."

Peroo would have moved, but the opium lay heavy upon him.

"Bah!" he said, spitting. "Here is Sitala herself; Mata—the small-pox. Has the Sahib a handkerchief to put over his face?"

"Little help! They fed me the corpses for a month, and I flung them out on my sand-bars, but their work went forward. Demons they are, and sons of demons! And ye left Mother Gunga alone for their fire-carriage to make a mock of the Justice of the Gods on the bridge-builders!"

The Bull turned the cud in his mouth and answered slowly: "If the Justice of the Gods caught all who made a mock of holy things there would be many dark altars in the land, mother."

"But this goes beyond a mock," said the Tigress, darting forward a griping paw. "Thou knowest, Shiv, and ye, too, Heavenly Ones; ye know that they have defiled Gunga. Surely they must come to the Destroyer. Let Indra judge."

The Buck made no movement as he answered: "How long has this evil been?

"Three years, as men count years," said the Mugger, close pressed to the earth.

"Does Mother Gunga die, then, in a year, that she is so anxious to see vengeance now? The deep sea was where she runs but yesterday, and tomorrow the sea shall cover her again as the Gods count that which men call time. Can any say that this their bridge endures till tomorrow?" said the Buck.

There was a long hush, and in the clearing of the storm the full moon stood up above the dripping trees.

"Judge ye, then," said the River, sullenly. "I have spoken my shame. The flood falls still. I can do no more."

"For my own part "—it was the voice of the great Ape seated within the shrine—" it pleases me well to watch these men, remembering that I also builded no small bridge in the world's youth."

"They say, too," snarled the Tiger, "that these men came of the wreck of thy armies, Hanuman, and therefore thou hast aided——"

"They toil as my armies toiled in Lanka, and they believe that their toil endures. Indra is too high, but Shiv, thou knowest how the land is threaded with their fire-carriages."

"Yea, I know," said the Bull. "Their Gods instructed them in the matter."

A laugh ran round the circle.

"Their Gods! What should their Gods know? They were born yesterday, and those that made them are scarcely yet cold," said the Mugger. "tomorrow their Gods will die."

"Ho!" said Peroo. "Mother Gunga talks good talk. I told that to the padre-sahib who preached on the *Mombassa*, and he asked the Burra Malum to put me in irons for a great rudeness."

"Surely they make these things to please their Gods," said the Bull again.

"Not altogether," the Elephant rolled forth. "It is for the profit of my mahajuns—my fat money-lenders that worship me at each new year, when they draw my image at the head of the account-books. I, looking over their shoulders by lamplight, see that the names in the books are those of men in far places—for all the towns are drawn together by the fire-carriage, and the money comes and goes swiftly, and the account-books grow as fat as—myself. And I, who am Ganesh of Good Luck, I bless my peoples."

"They have changed the face of the land—which is my land. They have killed and made new towns on my banks," said the Mugger.

"It is but the shifting of a little dirt. Let the dirt dig in the dirt if it pleases the dirt," answered the Elephant.

"But afterwards?" said the Tiger. "Afterwards they will see that Mother Gunga can avenge no insult, and they fall away from her first, and later from us all, one by one. In the end, Ganesh, we are left with naked altars."

The drunken Man staggered to his feet, and hiccupped vehemently.

"Kali lies. My sister lies. Also this my stick is the Kotwal of Kashi, and he keeps tally of my pilgrims. When the time comes to worship Bhairon—and it is always time—the fire-carriages move one by one, and each bears a thousand pilgrims. They do not come afoot any more, but rolling upon wheels, and my honour is increased."

"Gunga, I have seen thy bed at Pryag black with the pilgrims," said the Ape, leaning forward, "and but for the fire-carriage they would have come slowly and in fewer numbers. Remember."

"They come to me always," Bhairon went on thickly. "By day and night they pray to me, all the Common People in the fields and the roads. Who is like Bhairon today? What talk is this of changing faiths? Is my staff Kotwal of Kashi for nothing? He keeps the tally, and he says that never were so many altars as today, and the fire carriage serves them well. Bhairon am I—Bhairon of the Common People, and the chiefest of the Heavenly Ones today. Also my staff says——"

"Peace, thou" lowed the Bull. "The worship of the schools is mine, and they talk very wisely, asking whether I be one or many, as is the delight of my people, and ye know what I am. Kali, my wife, thou knowest also."

"Yea, I know," said the Tigress, with lowered head.

"Greater am I than Gunga also. For ye know who moved the minds of men that they should count Gunga holy among the rivers. Who die in that water—ye know how men say—come to us without punishment, and Gunga knows that the fire-carriage has borne to her scores upon scores of such anxious ones; and Kali knows that she has held her chiefest festivals among the pilgrimages that are fed by the fire-carriage. Who smote at Pooree, under the Image there, her thousands in a day and a night, and bound the sickness to the wheels of the fire-carriages, so that it ran from one end of the land to the other? Who but Kali? Before the fire-carriage came it was a heavy toil. The fire-carriages have served thee well, Mother of Death. But I speak for mine own altars, who am not Bhairon of the Common Folk, but Shiv. Men go to and fro, making words and telling talk of strange Gods, and I listen. Faith follows faith among my people in the schools, and I have no anger; for when all words are said, and the new talk is ended, to Shiv men return at the last."

"True. It is true," murmured Hanuman. "To Shiv and to the others, mother, they return. I creep from temple to temple in the North, where they worship one God and His Prophet; and presently my image is alone within their shrines."

"Small thanks," said the Buck, turning his head slowly. "I am that One and His Prophet also."

"Even so, father," said Hanuman. "And to the South I go who am the oldest of the Gods as men know the Gods, and presently I touch the shrines of the New Faith and the Woman whom we know is hewn twelve-armed, and still they call her Mary."

"Small thanks, brother," said the Tigress. "I am that Woman."

"Even so, sister; and I go West among the fire-carriages, and stand before the bridge-builders in many shapes, and because of me they change their faiths and are very wise.. Ho! ho! I am the builder of bridges, indeed—bridges between this and that, and each bridge leads surely to Us in the end. Be content, Gunga. Neither these men nor those that follow them mock thee at all."

"Am I alone, then, Heavenly Ones? Shall I smooth out my flood lest unhappily I bear away their walls? Will Indra dry my springs in the hills and make me crawl humbly between their wharfs? Shall I bury me in the sand ere I offend?"

"And all for the sake of a little iron bar with the fire-carriage atop. Truly, Mother Gunga is always young!" said Ganesh the Elephant. "A child had not spoken more foolishly. Let the dirt dig in the dirt ere it return to the dirt. I know only that my people grow rich and praise me. Shiv has said that the men of the schools do not forget; Bhairon is content for his crowd of the Common People; and Hanuman laughs."

"Surely I laugh," said the Ape. "My altars are few beside those of Ganesh or Bhairon, but the fire-carriages bring me new worshippers from beyond the Black Water—the men who believe that their God is toil. I run before them beckoning, and they follow Hanuman."

"Give them the toil that they desire, then," said the River. "Make a bar across my flood and throw the water back upon the bridge. Once thou wast strong in Lanka, Hanuman. Stoop and lift my bed."

"Who gives life can take life." The Ape scratched in the mud with a long forefinger. "And yet, who would profit by the killing? Very many would die."

There came up from the water a snatch of a love-song such as the boys sing when they watch their cattle in the noon heats of late spring. The parrot screamed joyously, sidling along his branch with lowered head as the song grew louder, and in a patch of clear moonlight stood revealed the young herd, the darling of the Gopis, the idol of dreaming maids and of mothers ere their children are born Krishna the Well-beloved. He stooped to knot up his long wet hair, and the Parrot fluttered to his shoulder.

"Fleeting and singing, and singing and fleeting," hiccupped Bhairon. "Those make thee late for the council, brother."

"And then?" said Krishna, with a laugh, throwing back his head. "Ye can do little without me or Karma here." He fondled the Parrot's plumage and laughed again. "What is this sitting and talking together? I heard Mother Gunga roaring in the dark, and so came quickly from a hut where I lay warm. And what have ye done to Karma, that he is so wet and silent? And what does Mother Gunga here? Are the heavens full that ye must come paddling in the mud beast-wise? Karma, what do they do?"

"Gunga has prayed for a vengeance on the bridge-builders, and Kali is with her. Now she bids Hanuman whelm the bridge, that her honour may be made great," cried the Parrot. "I waited here, knowing that thou wouldst come, O my master!"

"And the Heavenly Ones said nothing? Did Gunga and the Mother of Sorrows out-talk them? Did none speak for my people?"

"Nay," said Ganesh, moving uneasily from foot to foot; "I said it was but dirt at play, and why should we stamp it flat?"

"I was content to let them toil—well content," said Hanuman.

"What had I to do with Gunga's anger?" said the Bull.

"I am Bhairon of the Common Folk, and this my staff is Kotwal of all Kashi. I spoke for the Common People."

"Thou?" The young God's eyes sparkled.

"Am I not the first of the Gods in their mouths today?" returned Bhairon, unabashed. "For the sake of the Common People I said—very many wise things which I have now forgotten, but this my staff—"

Krishna turned impatiently, saw the Mugger at his feet, and kneeling, slipped an arm round the cold neck. "Mother," he said gently, "get thee to thy flood again. The matter is not for thee. What harm shall thy honour take of this live dirt? Thou hast given them their fields new year after year, and by thy flood they are made strong. They come all to thee at the last. What need to slay them now? Have pity, mother, for a little—and it is only for a little."

"If it be only for a little " the slow beast began.

"Are they Gods, then?" Krishna returned with a laugh, his eyes looking into the dull eyes of the River. "Be certain that it is only for a little. The Heavenly Ones have heard thee, and presently justice will be done. Go now, mother, to the flood again. Men and cattle are thick on the waters—the banks fall—the villages melt because of thee."

"But the bridge—the bridge stands." The Mugger turned grunting into the undergrowth as Krishna rose.

"It is ended," said the Tigress, viciously. "There is no more justice from the Heavenly Ones. Ye have made shame and sport of Gunga, who asked no more than a few score lives."

"Of *my* people—who lie under the leaf-roofs of the village yonder—of the young girls, and the young men who sing to them in the dark—of the child that will be born next morn—of that which was begotten tonight," said Krishna. "And when all is done, what profit? Tomorrow sees them at work. Ay, if ye swept the bridge out from end to end they would begin anew. Hear me! Bhairon is drunk always. Hanuman mocks his people with new riddles."

"Nay, but they are very old ones," the Ape said, laughing.

"Shiv hears the talk of the schools and the dreams of the holy men; Ganesh thinks only of his fat traders; but I—I live with these my people, asking for no gifts, and so receiving them hourly."

"And very tender art thou of thy people," said the Tigress.

"They are my own. The old women dream of me turning in their sleep; the maids look and listen for me when they go to fill their lotahs by the river. I walk by the young men waiting without the gates at dusk, and I call over my shoulder to the white-beards. Ye know, Heavenly Ones, that I alone of us all walk upon the earth continually, and have no pleasure in our heavens so long as a green blade springs here, or there are two voices at twilight in the standing crops. Wise are ye, but ye live far off; forgetting whence ye came. So do I not forget. And the fire-carriage feeds your shrines, ye say? And the fire-carriages bring a thousand pilgrims where but ten came in the old years? True. That is true, today."

"But tomorrow they are dead, brother," said Ganesh.

"Peace!" said the Bull, as Hanuman leaned forward again. "And tomorrow, beloved—what of tomorrow?"

"This only. A new word creeping from mouth to mouth among the Common Folk—a word that neither man nor God can lay hold of—an evil word—a little lazy word among the Common Folk, saying (and none know who set that word afoot) that they weary of ye, Heavenly Ones."

The Gods laughed together softly. "And then, beloved—" they said.

"And to cover that weariness they, my people, will bring to thee, Shiv, and to thee, Ganesh, at first greater offerings and a louder noise of worship. But the word has gone abroad, and, after, they will pay fewer dues to your fat Brahmins. Next they will forget your altars, but so slowly that no man can say how his forgetfulness began."

"I knew—I knew! I spoke this also, but they would not hear," said the Tigress. "We should have slain—we should have slain!"

"It is too late now. Ye should have slain at the beginning when the men from across the water had taught our folk nothing. Now my people see their work, and go away thinking. They do not think of the Heavenly Ones altogether. They think of the fire-carriage and the other things that the bridge-builders have done, and when your priests thrust forward hands asking alms, they give a little unwillingly. That is the beginning, among one or two, or five or ten—for I, moving among my people, know what is in their hearts."

"And the end, Jester of the Gods? What shall the end be?" said Ganesh.

"The end shall be as it was in the beginning, O slothful son of Shiv! The flame shall die upon the altars and the prayer upon the tongue till ye become little Gods again—Gods of the jungle—names that the hunters of rats and noosers of dogs whisper in the thicket and among the caves—rag-Gods, pot Godlings of the tree, and the village-mark, as ye were at the beginning. That is the end, Ganesh, for thee, and for Bhairon—Bhairon of the Common People."

"It is very far away," grunted Bhairon. "Also, it is a lie."

"Many women have kissed Krishna. They told him this to cheer their own hearts when the grey hairs came, and he has told us the tale," said the Bull, below his breath.

"Their Gods came, and we changed them. I took the Woman and made her twelve-armed. So shall we twist all their Gods," said Hanuman.

"Their Gods! This is no question of their Gods—one or three—man or woman. The matter is with the people. *They* move, and not the Gods of the bridge-builders," said Krishna.

"So be it. I have made a man worship the fire-carriage as it stood still breathing smoke, and he knew not that he worshipped me," said Hanuman the Ape. "They will only change a little the names of their Gods. I shall lead the builders of the bridges as of old; Shiv shall be worshipped in the schools by such as doubt and despise their fellows; Ganesh shall have his mahajuns, and Bhairon the donkey-drivers, the pilgrims, and the sellers of toys. Beloved, they will do no more than change the names, and that we have seen a thousand times."

"Surely they will do no more than change the names," echoed Ganesh; but there was an uneasy movement among the Gods.

"They will change more than the names. Me alone they cannot kill, so long as a maiden and a man meet together or the spring follows the winter rains. Heavenly Ones, not for nothing have I walked upon the earth. My people know not now what they know; but I, who live with them, I read their hearts. Great Kings, the beginning of the end is born already. The fire-carriages shout the names of new Gods that are *not* the old under new names. Drink now and eat greatly! Bathe your faces in the smoke of the altars before they grow cold! Take dues and listen to the cymbals and the drums, Heavenly Ones, while yet there are flowers and songs. As men count time the end is far off; but as we who know reckon it is today. I have spoken."

The young God ceased, and his brethren looked at each other long in silence.

"This I have not heard before," Peroo whispered in his companion's ear. "And yet sometimes, when I oiled the brasses in the engine-room of the *Goorkha*, I have wondered if our priests were so wise—so wise. The day is coming, Sahib. They will be gone by the morning."

A yellow light broadened in the sky, and the tone of the river changed as the darkness withdrew.

Suddenly the Elephant trumpeted aloud as though man had goaded him.

"Let Indra judge. Father of all, speak thou! What of the things we have heard? Has Krishna lied indeed? Or —"

"Ye know," said the Buck, rising to his feet. "Ye know the Riddle of the Gods. When Brahm ceases to dream, the Heavens and the Hells and

Earth disappear. Be content. Brahm dreams still. The dreams come and go, and the nature of the dreams changes, but still Brahm dreams. Krishna has walked too long upon earth, and yet I love him the more for the tale he has told. The Gods change, beloved—all save One!"

"Ay, all save one that makes love in the hearts of men," said Krishna, knotting his girdle. "It is but a little time to wait, and ye shall know if I lie."

"Truly it is but a little time, as thou sayest, and we shall know. Get thee to thy huts again, beloved, and make sport for the young things, for still Brahm dreams. Go, my children! Brahm dreams and till he wakes the Gods die not."

***

"Whither went they—" said the Lascar, awe-struck, shivering a little with the cold.

"God knows!" said Findlayson. The river and the island lay in full daylight now, and there was never mark of hoof or pug on the wet earth under the peepul. Only a parrot screamed in the branches, bringing down showers of water-drops as he fluttered his wings.

"Up! We are cramped with cold! Has the opium died out? Canst thou move, Sahib?"

Findlayson staggered to his feet and shook himself. His bead swam and ached, but the work of the opium was over, and, as he sluiced his forehead in a pool, the Chief Engineer of the Kashi Bridge was wondering how he had managed to fall upon the island, what chances the day offered of return, and, above all, how his work stood.

"Peroo, I have forgotten much I was under the guard-tower watching the river; and then——Did the flood sweep us away?"

"No. The boats broke loose, Sahib, and" (if the Sahib had forgotten about the opium, decidedly Peroo would not remind him) "in striving to retie them, so it seemed to me but it was dark—a rope caught the Sahib and threw him upon a boat. Considering that we two, with Hitchcock Sahib, built, as it were, that bridge, I came also upon the boat, which came riding on horseback, as it were, on the nose of this island, and so, splitting, cast us ashore. I made a great cry when the boat left the wharf and without doubt Hitchcock Sahib will come for us. As for the bridge, so many have died in the building that it cannot fall." A fierce sun, that drew out all the smell of the sodden land, had followed the storm, and in that clear light there was no room for a man to think of the dreams of the dark. Findlayson stared upstream, across the blaze of moving water, till his eyes ached. There was no sign of any bank to the Ganges, much less of a bridge-line.

"We came down far," he said. "It was wonderful that we were not drowned a hundred times."

"That was the least of the wonder, for no man dies before his time. I have seen Sydney, I have seen London, and twenty great ports, but "— Peroo looked at the damp, discoloured shrine under the peepul—"never man has seen that we saw here."

"What?"

"Has the Sahib forgotten; or do we black men only see the Gods?"

"There was a fever upon me." Findlayson was still looking uneasily across the water. "It seemed that the island was full of beasts and men talking, but I do not remember. A boat could live in this water now, I think."

"Oho! Then it is true. 'When Brahm ceases to dream, the Gods die.' Now I know, indeed, what he meant. Once, too, the *guru* said as much to me; but then I did not understand. Now I am wise."

"What?" said Findlayson, over his shoulder.

Peroo went on as if he were talking to himself "Six—seven—ten monsoons since, I was watch on the fo'c'sle of the *Rewah*—the Kumpani's big boat—and there was a big *tufan*; green and black water beating, and I held fast to the life-lines, choking under the waters. Then I thought of the Gods—of Those whom we saw tonight"—he stared curiously at Findlayson's back, but the white man was looking across the flood. "Yes, I say of Those whom we saw this night past, and I called upon Them to protect me. And while I prayed, still keeping my lookout, a big wave came and threw me forward upon the ring of the great black bow-anchor, and the *Rewah* rose high and high, leaning towards the left-hand side, and the water drew away from beneath her nose, and I lay upon my belly, holding the ring, and looking down into those great deeps. Then I thought, even in the face of death: If I lose hold I die, and for me neither the *Rewah* nor my place by the galley where the rice is cooked, nor Bombay, nor Calcutta, nor even London, will be any more for me. 'How shall I be sure,' I said, 'that the Gods to whom I pray will abide at all?' This I thought, and the *Rewah* dropped her nose as a hammer falls, and all the sea came in and slid me backwards along the fo'c'sle and over the break of the fo'c'sle, and I very badly bruised my shin against the donkey-engine: but I did not die, and I have seen the Gods. They are good for live men, but for the dead—— They have spoken Themselves. Therefore, when I come to the village I will beat the *guru* for talking riddles which are no riddles. When Brahm ceases to dream the Gods go."

"Look up-stream. The light blinds. Is there smoke yonder?"

Peroo shaded his eyes with his hands. "He is a wise man and quick. Hitchcock Sahib would not trust a rowboat. He has borrowed the Rao Sahib's steam-launch, and comes to look for us. I have always said that there should have been a steam-launch on the bridge works for us."

The territory of the Rao of Baraon lay within ten miles of the bridge; and Findlayson and Hitchcock had spent a fair portion of their scanty leisure in playing billiards and shooting blackbuck with the young man. He had been bearled by an English tutor of sporting tastes for some five or six years, and was now royally wasting the revenues accumulated during his minority by the Indian Government. His steam-launch, with its silver-plated rails, striped silk awning, and mahogany decks, was a new toy which Findlayson had found horribly in the way when the Rao came to look at the bridge works.

"It's great luck," murmured Findlayson, but he was none the less afraid, wondering what news might be of the bridge.

The gaudy blue-and-white funnel came downstream swiftly. They could see Hitchcock in the bows, with a pair of opera-glasses, and his face was unusually white. Then Peroo hailed, and the launch made for the tail of the island. The Rao Sahib, in tweed shooting-suit and a seven-hued turban, waved his royal hand, and Hitchcock shouted. But he need have asked no questions, for Findlayson's first demand was for his bridge.

"All serene! 'Gad, I never expected to see you again, Findlayson. You're seven koss downstream. Yes; there's not a stone shifted anywhere; but how are you? I borrowed the Rao Sahib's launch, and he was good enough to come along. Jump in."

"Ah, Finlinson, you are very well, eh? That was most unprecedented calamity last night, eh? My royal palace, too, it leaks like the devil, and the crops will also be short all about my country. Now you shall back her out, Hitchcock. I—I do not understand steam-engines. You are wet? You are cold, Finlinson? I have some things to eat here, and you will take a good drink."

"I'm immensely grateful, Rao Sahib. I believe you've saved my life. How did Hitchcock——"

"Oho! His hair was upon end. He rode to me in the middle of the night and woke me up in the arms of Morpheus. I was most truly concerned, Finlinson, so I came too. My head-priest he is very angry just now. We will go quick, Mister Hitchcock. I am due to attend at twelve forty-five in the state temple, where we sanctify some new idol. If not so I would have asked you to spend the day with me. They are dam-bore, these religious ceremonies, Finlinson, eh?"

Peroo, well known to the crew, had possessed himself of the inlaid wheel, and was taking the launch craftily up-stream. But while he steered he was, in his mind, handling two feet of partially untwisted wire-rope; and the back upon which he beat was the back of his *guru*.

Thoughts on The Bridge Builders

Laurence Davies wrote of this tale that it 'can stand interpretations by the dozen' (Cambridge Companion to Rudyard Kipling, 2011). In the most obvious of these the near completed bridge stands as a symbol for the West's attempt to conquer nature by imposing its will upon an alien land and its ancient gods. But Kipling is too shrewd to employ so straightforward a metaphor as that. Findlayson is, indeed, a representative of 'the new' who is happy to describe the Ganges ('Mother Gunga') as nothing more than a 'hill-fed sewer'. Peroo, on the other hand, though sympathetic to the ancient gods, has doubts about his faith is open to the possibilities of western technology, and is clearly the more long sighted of the two men.

But what are we to make of the debate of the Hindu gods and their discussion of the benefits or otherwise of British rule? Did it take place on some spiritual plane or only in the minds of two drug confused men? Both are depicted as conversing with the gods, albeit not very consciously. When they awake both, but particularly Peroo, assume that their vision was real. The late Philip Mason C.I.E., a former Indian civil servant, thought otherwise when he wrote, 'all is illusion, the dream of Brahm. In the extremity of stress, when the bridge which was his life might be destroyed and his honour washed down with it to the sea, Findlayson had perceived that in the eyes even of the man-made gods its life was nothing; the sea had once rolled where Ganges ran. And then, even beyond that, for a moment eternity had seemed real and all these things of no account.' As the Buck asks, 'Can any say that this their bridge endures till tomorrow?'

Engineering was a skill close to Kipling's heart. At the request of the Canadians he composed their 'Ritual for the Calling of an Engineer' that is still in use today. Seldom has an engineering construction been portrayed so convincingly as in this story. Kipling no doubt lifted much of the detail from his experience as a cub reporter writing about the building of a new bridge over the Ganges at Benares. We might note that in a story written nearly four decades after the Indian mutiny the fictional bridge, like the historical bridge over the Indus at Attock, was fortified by 'towers, of red brick, loopholed for musketry and pierced for big guns'.

Among the gods, the bull is Shiva the great god and the tigress is his wife, and Kali the goddess of time. The crocodile is mother Gunga. The black buck is Indra, the parrot is Kama and the ape is Hanuman.

Kashi was an earlier name for Benares (now Varanasi). A lascar was an Indian working in a European ship. The 'black water' referred to the sea. A 'tar' was a telegram. 'Raffle' meant rubbish. The 'peepul' is the sacred fig. And a 'tufan' is a typhoon.

Findlayson's C.I.E. meant that he was, like Philip Mason, a Companion of the Most Eminent Order of the Indian Empire. C.E. was the designation of a civil engineer.

The Return of the Children

Neither the harps nor the crowns amused, nor the cherubs' dove-winged races--
Holding hands forlornly the Children wandered beneath the Dome,
Plucking the splendid robes of the passers-by, and with pitiful! faces
Begging what Princes and Powers refused:--"Ah, please will you let us go home?"

Over the jewelled floor, nigh weeping, ran to them Mary the Mother,
Kneeled and caressed and made promise with kisses, and drew them along to the gateway--
Yea, the all-iron unbribeable Door which Peter must guard and none other.
Straightway She took the Keys from his keeping, and opened and freed them straightway.

Then, to Her Son, Who had seen and smiled, She said: "On the night that I bore Thee,
What didst Thou care for a love beyond mine or a heaven that was not my arm?
Didst Thou push from the nipple, O Child, to hear the angels adore Thee
When we two lay in the breath of the kine?" And He said -- "Thou hast done no harm."

So through the Void the Children ran homeward merrily hand in hand,
Looking neither to left nor right where the breathless Heavens stood still.
And the Guards of the Void resheathed their swords, for they heard the Command:
"Shall I that have suffered the Children to come to Me hold them against their will? "

"THEY"

One view called me to another; one hill top to its fellow, half across the county, and since I could answer at no more trouble than the snapping forward of a lever, I let the county flow under my wheels. The orchid-studded flats of the East gave way to the thyme, ilex, and grey grass of the Downs; these again to the rich cornland and fig-trees of the lower coast, where you carry the beat of the tide on your left hand for fifteen level miles; and when at last I turned inland through a huddle of rounded hills and woods I had run myself clean out of my known marks. Beyond that precise hamlet which stands godmother to the capital of the United States, I found hidden villages where bees, the only things awake, boomed in eighty-foot lindens that overhung grey Norman churches; miraculous brooks diving under stone bridges built for heavier traffic than would ever vex them again; tithe-barns larger than their churches, and an old smithy that cried out aloud how it had once been a hall of the Knights of the Temple. Gipsies I found on a common where the gorse, bracken, and heath fought it out together up a mile of Roman road; and a little further on I disturbed a red fox rolling dog-fashion in the naked sunlight.

As the wooded hills closed about me I stood up in the car to take the bearings of that great Down whose ringed head is a landmark for fifty miles across the low countries. I judged that the lie of the country would bring me across some westward running road that went to his feet, but I did not allow for the confusing veils of the woods. A quick turn plunged me first into a green cutting brimful of liquid sunshine, next into a gloomy tunnel where last year's dead leaves whispered and scuffled about my tyres. The strong hazel stuff meeting overhead had not been cut for a couple of generations at least, nor had any axe helped the moss-cankered oak and beech to spring above them. Here the road changed frankly into a carpeted ride on whose brown velvet spent primrose-clumps showed like jade, and a few sickly, white-stalked blue-bells nodded together. As the slope favoured I shut off the power and slid over the whirled leaves, expecting every moment to meet a keeper; but I only heard a jay, far off, arguing against the silence under the twilight of the trees.

Still the track descended. I was on the point of reversing and working my way back on the second speed ere I ended in some swamp, when I saw sunshine through the tangle ahead and lifted the brake.

It was down again at once. As the light beat across my face my fore-wheels took the turf of a great still lawn from which sprang horsemen ten feet high with levelled lances, monstrous peacocks, and sleek round-headed maids of honour—blue, black, and glistening—all of clipped yew. Across the lawn—the marshalled woods besieged it on three sides—stood an ancient house of lichened and weather-worn stone, with mullioned windows and roofs of rose-red tile. It was flanked by semi-circular walls, also rose-red, that closed the lawn on the fourth side, and at their feet a box hedge grew man-high. There were doves on the roof about the slim brick chimneys, and I caught a glimpse of an octagonal dove-house behind the screening wall.

Here, then, I stayed; a horseman's green spear laid at my breast; held by the exceeding beauty of that jewel in that setting.

"If I am not packed off for a trespasser, or if this knight does not ride a wallop at me," thought I, "Shakespeare and Queen Elizabeth at least must come out of that half-open garden door and ask me to tea."

A child appeared at an upper window, and I thought the little thing waved a friendly hand. But it was to call a companion, for presently another bright head showed. Then I heard a laugh among the yew-peacocks, and turning to make sure (till then I had been watching the house only) I saw the silver of a fountain behind a hedge thrown up against the sun. The doves on the roof cooed to the cooing water; but between the two notes I caught the utterly happy chuckle of a child absorbed in some light mischief.

The garden door—heavy oak sunk deep in the thickness of the wall—opened further: a woman in a big garden hat set her foot slowly on the time-hollowed stone step and as slowly walked across the turf. I was forming some apology when she lifted up her head and I saw that she was blind.

"I heard you," she said. "Isn't that a motor car?"

"I'm afraid I've made a mistake in my road. I should have turned off up above—I never dreamed——" I began.

"But I'm very glad. Fancy a motor car coming into the garden! It will be such a treat——" She turned and made as though looking about her. "You—you haven't seen any one, have you—perhaps?"

"No one to speak to, but the children seemed interested at a distance."

"Which?"

"I saw a couple up at the window just now, and I think I heard a little chap in the grounds."

"Oh, lucky you!" she cried, and her face brightened. "I hear them, of course, but that's all. You've seen them and heard them?"

"Yes," I answered. "And if I know anything of children one of them's having a beautiful time by the fountain yonder. Escaped, I should imagine."

"You're fond of children?"

I gave her one or two reasons why I did not altogether hate them.

"Of course, of course," she said. "Then you understand. Then you won't think it foolish if I ask you to take your car through the gardens, once or twice—quite slowly. I'm sure they'd like to see it. They see so little, poor things. One tries to make their life pleasant, but—" she threw out her hands towards the woods. "We're so out of the world here."

"That will be splendid," I said. "But I can't cut up your grass."

She faced to the right. "Wait a minute," she said. "We're at the South gate, aren't we? Behind those peacocks there's a flagged path. We call it the Peacock's Walk. You can't see it from here, they tell me, but if you squeeze along by the edge of the wood you can turn at the first peacock and get on to the flags."

It was sacrilege to wake that dreaming house-front with the clatter of machinery, but I swung the car to clear the turf, brushed along the edge of the wood and turned in on the broad stone path where the fountain-basin lay like one star-sapphire.

"May I come too?" she cried. "No, please don't help me. They'll like it better if they see me."

She felt her way lightly to the front of the car, and with one foot on the step she called: "Children, oh, children! Look and see what's going to happen!"

The voice would have drawn lost souls from the Pit, for the yearning that underlay its sweetness, and I was not surprised to hear an answering shout behind the yews. It must have been the child by the fountain, but he fled at our approach, leaving a little toy boat in the water. I saw the glint of his blue blouse among the still horsemen.

Very disposedly we paraded the length of the walk and at her request backed again. This time the child had got the better of his panic, but stood far off and doubting.

"The little fellow's watching us," I said. "I wonder if he'd like a ride."

"They're very shy still. Very shy. But, oh, lucky you to be able to see them! Let's listen."

I stopped the machine at once, and the humid stillness, heavy with the scent of box, cloaked us deep. Shears I could hear where some gardener was clipping; a mumble of bees and broken voices that might have been the doves.

"Oh, unkind!" she said weariedly.

"Perhaps they're only shy of the motor. The little maid at the window looks tremendously interested."

"Yes?" She raised her head. "It was wrong of me to say that. They are really fond of me. It's the only thing that makes life worth living—when they're fond of you, isn't it? I daren't think what the place would be without them. By the way, is it beautiful?"

"I think it is the most beautiful place I have ever seen."

"So they all tell me. I can feel it, of course, but that isn't quite the same thing."

"Then have you never?——" I began, but stopped abashed.

"Not since I can remember. It happened when I was only a few months old, they tell me. And yet I must remember something, else how could I dream about colours? I see light in my dreams, and colours, but I never see *them*. I only hear them just as I do when I'm awake."

"It's difficult to see faces in dreams. Some people can, but most of us haven't the gift," I went on, looking up at the window where the child stood all but hidden.

"I've heard that too," she said. "And they tell me that one never sees a dead person's face in a dream. Is that true?"

"I believe it is—now I come to think of it."

"But how is it with yourself—yourself?" The blind eyes turned towards me.

"I have never seen the faces of my dead in any dream," I answered.

"Then it must be as bad as being blind."

The sun had dipped behind the woods and the long shades were possessing the insolent horsemen one by one. I saw the light die from off the top of a glossy-leaved lance and all the brave hard green turn to soft black. The house, accepting another day at end, as it had accepted an hundred thousand gone, seemed to settle deeper into its rest among the shadows.

"Have you ever wanted to?" she said after the silence.

"Very much sometimes," I replied. The child had left the window as the shadows closed upon it.

"Ah! So've I, but I don't suppose it's allowed. . . . Where d'you live?"

"Quite the other side of the county—sixty miles and more, and I must be going back. I've come without my big lamp."

"But it's not dark yet. I can feel it."

"I'm afraid it will be by the time I get home. Could you lend me some one to set me on my road at first? I've utterly lost myself."

"I'll send Madden with you to the cross-roads. We are so out of the world, I don't wonder you were lost! I'll guide you round to the front of the house; but you will go slowly, won't you, till you're out of the grounds? It isn't foolish, do you think?"

"I promise you I'll go like this," I said, and let the car start herself down the flagged path.

We skirted the left wing of the house, whose elaborately cast lead guttering alone was worth a day's journey; passed under a great rose-grown gate in the red wall, and so round to the high front of the house which in beauty and stateliness as much excelled the back as that all others I had seen.

"Is it so very beautiful?" she said wistfully when she heard my raptures. "And you like the lead-figures too? There's the old azalea garden behind. They say that this place must have been made for children. Will you help me out, please? I should like to come with you as far as the cross-roads, but I mustn't leave them. Is that you, Madden? I want you to show this gentleman the way to the cross-roads. He has lost his way but—he has seen them."

A butler appeared noiselessly at the miracle of old oak that must be called the front door, and slipped aside to put on his hat. She stood looking at me with open blue eyes in which no sight lay, and I saw for the first time that she was beautiful.

"Remember," she said quietly, "if you are fond of them you will come again," and disappeared within the house.

The butler in the car said nothing till we were nearly at the lodge gates, where, catching a glimpse of a blue blouse in a shrubbery, I swerved amply lest the devil that leads little boys to play should drag me into child-murder.

"Excuse me," he asked of a sudden, "but why did you do that, Sir?"

"The child yonder."

"Our young gentleman in blue?"

"Of course."

"He runs about a good deal. Did you see him by the fountain, Sir?"

"Oh, yes, several times. Do we turn here?"

"Yes, Sir. And did you 'appen to see them upstairs too?"

"At the upper window? Yes."

"Was that before the mistress come out to speak to you, Sir?"

"A little before that. Why d'you want to know?"

He paused a little. "Only to make sure that—that they had seen the car, Sir, because with children running about, though I'm sure you're driving particularly careful, there might be an accident. That was all, Sir. Here are the cross-roads. You can't miss your way from now on. Thank you, Sir, but that isn't *our* custom, not with——"

"I beg your pardon," I said, and thrust away the British silver.

"Oh, it's quite right with the rest of 'em as a rule. Good-bye, Sir."

He retired into the armour-plated conning tower of his caste and walked away. Evidently a butler solicitous for the honour of his house, and interested, probably through a maid, in the nursery.

Once beyond the signposts at the cross-roads I looked back, but the crumpled hills interlaced so jealously that I could not see where the house had lain. When I asked its name at a cottage along the road, the fat woman who sold sweetmeats there gave me to understand that people with motor cars had small right to live—much less to "go about talking like carriage folk." They were not a pleasant-mannered community.

When I retraced my route on the map that evening I was little wiser. Hawkin's Old Farm appeared to be the survey title of the place, and the old County Gazetteer, generally so ample, did not allude to it. The big house of those parts was Hodnington Hall, Georgian with early Victorian embellishments, as an atrocious steel engraving attested. I carried my difficulty to a neighbour—a deep-rooted tree of that soil—and he gave me a name of a family which conveyed no meaning.

A month or so later—I went again, or it may have been that my car took the road of her own volition. She over-ran the fruitless Downs, threaded every turn of the maze of lanes below the hills, drew through the high-walled woods, impenetrable in their full leaf, came out at the cross-roads where the butler had left me, and a little further on developed an internal trouble which forced me to turn her in on a grass way-waste that cut into a summer-silent hazel wood. So far as I could make sure by the sun and a six-inch Ordnance map, this should be the road flank of that wood which I had first explored from the heights above. I made a mighty serious business of my repairs and a glittering shop of my repair kit, spanners, pump, and the like, which I spread out orderly upon a rug. It was a trap to catch all childhood, for on such a day, I argued, the children would not be far off. When I paused in my work I listened, but the wood was so full of the noises of summer (though the birds had mated) that I could not at first distinguish these from the tread of small cautious feet stealing across the dead leaves. I rang my bell in an alluring manner, but the feet fled, and I repented, for to a child a sudden noise is very real terror. I must have been at work half an hour when I heard in the wood the voice of the blind woman crying: "Children, oh, children, where are you?" and the stillness made slow to close on the perfection of that cry. She came towards me, half feeling her way between the tree-boles, and though a child, it seemed, clung to her skirt, it swerved into the leafage like a rabbit as she drew nearer.

"Is that you?" she said, "from the other side of the county?"

"Yes, it's me from the other side of the county."

"Then why didn't you come through the upper woods? They were there just now."

"They were here a few minutes ago. I expect they knew my car had broken down, and came to see the fun."

"Nothing serious, I hope? How do cars break down?"

"In fifty different ways. Only mine has chosen the fifty-first."

She laughed merrily at the tiny joke, cooed with delicious laughter, and pushed her hat back.

"Let me hear," she said.

"Wait a moment," I cried, "and I'll get you a cushion."

She set her foot on the rug all covered with spare parts, and stooped above it eagerly. "What delightful things!" The hands through which she saw glanced in the chequered sunlight. "A box here—another box! Why you've arranged them like playing shop!"

"I confess now that I put it out to attract them. I don't need half those things really."

"How nice of you! I heard your bell in the upper wood. You say they were here before that?"

"I'm sure of it. Why are they so shy? That little fellow in blue who was with you just now ought to have got over his fright. He's been watching me like a Red Indian."

"It must have been your bell," she said. "I heard one of them go past me in trouble when I was coming down. They're shy—so shy even with me." She turned her face over her shoulder and cried again: "Children! Oh, children! Look and see!"

"They must have gone off together on their own affairs," I suggested, for there was a murmur behind us of lowered voices broken by the sudden squeaking giggles of childhood. I returned to my tinkerings and she leaned forward, her chin on her hand, listening interestedly.

"How many are they?" I said at last. The work was finished, but I saw no reason to go.

Her forehead puckered a little in thought. "I don't quite know," she said simply. "Sometimes more—sometimes less. They come and stay with me because I love them, you see."

"That must be very jolly," I said, replacing a drawer, and as I spoke I heard the inanity of my answer.

"You—you aren't laughing at me," she cried. "I—I haven't any of my own. I never married. People laugh at me sometimes about them because—because—"

"Because they're savages," I returned. "It's nothing to fret for. That sort laugh at everything that isn't in their own fat lives."

"I don't know. How should I? I only don't like being laughed at about *them*. It hurts; and when one can't see. . . . I don't want to seem silly," her chin quivered like a child's as she spoke, "but we blindies have only one skin, I think. Everything outside hits straight at our souls. It's different with you. You've such good defences in your eyes—looking out—before any one can really pain you in your soul. People forget that with us."

I was silent, reviewing that inexhaustible matter—the more than inherited (since it is also carefully taught) brutality of the Christian peoples, beside which the mere heathendom of the West Coast nigger is clean and restrained. It led me a long distance into myself.

"Don't do that!" she said of a sudden, putting her hands before her eyes.

"What?"

She made a gesture with her hand.

"That! It's—it's all purple and black. Don't! That colour hurts."

"But how in the world do you know about colours?" I exclaimed, for here was a revelation indeed.

"Colours as colours?" she asked.

"No. *Those* Colours which you saw just now."

"You know as well as I do," she laughed, "else you wouldn't have asked that question. They aren't in the world at all. They're in *you*—when you went so angry."

"D'you mean a dull purplish patch, like port-wine mixed with ink?" I said.

"I've never seen ink or port-wine, but the colours aren't mixed. They are separate—all separate."

"Do you mean black streaks and jags across the purple?"

She nodded. "Yes—if they are like this," and zigzagged her finger again, "but it's more red than purple—that bad colour."

"And what are the colours at the top of the—whatever you see?"

Slowly she leaned forward and traced on the rug the figure of the Egg itself.

"I see them so," she said, pointing with a grass stem, "white, green, yellow, red, purple, and when people are angry or bad, black across the red—as you were just now."

"Who told you anything about it—in the beginning?" I demanded.

"About the colours? No one. I used to ask what colours were when I was little—in table-covers and curtains and carpets, you see—because some colours hurt me and some made me happy. People told me; and when I got older that was how I saw people." Again she traced the outline of the Egg which it is given to very few of us to see.

"All by yourself?" I repeated.

"All by myself. There wasn't any one else. I only found out afterwards that other people did not see the Colours."

She leaned against the tree-bole plaiting and unplaiting chance-plucked grass stems. The children in the wood had drawn nearer. I could see them with the tail of my eye frolicking like squirrels.

"Now I am sure you will never laugh at me," she went on after a long silence. "Nor at *them*."

"Goodness! No!" I cried, jolted out of my train of thought. "A man who laughs at a child—unless the child is laughing too—is a heathen!"

"I didn't mean that of course. You'd never laugh *at* children, but I thought—I used to think—that perhaps you might laugh about *them*. So now I beg your pardon. . . . What are you going to laugh at?"

I had made no sound, but she knew.

"At the notion of your begging my pardon. If you had done your duty as a pillar of the state and a landed proprietress you ought to have summoned me for trespass when I barged through your woods the other day. It was disgraceful of me—inexcusable."

She looked at me, her head against the tree trunk—long and steadfastly—this woman who could see the naked soul.

"How curious," she half whispered. "How very curious."

"Why, what have I done?"

"You don't understand . . . and yet you understood about the Colours. Don't you understand?"

She spoke with a passion that nothing had justified, and I faced her bewilderedly as she rose. The children had gathered themselves in a roundel behind a bramble bush. One sleek head bent over something smaller, and the set of the little shoulders told me that fingers were on lips. They, too, had some child's tremendous secret. I alone was hopelessly astray there in the broad sunlight.

"No," I said, and shook my head as though the dead eyes could note. "Whatever it is, I don't understand yet. Perhaps I shall later—if you'll let me come again."

"You will come again," she answered. "You will surely come again and walk in the wood."

"Perhaps the children will know me well enough by that time to let me play with them—as a favour. You know what children are like."

"It isn't a matter of favour but of right," she replied, and while I wondered what she meant, a dishevelled woman plunged round the bend of the road, loose-haired, purple, almost lowing with agony as she ran. It was my rude, fat friend of the sweetmeat shop. The blind woman heard and stepped forward. "What is it, Mrs. Madehurst?" she asked.

The woman flung her apron over her head and literally grovelled in the dust, crying that her grandchild was sick to death, that the local doctor was away fishing, that Jenny the mother was at her wits' end, and so forth, with repetitions and bellowings.

"Where's the next nearest doctor?" I asked between paroxysms.

"Madden will tell you. Go round to the house and take him with you. I'll attend to this. Be quick!" She half-supported the fat woman into the shade. In two minutes I was blowing all the horns of Jericho under the front of the House Beautiful, and Madden, in the pantry, rose to the crisis like a butler and a man.

A quarter of an hour at illegal speeds caught us a doctor five miles away. Within the half-hour we had decanted him, much interested in motors, at the door of the sweetmeat shop, and drew up the road to await the verdict.

"Useful things cars," said Madden, all man and no butler. "If I'd had one when mine took sick she wouldn't have died."

"How was it?" I asked.

"Croup. Mrs. Madden was away. No one knew what to do. I drove eight miles in a tax cart for the Doctor. She was choked when we came back. This car 'd ha' saved her. She'd have been close on ten now."

"I'm sorry," I said. "I thought you were rather fond of children from what you told me going to the cross-roads the other day."

"Have you seen 'em again, Sir—this mornin'?"

"Yes, but they're well broke to cars. I couldn't get any of them within twenty yards of it."

He looked at me carefully as a scout considers a stranger—not as a menial should lift his eyes to his divinely appointed superior.

"I wonder why," he said just above the breath that he drew.

We waited on. A light wind from the sea wandered up and down the long lines of the woods, and the wayside grasses, whitened already with summer dust, rose and bowed in sallow waves.

A woman, wiping the suds off her arms, came out of the cottage next the sweetmeat shop.

"I've be'n listenin' in de back-yard," she said cheerily. "He says Arthur's unaccountable bad. Did ye hear him shruck just now? Unaccountable bad. I reckon t'will come Jenny's turn to walk in de wood nex' week along, Mr. Madden."

"Excuse me, Sir, but your lap-robe is slipping," said Madden deferentially. The woman started, dropped a curtsey, and hurried away.

"What does she mean by 'walking in the wood'?" I asked.

"It must be some saying they use hereabouts. I'm from Norfolk myself," said Madden. "They're an independent lot in this county. She took you for a chauffeur, Sir."

I saw the Doctor come out of the cottage followed by a draggle-tailed wench who clung to his arm as though he could make treaty for her with Death. "Dat sort," she wailed—"dey're just as much to us dat has 'em as if dey was lawful born. Just as much—just as much! An' God he'd be just as pleased if you saved 'un, Doctor. Don't take it from me. Miss Florence will tell ye de very same. Don't leave 'im, Doctor!"

"I know. I know," said the man, "but he'll be quiet for a while now. We'll get the nurse and the medicine as fast as we can." He signalled me to come forward with the car, and I strove not to be privy to what followed; but I saw the girl's face, blotched and frozen with grief, and I felt the hand without a ring clutching at my knees when we moved away.

The Doctor was a man of some humour, for I remember he claimed my car under the Oath of Aesculapius, and used it and me without mercy. First we convoyed Mrs. Madehurst and the blind woman to wait by the sick-bed till the nurse should come. Next we invaded a neat county town for prescriptions (the Doctor said the trouble was cerebro-spinal meningitis), and when the County Institute, banked and flanked with scared market cattle, reported itself out of nurses, for the moment we literally flung ourselves loose upon the county. We conferred with the owners of great houses—magnates at the ends of overarching avenues whose big-boned womenfolk strode away from their tea-tables to listen to the imperious Doctor. At last a white-haired lady sitting under a cedar of Lebanon and surrounded by a court of magnificent Borzois—all hostile to motors—gave the Doctor, who received them as from a princess, written orders which we bore many miles at top speed, through a park, to a French nunnery, where we took over in exchange a pallid-faced and trembling Sister. She knelt at the bottom of the tonneau telling her beads without pause till, by short cuts of the Doctor's invention, we had her to the sweetmeat shop once more. It was a long afternoon crowded with mad episodes that rose and dissolved like the dust of our wheels; cross-sections of remote and incomprehensible lives through which we raced at right angles; and I went home in the dusk, wearied out, to dream of the clashing horns of cattle; round-eyed nuns walking in a garden of graves; pleasant tea-parties beneath shaded trees; the carbolic-scented, grey-painted corridors of the County Institute; the steps of shy children in the wood, and the hands that clung to my knees as the motor began to move.

***

I had intended to return in a day or two, but it pleased Fate to hold me from that side of the county, on many pretexts, till the elder and the wild rose had fruited. There came at last a brilliant day, swept clear from the south-west, that brought the hills within hand's reach—a day of unstable airs and high filmy clouds. Through no merit of my own I was free, and set the car for the third time on that known road. As I reached the crest of the Downs I felt the soft air change, saw it glaze under the sun; and, looking down at the sea, in that instant beheld the blue of the Channel turn through polished silver and dulled steel to dingy pewter. A laden collier hugging the coast steered outward for deeper water and, across copper-coloured haze, I saw sails rise one by one on the anchored fishing-fleet. In a deep dene behind me an eddy of sudden wind drummed through sheltered oaks, and spun aloft the first dry sample of autumn leaves. When I reached the beach road the sea-fog fumed over the brickfields, and the tide was telling all the groins of the gale beyond Ushant. In less than an hour summer England vanished in chill grey. We were again the shut island of the North, all the ships of the world bellowing at our perilous gates; and between their outcries ran the piping of bewildered gulls. My cap dripped moisture, the folds of the rug held it in pools or sluiced it away in runnels, and the salt-rime stuck to my lips.

Inland the smell of autumn loaded the thickened fog among the trees, and the drip became a continuous shower. Yet the late flowers—mallow of the wayside, scabious of the field, and dahlia of the garden—showed gay in the mist, and beyond the sea's breath there was little sign of decay in the leaf. Yet in the villages the house doors were all open, and bare-legged, bare-headed children sat at ease on the damp doorsteps to shout "pip-pip" at the stranger.

I made bold to call at the sweetmeat shop, where Mrs. Madehurst met me with a fat woman's hospitable tears. Jenny's child, she said, had died two days after the nun had come. It was, she felt, best out of the way, even though insurance offices, for reasons which she did not pretend to follow, would not willingly insure such stray lives. "Not but what Jenny didn't tend to Arthur as though he'd come all proper at de end of de first year—like Jenny herself." Thanks to Miss Florence, the child had been buried with a pomp which, in Mrs. Madehurst's opinion, more than covered the small irregularity of its birth. She described the coffin, within and without, the glass hearse, and the evergreen lining of the grave.

"But how's the mother?" I asked.

"Jenny? Oh, she'll get over it. I've felt dat way with one or two o' my own. She'll get over. She's walkin' in de wood now."

"In this weather?"

Mrs. Madehurst looked at me with narrowed eyes across the counter.

"I dunno but it opens de 'eart like. Yes, it opens de 'eart. Dat's where losin' and bearin' comes so alike in de long run, we do say."

Now the wisdom of the old wives is greater than that of all the Fathers, and this last oracle sent me thinking so extendedly as I went up the road that I nearly ran over a woman and a child at the wooded corner by the lodge gates of the House Beautiful.

"Awful weather!" I cried, as I slowed dead for the turn.

"Not so bad," she answered placidly out of the fog. "Mine's used to 'un. You'll find yours indoors, I reckon."

Indoors, Madden received me with professional courtesy, and kind inquiries for the health of the motor, which he would put under cover.

I waited in a still, nut-brown hall, pleasant with late flowers and warmed with a delicious wood fire—a place of good influence and great peace. (Men and women may sometimes, after great effort, achieve a creditable lie; but the house, which is their temple, cannot say anything save the truth of those who have lived in it.) A child's cart and a doll lay on the black-and-white floor, where a rug had been kicked back. I felt that the children had only just hurried away—to hide themselves, most like—in the many turns of the great adzed staircase that climbed statelily out of the hall, or to crouch at gaze behind the lions and roses of the carven gallery above. Then I heard her voice above me, singing as the blind sing—from the soul:—

In the pleasant orchard-closes.

And all my early summer came back at the call.

In the pleasant orchard-closes,

  God bless all our gains say we—

But may God bless all our losses,

  Better suits with our degree.

She dropped the marring fifth line, and repeated—

Better suits with our degree!

I saw her lean over the gallery, her linked hands white as pearl against the oak.

"Is that you—from the other side of the county?" she called.

"Yes, me from the other side of the county," I answered, laughing.

"What a long time before you had to come here again." She ran down the stairs, one hand lightly touching the broad rail. "It's two months and four days. Summer's gone!"

"I meant to come before, but Fate prevented."

"I knew it. Please do something to that fire. They won't let me play with it, but I can feel it's behaving badly. Hit it!"

I looked on either side of the deep fireplace, and found but a half-charred hedge-stake with which I punched a black log into flame.

"It never goes out, day or night," she said, as though explaining. "In case any one comes in with cold toes, you see."

"It's even lovelier inside than it was out," I murmured. The red light poured itself along the age-polished dusky panels till the Tudor roses and lions of the gallery took colour and motion. An old eagle-topped convex mirror gathered the picture into its mysterious heart, distorting afresh the distorted shadows, and curving the gallery lines into the curves of a ship. The day was shutting down in half a gale as the fog turned to stringy scud. Through the uncurtained mullions of the broad window I could see valiant horsemen of the lawn rear and recover against the wind that taunted them with legions of dead leaves.

"Yes, it must be beautiful," she said. "Would you like to go over it? There's still light enough upstairs."

I followed her up the unflinching, wagon-wide staircase to the gallery, whence opened the thin fluted Elizabethan doors.

"Feel how they put the latch low down for the sake of the children." She swung a light door inward.

"By the way, where are they?" I asked. "I haven't even heard them to-day."

She did not answer at once. Then, "I can only hear them," she replied softly. "This is one of their rooms—everything ready, you see."

She pointed into a heavily-timbered room. There were little low gate tables and children's chairs. A doll's house, it's hooked front half open, faced a great dappled rocking-horse, from whose padded saddle it was but a child's scramble to the broad window-seat overlooking the lawn. A toy gun lay in a corner beside a gilt wooden cannon.

"Surely they've only just gone," I whispered. In the failing light a door creaked cautiously. I heard the rustle of a frock and the patter of feet— quick feet through a room beyond.

"I heard that," she cried triumphantly. "Did you? Children, oh, children, where are you?"

The voice filled the walls that held it lovingly to the last perfect note, but there came no answering shout such as I had heard in the garden. We hurried on from room to oak-floored room; up a step here, down three steps there; among a maze of passages; always mocked by our quarry. One might as well have tried to work an unstopped warren with a single ferret. There were bolt-holes innumerable—recesses in walls, embrasures of deep slit-ten windows now darkened, whence they could start up behind us; and abandoned fireplaces, six feet deep in the masonry, as well as the tangle of communicating doors. Above all, they had the twilight for their helper in our game. I had caught one or two joyous chuckles of evasion, and once or twice had seen the silhouette of a child's frock against some darkening window at the end of a passage; but we returned empty-handed to the gallery, just as a middle-aged woman was setting a lamp in its niche.

"No, I haven't seen her either this evening, Miss Florence," I heard her say, "but that Turpin he says he wants to see you about his shed."

"Oh, Mr. Turpin must want to see me very badly. Tell him to come to the hall, Mrs. Madden."

I looked down into the hall whose only light was the dulled fire, and deep in the shadow I saw them at last. They must have slipped down while we were in the passages, and now thought themselves perfectly hidden behind an old gilt leather screen. By child's law, my fruitless chase was as good as an introduction, but since I had taken so much trouble I resolved to force them to come forward later by the simple trick, which children detest, of pretending not to notice them. They lay close, in a little huddle, no more than shadows except when a quick flame betrayed an outline.

"And now we'll have some tea," she said. "I believe I ought to have offered it you at first, but one doesn't arrive at manners, somehow, when one lives alone and is considered—h'm—peculiar." Then with very pretty scorn, "would you like a lamp to see to eat by?"

"The firelight's much pleasanter, I think." We descended into that delicious gloom and Madden brought tea.

I took my chair in the direction of the screen, ready to surprise or be surprised as the game should go, and at her permission, since a hearth is always sacred, bent forward to play with the fire.

"Where do you get these beautiful short faggots from?" I asked idly. "Why, they are tallies!"

"Of course," she said. "As I can't read or write I'm driven back on the early English tally for my accounts. Give me one and I'll tell you what it meant."

I passed her an unburnt hazel-tally, about a foot long, and she ran her thumb down the nicks.

"This is the milk-record for the home farm for the month of April last year, in gallons," said she. "I don't know what I should have done without tallies. An old forester of mine taught me the system. It's out of date now for every one else; but my tenants respect it. One of them's coming now to see me. Oh, it doesn't matter. He has no business here out of office hours. He's a greedy, ignorant man—very greedy or—he wouldn't come here after dark."

"Have you much land then?"

"Only a couple of hundred acres in hand, thank goodness. The other six hundred are nearly all let to folk who knew my folk before me, but this Turpin is quite a new man—and a highway robber."

"But are you sure I sha'n't be -?"

"Certainly not. You have the right. He hasn't any children."

"Ah, the children!" I said, and slid my low chair back till it nearly touched the screen that hid them. "I wonder whether they'll come out for me."

There was a murmur of voices—Madden's and a deeper note—at the low, dark side door, and a ginger-headed, canvas-gaitered giant of the unmistakable tenant farmer type stumbled or was pushed in.

"Come to the fire, Mr. Turpin," she said.

"If—if you please, Miss, I'll—I'll be quite as well by the door." He clung to the latch as he spoke, like a frightened child. Of a sudden I realised that he was in the grip of some almost overpowering fear.

"Well?"

"About that new shed for the young stock—that was all. These first autumn storms settin' in . . . but I'll come again, Miss." His teeth did not chatter much more than the door latch.

"I think not," she answered levelly. "The new shed—m'm. What did my agent write you on the 15th?"

"I—fancied p'r'aps that if I came to see you—ma—man to man like, Miss—but——"

His eyes rolled into every corner of the room, wide with horror. He half opened the door through which he had entered, but I noticed it shut again—from without and firmly.

"He wrote what I told him," she went on. "You are overstocked already. Dunnett's Farm never carried more than fifty bullocks—even in Mr. Wright's time. And *he* used cake. You've sixty-seven and you don't cake. You've broken the lease in that respect. You're dragging the heart out of the farm."

"I'm—I'm getting some minerals—superphosphates—next week. I've as good as ordered a truck-load already. I'll go down to the station to-morrow about 'em. Then I can come and see you man to man like, Miss, in the daylight. . . . That gentleman's not going away, is he?" He almost shrieked.

I had only slid the chair a little further back, reaching behind me to tap on the leather of the screen, but he jumped like a rat.

"No. Please attend to me, Mr. Turpin." She turned in her chair and faced him with his back to the door. It was an old and sordid little piece of scheming that she forced from him—his plea for the new cowshed at his landlady's expense, that he might with the covered manure pay his next year's rent out of the valuation after, as she made clear, he had bled the enriched pastures to the bone. I could not but admire the intensity of his greed, when I saw him out-facing for its sake whatever terror it was that ran wet on his forehead.

I ceased to tap the leather—was, indeed, calculating the cost of the shed—when I felt my relaxed hand taken and turned softly between the soft hands of a child. So at last I had triumphed. In a moment I would turn and acquaint myself with those quick-footed wanderers. . . .

The little brushing kiss fell in the centre of my palm—as a gift on which the fingers were, once, expected to close: as the all faithful half-reproachful signal of a waiting child not used to neglect even when grown-ups were busiest—a fragment of the mute code devised very long ago.

Then I knew. And it was as though I had known from the first day when I looked across the lawn at the high window.

I heard the door shut. The woman turned to me in silence, and I felt that she knew.

What time passed after this I cannot say. I was roused by the fall of a log, and mechanically rose to put it back. Then I returned to my place in the chair very close to the screen.

"Now you understand," she whispered, across the packed shadows.

"Yes, I understand—now. Thank you."

"I—I only hear them." She bowed her head in her hands. "I have no right, you know—no other right. I have neither borne nor lost—neither borne nor lost!"

"Be very glad then," said I, for my soul was torn open within me.

"Forgive me!"

She was still, and I went back to my sorrow and my joy.

"It was because I loved them so," she said at last, brokenly. "*That* was why it was, even from the first—even before I knew that they—they were all I should ever have. And I loved them so!"

She stretched out her arms to the shadows and the shadows within the shadow.

"They came because I loved them—because I needed them. I—I must have made them come. Was that wrong, think you?"

"No—no."

"I—I grant you that the toys and—and all that sort of thing were nonsense, but—but I used to so hate empty rooms myself when I was little." She pointed to the gallery. "And the passages all empty. . . . And how could I ever bear the garden door shut? Suppose——"

"Don't! For pity's sake, don't!" I cried. The twilight had brought a cold rain with gusty squalls that plucked at the leaded windows.

"And the same thing with keeping the fire in all night. *I* don't think it so foolish—do you?"

I looked at the broad brick hearth, saw, through tears I believe, that there was no unpassable iron on or near it, and bowed my head.

"I did all that and lots of other things—just to make believe. Then they came. I heard them, but I didn't know that they were not mine by right till Mrs. Madden told me——"

"The butler's wife? What?"

"One of them—I heard—she saw—and knew. Hers! *Not* for me. I didn't know at first. Perhaps I was jealous. Afterwards, I began to understand that it was only because I loved them, not because——. . . Oh, you *must* bear or lose," she said piteously. "There is no other way—and yet they love me. They must! Don't they?"

There was no sound in the room except the lapping voices of the fire, but we two listened intently, and she at least took comfort from what she heard. She recovered herself and half rose. I sat still in my chair by the screen.

"Don't think me a wretch to whine about myself like this, but—but I'm all in the dark, you know, and *you* can see."

In truth I could see, and my vision confirmed me in my resolve, though that was like the very parting of spirit and flesh. Yet a little longer I would stay since it was the last time.

"You think it is wrong, then?" she cried sharply, though I had said nothing.

"Not for you. A thousand times no. For you it is right. . . . I am grateful to you beyond words. For me it would be wrong. For me only. . . ."

"Why?" she said, but passed her hand before her face as she had done at our second meeting in the wood. "Oh, I see," she went on simply as a child. "For you it would be wrong." Then with a little indrawn laugh, "and, d'you remember, I called you lucky—once—at first. You who must never come here again!"

She left me to sit a little longer by the screen, and I heard the sound of her feet die out along the gallery above.

Thoughts on 'They'

In 1899, five years before this story was written, the Kipling family had arrived in New York by steamer, only to be struck down with illness that developed swiftly into pneumonia. Their beloved daughter, the six year old Josephine, succumbed and Kipling himself nearly died. When he was fit enough to be told of the loss it hit him like a thunderbolt. His cousin, Angela Thirkell commented, 'Much of the beloved Cousin Ruddy of our childhood died with Josephine.' At their home in Rottingdean, Rudyard, still not fully recovered, 'saw' Josephine 'every time a door was opened, every time a place was empty at table, saw her in every green corner of the garden, radiant and heart-breaking.'

Three years after Josephine's death Kipling gave voice to his grief in a beautiful poem, 'Merrow Down', which takes the form of a pre-historic fable recalling the times the two of them had enjoyed together in a cherished corner of Surrey. But it was not until he had written 'They' that he was able to begin the process of disengaging himself from the memories of one he had loved so dearly.

There are obvious parallels between the narrator of 'They' and the author. Both lived in Sussex, which county they were fond of exploring by motor car, and both had lost a beloved girl child. As Philip Mason observed, the house beautiful was 'like Bateman's but with a little bit more of everything'. It almost has a character of its own, with 'horsemen ten feet high with levelled lances, monstrous peacocks, and sleek round-headed maids of honour - blue, black, and glistening - all of clipped yew'. Significantly, the narrator is stopped at the entrance by a green spear.

On first reading, it is easy to miss the blind woman's comment that 'You'll find yours indoors, I reckon'. However, when the narrator finally comprehends the identity of 'his' child he realizes that he will never be able to return to the house. The mistress of the house understands why, but the reader is left to make up his own mind. Joyce Tompkins suggests that, like the road to En-Dor, 'one must turn one's back on that road and return to the living world to which one belongs.'

Not all the epigraphs to Kipling's stories are as relevant and moving as the poem, 'The Return of the Children' which precedes this.

Echoes of this deeply autobiographical story can be found in T.S. Eliot's 'Burnt Norton' (1935), a poem concerning the enigma of time: 'for the leaves were full of children, /Hidden excitedly, containing laughter'.

REGULUS

Regulus, a Roman general, defeated the Carthaginians 256 B.C., but was next year defeated and taken prisoner by the Carthaginians, who sent him to Rome with an embassy to ask for peace or an exchange of prisoners. Regulus strongly advised the Roman Senate to make no terms with the enemy. He then returned to Carthage and was put to death.

The Fifth Form had been dragged several times in its collective life, from one end of the school Horace to the other. Those were the years when Army examiners gave thousands of marks for Latin, and it was Mr. King's hated business to defeat them.

Hear him, then, on a raw November morning at second lesson.

'Aha!' he began, rubbing his hands. 'Cras ingens iterabimus aequor. Our portion to-day is the Fifth Ode of the Third Book, I believe—concerning one Regulus, a gentleman. And how often have we been through it?'

'Twice, sir,' said Malpass, head of the Form.

Mr. King shuddered. 'Yes, twice, quite literally,' he said. 'To-day, with an eye to your Army viva-voce examinations—ugh!—I shall exact somewhat freer and more florid renditions. With feeling and comprehension if that be possible. I except'—here his eye swept the back benches—'our friend and companion Beetle, from whom, now as always, I demand an absolutely literal translation.' The form laughed subserviently.

'Spare his blushes! Beetle charms us first.'

207

Beetle stood up, confident in the possession of a guaranteed construe, left behind by M'Turk, who had that day gone into the sick-house with a cold. Yet he was too wary a hand to show confidence.

'Credidimus, we—believe—we have believed,' he opened in hesitating slow time, 'tonantem Jovem, thundering Jove—regnare, to reign—caelo, in heaven. Augustus,—Augustus—habebitur, will be held or considered praesens divus, a present God—adjectis Britannis, the Britons being added—imperio, to the Empire—gravibusque Persis, with the heavy—er, stern Persians.'

'What?'

'The grave or stern Persians.' Beetle pulled up with the 'Thank-God-I-have-done-my-duty' air of Nelson in the cockpit.

'I am quite aware,' said King, 'that the first stanza is about the extent of your knowledge, but continue, sweet one, continue. Gravibus, by the way, is usually translated as "troublesome."'

Beetle drew along and tortured breath. The second stanza (which carries over to the third) of that Ode is what is technically called a 'stinker.' But M'Turk had done him handsomely.

'Milesne Crassi, had—has the soldier of Crassus—vixit, lived—lurpis maritus, a disgraceful husband——'

'You slurred the quantity of the word after turpis,' said King. 'Let's hear it.'

Beetle guessed again, and for a wonder hit the correct quantity. 'Er—a disgraceful husband—conjuge barbara, with a barbarous spouse.'

'Why do you select that disgustful equivalent out of all the dictionary?' King snapped. 'Isn't "wife "good enough for you?'

'Yes, sir. But what do I do about this bracket, sir? Shall I take it now?'

'Confine yourself at present to the soldier of Crassus.'

'Yes, Sir. Et, and—consenuit, has he grown old—in armis, in the—er—arms—hostium socerorum, of his father-in-law's enemies.'

'Who? How? Which?'

'Arms of his enemies' fathers-in-law, sir.'

'Tha-anks. By the way, what meaning might you attach to in armis?'

'Oh, weapons—weapons of war, sir.' There was a virginal note in Beetle's voice as though he had been falsely accused of uttering indecencies. 'Shall I take the bracket now, sir?'

'Since it seems to be troubling you.'

'Pro Curia, O for the Senate House—inversique mores, and manners up-set—upside down.'

'Ve-ry like your translation. Meantime, the soldier of Crassus?'

'Sub rege Medo, under a Median King—Marsus et Apulus, he being a Marsian and an Apulian.'

'Who? The Median King?'

'No, sir. The soldier of Crassus. Oblittus agrees with milesne Crassi, sir,' volunteered too hasty Beetle.

'Does it? It doesn't with me.'

'Oh-blight-us,' Beetle corrected hastily, 'forgetful—anciliorum, of the shields, or trophies—et nominis, and the—his name—et togae, and the toga—eternaeque Vestae, and eternal Vesta—incolumi Jove, Jove being safe—et urbe Roma, and the Roman city.' With an air of hardly re-strained zeal—'Shall I go on, sir?'

Mr. King winced. 'No, thank you. You have indeed given us a translation! May I ask if it conveys any meaning whatever to your so-called mind?'

'Oh, I think so, sir.' This with gentle toleration for Horace and all his works.

'We envy you. Sit down.'

Beetle sat down relieved, well knowing that a reef of uncharted genitives stretched ahead of him, on which in spite of M'Turk's sailing-directions he would infallibly have been wrecked.

Rattray, who took up the task, steered neatly through them and came unscathed to port.

'Here we require drama,' said King. 'Regulus himself is speaking now. Who shall represent the provident-minded Regulus? Winton, will you kindly oblige?'

Winton of King's House, a long, heavy, towheaded Second Fifteen forward, overdue for his First Fifteen colours, and in aspect like an earnest, elderly horse, rose up, and announced, among other things, that he had seen 'signs affixed to Punic deluges.' Half the Form shouted for joy, and the other half for joy that there was something to shout about.

Mr. King opened and shut his eyes with great swiftness. 'Signa adfixa delubris,' he gasped. 'So delubris is "deluges" is it? Winton, in all our dealings, have I ever suspected you of a jest?'

'No, sir,' said the rigid and angular Winton, while the Form rocked about him.

'And yet you assert delubris means "deluges." Whether I am a fit subject for such a jape is, of course, a matter of opinion, but . . . . Winton, you are normally conscientious. May we assume you looked out delubris?'

'No, sir.' Winton was privileged to speak that truth dangerous to all who stand before Kings.

''Made a shot at it then? '

Every line of Winton's body showed he had done nothing of the sort. Indeed, the very idea that 'Pater' Winton (and a boy is not called 'Pater' by companions for his frivolity) would make a shot at anything was beyond belief. But he replied, 'Yes,' and all the while worked with his right heel as though he were heeling a ball at punt-about.

Though none dared to boast of being a favourite with King, the taciturn, three-cornered Winton stood high in his House-Master's opinion. It seemed to save him neither rebuke nor punishment, but the two were in some fashion sympathetic.

'Hm!' said King drily. 'I was going to say—Flagitio additis damnum, but I think—I think I see the process. Beetle, the translation of delubris, please.'

Beetle raised his head from his shaking arm long enough to answer: 'Ruins, sir.'

There was an impressive pause while King checked off crimes on his fingers. Then to Beetle the much-enduring man addressed winged words:

'Guessing,' said he. 'Guessing, Beetle, as usual, from the look of delubris that it bore some relation to diluvium or deluge, you imparted the result of your half-baked lucubrations to Winton who seems to have been lost enough to have accepted it. Observing next, your companion's fall, from the presumed security of your undistinguished position in the rear-guard, you took another pot-shot. The turbid chaos of your mind threw up some memory of the word "dilapidations" which you have pitifully attempted to disguise under the synonym of "ruins."'

As this was precisely what Beetle had done he looked hurt but forgiving. 'We will attend to this later,' said King. 'Go on, Winton, and retrieve yourself.'

Delubris happened to be the one word which Winton had not looked out and had asked Beetle for, when they were settling into their places. He forged ahead with no further trouble. Only when he rendered scilicet as 'forsooth,' King erupted.

'Regulus,' he said, 'was not a leader-writer for the penny press, nor, for that matter, was Horace. Regulus says: "The soldier ransomed by gold will come keener for the fight—will he by—by gum!" That's the meaning of scilicet. It indicates contempt—bitter contempt. "Forsooth," forsooth! You'll be talking about "speckled beauties "and "eventually transpire" next. Howell, what do you make of that doubled "Vidi ego—ego vidi"? It wasn't put in to fill up the metre, you know.'

'Isn't it intensive, sir? 'said Howell, afflicted by a genuine interest in what he read. 'Regulus was a bit in earnest about Rome making no terms with Carthage—and he wanted to let the Romans understand it, didn't he, sir?'

'Less than your usual grace, but the fact. Regulus was in earnest. He was also engaged at the same time in cutting his own throat with every word he uttered. He knew Carthage which (your examiners won't ask you this so you needn't take notes) was a sort of God-forsaken nigger Manchester. Regulus was not thinking about his own life. He was telling Rome the truth. He was playing for his side. Those lines from the eighteenth to the fortieth ought to be written in blood. Yet there are things in human garments which will tell you that Horace was a flaneur—a man about town. Avoid such beings. Horace knew a very great deal. He knew! Erit ille fortis—"will he be brave who once to faithless foes has knelt?" And again (stop pawing with your hooves, Thornton!) hic unde vitam sumeret inscius. That means roughly—but I perceive I am ahead of my translators. Begin at hic unde, Vernon, and let us see if you have the spirit of Regulus.'

Now no one expected fireworks from gentle Paddy Vernon, sub-prefect of Hartopp's House, but, as must often be the case with growing boys, his mind was in abeyance for the time being, and he said, all in a rush, on behalf of Regulus: 'O magna Carthago probrosis altior Italiae ruinis, O Carthage, thou wilt stand forth higher than the ruins of Italy.'

Even Beetle, most lenient of critics, was interested at this point, though he did not join the half-groan of reprobation from the wiser heads of the Form.

'Please don't mind me,' said King, and Vernon very kindly did not. He ploughed on thus: He (Regulus) is related to have removed from himself the kiss of the shameful wife and of his small children as less by the head, and, being stern, to have placed his virile visage on the ground.'

Since King loved 'virile' about as much as he did 'spouse' or 'forsooth' the Form looked up hopefully. But Jove thundered not.

'Until,' Vernon continued, 'he should have confirmed the sliding fathers as being the author of counsel never given under an alias.'

He stopped, conscious of stillness round him like the dread calm of the typhoon's centre. King's opening voice was sweeter than honey.

'I am painfully aware by bitter experience that I cannot give you any idea of the passion, the power, the—the essential guts of the lines which you have so foully outraged in our presence. But——' the note changed, 'so far as in me lies, I will strive to bring home to you, Vernon, the fact that there exist in Latin a few pitiful rules of grammar, of syntax, nay, even of declension, which were not created for your incult sport—your Bœotian diversion. You will, therefore, Vernon, write out and bring to me to-morrow a word-for-word English-Latin translation of the Ode, together with a full list of all adjectives—an adjective is not a verb, Vernon, as the Lower Third will tell you—all adjectives, their number, case, and gender. Even now I haven't begun to deal with you faithfully.'

'I—I'm very sorry, sir,' Vernon stammered.

'You mistake the symptoms, Vernon. You are possibly discomfited by the imposition, but sorrow postulates some sort of mind, intellect, nous. Your rendering of probrosis alone stamps you as lower than the beasts of the field. Will some one take the taste out of our mouths? And—talking of tastes——' He coughed. There was a distinct flavour of chlorine gas in the air. Up went an eyebrow, though King knew perfectly well what it meant.

'Mr. Hartopp's st—science class next door,' said Malpass.

'Oh yes. I had forgotten. Our newly established Modern Side, of course. Perowne, open the windows; and Winton, go on once more from inter-que maerentes.'

'And hastened away,' said Winton, 'surrounded by his mourning friends, into—into illustrious banishment. But I got that out of Conington, sir,' he added in one conscientious breath.

'I am aware. The master generally knows his ass's crib, though I acquit you of any intention that way. Can you suggest anything for egregius exul? Only "egregious exile'? I fear "egregious "is a good word ruined. No! You can't in this case improve on Conington. Now then for atqui sciebat quae sibi barbarus tortor par aret. The whole force of it lies in the atqui.'

'Although he knew,' Winton suggested.

'Stronger than that, I think.'

'He who knew well,' Malpass interpolated.

'Ye-es. "Well though he knew." I don't like Conington's "well-witting." It's Wardour Street.'

'Well though he knew what the savage torturer was—was getting ready for him,' said Winton.

'Ye-es. Had in store for him.'

'Yet he brushed aside his kinsmen and the people delaying his return.'

'Ye-es; but then how do you render obstantes?'

'If it's a free translation mightn't obstantes and morantem come to about the same thing, sir??'

'Nothing comes to "about the same thing" with Horace, Winton. As I have said, Horace was not a journalist. No, I take it that his kinsmen bodily withstood his departure, whereas the crowd—populumque—the democracy stood about futilely pitying him and getting in the way. Now for that noblest of endings—quam si clientum,' and King ran off into the quotation:

'As though some tedious business o'er

Of clients' court, his journey lay

Towards Venafrum's grassy floor

Or Sparta-built Tarentum's bay.

All right, Winton. Beetle, when you've quite finished dodging the fresh air yonder, give me the meaning of tendens—and turn down your collar.'

'Me, sir? Tendens, sir? Oh! Stretching away in the direction of, sir.'

'Idiot! Regulus was not a feature of the landscape. He was a man, self-doomed to death by torture. Atqui sciebat—knowing it—having achieved it for his country's sake—can't you hear that atqui cut like a knife?—he moved off with some dignity. That is why Horace out of the whole golden Latin tongue chose the one word "tendens"—which is utterly untranslatable.'

The gross injustice of being asked to translate it, converted Beetle into a young Christian martyr, till King buried his nose in his handkerchief again.

'I think they've broken another gas-bottle next door, sir,' said Howell. 'They're always doing it.' The Form coughed as more chlorine came in.

'Well, I suppose we must be patient with the Modern Side,' said King. 'But it is almost insupportable for this Side. Vernon, what are you grinning at?'

Vernon's mind had returned to him glowing and inspired. He chuckled as he underlined his Horace.

'It appears to amuse you,' said King. 'Let us participate. What is it? '

'The last two lines of the Tenth Ode, in this book, sir,' was Vernon's amazing reply.

'What? Oh, I see. Non hoc semper erit liminis aut aquae caelestis patiens latus.' King's mouth twitched to hide a grin. 'Was that done with intention?'

'I—I thought it fitted, sir.'

'It does. It's distinctly happy. What put it into your thick head, Paddy?'

'I don't know, sir, except we did the Ode last term.'

'And you remembered? The same head that minted probrosis as a verb! Vernon, you are an enigma. No! This Side will not always be patient of unheavenly gases and waters. I will make representations to our so-called Moderns. Meantime (who shall say I am not just?) I remit you your accrued pains and penalties in regard to probrosim, probrosis, probrosit and other enormities. I oughtn't to do it, but this Side is occasionally human. By no means bad, Paddy.'

'Thank you, sir,' said Vernon, wondering how inspiration had visited him.

Then King, with a few brisk remarks about Science, headed them back to Regulus, of whom and of Horace and Rome and evil-minded commercial Carthage and of the democracy eternally futile, he explained, in all ages and climes, he spoke for ten minutes; passing thence to the next Ode—Delicta majorum—where he fetched up, full-voiced, upon—'Dis te minorem quod geris imperas' (Thou rulest because thou bearest thyself as lower than the Gods)—making it a text for a discourse on manners, morals, and respect for authority as distinct from bottled gases, which lasted till the bell rang. Then Beetle, concertinaing his books, observed to Winton, 'When King's really on tap he's an interestin' dog. Hartopp's chlorine uncorked him.'

'Yes; but why did you tell me delubris was "deluges," you silly ass?' said Winton.

'Well, that uncorked him too. Look out, you hoof-handed old owl!' Winton had cleared for action as the Form poured out like puppies at play and was scragging Beetle. Stalky from behind collared Winton low. The three fell in confusion.

'Dis te minorem quod geris imperas,' quoth Stalky, ruffling Winton's lint-whitelocks. ''Mustn't jape with Number Five study. Don't be too virtuous. Don't brood over it. 'Twon't count against you in your future caree-ah. Cheer up, Pater.'

'Pull him off my—er—essential guts, will you?' said Beetle from beneath. 'He's squashin' 'em.'

They dispersed to their studies.

***

No one, the owner least of all, can explain what is in a growing boy's mind. It might have been the blind ferment of adolescence; Stalky's random remarks about virtue might have stirred him; like his betters he might have sought popularity by way of clowning; or, as the Head asserted years later, the only known jest of his serious life might have worked on him, as a sober-sided man's one love colours and dislocates all his after days. But, at the next lesson, mechanical drawing with Mr.

Lidgett who as drawing-master had very limited powers of punishment, Winton fell suddenly from grace and let loose a live mouse in the form-room. The whole form, shrieking and leaping high, threw at it all the plaster cones, pyramids, and fruit in high relief—not to mention ink-pots—that they could lay hands on. Mr. Lidgett reported at once to the Head; Winton owned up to his crime, which, venial in the Upper Third, pardonable at a price in the Lower Fourth, was, of course, rank ruffianism on the part of a Fifth Form boy; and so, by graduated stages, he arrived at the Head's study just before lunch, penitent, perturbed, annoyed with himself and—as the Head said to King in the corridor after the meal—more human than he had known him in seven years.

'You see,' the Head drawled on, 'Winton's only fault is a certain costive and unaccommodating virtue. So this comes very happily.'

'I've never noticed any sign of it,' said King. Winton was in King's House, and though King as pro-consul might, and did, infernally oppress his own Province, once a black and yellow cap was in trouble at the hands of the Imperial authority King fought for him to the very last steps of Caesar's throne.

'Well, you yourself admitted just now that a mouse was beneath the occasion,' the Head answered.

'It was.' Mr. King did not love Mr. Lidgett. 'It should have been a rat. But—but—I hate to plead it—it's the lad's first offence.'

'Could you have damned him more completely, King?'

'Hm. What is the penalty?' said King, in retreat, but keeping up a rear-guard action.

'Only my usual few lines of Virgil to be shown up by tea-time.'

The Head's eyes turned slightly to that end of the corridor where Mullins, Captain of the Games ('Pot,' 'old Pot,' or 'Potiphar' Mullins), was pinning up the usual Wednesday notice—'Big, Middle, and Little Side Football—A to K, L to Z, 3 to 4.45 p.m.

You cannot write out the Head's usual few (which means five hundred) Latin lines and play football for one hour and three-quarters between the hours of 1.30 and 5 p.m. Winton had evidently no intention of trying to do so, for he hung about the corridor with a set face and an uneasy foot. Yet it was law in the school, compared with which that of the Medes and Persians was no more than a non-committal resolution, that any boy, outside the First Fifteen, who missed his football for any reason whatever, and had not a written excuse, duly signed by competent authority to explain his absence, would receive not less than three strokes with a ground-ash from the Captain of the Games, generally a youth between seventeen and eighteen years, rarely under eleven stone ('Pot' was nearer thirteen), and always in hard condition.

King knew without inquiry that the Head had given Winton no such excuse.

'But he is practically a member of the First Fifteen. He has played for it all this term,' said King. 'I believe his Cap should have arrived last week.'

'His Cap has not been given him. Officially, therefore, he is naught. I rely on old Pot.'

'But Mullins is Winton's study-mate,' King persisted.

Pot Mullins and Pater Winton were cousins and rather close friends.

'That will make no difference to Mullins'or Winton, if I know 'em,' said the Head.

'But—but,' King played his last card desperately, 'I was going to recommend Winton for extra sub-prefect in my House, now Carton has gone.'

'Certainly,' said the Head. 'Why not? He will be excellent by tea-time, I hope.'

At that moment they saw Mr. Lidgett, tripping down the corridor, way-laid by Winton.

'It's about that mouse-business at mechanical drawing,' Winton opened, swinging across his path.

'Yes, yes, highly disgraceful,' Mr. Lidgett panted.

'I know it was,' said Winton. 'It—it was a cad's trick because——'

'Because you knew I couldn't give you more than fifty lines,' said Mr. Lidgett.

'Well, anyhow I've come to apologise for it.'

'Certainly,' said Mr. Lidgett, and added, for he was a kindly man, 'I think that shows quite right feeling. I'll tell the Head at once I'm satisfied.'

'No—no!' The boy's still unmended voice jumped from the growl to the squeak. 'I didn't mean that! I—I did it on principle. Please don't—er—do anything of that kind.'

Mr. Lidgett looked him up and down and, being an artist, understood.

'Thank you, Winton,' he said. 'This shall be between ourselves.'

'You heard?' said King, indecent pride in his voice.

'Of course. You thought he was going to get Lidgett to beg him off the impot.'

King denied this with so much warmth that the Head laughed and King went away in a huff.

'By the way,' said the Head, 'I've told Winton to do his lines in your form-room—not in his study.'

'Thanks,' said King over his shoulder, for the Head's orders had saved Winton and Mullins, who was doing extra Army work in the study, from an embarrassing afternoon together.

An hour later, King wandered into his still form-room as though by accident. Winton was hard at work.

'Aha!' said King, rubbing his hands. 'This does not look like games, Winton. Don't let me arrest your facile pen. Whence this sudden love for Virgil?'

'Impot from the Head, sir, for that mouse-business this morning.'

'Rumours thereof have reached us. That was a lapse on your part into Lower Thirdery which I don't quite understand.'

The 'tump-tump' of the puntabouts before the sides settled to games came through the open window. Winton, like his House-master, loved fresh air. Then they heard Paddy Vernon, sub-prefect on duty, calling the roll in the field and marking defaulters. Winton wrote steadily. King curled himself up on a desk, hands round knees. One would have said that the man was gloating over the boy's misfortune, but the boy understood.

'Dis te minorem quad geris imperas,' King quoted presently. 'It is necessary to bear oneself as lower than the local gods—even than drawing-masters who are precluded from effective retaliation. I do wish you'd tried that mouse-game with me, Pater.'

Winton grinned; then sobered. 'It was a cad's trick, sir, to play on Mr. Lidgett.' He peered forward at the page he was copying.

'Well, "the sin I impute to each frustrate ghost"——s' King stopped himself: 'Why do you goggle like an owl? Hand me the Mantuan and I'll dictate. No matter. Any rich Virgilian measures will serve. I may peradventure recall a few.' He began:

'Tu regere imperio populos Romane memento

    Hae tibi erunt artes pacisque imponere morem,

Parcere subjectis et debellare superbos.

There you have it all, Winton. Write that out twice and yet once again.'

For the next forty minutes, with never a glance at the book, King paid out the glorious hexameters (and King could read Latin as though it were alive), Winton hauling them in and coiling them away behind him as trimmers in a telegraph-ship's hold coil away deep-sea cable. King broke from the Aeneid to the Georgics and back again, pausing now and then to translate some specially loved line or to dwell on the treble-shot texture of the ancient fabric. He did not allude to the coming interview with Mullins except at the last, when he said, 'I think at this juncture, Pater, I need not ask you for the precise significance of atqui sciebat quae sibi barbarus tortor.'

The ungrateful Winton flushed angrily, and King loafed out to take five o'clock call-over, after which he invited little Hartopp to tea and a talk on chlorine-gas. Hartopp accepted the challenge like a bantam, and the two went up to King's study about the same time as Winton returned to the form-room beneath it to finish his lines.

Then half a dozen of the Second Fifteen who should have been washing strolled in to condole with 'Pater' Winton, whose misfortune and its consequences were common talk. No one was more sincere than the long, red-headed, knotty-knuckled 'Paddy' Vernon, but, being a careless animal, he joggled Winton's desk.

'Curse you for a silly ass! 'said Winton. 'Don't do that.'

No one is expected to be polite while under punishment, so Vernon, sinking his sub-prefectship, replied peacefully enough:

'Well, don't be wrathy, Pater.'

'I'm not,' said Winton. 'Get out! This ain't your House form-room.'

'Form-room don't belong to you. Why don't you go to your own study?' Vernon replied.

'Because Mullins is there waitin' for the victim,' said Stalky delicately, and they all laughed. 'You ought to have shaken that mouse out of your trouser-leg, Pater. That's the way I did in my youth. Pater's revertin' to his second childhood. Never mind, Pater, we all respect you and your future caree-ah.'

Winton, still writhing, growled. Vernon leaning on the desk somehow shook it again. Then he laughed.

'What are you grinning at?' Winton asked.

'I was only thinkin' of you being sent up to take a lickin' from Pot. I swear I don't think it's fair. You've never shirked a game in your life, and you're as good as in the First Fifteen already. Your Cap ought to have been delivered last week, oughtn't it?'

It was law in the school that no man could by any means enjoy the privileges and immunities of the First Fifteen till the black velvet cap with the gold tassel, made by dilatory Exeter outfitters, had been actually set on his head. Ages ago, a large-built and unruly Second Fifteen had attempted to change this law, but the prefects of that age were still larger, and the lively experiment had never been repeated.

'Will you,' said Winton very slowly, 'kindly mind your own damned business, you cursed, clumsy, fat-headed fool?'

The form-room was as silent as the empty field in the darkness outside. Vernon shifted his feet uneasily.

'Well, I shouldn't like to take a lickin' from Pot,' he said.

'Wouldn't you?' Winton asked, as he paged the sheets of lines with hands that shook.

'No, I shouldn't,' said Vernon, his freckles growing more distinct on the bridge of his white nose.

'Well, I'm going to take it'—Winton moved clear of the desk as he spoke. 'But you're going to take a lickin' from me first.' Before any one realised it, he had flung himself neighing against Vernon. No decencies were observed on either side, and the rest looked on amazed. The two met confusedly, Vernon trying to do what he could with his longer reach; Winton, insensible to blows, only concerned to drive his enemy into a corner and batter him to pulp. This he managed over against the fire-place, where Vernon dropped half-stunned. 'Now I'm going to give you your lickin',' said Winton. 'Lie there till I get a ground-ash and I'll cut you to pieces. If you move, I'll chuck you out of the window.' He wound his hand s into the boy's collar and waistband, and had actually heaved him half off the ground before the others with one accord dropped on his head, shoulders, and legs. He fought them crazily in an awful hissing silence, Stalky's sensitive nose was rubbed along the floor; Beetle received a jolt in the wind that sent him whistling and crowing against the wall; Perowne's forehead was cut, and Malpass came out with an eye that explained itself like a dying rainbow through a whole week.

'Mad! Quite mad!' said Stalky, and for the third time wriggled back to Winton's throat. The door opened and King came in, Hartopp's little figure just behind him. The mound on the floor panted and heaved but did not rise, for Winton still squirmed vengefully. 'Only a little play, sir,' said Perowne. ''Only hit my head against a form.' This was quite true.

'Oh,' said King. 'Dimovit obstantes propinquos. You, I presume, are the populus delaying Winton's return to—Mullins, eh?'

'No, sir,' said Stalky behind his claret-coloured handkerchief. 'We're the maerentes amicos.'

'Not bad! You see, some of it sticks after all,' King chuckled to Hartopp, and the two masters left without further inquiries.

The boys sat still on the now passive Winton.

'Well,' said Stalky at last, 'of all the putrid he-asses, Pater, you are the—'

'I'm sorry. I'm awfully sorry,' Winton began, and they let him rise. He held out his hand to the bruised and bewildered Vernon. 'Sorry, Paddy. I—I must have lost my temper. I—I don't know what's the matter with me.'

''Fat lot of good that'll do my face at tea,' Vernon grunted. 'Why couldn't you say there was something wrong with you instead of lamming out like a lunatic? Is my lip puffy?'

'Just a trifle. Look at my beak! Well, we got all these pretty marks at footer-owin' to the zeal with which we played the game,' said Stalky, dusting himself. 'But d'you think you're fit to be let loose again, Pater? 'Sure you don't want to kill another sub-prefect? I wish I was Pot. I'd cut your sprightly young soul out.'

'I s'pose I ought to go to Pot now,' said Winton.

'And let all the other asses see you lookin' like this! Not much. We'll all come up to Number Five Study and wash off in hot water. Beetle, you aren't damaged. Go along and light the gasstove.'

'There's a tin of cocoa in my study somewhere,' Perowne shouted after him. 'Rootle round till you find it, and take it up.'

Separately, by different roads, Vernon's jersey pulled half over his head, the boys repaired to Number Five Study. Little Hartopp and King, I am sorry to say, leaned over the banisters of King's landing and watched.

'Ve-ry human,' said little Hartopp. 'Your virtuous Winton, having got himself into trouble, takes it out of my poor old Paddy. I wonder what precise lie Paddy will tell about his face.'

'But surely you aren't going to embarrass him by asking?' said King.

'Your boy won,' said Hartopp.

'To go back to what we were discussing,' said King quickly, 'do you pretend that your modern system of inculcating unrelated facts about chlorine, for instance, all of which may be proved fallacies by the time the boys grow up, can have any real bearing on education—even the low type of it that examiners expect?'

'I maintain nothing. But is it any worse than your Chinese reiteration of uncomprehended syllables in a dead tongue?'

'Dead, forsooth!' King fairly danced. 'The only living tongue on earth! Chinese! On my word, Hartopp!'

'And at the end of seven years—how often have I said it?' Hartopp went on,—'seven years of two hundred and twenty days of six hours each, your victims go away with nothing, absolutely nothing, except, perhaps, if they've been very attentive, a dozen—no, I'll grant you twenty—one score of totally unrelated Latin tags which any child of twelve could have absorbed in two terms.'

'But—but can't you realise that if our system brings later—at any rate—at a pinch-—a simple understanding—grammar and Latinity apart—a mere glimpse of the significance (foul word!) of, we'll say, one Ode of Horace, one twenty lines of Virgil, we've got what we poor devils of ushers are striving after?'

'And what might that be?' said Hartopp.

'Balance, proportion, perspective—life. Your scientific man is the unrelated animal—the beast without background. Haven't you ever realised that in your atmosphere of stinks?'

'Meantime you make them lose life for the sake of living, eh?'

'Blind again, Hartopp! I told you about Paddy's quotation this morning. (But he made probrosis a verb, he did!) You yourself heard young Corkran's reference to maerentes amicos. It sticks—a little of it sticks among the barbarians.'

'Absolutely and essentially Chinese,' said little Hartopp, who, alone of the common-room, refused to be outfaced by King. 'But I don't yet understand how Paddy came to be licked by Winton. Paddy's supposed to be something of a boxer.'

'Beware of vinegar made from honey,' King replied. 'Pater, like some other people, is patient and long-suffering, but he has his limits. The Head is oppressing him damnably, too. As I pointed out, the boy has practically been in the First Fifteen since term began.'

'But, my dear fellow, I've known you give a boy an impot and refuse him leave off games, again and again.'

'Ah, but that was when there was real need to get at some oaf who couldn't be sensitised in any other way. Now, in our esteemed Head's action I see nothing but——'

The conversation from this point does not concern us.

Meantime Winton, very penitent and especially polite towards Vernon, was being cheered with cocoa in Number Five Study. They had some difficulty in stemming the flood of his apologies. He himself pointed out to Vernon that he had attacked a sub-prefect for no reason whatever, and, therefore, deserved official punishment.

'I can't think what was the matter with me to-day,' he mourned. 'Ever since that blasted mouse business——'

'Well, then, don't think,' said Stalky. 'Or do you want Paddy to make a row about it before all the school?'

Here Vernon was understood to say that he would see Winton and all the school somewhere else.

'And if you imagine Perowne and Malpass and me are goin' to give evidence at a prefects' meeting just to soothe your beastly conscience, you jolly well err,' said Beetle. 'I know what you did.'

'What?' croaked Pater, out of the valley of his humiliation.

'You went Berserk. I've read all about it in Hypatia.'

'What's "going Berserk"?' Winton asked.

'Never you mind,' was the reply. 'Now, don't you feel awfully weak and seedy?'

'I am rather tired,' said Winton, sighing.

'That's what you ought to be. You've gone Berserk and pretty soon you'll go to sleep. But you'll probably be liable to fits of it all your life,' Beetle concluded. "Shouldn't wonder if you murdered some one some day.'

'Shut up—you and your Berserks! 'said Stalky. 'Go to Mullins now and get it over, Pater.'

'I call it filthy unjust of the Head,' said Vernon. 'Anyhow, you've given me my lickin', old man. I hope Pot'll give you yours.'

'I'm awfully sorry—awfully sorry,' was Winton's last word.

It was the custom in that consulship to deal with games' defaulters between five o'clock call-over and tea. Mullins, who was old enough to pity, did not believe in letting boys wait through the night till the chill of the next morning for their punishments. He was finishing off the last of the small fry and their excuses when Winton arrived.

'But, please, Mullins'—this was Babcock tertius, a dear little twelve-year-old mother's darling—'I had an awful hack on the knee. I've been to the Matron about it and she gave me some iodine. I've been rubbing it in all day. I thought that would be an excuse off'

'Let's have a look at it,' said the impassive Mullins. 'That's a shin-bruise—about a week old. Touch your toes. I'll give you the iodine.'

Babcock yelled loudly as he had many times before. The face of Jevons, aged eleven, a new boy that dark wet term, low in the House, low in the Lower School, and lowest of all in his homesick little mind, turned white at the horror of the sight. They could hear his working lips part stickily as Babcock wailed his way out of hearing.

'Hullo, Jevons! What brings you here?' said Mullins.

'Pl-ease, sir, I went for a walk with Babcock tertius.'

'Did you? Then I bet you went to the tuckshop—and you paid, didn't you?'

A nod. Jevons was too terrified to speak.

'Of course, and I bet Babcock told you that old Pot 'ud let you off because it was the first time.'

Another nod with a ghost of a smile in it.

'All right.' Mullins picked Jevons up before he could guess what was coming, laid him on the table with one hand, with the other gave him three emphatic spanks, then held him high in air.

'Now you tell Babcock tertius that he's got you a licking from me, and see you jolly well pay it back to him. And when you're prefect of games don't you let any one shirk his footer without a written excuse. Where d'you play in your game?'

'Forward, sir.'

'You can do better than that. I've seen you run like a young buck-rabbit. Ask Dickson from me to try you as three-quarter next game, will you? Cut along.'

Jevons left, warm for the first time that day, enormously set up in his own esteem, and very hot against the deceitful Babcock.

Mullins turned to Winton. 'Your name's on the list, Pater.' Winton nodded.

'I know it. The Head landed me with an impot for that mouse-business at mechanical drawing. No excuse.'

'He meant it then?' Mullins jerked his head delicately towards the ground-ash on the table. 'I heard something about it.'

Winton nodded. 'A rotten thing to do,' he said. 'Can't think what I was doing ever to do it. It counts against a fellow so; and there's some more too——'

'All right, Pater. Just stand clear of our photobracket, will you?'

The little formality over, there was a pause. Winton swung round, yawned in Pot's astonished face and staggered towards the window-seat.

'What's the matter with you, Dick? Ill?'

'No. Perfectly all right, thanks. Only—only a little sleepy.' Winton stretched himself out, and then and there fell deeply and placidly asleep.

'It isn't a faint,' said the experienced Mullins, 'or his pulse wouldn't act. 'Tisn't a fit or he'd snort and twitch. It can't be sunstroke, this term, and he hasn't been over-training for anything.' He opened Winton's collar, packed a cushion under his head, threw a rug over him and sat down to listen to the regular breathing. Before long Stalky arrived, on pretence of borrowing a book. He looked at the window-seat.

"Noticed anything wrong with Winton lately?' said Mullins.

"Notice anything wrong with my beak?' Stalky replied. 'Pater went Berserk after call-over, and fell on a lot of us for jesting with him about his impot. You ought to see Malpass's eye.'

'You mean that Pater fought?' said Mullins.

'Like a devil. Then he nearly went to sleep in our study just now. I expect he'll be all right when he wakes up. Rummy business! Conscientious old bargee. You ought to have heard his apologies.'

'But Pater can't fight one little bit,' Mullins repeated.

"Twasn't fighting. He just tried to murder every one.' Stalky described the affair, and when he left Mullins went off to take counsel with the Head, who, out of a cloud of blue smoke, told him that all would yet be well.

'Winton,' said he, 'is a little stiff in his moral joints. He'll get over that. If he asks you whether to-day's doings will count against him in his—'

'But you know it's important to him, sir. His people aren't—very well off,' said Mullins.

'That's why I'm taking all this trouble. You must reassure him, Pot. I have overcrowded him with new experiences. Oh, by the way, has his Cap come?'

'It came at dinner, sir.' Mullins laughed.

Sure enough, when he waked at tea-time, Winton proposed to take Mullins all through every one of his day's lapses from grace, and 'Do you think it will count against me?' said he.

'Don't you fuss so much about yourself and your silly career,' said Mullins. 'You're all right. And oh—here's your First Cap at last. Shove it up on the bracket and come on to tea.'

They met King on their way, stepping statelily and rubbing his hands. 'I have applied,' said he, 'for the services of an additional sub-prefect in Carton's unlamented absence. Your name, Winton, seems to have found favour with the powers that be, and—and all things considered— I am disposed to give my support to the nomination. You are therefore a quasi-lictor.'

'Then it didn't count against me,' Winton gasped as soon as they were out of hearing.

A Captain of Games can jest with a sub-prefect publicly.

'You utter ass!' said Mullins, and caught him by the back of his stiff neck and ran him down to the hall where the sub-prefects, who sit below the salt, made him welcome with the economical bloater-paste of mid-term.

***

King and little Hartopp were sparring in the Reverend John Gillett's study at 10 p.m.—classical versus modern as usual.

'Character—proportion—background,' snarled King. 'That is the essence of the Humanities.'

'Analects of Confucius,' little Hartopp answered,

'Time,' said the Reverend John behind the soda-water. 'You men oppress me. Hartopp, what did you say to Paddy in your dormitories tonight? Even you couldn't have overlooked his face.'

'But I did,' said Hartopp calmly. 'I wasn't even humorous about it, as some clerics might have been. I went straight through and said naught.'

'Poor Paddy! Now, for my part,' said King, 'and you know I am not lavish in my praises, I consider Winton a first-class type; absolutely first-class.'

'Ha-ardly,' said the Reverend John. 'First-class of the second class, I admit. The very best type of second class but'—he shook his head—'it should have been a rat. Pater'll never be anything more than a Colonel of Engineers.'

'What do you base that verdict on?' said King stiffly.

'He came to me after prayers—with all his conscience.'

'Poor old Pater. Was it the mouse?' said little Hartopp.

'That, and what he called his uncontrollable temper, and his responsibilities as sub-prefect.'

'And you?'

'If we had had what is vulgarly called a pi-jaw he'd have had hysterics. So I recommended a dose of Epsom salts. He'll take it, too—conscientiously. Don't eat me, King. Perhaps he'll be a K.C.B.'

Ten o'clock struck and the Army class boys in the further studies coming to their houses after an hour's extra work passed along the gravel path below. Some one was chanting, to the tune of 'White sand and grey sand,' Dis to minorem quod geris imperas. He stopped outside Mullins' study. They heard Mullins' window slide up and then Stalky's voice:

'Ah! Good-evening, Mullins, my barbarus tortor. We're the waits. We have come to inquire after the local Berserk. Is he doin' as well as can be expected in his new caree-ah?'

'Better than you will, in a sec, Stalky,' Mullins grunted.

''Glad of that. We thought he'd like to know that Paddy has been carried to the sick-house in ravin' delirium. They think it's concussion of the brain.'

'Why, he was all right at prayers,' Winton began earnestly, and they heard a laugh in the background as Mullins slammed down the window.

''Night, Regulus,' Stalky sang out, and the light footsteps went on.

'You see. It sticks. A little of it sticks among the barbarians,' said King.

'Amen,' said the Reverend John. 'Go to bed.'

A Translation

Horace, BK. V., Ode 3
"Regulus"-- A Diversity of Creatures

There are whose study is of smells,
And to attentive schools rehearse
How something mixed with something else
Makes something worse.

Some cultivate in broths impure
The clients of our body--these,
Increasing without Venus, cure,
Or cause, disease.

Others the heated wheel extol,
And all its offspring, whose concern
Is how to make it farthest roll
And fastest turn.

Me, much incurious if the hour
Present, or to be paid for, brings
Me to Brundusium by the power
Of wheels or wings;

Me, in whose breast no flame hath burned
Life-long, save that by Pindar lit,
Such lore leaves cold. I am not turned
Aside to it

More than when, sunk in thought profound
Of what the unaltering Gods require,
My steward (friend but slave) brings round
Logs for my fire.

Thoughts on Regulus

The years that Kipling spent at the United Services College formed the inspiration for a collection of stories entitled 'Stalky & Co.', first published in 1899 when he was 34. Enjoyed by many, criticized by others for their 'youthful brutality', anti-intellectualism and crude humour, these stories are also among his most enjoyed.

Eighteen years after' Stalky & Co.' was published, when the great European war was at its height, Kipling produced this final story in the series. Of a more thoughtful nature than the rest, it is called simply, 'Regulus' after the roman general of that name, a model of military honour and thus an exemplar to the young men England so badly needed. The inspiration for the tale came from the author's admiration of 'C----, my English and Classics Master, a rowing-man of splendid physique, and a scholar who lived in secret hope of translating Theocritus worthily ... I tried to give a pale rendering of his style when heated in a 'Stalky' tale, 'Regulus,' but I wish I could have presented him as he blazed forth once on the great Cleopatra Ode--the 27th of the Third Book.' ('Something of Myself')

Such was the gift that C--- gave to the young man that Kipling and a friend, Charles Graves were to write an imaginary Fifth Book of Horace. It was probably on the strength of this that the editors of Penguin's magnificent 'Horace in English' described the author as 'insufficiently recognised as one of our great Horation poets'.

Much ink has been spilled promoting and condemning the value of the Classics and sport in preparing England's youth for their role in life, and I do not intend to get involved in that controversy here. In a letter to a friend the older Kipling was to make this defence of Latin: '... every last thing I got out of the schools, came to me after - years after – the enforced study of two out of date authors one called Virgil and t'other Horace. I didn't understand 'em at the time. I firmly believed they constructed their sentences, same as Euclid did his problems, to annoy and defeat the likes of me: but I got the good of them, as I say, afterwards.'

MARY POSTGATE

[1915]

Of Miss Mary Postgate, Lady McCausland wrote that she was 'thoroughly conscientious, tidy, companionable, and ladylike. I am very sorry to part with her, and shall always be interested in her welfare.'

Miss Fowler engaged her on this recommendation, and to her surprise, for she had had experience of companions, found that it was true. Miss Fowler was nearer sixty than fifty at the time, but though she needed care she did not exhaust her attendant's vitality. On the contrary, she gave out, stimulatingly and with reminiscences. Her father had been a minor Court official in the days when the Great Exhibition of 1851 had just set its seal on Civilisation made perfect. Some of Miss Fowler's tales, none the less, were not always for the young. Mary was not young, and though her speech was as colourless as her eyes or her hair, she was never shocked. She listened unflinchingly to every one; said at the end, 'How interesting!' or 'How shocking!' as the case might be, and never again referred to it, for she prided herself on a trained mind, which 'did not dwell on these things.' She was, too, a treasure at domestic accounts, for which the village tradesmen, with their weekly books, loved her not. Otherwise she had no enemies; provoked no jealousy even among the plainest; neither gossip nor slander had ever been traced to her; she supplied the odd place at the Rector's or the Doctor's table at half an hour's notice; she was a sort of public aunt to very many small children of the village street, whose parents, while accepting everything, would have been swift to resent what they called 'patronage'; she served on the Village Nursing Committee as Miss Fowler's nominee when Miss

Fowler was crippled by rheumatoid arthritis, and came out of six months' fortnightly meetings equally respected by all the cliques.

And when Fate threw Miss Fowler's nephew, an unlovely orphan of eleven, on Miss Fowler's hands, Mary Postgate stood to her share of the business of education as practised in private and public schools. She checked printed clothes-lists, and unitemised bills of extras; wrote to Head and House masters, matrons, nurses and doctors, and grieved or rejoiced over half-term reports. Young Wyndham Fowler repaid her in his holidays by calling her 'Gatepost,' 'Postey,' or 'Packthread,' by thumping her between her narrow shoulders, or by chasing her bleating, round the garden, her large mouth open, her large nose high in air, at a stiff necked shamble very like a camel's. Later on he filled the house with clamour, argument, and harangues as to his personal needs, likes and dislikes, and the limitations of 'you women,' reducing Mary to tears of physical fatigue, or, when he chose to be humorous, of helpless laughter. At crises, which multiplied as he grew older, she was his ambassadress and his interpretress to Miss Fowler, who had no large sympathy with the young; a vote in his interest at the councils on his future; his sewing-woman, strictly accountable for mislaid boots and garments; always his butt and his slave.

And when he decided to become a solicitor, and had entered an office in London; when his greeting had changed from 'Hullo, Postey, you old beast,' to 'Mornin', Packthread,' there came a war which, unlike all wars that Mary could remember, did not stay decently outside England and in the newspapers, but intruded on the lives of people whom she knew. As she said to Miss Fowler, it was 'most vexatious.' It took the Rector's son who was going into business with his elder brother; it took the Colonel's nephew on the eve of fruit-farming in Canada; it took Mrs. Grant's son who, his mother said, was devoted to the ministry; and, very early indeed, it took Wynn Fowler, who announced on a postcard that he had joined the Flying Corps and wanted a cardigan waistcoat.

'He must go, and he must have the waistcoat,' said Miss Fowler. So Mary got the proper-sized needles and wool, while Miss Fowler told the men of her establishment—two gardeners and an odd man, aged sixty—that those who could join the Army had better do so. The gardeners left. Cheape, the odd man, stayed on, and was promoted to the gardener's cottage. The cook, scorning to be limited in luxuries, also left, after a spirited scene with Miss Fowler, and took the housemaid with her. Miss Fowler gazetted Nellie, Cheape's seventeen-year-old daughter, to the vacant post; Mrs. Cheape to the rank of cook, with occasional cleaning bouts; and the reduced establishment moved forward smoothly.

Wynn demanded an increase in his allowance. Miss Fowler, who always looked facts in the face, said, 'He must have it. The chances are he won't live long to draw it, and if three hundred makes him happy——'

Wynn was grateful, and came over, in his tight-buttoned uniform, to say so. His training centre was not thirty miles away, and his talk was so technical that it had to be explained by charts of the various types of machines. He gave Mary such a chart.

'And you'd better study it, Postey,' he said. 'You'll be seeing a lot of 'em soon.' So Mary studied the chart, but when Wynn next arrived to swell and exalt himself before his womenfolk, she failed badly in cross-examination, and he rated her as in the old days.

'You *look* more or less like a human being,' he said in his new Service voice. 'You *must* have had a brain at some time in your past. What have you done with it? Where d'you keep it? A sheep would know more than you do, Postey. You're lamentable. You are less use than an empty tin can, you dowey old cassowary.'

'I suppose that's how your superior officer talks to *you*?' said Miss Fowler from her chair.

'But Postey doesn't mind,' Wynn replied. 'Do you, Packthread?'

'Why? Was Wynn saying anything? I shall get this right next time you come,' she muttered, and knitted her pale brows again over the diagrams of Taubes, Farmans, and Zeppelins.

In a few weeks the mere land and sea battles which she read to Miss Fowler after breakfast passed her like idle breath. Her heart and her interest were high in the air with Wynn, who had finished 'rolling' (whatever that might be) and had gone on from a 'taxi' to a machine more or less his own. One morning it circled over their very chimneys, alighted on Vegg's Heath, almost outside the garden gate, and Wynn came in, blue with cold, shouting for food. He and she drew Miss Fowler's bath-chair, as they had often done, along the Heath foot-path to look at the biplane. Mary observed that 'it smelt very badly.'

'Postey, I believe you think with your nose,' said Lynn. 'I know you don't with your mind. Now, what type's that?'

'I'll go and get the chart,' said Mary.

'You're hopeless! You haven't the mental capacity of a white mouse,' he cried, and explained the dials and the sockets for bomb-dropping till it was time to mount and ride the wet clouds once more.

'Ah!' said Mary, as the stinking thing flared upward. 'Wait till our Flying Corps gets to work! Wynn says it's much safer than in the trenches.'

'I wonder,' said Miss Fowler. 'Tell Cheape to come and tow me home again.'

'It's all downhill. I can do it,' said Mary, 'if you put the brake on.' She laid her lean self against the pushing-bar and home they trundled.

'Now, be careful you aren't heated and catch a chill,' said overdressed Miss Fowler.

'Nothing makes me perspire,' said Mary. As she bumped the chair under the porch she straightened her long back. The exertion had given her a colour, and the wind had loosened a wisp of hair across her forehead. Miss Fowler glanced at her.

'What do you ever think of, Mary?' she demanded suddenly.

'Oh, Wynn says he wants another three pairs of stockings—as thick as we can make them.'

'Yes. But I mean the things that women think about. Here you are, more than forty—'

'Forty-four,' said truthful Mary.

'Well?'

'Well?' Mary offered Miss Fowler her shoulder as usual.

'And you've been with me ten years now.'

'Let's see,' said Mary. 'Wynn was eleven when he came. He's twenty now, and I came two years before that. It must be eleven.'

'Eleven! And you've never told me anything that matters in all that while. Looking back, it seems to me that *I*'ve done all the talking.'

'I'm afraid I'm not much of a conversationalist. As Wynn says, I haven't the mind. Let me take your hat.'

Miss Fowler, moving stiffly from the hip, stamped her rubber-tipped stick on the tiled hall floor. 'Mary, aren't you *anything* except a companion? Would you *ever* have been anything except a companion?'

Mary hung up the garden hat on its proper peg. 'No,' she said after consideration. 'I don't imagine I ever should. But I've no imagination, I'm afraid.'

She fetched Miss Fowler her eleven-o'clock glass of Contrexeville.

That was the wet December when it rained six inches to the month, and the women went abroad as little as might be. Wynn's flying chariot visited them several times, and for two mornings (he had warned her by postcard) Mary heard the thresh of his propellers at dawn. The second time she ran to the window, and stared at the whitening sky. A little blur passed overhead. She lifted her lean arms towards it.

That evening at six o'clock there came an announcement in an official envelope that Second Lieutenant W. Fowler had been killed during a trial flight. Death was instantaneous. She read it and carried it to Miss Fowler.

'I never expected anything else,' said Miss Fowler; 'but I'm sorry it happened before he had done anything.'

The room was whirling round Mary Postgate, but she found herself quite steady in the midst of it.

'Yes,' she said. 'It's a great pity he didn't die in action after he had killed somebody.'

'He was killed instantly. That's one comfort,' Miss Fowler went on.

'But Wynn says the shock of a fall kills a man at once—whatever happens to the tanks,' quoted Mary.

The room was coming to rest now. She heard Miss Fowler say impatiently, 'But why can't we cry, Mary?' and herself replying, 'There's nothing to cry for. He has done his duty as much as Mrs. Grant's son did.'

'And when he died, *she* came and cried all the morning,' said Miss Fowler. 'This only makes me feel tired—terribly tired. Will you help me to bed, please, Mary?—And I think I'd like the hot-water bottle.'

So Mary helped her and sat beside, talking of Wynn in his riotous youth.

'I believe,' said Miss Fowler suddenly, 'that old people and young people slip from under a stroke like this. The middle-aged feel it most.'

'I expect that's true,' said Mary, rising. 'I'm going to put away the things in his room now. Shall we wear mourning?'

'Certainly not,' said Miss Fowler. 'Except, of course, at the funeral. I can't go. You will. I want you to arrange about his being buried here. What a blessing it didn't happen at Salisbury!'

Every one, from the Authorities of the Flying Corps to the Rector, was most kind and sympathetic. Mary found herself for the moment in a world where bodies were in the habit of being despatched by all sorts of conveyances to all sorts of places. And at the funeral two young men in buttoned-up uniforms stood beside the grave and spoke to her afterwards.

'You're Miss Postgate, aren't you?' said one.

'Fowler told me about you. He was a good chap—a first-class fellow—a great loss.'

'Great loss!' growled his companion. 'We're all awfully sorry.'

'How high did he fall from?' Mary whispered.

'Pretty nearly four thousand feet, I should think, didn't he? You were up that day, Monkey?'

'All of that,' the other child replied. 'My bar made three thousand, and I wasn't as high as him by a lot.'

'Then *that's* all right,' said Mary. 'Thank you very much.'

They moved away as Mrs. Grant flung herself weeping on Mary's flat chest, under the lych-gate, and cried, '*I* know how it feels! *I* know how it feels!'

'But both his parents are dead,' Mary returned, as she fended her off. 'Perhaps they've all met by now,' she added vaguely as she escaped towards the coach.

'I've thought of that too,' wailed Mrs. Grant; 'but then he'll be practically a stranger to them. Quite embarrassing!'

Mary faithfully reported every detail of the ceremony to Miss Fowler, who, when she described Mrs. Grant's outburst, laughed aloud.

'Oh, how Wynn would have enjoyed it! He was always utterly unreliable at funerals. D'you remember——' And they talked of him again, each piecing out the other's gaps. 'And now,' said Miss Fowler, 'we'll pull up the blinds and we'll have a general tidy. That always does us good. Have you seen to Wynn's things?'

'Everything—since he first came,' said Mary. 'He was never destructive—even with his toys.'

They faced that neat room.

'It can't be natural not to cry,' Mary said at last. 'I'm *so* afraid you'll have a reaction.'

'As I told you, we old people slip from under the stroke. It's you I'm afraid for. Have you cried yet?'

'I can't. It only makes me angry with the Germans.'

'That's sheer waste of vitality,' said Miss Fowler. 'We must live till the war's finished.' She opened a full wardrobe. 'Now, I've been thinking things over. This is my plan. All his civilian clothes can be given away— Belgian refugees, and so on.'

Mary nodded. 'Boots, collars, and gloves?'

'Yes. We don't need to keep anything except his cap and belt.'

'They came back yesterday with his Flying Corps clothes'—Mary pointed to a roll on the little iron bed.

'Ah, but keep his Service things. Some one may be glad of them later. Do you remember his sizes?'

'Five feet eight and a half; thirty-six inches round the chest. But he told me he's just put on an inch and a half. I'll mark it on a label and tie it on his sleeping-bag.'

'So that disposes of *that*,' said Miss Fowler, tapping the palm of one hand with the ringed third finger of the other. 'What waste it all is! We'll get his old school trunk to-morrow and pack his civilian clothes.'

'And the rest?' said Mary. 'His books and pictures and the games and the toys—and—and the rest?'

'My plan is to burn every single thing,' said Miss Fowler. 'Then we shall know where they are and no one can handle them afterwards. What do you think?'

'I think that would be much the best,' said Mary. 'But there's such a lot of them.'

'We'll burn them in the destructor,' said Miss Fowler.

This was an open-air furnace for the consumption of refuse; a little circular four-foot tower of pierced brick over an iron grating. Miss Fowler had noticed the design in a gardening journal years ago, and had had it built at the bottom of the garden. It suited her tidy soul, for it saved unsightly rubbish-heaps, and the ashes lightened the stiff clay soil.

Mary considered for a moment, saw her way clear, and nodded again. They spent the evening putting away well-remembered civilian suits, underclothes that Mary had marked, and the regiments of very gaudy socks and ties. A second trunk was needed, and, after that, a little packing-case, and it was late next day when Cheape and the local carrier lifted them to the cart. The Rector luckily knew of a friend's son, about five feet eight and a half inches high, to whom a complete Flying Corps outfit would be most acceptable, and sent his gardener's son down with a barrow to take delivery of it. The cap was hung up in Miss Fowler's bedroom, the belt in Miss Postgate's; for, as Miss Fowler said, they had no desire to make tea-party talk of them.

'That disposes of *that*,' said Miss Fowler. 'I'll leave the rest to you, Mary. I can't run up and down the garden. You'd better take the big clothes-basket and get Nellie to help you.'

'I shall take the wheel-barrow and do it myself,' said Mary, and for once in her life closed her mouth.

Miss Fowler, in moments of irritation, had called Mary deadly methodical. She put on her oldest waterproof and gardening-hat and her ever-slipping goloshes, for the weather was on the edge of more rain. She gathered fire-lighters from the kitchen, a half-scuttle of coals, and a faggot of brushwood. These she wheeled in the barrow down the mossed paths to the dank little laurel shrubbery where the destructor stood under the drip of three oaks. She climbed the wire fence into the Rector's glebe just behind, and from his tenant's rick pulled two large armfuls of good hay, which she spread neatly on the fire-bars. Next, journey by journey, passing Miss Fowler's white face at the morning-room window each time, she brought down in the towel-covered clothes-basket, on the wheelbarrow, thumbed and used Hentys, Marryats, Levers, Stevensons, Baroness Orczys, Garvices, schoolbooks, and atlases, unrelated piles of the *Motor Cyclist*, the *Light Car*, and catalogues of Olympia Exhibitions; the remnants of a fleet of sailing-ships from nine-penny cutters to a three-guinea yacht; a prep. school dressing-gown; bats from three-and-sixpence to twenty-four shillings; cricket and tennis balls; disintegrated steam and clockwork locomotives with their twisted rails; a grey and red tin model of a submarine; a dumb gramophone and cracked records; golf-clubs that had to be broken across the knee, like his walking-sticks, and an assegai; photographs of private and public school cricket and football elevens, and his O.T.C. on the line of march; kodaks, and film-rolls; some pewters, and one real silver cup, for boxing competitions and junior Hurdles; sheaves of school photographs; Miss Fowler's photograph; her own which he had borne off in fun and (good care she took not to ask!) had never returned; a playbox with a secret drawer; a load of flannels, belts, and jerseys, and a pair of spiked shoes unearthed in the attic; a packet of all the letters that Miss Fowler and she had ever written to him, kept for some absurd reason through all these years; a five-day attempt at a diary; framed pictures of racing motors in full Brooklands career, and load upon load of undistinguishable wreckage of tool-boxes, rabbit-hutches, electric batteries, tin soldiers, fret-saw outfits, and jig-saw puzzles.

Miss Fowler at the window watched her come and go, and said to herself, 'Mary's an old woman. I never realised it before.'

After lunch she recommended her to rest.

'I'm not in the least tired,' said Mary. 'I've got it all arranged. I'm going to the village at two o'clock for some paraffin. Nellie hasn't enough, and the walk will do me good.'

She made one last quest round the house before she started, and found that she had overlooked nothing. It began to mist as soon as she had skirted Vegg's Heath, where Wynn used to descend—it seemed to her that she could almost hear the beat of his propellers overhead, but there was nothing to see. She hoisted her umbrella and lunged into the blind wet till she had reached the shelter of the empty village. As she came out of Mr. Kidd's shop with a bottle full of paraffin in her string shopping-bag, she met Nurse Eden, the village nurse, and fell into talk with her, as usual, about the village children. They were just parting opposite the 'Royal Oak,' when a gun, they fancied, was fired immediately behind the house. It was followed by a child's shriek dying into a wail.

'Accident!' said Nurse Eden promptly, and dashed through the empty bar, followed by Mary. They found Mrs. Gerritt, the publican's wife, who could only gasp and point to the yard, where a little cart-lodge was sliding sideways amid a clatter of tiles. Nurse Eden snatched up a sheet drying before the fire, ran out, lifted something from the ground, and flung the sheet round it. The sheet turned scarlet and half her uniform too, as she bore the load into the kitchen. It was little Edna Gerritt, aged nine, whom Mary had known since her perambulator days.

'Am I hurted bad?' Edna asked, and died between Nurse Eden's dripping hands. The sheet fell aside and for an instant, before she could shut her eyes, Mary saw the ripped and shredded body.

'It's a wonder she spoke at all,' said Nurse Eden. 'What in God's name was it?'

'A bomb,' said Mary.

'One o' the Zeppelins?'

'No. An aeroplane. I thought I heard it on the Heath, but I fancied it was one of ours. It must have shut of its engines as it came down. That's why we didn't notice it.'

'The filthy pigs!' said Nurse Eden, all white and shaken. 'See the pickle I'm in! Go and tell Dr. Hennis, Miss Postgate.' Nurse looked at the mother, who had dropped face down on the floor. 'She's only in a fit. Turn her over.'

Mary heaved Mrs. Gerritt right side up, and hurried off for the doctor. When she told her tale, he asked her to sit down in the surgery till he got her something.

'But I don't need it, I assure you,' said she. 'I don't think it would be wise to tell Miss Fowler about it, do you? Her heart is so irritable in this weather.'

Dr. Hennis looked at her admiringly as he packed up his bag.

'No. Don't tell anybody till we're sure,' he said, and hastened to the 'Royal Oak,' while Mary went on with the paraffin. The village behind her was as quiet as usual, for the news had not yet spread. She frowned a little to herself, her large nostrils expanded uglily, and from time to time she muttered a phrase which Wynn, who never restrained himself before his women-folk, had applied to the enemy. 'Bloody pagans! They *are* bloody pagans. But,' she continued, falling back on the teaching that had made her what she was, 'one mustn't let one's mind dwell on these things.'

Before she reached the house Dr. Hennis, who was also a special constable, overtook her in his car.

'Oh, Miss Postgate,' he said, 'I wanted to tell you that that accident at the "Royal Oak" was due to Gerritt's stable tumbling down. It's been dangerous for a long time. It ought to have been condemned.'

'I thought I heard an explosion too,' said Mary.

'You might have been misled by the beams snapping. I've been looking at 'em. They were dry-rotted through and through. Of course, as they broke, they would make a noise just like a gun.'

'Yes?' said Mary politely.

'Poor little Edna was playing underneath it,' he went on, still holding her with his eyes, 'and that and the tiles cut her to pieces, you see?'

'I saw it,' said Mary, shaking her head. 'I heard it too.'

'Well, we cannot be sure.' Dr. Hennis changed his tone completely. 'I know both you and Nurse Eden (I've been speaking to her) are perfectly trustworthy, and I can rely on you not to say anything—yet at least. It is no good to stir up people unless——'

'Oh, I never do—anyhow,' said Mary, and Dr. Hennis went on to the county town.

After all, she told herself, it might, just possibly, have been the collapse of the old stable that had done all those things to poor little Edna. She was sorry she had even hinted at other things, but Nurse Eden was discretion itself. By the time she reached home the affair seemed increasingly remote by its very monstrosity. As she came in, Miss Fowler told her that a couple of aeroplanes had passed half an hour ago.

'I thought I heard them,' she replied, 'I'm going down to the garden now. I've got the paraffin.'

'Yes, but—what *have* you got on your boots? They're soaking wet. Change them at once.'

Not only did Mary obey but she wrapped the boots in a newspaper, and put them into the string bag with the bottle. So, armed with the longest kitchen poker, she left.

'It's raining again,' was Miss Fowler's last word, 'but—I know you won't be happy till that's disposed of.'

'It won't take long. I've got everything down there, and I've put the lid on the destructor to keep the wet out.'

The shrubbery was filling with twilight by the time she had completed her arrangements and sprinkled the sacrificial oil. As she lit the match that would burn her heart to ashes, she heard a groan or a grunt behind the dense Portugal laurels.

'Cheape?' she called impatiently, but Cheape, with his ancient lumbago, in his comfortable cottage would be the last man to profane the sanctuary. 'Sheep,' she concluded, and threw in the fusee. The pyre went up in a roar, and the immediate flame hastened night around her.

'How Wynn would have loved this!' she thought, stepping back from the blaze.

By its light she saw, half hidden behind a laurel not five paces away, a bareheaded man sitting very stiffly at the foot of one of the oaks. A broken branch lay across his lap—one booted leg protruding from beneath it. His head moved ceaselessly from side to side, but his body was as still as the tree's trunk. He was dressed—she moved sideways to look more closely—in a uniform something like Wynn's, with a flap buttoned across the chest. For an instant, she had some idea that it might be one of the young flying men she had met at the funeral. But their heads were dark and glossy. This man's was as pale as a baby's, and so closely cropped that she could see the disgusting pinky skin beneath. His lips moved.

'What do you say?' Mary moved towards him and stooped.

'Laty! Laty! Laty!' he muttered, while his hands picked at the dead wet leaves. There was no doubt as to his nationality. It made her so angry that she strode back to the destructor, though it was still too hot to use the poker there. Wynn's books seemed to be catching well. She looked up at the oak behind the man; several of the light upper and two or three rotten lower branches had broken and scattered their rubbish on the shrubbery path. On the lowest fork a helmet with dependent strings, showed like a bird's-nest in the light of along-tongued flame. Evidently this person had fallen through the tree. Wynn had told her that it was quite possible for people to fall out of aeroplanes. Wynn told her too, that trees were useful things to break an aviator's fall, but in this case the aviator must have been broken or he would have moved from his queer position. He seemed helpless except for his horrible rolling head. On the other hand, she could see a pistol case at his belt—and Mary loathed pistols. Months ago, after reading certain Belgian reports together, she and Miss Fowler had had dealings with one—a huge revolver with flat-nosed bullets, which latter, Wynn said, were forbidden by the rules of war to be used against civilised enemies. 'They're good enough for us,' Miss Fowler had replied. 'Show Mary how it works.' And Wynn, laughing at the mere possibility of any such need, had led the craven winking Mary into the Rector's disused quarry, and had shown her how to fire the terrible machine. It lay now in the top-left-hand drawer of her toilet-table—a memento not included in the burning. Wynn would be pleased to see how she was not afraid.

She slipped up to the house to get it. When she came through the rain, the eyes in the head were alive with expectation. The mouth even tried to smile. But at sight of the revolver its corners went down just like Edna Gerritt's. A tear trickled from one eye, and the head rolled from shoulder to shoulder as though trying to point out something.

'Cassée. Tout cassée,' it whimpered.

'What do you say?' said Mary disgustedly, keeping well to one side, though only the head moved.

'Cassée,' it repeated. 'Che me rends. Le médicin! Toctor!'

'Nein! said she, bringing all her small German to bear with the big pistol. 'Ich haben der todt Kinder gesehn.'

The head was still. Mary's hand dropped. She had been careful to keep her finger off the trigger for fear of accidents. After a few moments' waiting, she returned to the destructor, where the flames were falling, and churned up Wynn's charring books with the poker. Again the head groaned for the doctor.

'Stop that! 'said Mary, and stamped her foot. 'Stop that, you bloody pagan!'

The words came quite smoothly and naturally. They were Wynn's own words, and Wynn was a gentleman who for no consideration on earth would have torn little Edna into those vividly coloured strips and strings. But this thing hunched under the oak-tree had done that thing. It was no question of reading horrors out of newspapers to Miss Fowler. Mary had seen it with her own eyes on the 'Royal Oak' kitchen table. She must not allow her mind to dwell upon it. Now Wynn was dead, and everything connected with him was lumping and rustling and tinkling under her busy poker into red black dust and grey leaves of ash. The thing beneath the oak would die too. Mary had seen death more than once. She came of a family that had a knack of dying under, as she told Miss Fowler, 'most distressing circumstances.' She would stay where she was till she was entirely satisfied that It was dead—dead as dear papa in the late 'eighties; aunt Mary in 'eighty-nine; mamma in 'ninety-one; cousin Dick in 'ninety-five; Lady McCausland's housemaid in 'ninety-nine; Lady McCausland's sister in nineteen hundred and one; Wynn buried five days ago; and Edna Gerritt still waiting for decent earth to hide her. As she thought—her underlip caught up by one faded canine, brows knit and nostrils wide—she wielded the poker with lunges that jarred the grating at the bottom, and careful scrapes round the brickwork above. She looked at her wrist-watch. It was getting on to half-past four, and the rain was coming down in earnest. Tea would be at five. If It did not die before that time, she would be soaked and would have to change. Meantime, and this occupied her, Wynn's things were burning well in spite of the hissing wet, though now and again a book-back with a quite distinguishable title would be heaved up out of the mass. The exercise of stoking had given her a glow which seemed to reach to the marrow of her bones. She hummed—Mary never had a voice—to herself. She had never believed in all those advanced views— though Miss Fowler herself leaned a little that way—of woman's work in the world; but now she saw there was much to be said for them. This, for instance, was *her* work—work which no man, least of all Dr. Hennis, would ever have done. A man, at such a crisis, would be what Wynn called a 'sportsman'; would leave everything to fetch help, and would certainly bring It into the house. Now a woman's business was to make a happy home for—for a husband and children. Failing these—it was not a thing one should allow ones mind to dwell upon—but—

'Stop it!' Mary cried once more across the shadows. 'Nein, I tell you! Ich haben der todt Kinder gesehn.'

But it was a fact. A woman who had missed these things could still be useful—more useful than a man in certain respects. She thumped like a pavior through the settling ashes at the secret thrill of it. The rain was damping the fire, but she could feel—it was too dark to see—that her work was done. There was a dull red glow at the bottom of the destructor, not enough to char the wooden lid if she slipped it half over against the driving wet. This arranged, she leaned on the poker and waited, while an increasing rapture laid hold on her. She ceased to think. She gave herself up to feel. Her long pleasure was broken by a sound that she had waited for in agony several times in her life. She leaned forward and listened, smiling. There could be no mistake. She closed her eyes and drank it in, Once it ceased abruptly.

'Go on,' she murmured, half aloud. 'That isn't the end.'

Then the end came very distinctly in a lull between two rain-gusts. Mary Postgate drew her breath short between her teeth and shivered from head to foot. 'That's all right,' said she contentedly, and went up to the house, where she scandalised the whole routine by taking a luxurious hot bath before tea, and came down looking, as Miss Fowler said when she saw her lying all relaxed on the other sofa, 'quite handsome!'

The Beginnings

It was not part of their blood,
It came to them very late
With long arrears to make good,
When the English began to hate.

They were not easily moved,
They were icy willing to wait
Till every count should be proved,
Ere the English began to hate.

Their voices were even and low,
Their eyes were level and straight.
There was neither sign nor show,
When the English began to hate.

It was not preached to the crowd,
It was not taught by the State.
No man spoke it aloud,
When the English began to hate.

It was not suddenly bred,
It will not swiftly abate,
Through the chill years ahead,
When Time shall count from the date
That the English began to hate.

Thoughts on Mary Postgate

Like 'They' and 'The Gardener', 'Mary Postgate' is a tale of unbearable loss. All three were written by a man who loved his children above all things, who had already lost one and was justifiably fearful of losing another. It shocks by reason of a single act of cruelty, or to be precise a cruel withholding of mercy. At the same time it is a bafflingly crafted mystery. Is it a succèss fou or a colossal failure?

'Mary Postgate' has to be understood in the context of its time, namely the first year of 'the great war for civilization' when stories abounded of German ill treatment of civilians in occupied Belgium, which we now know to have a basis in fact. Some have claimed that these were prompted by the invader's policy of 'frightfulness' (referred to in England by the supposed German word, 'Schrecklichkeit'), though nervous soldiers could be disposed to interpret even the slightest signs of civilian resentment as the action of francs tireurs, or partisans. What is clear is that the German reaction to the perceived resistance of civilians was swift and brutal to an extent that could never be justified. Kipling saw this as a feature of the German character so deep seated as to amount to a threat to the European civilization that it was Britain's duty to protect.

'Mary Postgate' was first collected in a volume entitled, 'A Diversity of Creatures' in which it was preceded by a tale about a German Hausfrau scrubbing the floor of her Berlin apartment to remove what she believed to be the blood of children killed by soldiers like her son. It was followed by a poem which commemorates the time 'When the English began to hate'. So is 'Mary Postgate' just a tale of anti-Hun venom (which Kipling certainly possessed), or is there more?

The story is full of enigmas. First, there is the mystery of the village girl; was her death the result of an aerial bomb or, as Mary was assured by the doctor, the collapse of a rotting stable? And, was the injured airman really a German? It is easy to overlook that he never spoke in that language, only in French and halting English. (The only person to use even poor German was Mary.) Could the 'aviator' actually have been a French ally?

But perhaps we should ask ourselves an even more fundamental question: did 'the aviator' actually exist outside of Mary's fevered mind? If he was real what would the gardener have thought when he next came to tidy up the shrubbery? Respected commentators have taken different positions, but the present editor is inclined to think that from the moment that Mary returned to the garden, paraffin can in hand, until the time she left the dying fire the events described took place entirely within her head. What is the case for this view?

Mary is at first painted as a bland mousy creature incapable of imagination - 'nothing makes me perspire'. This seems to be born out by her curiously cold and detached reaction to Wynn's death. 'It's a great pity he didn't die in action after he had killed somebody.' Our first hint that she is capable of deeper emotions is when on the day of the boy's death she hears 'the thresh of his propellers at dawn' and runs to the window only to see 'a little blur (passing) overhead'. In an age which shunned the undue expression of grief, 'She lift[ed] her lean arms towards it' in an obvious gesture of yearning. But that evening when she learns of Wynn's death her only outward reaction is concern about what to wear at the funeral.

Days later, only a short time after having witnessed the death of a village child, Mary stands in her employer's garden alone in the pouring rain and unable to grieve. Is it not likely that in this state she conjured up an imaginary act of revenge upon a representative of the race she had decided was responsible for so much cruelty? Her actions and emotions thereafter, as described by the narrator, are best explained as an acting out of the sexual act she had so long denied herself. (Consider the repeated references to the poker.) The story's last sentence underlines the point by describing how after the incident in the garden 'she scandalized the whole routine by taking a luxurious hot bath before tea, and came down looking, as Miss Fowler said when she saw her lying all relaxed on the other sofa, 'quite handsome!''

In my view 'Mary Postgate' is not a story of hatred leading to sadistic pleasure, but a study of the pathology of a sexually repressed woman fragile from bereavement and horrified by two recent brushes with death. In her imagined withholding of mercy from a representative, albeit imaginary, *of the hated perpetrators of cruelty she discovers a release both from her sexual frustration and from the feelings generated by the death of the boy she had secretly adored.*

As a footnote, few readers of this story will be unaffected by the list, so poignantly evocative of its time, of the dead lad's effects awaiting the fire. To what extent, one wonders, did the author draw upon the contents of his own son's room?

FRIENDLY BROOK

The valley was so choked with fog that one could scarcely see a cow's length across a field. Every blade, twig, bracken-frond, and hoof-print carried water, and the air was filled with the noise of rushing ditches and field-drains, all delivering to the brook below. A week's November rain on water-logged land had gorged her to full flood, and she proclaimed it aloud.

Two men in sackcloth aprons were considering an untrimmed hedge that ran down the hillside and disappeared into mist beside those roarings. They stood back and took stock of the neglected growth, tapped an elbow of hedge-oak here, a mossed beech-stub there, swayed a stooled ash back and forth, and looked at each other.

'I reckon she's about two rod thick,' said Jabez the younger, 'an' she hasn't felt iron since—when has she, Jesse?'

'Call it twenty-five year, Jabez, an' you won't be far out.'

'Umm!' Jabez rubbed his wet handbill on his wetter coat-sleeve. 'She ain't a hedge. She's all manner o' trees. We'll just about have to—' He paused, as professional etiquette required.

'Just about have to side her up an' see what she'll bear. But hadn't we best—?' Jesse paused in his turn; both men being artists and equals.

'Get some kind o' line to go by.' Jabez ranged up and down till he found a thinner place, and with clean snicks of the handbill revealed the original face of the fence. Jesse took over the dripping stuff as it fell forward, and, with a grasp and a kick, made it to lie orderly on the bank till it should be faggoted.

By noon a length of unclean jungle had turned itself into a cattle-proof barrier, tufted here and there with little plumes of the sacred holly which no woodman touches without orders.

'Now we've a witness-board to go by! 'said Jesse at last.

'She won't be as easy as this all along,' Jabez answered. 'She'll need plenty stakes and binders when we come to the brook.'

'Well, ain't we plenty?' Jesse pointed to the ragged perspective ahead of them that plunged downhill into the fog. 'I lay there's a cord an' a half o' firewood, let alone faggots, 'fore we get anywheres anigh the brook.'

'The brook's got up a piece since morning,' said Jabez. 'Sounds like's if she was over Wickenden's door-stones.'

Jesse listened, too. There was a growl in the brook's roar as though she worried something hard.

'Yes. She's over Wickenden's door-stones,' he replied. 'Now she'll flood acrost Alder Bay an' that'll ease her.'

'She won't ease Jim Wickenden's hay none if she do,' Jabez grunted. 'I told Jim he'd set that liddle hay-stack o' his too low down in the medder. I *told* him so when he was drawin' the bottom for it.'

'I told him so, too,' said Jesse. 'I told him 'fore ever you did. I told him when the County Council tarred the roads up along.' He pointed up-hill, where unseen automobiles and road-engines droned past continually. 'A tarred road, she shoots every drop o' water into a valley same's a slate roof. 'Tisn't as 'twas in the old days, when the waters soaked in and soaked out in the way o' nature. It rooshes off they tarred roads all of a lump, and naturally every drop is bound to descend into the valley. And there's tar roads both two sides this valley for ten mile. That's what

I told Jim Wickenden when they tarred the roads last year. But he's a valley-man. He don't hardly ever journey up-hill.'

'What did he say when you told him that?' Jabez demanded, with a little change of voice.

'Why? What did he say to you when *you* told him?' was the answer.

'What he said to you, I reckon, Jesse.'

Then, you don't need me to say it over again, Jabez.,

'Well, let be how 'twill, what was he gettin' *after* when he said what he said to me? 'Jabez insisted.

'I dunno; unless you tell me what manner o' words he said to *you*.'

Jabez drew back from the hedge—all hedges are nests of treachery and eavesdropping—and moved to an open cattle-lodge in the centre of the field.

'No need to go ferretin' around,' said Jesse. 'None can't see us here 'fore we see them.'

'What was Jim Wickenden gettin' at when I said he'd set his stack too near anigh the brook?' Jabez dropped his voice. 'He was in his mind.'

'He ain't never been out of it yet to my knowledge,' Jesse drawled, and uncorked his tea-bottle.

'But then Jim says: "I ain't goin' to shift my stack a yard," he says. "The Brook's been good friends to me, and if she be minded," he says, "to take a snatch at my hay, *I* ain't settin' out to withstand her." That's what Jim Wickenden says to me last—last June-end 'twas,' said Jabez.

'Nor he hasn't shifted his stack, neither,' Jesse replied. 'An' if there's more rain, the brook she'll shift it for him.'

'No need tell *me*! But I want to know what Jim was gettin' *at*?'

Jabez opened his clasp-knife very deliberately; Jesse as carefully opened his. They unfolded the newspapers that wrapped their dinners, coiled away and pocketed the string that bound the packages, and sat down on the edge of the lodge manger. The rain began to fall again through the fog, and the brook's voice rose.

***

'But I always allowed Mary was his lawful child, like,' said Jabez, after Jesse had spoken for a while.

"Tain't so. . . . Jim Wickenden's woman she never made nothing. She come out o' Lewes with her stockin's round her heels, an' she never made nor mended aught till she died. *He* had to light fire an' get breakfast every mornin' except Sundays, while she sowed it abed. Then she took an' died, sixteen, seventeen, year back; but she never had no childern.'

'They was valley-folk,' said Jabez apologetically. 'I'd no call to go in among 'em, but I always allowed Mary——'

'No. Mary come out o' one o' those Lunnon Childern Societies. After his woman died, Jim got his mother back from his sister over to Peasmarsh, which she'd gone to house with when Jim married. His mother kept house for Jim after his woman died. They do say 'twas his mother led him on toward adoptin' of Mary—to furnish out the house with a child, like, and to keep him off of gettin' a noo woman. He mostly done what his mother contrived. 'Cardenly, twixt 'em, they asked for a child from one o' those Lunnon societies—same as it might ha' been these Barnardo children—an' Mary was sent down to 'em, in a candle-box, I've heard.'

'Then Mary is chance-born. I never knowed that,' said Jabez. 'Yet I must ha' heard it some time or other . . .'

'No. She ain't. 'Twould ha' been better for some folk if she had been. She come to Jim in a candle-box with all the proper papers—lawful child o' some couple in Lunnon somewheres—mother dead, father drinkin'. *And* there was that Lunnon society's five shillin's a week for her. Jim's mother she wouldn't despise week-end money, but I never heard Jim was much of a muck-grubber. Let be how 'twill, they two mothered up Mary no bounds, till it looked at last like they'd forgot she wasn't their own flesh an' blood. Yes, I reckon they forgot Mary wasn't their'n by rights.'

'That's no new thing,' said Jabez. 'There's more'n one or two in this parish wouldn't surrender back their Bernarders. You ask Mark Copley an' his woman an' that Bernarder cripple-babe o' theirs.'

'Maybe they need the five shillin',' Jesse suggested.

'It's handy,' said Jabez. 'But the child's more. "Dada" he says, an' "Mumma" he says, with his great rollin' head-piece all hurdled up in that iron collar. *He* won't live long—his backbone's rotten, like. But they Copleys do just about set store by him—five bob or no five bob.'

'Same way with Jim an' his mother,' Jesse went on. 'There was talk betwixt 'em after a few years o' not takin' any more week-end money for Mary; but let alone *she* never passed a farden in the mire 'thout longin's, Jim didn't care, like, to push himself forward into the Society's remembrance. So naun came of it. The week-end money would ha' made no odds to Jim—not after his uncle willed him they four cottages at Eastbourne *an'* money in the bank.'

'That was true, too, then? I heard something in a scadderin' word-o'-mouth way,' said Jabez.

'I'll answer for the house property, because Jim he reequested my signed name at the foot o' some papers concernin' it. Regardin' the money in the bank, he nature-ally wouldn't like such things talked about all round the parish, so he took strangers for witnesses.'

'Then 'twill make Mary worth seekin' after?'

'She'll need it. Her Maker ain't done much for her outside nor yet in.'

'That ain't no odds.' Jabez shook his head till the water showered off his hat-brim. 'If Mary has money, she'll be wed before any likely pore maid. She's cause to be grateful to Jim.'

'She hides it middlin' close, then,' said Jesse. 'It don't sometimes look to me as if Mary has her natural rightful feelin's. She don't put on an apron o' Mondays 'thout being druv to it—in the kitchen *or* the hen-house. She's studyin' to be a school-teacher. She'll make a beauty! I never knowed her show any sort o' kindness to nobody—not even when Jim's mother was took dumb. No! 'Twadn't no stroke. It stifled the old lady in the throat here. First she couldn't shape her words no shape; then she clucked, like, an' lastly she couldn't more than suck down spoon-meat an' hold her peace. Jim took her to Doctor Harding, an' Harding he bundled her off to Brighton Hospital on a ticket, but they couldn't make no stay to her afflictions there; and she was bundled off to Lunnon, an' they lit a great old lamp inside her, and Jim told me they couldn't make out nothing in no sort there; and, along o' one thing an' another, an' all their spyin's and pryin's, she come back a hem sight worse than when she started. Jim said he'd have no more hospitalizin', so he give her a slate, which she tied to her waist-string, and what she was minded to say she writ on it.'

'Now, I never knowed that! But they're valley—folk;' Jabez repeated.

''Twadn't particular noticeable, for she wasn't a talkin' woman any time o' her days. Mary had all three's tongue . . . . Well, then, two years this summer, come what I'm tellin' you. Mary's Lunnon father, which they'd put clean out o' their minds, arrived down from Lunnon with the law on his side, sayin' he'd take his daughter back to Lunnon, after all. I was working for Mus' Dockett at Pounds Farm that summer, but I was obligin' Jim that evenin' muckin' out his pig-pen. I seed a stranger come traipsin' over the bridge agin' Wickenden's door-stones. 'Twadn't the new County Council bridge with the handrail. They hadn't given it in for a public right o' way then. 'Twas just a bit o' lathy old plank which Jim had throwed acrost the brook for his own conveniences. The man wasn't drunk—only a little concerned in liquor, like—an' his back was a mask where he'd slipped in the muck comin' along. He went up the bricks past Jim's mother, which was feedin' the ducks, an' set himself down at the table inside—Jim was just changin' his socks—an' the man let Jim know all his rights and aims regardin' Mary. Then there just about *was* a hurly-bulloo? Jim's fust mind was to pitch him forth, but he'd done that once in his young days, and got six months up to Lewes jail along o' the man fallin' on his head. So he swallowed his spittle an' let him talk. The law about Mary *was* on the man's side from fust to last, for he showed us all the papers. Then Mary come downstairs—she'd been studyin' for an examination—an' the man tells her who he was, an' she says he had ought to have took proper care of his own flesh and blood while he had it by him, an' not to think he could ree-claim it when it suited. He says somethin' or other, but she looks him up an' down, front an' backwent, an' she just tongues him scadderin' out o' doors, and he went away stuffin' all the papers back into his hat, talkin' most abusefully. Then she come back an' freed her mind against Jim an' his mother for not havin' warned her of her upbringin's, which it come out she hadn't ever been told. They didn't say naun to her. They never did. *I*'d ha' packed her off with any man that would ha' took her—an' God's pity on him!'

'Umm! 'said Jabez, and sucked his pipe.

'So then, that was the beginnin'. The man come back again next week or so, an' he catched Jim alone, 'thout his mother this time, an' he fair bea-zled him with his papers an' his talk—for the law *was* on his side—till Jim went down into his money-purse an' give him ten shillings hush-money—he told me—to withdraw away for a bit an' leave Mary with 'em.'

'But that's no way to get rid o' man or woman,' Jabez said.

'No more 'tis. I told Jim so. "What can I do?" Jim says.—"The law's *with* the man. I walk about daytimes thinkin' o' it till I sweats my under-clothes wringin', an' I lie abed nights thinkin' o' it till I sweats my sheets all of a sop. 'Tisn't as if I was a young man," he says, "nor yet as if I was a pore man. Maybe he'll drink hisself to death." I e'en a'most told him outright what foolishness he was enterin' into, but he knowed it—he knowed it—because he said next time the man come 'twould be fifteen shillin's. An' next time 'twas. Just fifteen shillin's!'

'An' *was* the man her father?' asked Jabez.

'He had the proofs an' the papers. Jim showed me what that Lunnon Childern's Society had answered when Mary writ up to 'em an' taxed 'em with it. I lay she hadn't been proper polite in her letters to 'em, for they answered middlin' short. They said the matter was out o' their hands, but—let's see if I remember—oh, yes,—they ree-gretted there had been an oversight. I reckon they had sent Mary out in the candle-box as a orphan instead o' havin' a father. Terrible awkward! Then, when he'd drinked up the money, the man come again—in his usuals—an' he kept hammerin' on and hammerin' on about his duty to his pore dear wife, an' what he'd do for his dear daughter in Lunnon, till the tears runnel down his two dirty cheeks an' he come away with more money. Jim used to slip it into his hand behind the door; but his mother she heard the chink. She didn't hold with hush-money. She'd write out all her feelin's on the slate, an' Jim 'ud be settin' up half the night answerin' back an showing that the man had the law with him.'

'Hadn't that man no trade nor business, then?'

'He told me he was a printer. I reckon, though, he lived on the rates like the rest of 'ern up there in Lunnon.'

'An' how did Mary take it?'

'She said she'd sooner go into service than go with the man. I reckon a mistress 'ud be middlin' put to it for a maid 'fore she put Mary into cap an' gown. She was studyin' to be a schoo-ool-teacher. A beauty she'll make! . . . Well, that was how things went that fall. Mary's Lunnon father kep' comin' an' comin' 'carden as he'd drinked out the money Jim gave him; an' each time he'd put up his price for not takin' Mary away. Jim's mother, she didn't like partin' with no money, an' bein' obliged to write her feelin's on the slate instead o' givin' 'em vent by mouth, she was just about mad. Just about she *was* mad!'

Come November, I lodged with Jim in the outside room over 'gainst his hen-house. I paid *her* my rent. I was workin' for Dockett at Pounds—gettin' chestnut-bats out o' Perry Shaw. Just such weather as this be-rain atop o' rain after a wet October. (An' I remember it ended in dry frostes right away up to Christmas.) Dockett he'd sent up to Perry Shaw for me—no, he comes puffin' up to me himself—because a big cornerpiece o' the bank had slipped into the brook where she makes that elber at the bottom o' the Seventeen Acre, an' all the rubbishy alders an' sallies which he ought to have cut out when he took the farm, they'd slipped with the slip, an' the brook was comin' rooshin' down atop of 'em, an' they'd just about back an' spill the waters over his winter wheat. The water was lyin' in the flats already. "Gor a-mighty, Jesse!" he bellers out at me, "get that rubbish away all manners you can. Don't stop for no fagottin', but give the brook play or my wheat's past salvation. I can't lend you no help," he says, "but work an' I'll pay ye.'"

'You had him there,' Jabez chuckled.

'Yes. I reckon I had ought to have drove my bargain, but the brook was backin' up on good bread-corn. So 'cardenly, I laid into the mess of it, workin' off the bank where the trees was drownin' themselves head-down in the roosh—just such weather as this—an' the brook creepin' up on me all the time. 'Long toward noon, Jim comes mowchin' along with his toppin' axe over his shoulder.

"'Be you minded for an extra hand at your job?" he says.

"'Be you minded to turn to?" I ses, an'—no more talk to it—Jim laid in alongside o' me. He's no bunger with a toppin' axe.'

'Maybe, but I've seed him at a job o' throwin' in the woods, an' he didn't seem to make out no shape,' said Jabez. 'He haven't got the shoulders, nor yet the judgment—*my* opinion—when he's dealin' with full-girt timber. He don't rightly make up his mind where he's goin' to throw her.'

'We wasn't throwin' nothin'. We was cuttin' out they soft alders, an' haulin' 'em up the bank 'fore they could back the waters on the wheat.

Jim didn't say much, 'less it was that he'd had a post-card from Mary's Lunnon father, night before, sayin' he was comin' down that mornin'. Jim, he'd sweated all night, an' he didn't reckon hisself equal to the talkin' an' the swearin' an' the cryin', an' his mother blamin' him afterwards on the slate. "It spiled my day to think of it," he ses, when we was eatin' our pieces. "So I've fair cried dunghill an' run. Mother'll have to tackle him by herself. I lay *she* won't give him no hush-money," he ses. "I lay he'll be surprised by the time he's done with *her*," he ses. An' that was e'en a'most all the talk we had concernin' it. But he's no bunger with the toppin' axe.

'The brook she'd crep' up an' up on us, an' she kep' creepin' upon us till we was workin' knee-deep in the shallers, cuttin' an' pookin' an' pullin' what we could get to o' the rubbish. There was a middlin' lot comin' down-stream, too—cattle-bars an' hop-poles and odds-ends bats, all poltin' down together; but they rooshed round the elber good shape by the time we'd backed out they drowned trees. Come four o'clock we reckoned we'd done a proper day's work, an' she'd take no harm if we left her. We couldn't puddle about there in the dark an' wet to no more advantage. Jim he was pourin' the water out of his boots—no, I was doin' that. Jim was kneelin' to unlace his'n. "Damn it all, Jesse," he ses, standin' up; "the flood must be over my doorsteps at home, for here comes my old white-top bee-skep!"'

'Yes. I allus heard he paints his bee-skeps,' Jabez put in. 'I dunno paint don't tarrify bees more'n it keeps 'em dry.'

'"I'll have a pook at it," he ses, an' he pooks at it as it comes round the elber. The roosh nigh jerked the pooker out of his hand-grips, an' he calls to me, an' I come runnin' barefoot. Then we pulled on the pooker, an' it reared up on eend in the roosh, an' we guessed what 'twas. 'Cardenly we pulled it in into a shaller, an' it rolled a piece, an' a great old stiff man's arm nigh hit me in the face. Then we was sure. "'Tis a man," ses Jim. But the face was all a mask. "I reckon it's Mary's Lunnon father," he ses presently. "Lend me a match and I'll make sure." He never used baccy. We lit three matches one by another, well's we could in the rain, an' he cleaned off some o' the slob with a tussick o' grass. "Yes," he ses. "It's

Mary's Lunnon father. He won't tarrify us no more. D'you want him, Jesse?" he ses.

"No," I ses. "If this was Eastbourne beach like, he'd be half-a-crown apiece to us 'fore the coroner; but now we'd only lose a day havin' to 'tend the inquest. I lay he fell into the brook."

"I lay he did," ses Jim. "I wonder if he saw mother." He turns him over, an' opens his coat and puts his fingers in the waistcoat pocket an' starts laugbin'. "He's seen mother, right enough," he ses. "An' he's got the best of her, too. *She* won't be able to crow no more over *me* 'bout givin' him money. *I* never give him more than a sovereign. She's give him two!" an' he trousers 'em, laughin' all the time. "An' now we'll pook him back again, for I've done with him," he ses.

'So we pooked him back into the middle of the brook, an' we saw he went round the elber 'thout balkin', an' we walked quite a piece beside of him to set him on his ways. When we couldn't see no more, we went home by the high road, because we knowed the brook 'u'd be out acrost the medders, an' we wasn't goin' to hunt for Jim's little rotten old bridge in that darkan' rainin' Heavens' hard, too. I was middlin' pleased to see light an' vittles again when we got home. Jim he pressed me to come insides for a drink. He don't drink in a generality, but he was rid of all his troubles that evenin', d'ye see? "Mother," he ses so soon as the door ope'd, "have you seen him? "She whips out her slate an' writes down— "No." "Oh, no," ses Jim. "You don't get out of it that way, mother. I lay you *have* seen him, an' I lay he's bested you for all your talk, same as he bested me. Make a clean breast of it, mother," he ses. "He got round you too." She was goin' for the slate again, but he stops her. "It's all right, mother," he ses. "I've seen him sense you have, an' he won't trouble us no more." The old lady looks up quick as a robin, an' she writes, "Did he say so?" "No," ses Jim, laughin'. "He didn't say so. That's how I know. But he bested *you*, mother. You can't have it in at *me* for bein' soft-heart-ed. You're twice as tender-hearted as what I be. Look!" he ses, an' he shows her the two sovereigns. "Put 'em away where they belong," he ses. "He won't never come for no more; an' now we'll have our drink," he ses, "for we've earned it."

'Nature-ally they weren't goin' to let me see where they kep' their monies. She went upstairs with it—for the whisky.'

'I never knowed Jim was a drinkin' man—in his own house, like,' said Jabez.

'No more he isn't; but what he takes he likes good. He won't tech no publican's hogwash acrost the bar. Four shillin's he paid for that bottle o' whisky. I know, because when the old lady brought it down there wasn't more'n jest a liddle few dreenin's an' dregs in it. Nothin' to set before neighbours, I do assure you.'

"Why, 'twas half full last week, mother," he ses. "You don't mean," he ses, " you've given him all that as well? It's two shillin's worth," he ses. (That's how I knowed he paid four.) "Well, well, mother, you be too tender-'earted to live. But I don't grudge it to him," he ses. "I don't grudge him nothin' he can keep." So, 'cardenly, we drinked up what little sup was left.'

'An' what come to Mary's Lunnon father?' said Jabez, after a full minute's silence.

'I be too tired to go readin' papers of evenin's; but Dockett he told me, that very week, I think, that they'd inquested on a man down at Robertsbridge which had polted and polted up agin' so many bridges an' banks, like, they couldn't make naun out of him.'

'An' what did Mary say to all these doin's?'

'The old lady bundled her off to the village 'fore her Lunnon father come, to buy week-end stuff (an' she forgot the half o' it). When we come in she was upstairs studyin' to be a schoolteacher. None told her naun about it. 'Twadn't girls' affairs.'

'Reckon *she* knowed?' Jabez went on.

'She? She must have guessed it middlin' close when she saw her money come back. But she never mentioned it in writing so far's I know. She were more worritted that night on account of two-three her chickens bein' drowned, for the flood had skewed their old hen-house round on her postes. I cobbled her up next mornin' when the brook shrinked.'

'An' where did you find the bridge? Some fur down-stream, didn't ye?'

'Just where she allus was. She hadn't shifted but very little. The brook had gulled out the bank a piece under one eend o' the plank, so's she was liable to tilt ye sideways if you wasn't careful. But I pocked three-four bricks under her, an' she was all plumb again.'

'Well, I dunno how it *looks* like, but let be how 'twill,' said Jabez, 'he hadn't no business to come down from Lunnon tarrifyin' people, an' threatenin' to take away children which they'd hobbed up for their law-ful own—even if 'twas Mary Wickenden.'

'He had the business right enough, an' he had the law with him—no gettin' over that,' said Jesse.

'But he had the drink with him, too, an' that was where he failed, like.'

'Well, well! Let be how 'twill, the brook was a good friend to Jim. I see it now. I allus *did* wonder what he was gettin' at when he said that, when I talked to him about shiftin' the stack. "You dunno everythin'," he ses. "The Brook's been a good friend to me," he ses, "an' if she's minded to have a snatch at my hay, *I* ain't settin' out to withstand her."'

'I reckon she's about shifted it, too, by now,' Jesse chuckled. 'Hark! That ain't any slip off the bank which she's got hold of.'

The Brook had changed her note again. It sounded as though she were mumbling something soft.

The Land

When Julius Fabricius, Sub-Prefect of the Weald,
In the days of Diocletian owned our Lower River-field,
He called to him Hobdenius—a Briton of the Clay,
Saying: "What about that River-piece for layin' in to hay?"

And the aged Hobden answered: "I remember as a lad
My father told your father that she wanted dreenin' bad.
An' the more that you neeglect her the less you'll get her clean.
Have it jest as you've a mind to, but, if I was you, I'd dreen."

So they drained it long and crossways in the lavish Roman style —
Still we find among the river-drift their flakes of ancient tile,
And in drouthy middle August, when the bones of meadows show,
We can trace the lines they followed sixteen hundred years ago.

Then Julius Fabricius died as even Prefects do,
And after certain centuries, Imperial Rome died too.
Then did robbers enter Britain from across the Northern main
And our Lower River-field was won by Ogier the Dane.

Well could Ogier work his war-boat—well could Ogier wield his brand—
Much he knew of foaming waters—not so much of farming land.
So he called to him a Hobden of the old unaltered blood,
Saying: "What about that River-piece; she doesn't look no good?"

And that aged Hobden answered "'Tain't for me to interfere.
But I've known that bit o' meadow now for five and fifty year.
Have it jest as you've a mind to, but I've proved it time on ' time,
If you want to change her nature you have got to give her lime!"

Ogier sent his wains to Lewes, twenty hours' solemn walk,
And drew back great abundance of the cool, grey, healing chalk.
And old Hobden spread it broadcast, never heeding what was in't—
Which is why in cleaning ditches, now and then we find a flint.

Ogier died. His sons grew English—Anglo-Saxon was their name—
Till out of blossomed Normandy another pirate came;
For Duke William conquered England and divided with his men,
And our Lower River-field he gave to William of Warenne.

But the Brook (you know her habit) rose one rainy autumn night
And tore down sodden flitches of the bank to left and right.
So, said William to his Bailiff as they rode their dripping rounds:
"Hob, what about that River-bit—the Brook's got up no bounds ?"

And that aged Hobden answered: "'Tain't my business to advise,
But ye might ha' known 'twould happen from the way the valley lies.
Where ye can't hold back the water you must try and save the sile.
Hev it jest as you've a mind to, but, if I was you, I'd spile!"

They spiled along the water-course with trunks of willow-trees,
And planks of elms behind 'em and immortal oaken knees.
And when the spates of Autumn whirl the gravel-beds away
You can see their faithful fragments, iron-hard in iron clay.

Georgii Quinti Anno Sexto, I, who own the River-field,
Am fortified with title-deeds, attested, signed and sealed,
Guaranteeing me, my assigns, my executors and heirs
All sorts of powers and profits which—are neither mine nor theirs,

I have rights of chase and warren, as my dignity requires.
I can fish—but Hobden tickles—I can shoot—but Hobden wires.
I repair, but he reopens, certain gaps which, men allege,
Have been used by every Hobden since a Hobden swapped a hedge.

Shall I dog his morning progress o'er the track-betraying dew ?
Demand his dinner-basket into which my pheasant flew ?
Confiscate his evening faggot under which my conies ran,
And summons him to judgment ? I would sooner summons Pan.

His dead are in the churchyard—thirty generations laid.
Their names were old in history when Domesday Book was made;
And the passion and the piety and prowess of his line
Have seeded, rooted, fruited in some land the Law calls mine.

Not for any beast that burrows, not for any bird that flies,
Would I lose his large sound counsel, miss his keen amending eyes.
He is bailiff, woodman, wheelwright, field-surveyor, engineer,
And if flagrantly a poacher—'tain't for me to interfere.

"Hob, what about that River-bit ?" I turn to him again,
With Fabricius and Ogier and William of Warenne.
"Hev it jest as you've a mind to, but"—and here he takes command.
For whoever pays the taxes old Mus' Hobden owns the land.

Thoughts on Friendly Brook

Like 'Mary Postgate', 'Friendly Brook' displays a maturity of emotion and confidence of style that could not have been written by a younger man; just re-read the opening paragraphs.

Mary, the Barnardo girl, could in the hands of a lesser writer have been painted in saccharine colours, but according to Jesse she is a slack house-keeper who lacks kindness.

The climax of the tale is tautly crafted, along with the men's act in consigning the body back into the flood. All the people in the story are rounded human beings, but from beginning to end the dominant character is the brook, which is painted in almost anthropomorphic colours. When the waters go over Wickenden's door-stones there was 'a growl in the brook's roar as though she worried something hard'. After the death the brook changes her note again to 'something soft'. The men's attitude towards the brook has caused some critics to read the plot in terms of animism. However, Philip Mason was surely correct when he suggested that it was superficial to dismiss the men's feelings in this way. 'They do not really think the Brook is a water-spirit, but they do think that something is due to something. It is just, it is retribution, and there is no need for revenge.'

'The Land', the poem that Kipling finished this story with, encapsulates his romantic attitude towards Sussex and its people. Angus Wilson has pointed out that even then 'his' Sussex was not as immutable as he supposed; and time has only confirmed that view. However, we do not read Kipling for his demographic insights, but for his love and understanding of the countryside and its people.

Hobden, a local name, though Latinized in the poem, was based on a real person of a different name.

THE EYE OF ALLAH

Untimely

Nothing in life has been made by man for man's using
But it was shown long since to man in ages
Lost as the name of the maker of it,

Who received oppression and scorn for his wages—
Hate, avoidance, and scorn in his daily dealings—
Until he perished, wholly confounded.

More to be pitied than he are the wise
Souls which foresaw the evil of loosing
Knowledge or Art before time, and aborted
Noble devices and deep-wrought healings,
Lest offence should arise.

Heaven delivers on earth the Hour that cannot be thwarted,
Neither advanced, at the price of a world or a soul, and its Prophet
Comes through the blood of the vanguards who dreamed—too soon—it
had sounded.

The Cantor of St. Illod's being far too enthusiastic a musician to con-cern himself with its Library, the Sub-Cantor, who idolised every detail of the work, was tidying up, after two hours' writing and dictation in the Scriptorium. The copying-monks handed him in their sheets—it was a plain Four Gospels ordered by an Abbot at Evesham—and filed out to vespers. John Otho, better known as John of Burgos, took no heed. He was burnishing a tiny boss of gold in his miniature of the Annunciation for his Gospel of St. Luke, which it was hoped that Cardinal Falcodi, the Papal Legate, might later be pleased to accept.

'Break off, John,' said the Sub-Cantor in an undertone.

'Eh? Gone, have they? I never heard. Hold a minute, Clement.'

The Sub-Cantor waited patiently. He had known John more than a dozen years, coming and going at St. Illod's, to which monastery John, when abroad, always said he belonged. The claim was gladly allowed, for, more even than other Fitz Othos, he seemed to carry all the Arts under his hand, and most of their practical receipts under his hood.

The Sub-Cantor looked over his shoulder at the pinned-down sheet where the first words of the Magnificat were built up in gold washed with red-lac for a background to the Virgin's hardly yet fired halo. She was shown, hands joined in wonder, at a lattice of infinitely intricate arabesque, round the edges of which sprays of orange-bloom seemed to load the blue hot air that carried back over the minute parched land-scape in the middle distance.

'You've made her all Jewess,' said the SubCantor, studying the olive-flushed cheek and the eyes charged with foreknowledge.

'What else was Our Lady?' John slipped out the pins. 'Listen, Clement. If I do not come back, this goes into my Great Luke, whoever finishes it.' He slid the drawing between its guard-papers.

'Then you're for Burgos again—as I heard?'

'In two days. The new Cathedral yonder—but they're slower than the Wrath of God, those masons—is good for the soul.'

'*Thy* soul?' The Sub-Cantor seemed doubtful.

'Even mine, by your permission. And down south—on the edge of the Conquered Countries—Granada way—there's some Moorish diaper-work that's wholesome. It allays vain thought and draws it toward the picture—as you felt, just now, in my Annunciation.'

'She—it was very beautiful. No wonder you go. But you'll not forget your absolution, John?'

'Surely.' This was a precaution John no more omitted on the eve of his travels than he did the recutting of the tonsure which he had provided himself with in his youth, somewhere near Ghent. The mark gave him privilege of clergy at a pinch, and a certain consideration on the road always.

'You'll not forget, either, what we need in the Scriptorium. There's no more true ultramarine in this world now. They mix it with that German blue. And as for vermilion——'

'I'll do my best always.'

'And Brother Thomas' (this was the Infirmarian in charge of the monastery hospital) 'he needs——'

'He'll do his own asking. I'll go over his side now, and get me re-tonsured.'

John went down the stairs to the lane that divides the hospital and cookhouse from the back-cloisters. While he was being barbered, Brother Thomas (St. Illod's meek but deadly persistent Infirmarian) gave him a list of drugs that he was to bring back from Spain by hook, crook, or lawful purchase. Here they were surprised by the lame, dark Abbot Stephen, in his fur-lined night-boots. Not that Stephen de Sautré was any spy; but as a young man he had shared an unlucky Crusade, which had ended, after a battle at Mansura, in two years' captivity among the Saracens at Cairo where men learn to walk softly. A fair huntsman and hawker, a reasonable disciplinarian, but a man of science above all, and a Doctor of Medicine under one Ranulphus, Canon of St. Paul's, his heart was more m the monastery's hospital work than its religious. He checked their list interestedly, adding items of his own. After the Infirmarian had withdrawn, he gave John generous absolution, to cover lapses by the way; for he did not hold with chance-bought Indulgences.

'And what seek you *this* journey?' he demanded, sitting on the bench beside the mortar and scales in the little warm cell for stored drugs.

'Devils, mostly,' said John, grinning.

'In Spain? Are not Abana and Phar-par——?'

John, to whom men were but matter for drawings, and well-born to boot (since he was a de Sanford on his mother's side), looked the Abbot full in the face and—'Did *you* find it so?' said he.

'No. They were in Cairo too. But what's your special need of 'em?'

'For my Great Luke. He's the masterhand of all Four when it comes to devils.'

'No wonder. He was a physician. You're not.'

'Heaven forbid! But I'm weary of our Church-pattern devils. They're only apes and goats and poultry conjoined. 'Good enough for plain red-and-black Hells and Judgment Days—but not for me.'

'What makes you so choice in them?'

'Because it stands to reason and Art that there are all musters of devils in Hell's dealings. Those Seven, for example, that were haled out of the Magdalene. They'd be she-devils—no kin at all to the beaked and horned and bearded devils-general.'

The Abbot laughed.

'And see again! The devil that came out of the dumb man. What use is snout or bill to *him*? He'd be faceless as a leper. Above all—God send I live to do it!—the devils that entered the Gadarene swine. They'd be—they'd be—I know not yet what they'd be, but they'd be surpassing devils. I'd have 'em diverse as the Saints themselves. But now, they're all one pattern, for wall, window, or picture-work.'

'Go on, John. You're deeper in this mystery than I'

'Heaven forbid! But I say there's respect due to devils, damned tho' they be.'

'Dangerous doctrine.'

'My meaning is that if the shape of anything be worth man's thought to picture to man, it's worth his best thought.'

'That's safer. But I'm glad I've given you Absolution.'

'There's less risk for a craftsman who deals with the outside shapes of things—for Mother Church's glory.'

'Maybe so, but, John'—the Abbot's hand almost touched John's sleeve—'tell me, now, is—is she Moorish or—or Hebrew?'

'She's mine,' John returned.

'Is that enough?'

'I have found it so.'

'Well—ah well! It's out of my jurisdiction, but—how do they look at it down yonder?'

'Oh, they drive nothing to a head in Spain—neither Church nor King, bless them! There's too many Moors and Jews to kill them all, and if they chased 'em away there'd be no trade nor farming. Trust me, in the Conquered Countries, from Seville to Granada, we live lovingly enough together—Spaniard, Moor, and Jew. Ye see, *we* ask no questions.'

'Yes—yes,' Stephen sighed. 'And always there's the hope she may be converted.'

'Oh yes, there's always hope.'

The Abbot went on into the hospital. It was an easy age before Rome tightened the screw as to clerical connections. If the lady were not too forward, or the son too much his father's beneficiary in ecclesiastical preferments and levies, a good deal was overlooked. But, as the Abbot had reason to recall, unions between Christian and Infidel led to sorrow. None the less, when John with mule, mails, and man, clattered off down the lane for Southampton and the sea, Stephen envied him.

***

He was back, twenty months later, in good hard case, and loaded down with fairings. A lump of richest lazuli, a bar of orange-hearted vermilion, and a small packet of dried beetles which make most glorious scarlet, for the SubCantor. Besides that, a few cubes of milky marble, with yet a pink flush in them, which could be slaked and ground down to incomparable background-stuff. There were quite half the drugs that the Abbot and Thomas had demanded, and there was a long deep-red cornelian necklace for the Abbot's Lady—Anne of Norton. She received it graciously, and asked where John had come by it.

'Near Granada,' he said.

'You left all well there?' Anne asked. (Maybe the Abbot had told her something of John's confession.)

'I left all in the hands of God.'

'Ah me! How long since?'

'Four months less eleven days.'

'Were you—with her?'

'In my arms. Childbed.'

'And?'

'The boy too. There is nothing now.'

Anne of Norton caught her breath.

'I think you'll be glad of that,' she said after a while.

'Give me time, and maybe I'll compass it. But not now.'

'You have your handiwork and your art, and—John—remember there's no jealousy in the grave.'

'Ye-es! I have my Art, and Heaven knows I'm jealous of none.'

'Thank God for that at least,' said Anne of Norton, the always ailing woman who followed the Abbot with her sunk eyes. 'And be sure I shall treasure this'—she touched the beads—'as long as I shall live.'

'I brought—trusted—it to you for that,' he replied, and took leave. When she told the Abbot how she had come by it, he said nothing, but as he and Thomas were storing the drugs that John handed over in the cell which backs on to the hospital kitchen-chimney, he observed, of a cake of dried poppy juice: 'This has power to cut off all pain from a man's body.'

'I have seen it,' said John.

'But for pain of the soul there is, outside God's Grace, but one drug; and that is a man's craft, learning, or other helpful motion of his own mind.'

'That is coming to me, too,' was the answer.

John spent the next fair May day out in the woods with the monastery swineherd and all the porkers; and returned loaded with flowers and sprays of spring, to his own carefully kept place in the north bay of the Scriptorium. There, with his travelling sketch-books under his left elbow, he sunk himself past all recollections in his Great Luke.

Brother Martin, Senior Copyist (who spoke about once a fortnight), ventured to ask, later, how the work was going.

'All here!' John tapped his forehead with his pencil. 'It has been only waiting these months to—ah God!—be born. Are ye free of your plain-copying, Martin?'

Brother Martin nodded. It was his pride that John of Burgos turned to him, in spite of his seventy years, for really good page-work.

'Then see!' John laid out a new vellum—thin but flawless. 'There's no better than this sheet from here to Paris. Yes! Smell it if you choose. Wherefore—give me the compasses and I'll set it out for you—if ye make one letter lighter or darker than its next, I'll stick ye like a pig.'

'Never, John!' The old man beamed happily. 'But I will! Now, follow! Here and here, as I prick, and in script of just this height to the hair's-breadth, yell scribe the thirty-first and thirty-second verses of Eighth Luke.'

'Yes, the Gadarene Swine! *"And they besought him that he would not command them to go out into the abyss. And there was a herd of many swine"*—— Brother Martin naturally knew all the Gospels by heart.

'Just so! Down to *"and he suffered them."* Take your time to it. My Magdalene has to come off my heart first.'

Brother Martin achieved the work so perfectly that John stole some soft sweetmeats from the Abbot's kitchen for his reward. The old man ate them; then repented; then confessed and insisted on penance. At which, the Abbot, knowing there was but one way to reach the real sinner, set him a book called *De Virtutibus Herbarum* to fair-copy. St. Illod's had borrowed it from the gloomy Cistercians, who do not hold with pretty things, and the crabbed text kept Martin busy just when John wanted him for some rather specially spaced letterings.

'See now,' said the Sub-Cantor improvingly. 'You should not do such things, John. Here's Brother Martin on penance for your sake——'

'No—for my Great Luke. But I've paid the Abbot's cook. I've drawn him till his own scullions cannot keep straight-faced. *He*'ll not tell again.'

'Unkindly done! And you're out of favour with the Abbot too. He's made no sign to you since you came back—never asked you to high table.'

'I've been busy. Having eyes in his head, Stephen knew it. Clement, there's no Librarian from Durham to Torre fit to clean up after you.'

The Sub-Cantor stood on guard; he knew where John's compliments generally ended.

'But outside the Scriptorium——'

'Where I never go.' The Sub-Cantor had been excused even digging in the garden, lest it should mar his wonderful book-binding hands.

'In all things outside the Scriptorium you are the master-fool of Christendie. Take it from me, Clement. I've met many.'

'I take everything from you,' Clement smiled benignly. 'You use me worse than a singing-boy.

They could hear one of that suffering breed in the cloister below, squalling as the Cantor pulled his hair.

'God love you! So I do! But have you ever thought how I lie and steal daily on my travels—yes, and for aught you know, murder—to fetch you colours and earths?'

'True,' said just and conscience-stricken Clement. 'I have often thought that were I in the world—which God forbid!—I might be a strong thief in some matters.'

Even Brother Martin, bent above his loathed *De Virtutibus*, laughed.

***

But about mid-summer, Thomas the Infirmarian conveyed to John the Abbot's invitation to supper in his house that night, with the request that he would bring with him anything that he had done for his Great Luke.

'What's toward?' said John, who had been wholly shut up in his work.

'Only one of his "wisdom" dinners. You've sat at a few since you were a man.'

'True: and mostly good. How would Stephen have us——?'

'Gown and hood over all. There will be a doctor from Salerno—one Roger, an Italian. Wise and famous with the knife on the body. He's been in the Infirmary some ten days, helping me—even me!'

"Never heard the name. But our Stephen's *physicus* before *sacerdos*, always.'

'And his Lady has a sickness of some time. Roger came hither in chief because of her.'

'Did he? Now I think of it, I have not seen the Lady Anne for a while.'

'Ye've seen nothing for a long while. She has been housed near a month—they have to carry her abroad now.'

'So bad as that, then?'

'Roger of Salerno will not yet say what he thinks. But——'

'God pity Stephen! . . . Who else at table, besides thee?'

'An Oxford friar. Roger is his name also. A learned and famous philosopher. And he holds his liquor too, valiantly.'

'Three doctors—counting Stephen. I've always found that means two atheists.'

Thomas looked uneasily down his nose. 'That's a wicked proverb,' he stammered. 'You should not use it.'

'Hoh! Never come you the monk over me, Thomas! You've been Infirmarian at St. Illod's eleven years—and a lay-brother still. Why have you never taken orders, all this while?'

'I—I am not worthy.'

'Ten times worthier than that new fat swine—Henry Who's-his-name— that takes the Infirmary Masses. He bullocks in with the Viaticum, under your nose, when a sick man's only faint from being bled. So the man dies—of pure fear. Ye know it! I've watched your face at such times. Take Orders, Didymus. You'll have a little more medicine and a little less Mass with your sick then; and they'll live longer.'

'I am unworthy—unworthy,' Thomas repeated pitifully.

'Not you—but—to your own master you stand or fall. And now that my work releases me for awhile, I'll drink with any philosopher out of any school. And, Thomas,' he coaxed, 'a hot bath for me in the Infirmary before vespers.'

***

When the Abbot's perfectly cooked and served meal had ended, and the deep-fringed naperies were removed, and the Prior had sent in the keys with word that all was fast in the Monastery, and the keys had been duly returned with the word, 'Make it so till Prime,' the Abbot and his guests went out to cool themselves in an upper cloister that took them, by way of the leads, to the South Choir side of the Triforium. The summer sun was still strong, for it was barely six o'clock, but the Abbey Church, of course, lay in her wonted darkness. Lights were being lit for choir-practice thirty feet below.

'Our Cantor gores them no rest,' the Abbot whispered. 'Stand by this pillar and we'll hear what he's driving them at now.'

'Remember, all!' the Cantor's hard voice came up. 'This is the soul of Bernard himself, attacking our evil world. Take it quicker than yesterday, and throw all your words clean-bitten from you. In the loft there! Begin!'

The organ broke out for an instant, alone and raging. Then the voices crashed together into that first fierce line of the 'De Contemptu Mundi.'

'*Hora novissima—tempora pessima*'—a dead pause till the assenting *sunt* broke, like a sob, out of the darkness, and one boy's voice, clearer than silver trumpets, returned the long-drawn *vigilemus.*

'*Ecce minaciter, imminet Arbiter*' (organ and voices were leashed together in terror and warning, breaking away liquidly to the '*ille supremus*'). Then the tone-colours shifted for the prelude to '*Imminet, imminet, ut mala terminet*——'

'Stop! Again!' cried the Cantor; and gave his reasons a little more roundly than was natural at choir-practice.

'Ah! Pity o' man's vanity! He's guessed we are here. Come away!' said the Abbot. Anne of Norton, in her carried chair, had been listening too, further along the dark Triforium, with Roger of Salerno. John heard her sob. On the way back, he asked Thomas how her health stood. Before Thomas could reply the sharp-featured Italian doctor pushed between them. 'Following on our talk together, I judged it best to tell her,' said he to Thomas.

'What?' John asked simply enough.

'What she knew already.' Roger of Salerno launched into a Greek quotation to the effect that every woman knows all about everything.

'I have no Greek,' said John stiffly. Roger of Salerno had been giving them a good deal of it, at dinner.

'Then I'll come to you in Latin. Ovid hath it neatly. *"Utque malum late solet immedicabile cancer—"* but doubtless you know the rest, worthy Sir.'

'Alas! My school-Latin's but what I've gathered by the way from fools professing to heal sick women. *"Hocus-pocus—"* but doubtless you know the rest, worthy Sir.'

Roger of Salerno was quite quiet till they regained the dining-room, where the fire had been comforted and the dates, raisins, ginger, figs, and cinnamon-scented sweetmeats set out, with the choicer wines, on the after-table. The Abbot seated himself, drew off his ring, dropped it, that all might hear the tinkle, into an empty silver cup, stretched his feet towards the hearth, and looked at the great gilt and carved rose in the barrel-roof. The silence that keeps from Compline to Matins had closed on their world. The bull-necked Friar watched a ray of sunlight split itself into colours on the rim of a crystal salt-cellar; Roger of Salerno had re-opened some discussion with Brother Thomas on a type of spotted fever that was baffling them both in England and abroad; John took note of the keen profile, and—it might serve as a note for the Great Luke—his hand moved to his bosom. The Abbot saw, and nodded permission. John whipped out silver-point and sketch-book.

'Nay—modesty is good enough—but deliver your own opinion,' the Italian was urging the Infirmarian. Out of courtesy to the foreigner nearly all the talk was in table-Latin; more formal and more copious than monk's patter. Thomas began with his meek stammer.

'I confess myself at a loss for the cause of the fever unless—as Varro saith in his *De Re Rustica*—certain small animals which the eye cannot follow enter the body by the nose and mouth, and set up grave diseases. On the other hand, this is not in Scripture.'

Roger of Salerno hunched head and shoulders like an angry cat. 'Always *that*!' he said, and John snatched down the twist of the thin lips.

'Never at rest, John.' The Abbot smiled at the artist. 'You should break off every two hours for prayers, as we do. St. Benedict was no fool. Two hours is all that a man can carry the edge of his eye or hand.'

'For copyists—yes. Brother Martin is not sure after one hour. But when a man's work takes him, he must go on till it lets him go.'

'Yes, that is the Demon of Socrates,' the Friar from Oxford rumbled above his cup.

'The doctrine leans toward presumption,' said the Abbot. 'Remember, "Shall mortal man be more just than his Maker?"'

'There is no danger of justice'; the Friar spoke bitterly. 'But at least Man might be suffered to go forward in his Art or his thought. Yet if Mother Church sees or hears him move anyward, what says she? "No!" Always "No."'

'But if the little animals of Varro be invisible'—this was Roger of Salerno to Thomas—'how are we any nearer to a cure?'

'By experiment'—the Friar wheeled round on them suddenly. 'By reason and experiment. The one is useless without the other. But Mother Church——'

'Ay !' Roger de Salerno dashed at the fresh bait like a pike. 'Listen, Sirs. Her bishops—our Princes—strew our roads in Italy with carcasses that they make for their pleasure or wrath. Beautiful corpses! Yet if I—if we doctors—so much as raise the skin of one of them to look at God's fabric beneath, what says Mother Church? "Sacrilege! Stick to your pigs and dogs, or you burn!"'

'And not Mother Church only!' the Friar chimed in. '*Every* way we are barred—barred by the words of some man, dead a thousand years, which are held final. Who is any son of Adam that his one say—so should close a door towards truth? I would not except even Peter Peregrinus, my own great teacher.'

'Nor I Paul of Aegina,' Roger of Salerno cried. 'Listen, Sirs! Here is a case to the very point. Apuleius affirmeth, if a man eat fasting of the juice of the cut-leaved buttercup—*sceleratus* we call it, which means "rascal-ly"'—this with a condescending nod towards John—'his soul will leave his body laughing. Now this is the lie more dangerous than truth, since truth of a sort is in it.'

'He's away!' whispered the Abbot despairingly.

'For the juice of that herb, I know by experiment, burns, blisters, and wries the mouth. I know also the *rictus*, or pseudo-laughter, on the face of such as have perished by the strong poisons of herbs al-lied to this ranunculus. Certainly that spasm resembles laughter. It seems then, in my judgment, that Apuleius, having seen the body of one thus poisoned, went off at score and wrote that the man died laughing.'

'Neither staying to observe, nor to confirm observation by experiment,' added the Friar, frowning.

Stephen the Abbot cocked an eyebrow toward John.

'How think *you*?' said he.

'I'm no doctor,' John returned, 'but I'd say Apuleius in all these years might have been betrayed by his copyists. They take short-cuts to save 'emselves trouble. Put case that Apuleius wrote the soul *seems to* leave the body laughing, after this poison. There's not three copyists in five (*my* judgment) would not leave out the "seems to." For who'd question Apuleius? If it seemed so to him, so it must be. Otherwise any child knows cut-leaved buttercup.'

'Have you knowledge of herbs?' Roger of Salerno asked curtly.

'Only that, when I was a boy in convent, I've made tetters round my mouth and on my neck with buttercup juice, to save going to prayer o' cold nights.'

'Ah!' said Roger. 'I profess no knowledge of tricks.' He turned aside, stiffly.

'No matter! Now for your own tricks, John,' the tactful Abbot broke in. 'You shall show the doctors your Magdalene and your Gadarene Swine and the devils.'

'Devils? Devils? *I* have produced devils by means of drugs; and have abolished them by the same means. Whether devils be external to mankind or immanent, I have not yet pronounced.' Roger of Salerno was still angry.

'Ye dare not,' snapped the Friar from Oxford. 'Mother Church makes Her own devils.'

'Not wholly! Our John has come back from Spain with brand-new ones.' Abbot Stephen took the vellum handed to him, and laid it tenderly on the table. They gathered to look. The Magdalene was drawn in palest, almost transparent, grisaille, against a raging, swaying background of woman-faced devils, each broke to and by her special sin, and each, one could see, frenziedly straining against the Power that compelled her.

'I've never seen the like of this grey shadowwork,' said the Abbot. 'How came you by it?'

'*Non nobis*! It came to me,' said John, not knowing he was a generation or so ahead of his time in the use of that medium.

'Why is she so pale?' the Friar demanded.

'Evil has all come out of her—she'd take any colour now.'

'Ay, like light through glass. *I* see.'

Roger of Salerno was looking in silence—his nose nearer and nearer the page. 'It is so,' he pronounced finally. 'Thus it is in epilepsy—mouth, eyes, and forehead—even to the droop of her wrist there. Every sign of it! She will need restoratives, that woman, and, afterwards, sleep natural. No poppy juice, or she will vomit on her waking. And thereafter—but I am not in my Schools.' He drew himself up. 'Sir,' said he, 'you should be of Our calling. For, by the Snakes of Aesculapius, you *see!*'

The two struck hands as equals.

'And how think you of the Seven Devils?' the Abbot went on.

These melted into convoluted flower—or flame-like bodies, ranging in colour from phosphorescent green to the black purple of outworn iniquity, whose hearts could be traced beating through their substance. But, for sign of hope and the sane workings of life, to be regained, the deep border was of conventionalised spring flowers and birds, all crowned by a kingfisher in haste, atilt through a clump of yellow iris.

Roger of Salerno identified the herbs and spoke largely of their virtues.

'And now, the Gadarene Swine,' said Stephen. John laid the picture on the table.

Here were devils dishoused, in dread of being abolished to the Void, huddling and hurtling together to force lodgment by every opening into the brute bodies offered. Some of the swine fought the invasion, foaming and jerking; some were surrendering to it, sleepily, as to a luxurious back-scratching; others, wholly possessed, whirled off in bucking droves for the lake beneath. In one corner the freed man stretched out his limbs all restored to his control, and Our Lord, seated, looked at him as questioning what he would make of his deliverance.

'Devils indeed!' was the Friar's comment. 'But wholly a new sort.'

Some devils were mere lumps, with lobes and protuberances—a hint of a fiend's face peering through jelly-like walls. And there was a family of impatient, globular devillings who had burst open the belly of their smirking parent, and were revolving desperately toward their prey. Others patterned themselves into rods, chains and ladders, single or conjoined, round the throat and jaws of a shrieking sow, from whose ear emerged the lashing, glassy tail of a devil that had made good his refuge. And there were granulated and conglomerate devils, mixed up with the foam and slaver where the attack was fiercest. Thence the eye carried on to the insanely active backs of the downward-racing swine, the swineherd's aghast face, and his dog's terror.

Said Roger of Salerno, 'I pronounce that these were begotten of drugs. They stand outside the rational mind.'

'Not these,' said Thomas the Infirmarian, who as a servant of the Monastery should have asked his Abbot's leave to speak. 'Not these— look!—in the bordure.'

The border to the picture was a diaper of irregular but balanced compartments or cellules, where sat, swam, or weltered, devils in blank, so to say—things as yet uninspired by Evil—indifferent, but lawlessly outside imagination. Their shapes resembled, again, ladders, chains, scourges, diamonds, aborted buds, or gravid phosphorescent globes- some well-nigh starlike.

Roger of Salerno compared them to the obsessions of a Churchman's mind.

'Malignant?' the Friar from Oxford questioned.

'"Count everything unknown for horrible,"' Roger quoted with scorn.

'Not I. But they are marvellous—marvellous. I think——'

The Friar drew back. Thomas edged in to see better, and half opened his mouth.

'Speak,' said Stephen, who had been watching him. 'We are all in a sort doctors here.'

'I would say then'—Thomas rushed at it as one putting out his life's belief at the stake—'that these lower shapes in the bordure may not be so much hellish and malignant as models and patterns upon which John has tricked out and embellished his proper devils among the swine above there!'

'And that would signify?' said Roger of Salerno sharply.

'In my poor judgment, that he may have seen such shapes—without help of drugs.'

'Now who—*who*,' said John of Burgos, after a round and unregarded oath, 'has made thee so wise of a sudden, my Doubter?'

'I wise? God forbid! Only John, remember—one winter six years ago—the snow-flakes melting on your sleeve at the cookhouse-door. You showed me them through a little crystal, that made small things larger.'

'Yes. The Moors call such a glass the Eye of Allah,' John confirmed.

'You showed me them melting—six-sided. You called them, then, your patterns.'

'True. Snow-flakes melt six-sided. I have used them for diaper-work often.'

'Melting snow-flakes as seen through a glass? By art optical?' the Friar asked.

'Art optical? *I* have never heard!' Roger of Salerno cried.

'John,' said the Abbot of St. Illod's commandingly, 'was it—is it so?'

'In some sort,' John replied, 'Thomas has the right of it. Those shapes in the bordure were my workshop-patterns for the devils above. In *my* craft, Salerno, we dare not drug. It kills hand and eye. My shapes are to be seen honestly, in nature.'

The Abbot drew a bowl of rose-water towards him. 'When I was prisoner with—with the Saracens after Mansura,' he began, turning up the fold of his long sleeve, 'there were certain magicians—physicians—who could show—' he dipped his third finger delicately in the water—'all the firmament of Hell, as it were, in—' he shook off one drop from his polished nail on to the polished table—'even such a supernaculum as this.'

'But it must be foul water—not clean,' said John.

'Show us then—all—all,' said Stephen. 'I would make sure—once more.' The Abbot's voice was official.

John drew from his bosom a stamped leather box, some six or eight inches long, wherein, bedded on faded velvet, lay what looked like silver-bound compasses of old box-wood, with a screw at the head which opened or closed the legs to minute fractions. The legs terminated, not in points, but spoon-shapedly, one spatula pierced with a metal-lined hole less than a quarter of an inch across, the other with a half-inch hole. Into this latter John, after carefully wiping with a silk rag, slipped a metal cylinder that carried glass or crystal, it seemed, at each end.

'Ah! Art optic!' said the Friar. 'But what is that beneath it?'

It was a small swivelling sheet of polished silver no bigger than a florin, which caught the light and concentrated it on the lesser hole. John adjusted it without the Friar's proffered help.

'And now to find a drop of water,' said he, picking up a small brush.

'Come to my upper cloister. The sun is on the leads still,' said the Abbot, rising.

They followed him there. Half-way along, a drip from a gutter had made a greenish puddle in a worn stone. Very carefully, John dropped a drop of it into the smaller hole of the compassleg, and, steadying the apparatus on a coping, worked the screw m the compass joint, screwed the cylinder, and swung the swivel of the mirror till he was satisfied.

'Good!' He peered through the thing. 'My Shapes are all here. Now look, Father! If they do not meet your eye at first, turn this nicked edge here, left- or right-handed.'

'I have not forgotten,' said the Abbot, taking his place. 'Yes! They are here—as they were in my time—my time past. There is no end to them, I was told . . . . There *is* no end!'

'The light will go. Oh, let me look! Suffer me to see, also!' the Friar pleaded, almost shouldering Stephen from the eye-piece. The Abbot gave way. His eyes were on time past. But the Friar, instead of looking, turned the apparatus in his capable hands.

'Nay, nay,' John interrupted, for the man was already fiddling at the screws. 'Let the Doctor see.'

Roger of Salerno looked, minute after minute. John saw his blue-veined cheek-bones turn white. He stepped back at last, as though stricken.

'It is a new world—a new world, and—Oh, God Unjust!—I am old!'

'And now Thomas,' Stephen ordered.

John manipulated the tube for the Infirmarian, whose hands shook, and he too looked long. 'It is Life,' he said presently in a breaking voice. 'No Hell! Life created and rejoicing—the work of the Creator. They live, even as I have dreamed. Then it was no sin for me to dream. No sin—O God—no sin!'

He flung himself on his knees and began hysterically the *Benedicite omnia Opera*.

'And now I will see how it is actuated,' said the Friar from Oxford, thrusting forward again.

'Bring it within. The place is all eyes and ears,' said Stephen.

They walked quietly back along the leads, three English counties laid out in evening sunshine around them; church upon church, monastery upon monastery, cell after cell, and the bulk of a vast cathedral moored on the edge of the banked shoals of sunset.

When they were at the after-table once more they sat down, all except the Friar, who went to the window and huddled bat-like over the thing. 'I see! I see!' he was repeating to himself.

'He'll not hurt it,' said John. But the Abbot, staring in front of him, like Roger of Salerno, did not hear. The Infirmarian's head was on the table between his shaking arms.

John reached for a cup of wine.

'It was shown to me,' the Abbot was speaking to himself, 'in Cairo, that man stands ever between two Infinities—of greatness and littleness. Therefore, there is no end—either to life—or—'

'And *I* stand on the edge of the grave,' snarled Roger of Salerno. 'Who pities *me*?'

'Hush!' said Thomas the Infirmarian. 'The little creatures shall be sanctified—sanctified to the service of His sick.'

'What need?' John of Burgos wiped his lips. 'It shows no more than the shapes of things. It gives good pictures. I had it at Granada. It was brought from the East, they told me.'

Roger of Salerno laughed with an old man's malice. 'What of Mother Church? Most Holy Mother Church? If it comes to Her ears that we have spied into Her Hell without Her leave, where do we stand?'

'At the stake,' said the Abbot of St. Illod's, and, raising his voice a trifle 'You hear that? Roger Bacon, heard you that?'

The Friar turned from the window, clutching the compasses tighter.

'No, no!' he appealed. 'Not with Falcodi—not with our English-hearted Foulkes made Pope. He's wise—he's learned. He reads what I have put forth. Foulkes would never suffer it.'

'"Holy Pope is one thing, Holy Church another,"' Roger quoted.

'But I—*I* can bear witness it is no Art Magic,' the Friar went on. 'Nothing is it, except Art optical-wisdom after trial and experiment, mark you. I can prove it, and—my name weighs with men who dare think.'

'Find them!' croaked Roger of Salerno. 'Five or six in all the world. That makes less than fifty pounds by weight of ashes at the stake. I have watched such men—reduced.'

'I will not give this up!' The Friar's voice cracked in passion and despair. 'It would be to sin against the Light.'

'No, no! Let us—let us sanctify the little animals of Varro,' said Thomas.

Stephen leaned forward, fished his ring out of the cup, and slipped it on his finger. 'My sons,' said he, 'we have seen what we have seen.'

'That it is no magic but simple Art,' the Friar persisted.

"Avails nothing. In the eyes of Mother Church we have seen more than is permitted to man.'

'But it was Life—created and rejoicing,' said Thomas.

'To look into Hell as we shall be judged—as we shall be proved—to have looked, is for priests only.'

'Or green-sick virgins on the road to sainthood who, for cause any midwife could give you—'

The Abbot's half-lifted hand checked Roger of Salerno's outpouring.

'Nor may even priests see more in Hell than Church knows to be there. John, there is respect due to Church as well as to Devils.'

'My trade's the outside of things,' said John quietly. 'I have my patterns.'

'But you may need to look again for more,' the Friar said.

'In my craft, a thing done is done with. We go on to new shapes after that.'

'And if we trespass beyond bounds, even in thought, we lie open to the judgment of the Church,' the Abbot continued.

'But thou knowest—*knowest*!' Roger of Salerno had returned to the attack. 'Here's all the world in darkness concerning the causes of things—from the fever across the lane to thy Lady's—throe own Lady's—eating malady. Think!'

'I have thought upon it, Salerno! I have thought indeed.'

Thomas the Infirmarian lifted his head again; and this time he did not stammer at all. 'As in the water, so in the blood must they rage and war with each other! I have dreamed these ten years—I thought it was a sin—but my dreams and Varro's are true! Think on it again! Here's the Light under our very hand!'

'Quench it! You'd no more stand to roasting than—any other. I'll give you the case as Church—as I myself—would frame it. Our John here returns from the Moors, and shows us a hell of devils contending in the compass of one drop of water. Magic past clearance! You can hear the faggots crackle.'

'But thou knowest! Thou hast seen it all before! For man's poor sake! For old friendship's sake—Stephen !' The Friar was trying to stuff the compasses into his bosom as he appealed.

'What Stephen de Sautré knows, you his friends know also. I would have you, now, obey the Abbot of St. Illod's. Give to me!' He held out his ringed hand.

'May I—may John here—not even make a drawing of one—one screw?' said the broken Friar, in spite of himself.

'Nowise!' Stephen took it over. 'Your dagger, John. Sheathed will serve.'

He unscrewed the metal cylinder, laid it on the table, and with the dagger's hilt smashed some crystal to sparkling dust which he swept into a scooped hand and cast behind the hearth.

'It would seem,' said he, 'the choice lies between two sins. To deny the world a Light which is under our hand, or to enlighten the world before her time. What you have seen, I saw long since among the physicians at Cairo. And I know what doctrine they drew from it. Hast *thou* dreamed, Thomas? I also—with fuller knowledge. But this birth, my sons, is untimely. It will be but the mother of more death, more torture, more division, and greater darkness in this dark age. Therefore I, who know both my world and the Church, take this Choice on my conscience. Go! It is finished.'

He thrust the wooden part of the compasses deep among the beech logs till all was burned.

THE LAST ODE

(Nov. 27, 8 B.C.)
Horace, BK. V. Ode 31

As watchers couched beneath a Bantine oak,
Hearing the dawn-wind stir,
Know that the present strength of night is broke
Though no dawn threaten her
Till dawn's appointed hour--so Virgil died,
Aware of change at hand, and prophesied

Change upon all the Eternal Gods had made
And on the Gods alike--
Fated as dawn but, as the dawn, delayed
Till the just hour should strike--

A Star new-risen above the living and dead;
And the lost shades that were our loves restored
As lovers, and for ever. So he said;
Having received the word...

Maecenas waits me on the Esquiline:
Thither to-night go I....
And shall this dawn restore us, Virgil mine
To dawn? Beneath what sky?

Thoughts on The Eye of Allah

On the face of it 'The Eye of Allah' is about whether there is a time or-dained for new inventions, 'the hour that cannot be thwarted' as the epi-graph puts it. It is an idea that is as old as Ecclesiastes ('To every thing there is a season, and a time to every purpose under the heaven'.) But the story is about more, much more.

Carl Bodelsen described it as being 'on one level, a story about what hap-pens to a group of people in a mediaeval monastery; on another level it is a story about a premature discovery; on a third it is about the impact of the Renaissance on the mediaeval world picture; on a fourth about the attitude of the artist, the physician, and the philosopher to science; and on the fifth about four aspects of civilization, personified as the artist, the scientist, the philosopher and the church dignitary and statesman, and illustrated by confronting them with an emblem of the new science: the microscope.' (Aspects of Kipling's Art, 1964.) The Abbot understands the arguments for releasing the discovery, but after destroying the invention points out that not to do so would 'be but the mother of more death, more torture, more division, and greater darkness in this dark age.'

John Coates describes the monastery as catching 'the very moment of poise in a civilization between germination and decay, when the circle of buildings, complete in its elaborate particulars, holds back the 'sea of dreams'.' ('Memories of Mansura: The 'Tints and Textures' of Kipling's Late Art in The Eye of Allah'. 85 Modern Language Review 3, 1990).

And all this against the background of a complex love story.

Kipling has left an enlightening account of the story's creation. '[It] went dead under my hand, and for the life of me I could not see why. I put it away and waited. Then said my Daemon—and I was meditating some-thing else at the time—'Treat it as an illuminated manuscript.' I had rid-den off on hard black-and-white decoration, instead of pumicing the whole thing ivory-smooth, and loading it with thick colour and gilt.' ('Something of Myself') Every word, every image fulfills a purpose. Consider, for example, the eyes of the figure in John of Burgos's miniature which are described as 'charged with foreknowledge'.

Lisa Lewis has convincingly suggested 1266 or1267 as the date of the story. The two Rogers were historical figures, although Roger of Salerno lived a century before their time.

The description of the fictional device has been said to resemble a microscope of a type which was not invented until about 1600.

'The Last Ode' at the end of the story was written by the author in imitation of the poet, Horace. (Maecanas was his patron). It concerns the death 'at the appointed hour' of his friend, the great Virgil. The Ode refers to one of Virgil's poems that has been interpreted as foreseeing the birth of Christ and the promise of the resurrection, though the last two lines express Kipling's own doubts.

THE GARDENER

One grave to me was given,
One watch till Judgement Day;
And God looked down from Heaven
And rolled the stone away.

One day in all the years,
One hour in that one day,
His Angel saw my tears,
And rolled the stone away!

Every one in the village knew that Helen Turrell did her duty by all her world, and by none more honourably than by her only brother's unfortunate child. The village knew, too, that George Turrell had tried his family severely since early youth, and were not surprised to be told that, after many fresh starts given and thrown away, he, an Inspector of Indian Police, had entangled himself with the daughter of a retired noncommissioned officer, and had died of a fall from a horse a few weeks before his child was born. Mercifully, George's father and mother were both dead, and though Helen, thirty-five and independent, might well have washed her hands of the whole disgraceful affair, she most nobly took charge, though she was, at the time, under threat of lung trouble which had driven her to the South of France. She arranged for the passage of the child and a nurse from Bombay, met them at Marseilles, nursed the baby through an attack of infantile dysentery due to the carelessness of the nurse, whom she had had to dismiss, and at last, thin and worn but triumphant, brought the boy late in the autumn, wholly restored, to her Hampshire home.

All these details were public property, for Helen was as open as the day, and held that scandals are only increased by hushing them up. She admitted that George had always been rather a black sheep, but things might have been much worse if the mother had insisted on her right to keep the boy. Luckily, it seemed that people of that class would do almost anything for money, and, as George had always turned to her in his scrapes, she felt herself justified—her friends agreed with her— in cutting the whole non-commissioned officer connection, and giving the child every advantage. A christening, by the Rector, under the name of Michael, was the first step. So far as she knew herself, she was not, she said, a child-lover, but, for all his faults, she had been very fond of George, and she pointed out that little Michael had his father's mouth to a line; which made something to build upon.

As a matter of fact, it was the Turrell forehead, broad, low, and well-shaped, with the widely spaced eyes beneath it, that Michael had most faithfully reproduced. His mouth was somewhat better cut than the family type. But Helen, who would concede nothing good to his mother's side, vowed he was a Turrell all over, and, there being no one to contradict, the likeness was established.

In a few years Michael took his place, as accepted as Helen had always been—fearless, philosophical, and fairly good-looking. At six, he wished to know why he could not call her 'Mummy', as other boys called their mothers. She explained that she was only his auntie, and that aunties were not quite the same as mummies, but that, if it gave him pleasure, he might call her 'Mummy' at bedtime, for a pet-name between themselves.

Michael kept his secret most loyally, but Helen, as usual, explained the fact to her friends; which when Michael heard, he raged.

'Why did you tell? *Why* did you tell?' came at the end of the storm.

'Because it's always best to tell the truth,' Helen answered, her arm round him as he shook in his cot.

'All right, but when the troof's ugly I don't think it's nice.'

'Don't *you*, dear!'

'No, I don't, and'—she felt the small body stiffen—'now you've told, I won't call you "Mummy" any more—not even at bedtimes.

'But isn't that rather unkind?' said Helen softly.

'I don't care! You've hurted me in my insides and I'l hurt you back. I'll hurt you as long as I live!'

'Don't, oh, don't talk like that, dear! You don't know what—'

'I will! And when I'm dead I'll hurt you worse!'

'Thank goodness, I shall be dead long before you, darling.'

'Huh! Emma says, '"Never know your luck."' (Michael had been talking to Helen's elderly flat-faced maid.) 'Lots of little boys die quite soon. So'll I. *Then* you'll see!'

Helen caught her breath and moved towards the door, but the wail of 'Mummy! Mummy!' drew her back again, and the two wept together.

At ten years old, after two terms at a prep. school, something or somebody gave him the idea that his civil status was not quite regular. He attacked Helen on the subject, breaking down her stammered defences with the family directness.

'Don't believe a word of it,' he said, cheerily, at the end. 'People wouldn't have talked like they did if my people had been married. But don't you bother, Auntie. I've found out all about my sort in English Hist'ry and the Shakespeare bits. There was William the Conqueror to begin with, and—oh, heaps more, and they all got on first-rate. 'Twon't make any difference to you, my being *that*—will it?'

'As if anything could—' she began.

'All right. We won't talk about it any more if it makes you cry.' He never mentioned the thing again of his own will, but when, two years later, he skilfully managed to have measles in the holidays, as his temperature went up to the appointed one hundred and four he muttered of nothing else, till Helen's voice, piercing at last his delirium, reached him with assurance that nothing on earth or beyond could make any difference between them.

The terms at his public school and the wonderful Christmas, Easter, and Summer holidays followed each other, variegated and glorious as jewels on a string; and as jewels Helen treasured them. In due time Michael developed his own interests, which ran their courses and gave way to others; but his interest in Helen was constant and increasing throughout. She repaid it with all that she had of affection or could command of counsel and money; and since Michael was no fool, the War took him just before what was like to have been a most promising career.

He was to have gone up to Oxford, with a scholarship, in October. At the end of August he was on the edge of joining the first holocaust of public-school boys who threw themselves into the Line; but the captain of his OTC, where he had been sergeant for nearly a year, headed him off and steered him directly to a commission in a battalion so new that half of it still wore the old Army red, and the other half was breeding meningitis through living overcrowdedly in damp tents. Helen had been shocked at the idea of direct enlistment. 'But it's in the family,' Michael laughed.

'You don't mean to tell me that you believed that old story all this time?' said Helen. (Emma, her maid, had been dead now several years.) 'I gave you my word of honour—and I give it again—that—that it's all right. It is indeed.'

'Oh, *that* doesn't worry me. It never did,' he replied valiantly. 'What I meant was, I should have got into the show earlier if I'd enlisted—like my grandfather.

'Don't talk like that! Are you afraid of its ending so soon, then!'

'No such luck. You know what K says.'

'Yes. But my banker told me last Monday it couldn't *possibly* last beyond Christmas—for financial reasons.'

'Hope he's right, but our Colonel—and he's a Regular—says it's going to be a long job.'

Michael's battalion was fortunate in that, by some chance which meant several 'leaves', it was used for coast-defence among shallow trenches on the Norfolk coast; thence sent north to watch the mouth of a Scotch estuary, and, lastly, held for weeks on a baseless rumour of distant service. But, the very day that Michael was to have met Helen for four whole hours at a railway-junction up the line, it was hurled out, to help make good the wastage of Loos, and he had only just time to send her a wire of farewell.

In France luck again helped the battalion. It was put down near the Salient, where it led a meritorious and unexacting life, while the Somme was being manufactured; and enjoyed the peace of the Armentieres and Laventie sectors when that battle began. Finding that it had sound views on protecting its own flanks and could dig, a prudent Commander stole it out of its own Division, under pretence of helping to lay telegraphs, and used it round Ypres at large.

A month later, just after Michael had written Helen that there was nothing special doing and therefore no need to worry, a shell-splinter dropping out of a wet dawn killed him at once. The next shell uprooted and laid down over the body what had been the foundation of a barn wall, so neatly that none but an expert would have guessed that anything unpleasant had happened.

By this time the village was old in experience of war, and, English fashion, had evolved a ritual to meet it. When the postmistress handed her seven-year-old daughter the official telegram to take to Miss Turrell, she observed to the Rector's gardener: 'It's Miss Helen's turn now.' He replied, thinking of his own son: 'Well, he's lasted longer than some.' The child herself came to the front-door weeping aloud, because Master Michael had often given her sweets. Helen, presently, found herself pulling down the house-blinds one after one with great care, and saying earnestly to each: 'Missing *always* means dead.' Then she took her place in the dreary procession that was impelled to go through an inevitable series of unprofitable emotions. The Rector, of course, preached hope and prophesied word, very soon, from a prison camp. Several friends, too, told her perfectly truthful tales, but always about other women, to whom, after months and months of silence, their missing had been miraculously restored. Other people urged her to communicate with infallible Secretaries of organizations who could communicate with benevolent neutrals, who could extract accurate information from the most secretive of Hun prison commandants. Helen did and wrote and signed everything that was suggested or put before her.

Once, on one of Michael's leaves, he had taken her over munition factory, where she saw the progress of a shell from blank-iron to the all but finished article. It struck her at the time that the wretched thing was never left alone for a single second; and 'I'm being manufactured into a bereaved next of kin,' she told herself, as she prepared her documents.

In due course, when all the organizations had deeply or sincerely regretted their inability to trace, etc., something gave way within her and all sensation—save of thankfulness for the release—came to an end in blessed passivity. Michael had died and her world had stood still and she had been one with the full shock of that arrest. Now she was standing still and the world was going forward, but it did not concern her— in no way or relation did it touch her. She knew this by the ease with which she could slip Michael's name into talk and incline her head to the proper angle, at the proper murmur of sympathy.

In the blessed realization of that relief, the Armistice with all its bells broke over her and passed unheeded. At the end of another year she had overcome her physical loathing of the living and returned young, so that she could take them by the hand and almost sincerely wish them well.

She had no interest in any aftermath, national or personal, of the war, but, moving at an immense distance, she sat on various relief committees and held strong views—she heard herself delivering them—about the site of the proposed village War Memorial.

Then there came to her, as next of kin, an official intimation, backed by a page of a letter to her in indelible pencil, a silver identity-disc, and a watch, to the effect that the body of Lieutenant Michael Turrell had been found, identified, and re-interred in Hagenzeele Third Military Cemetery—the letter of the row and the grave's number in that row duly given.

So Helen found herself moved on to another process of the manufacture—to a world full of exultant or broken relatives, now strong in the certainty that there was an altar upon earth where they might lay their love. These soon told her, and by means of time-tables made clear, how easy it was and how little it interfered with life's affairs to go and see one's grave.

'*So* different,' as the Rector's wife said, 'if he'd been killed in Mesopotamia, or even Gallipoli.'

The agony of being waked up to some sort of second life drove Helen across the Channel, where, in a new world of abbreviated titles, she learnt that Hagenzeele Third could be comfortably reached by an afternoon train which fitted in with the morning boat, and that there was a comfortable little hotel not three kilometres from Hagenzeele itself, where one could spend quite a comfortable night and see one's grave next morning. All this she had from a Central Authority who lived in a board and tar-paper shed on the skirts of a razed city full of whirling lime-dust and blown papers.

'By the way,' said he, 'you know your grave, of course!'

'Yes, thank you,' said Helen, and showed its row and number typed on Michael's own little typewriter. The officer would have checked it, out of one of his many books; but a large Lancashire woman thrust between them and bade him tell her where she might find her son, who had been corporal in the A.S.C. His proper name, she sobbed, was Anderson, but, coming of respectable folk, he had of course enlisted under the name of Smith; and had been killed at Dickiebush, in early 'Fifteen. She had not his number nor did she know which of his two Christian names he might have used with his alias; but her Cook's tourist ticket expired at the end of Easter week, and if by then she could not find her child she should go mad. Whereupon she fell forward on Helen's breast; but the officer's wife came out quickly from a little bedroom behind the office, and the three of them lifted the woman on to the cot.

'They are often like this,' said the officer's wife, loosening the tight bonnet-strings. 'Yesterday she said he'd been killed at Hooge. Are you sure you know your grave? It makes such a difference.'

'Yes, thank you,' said Helen, and hurried out before the woman on the bed should begin to lament again.

Tea in a crowded mauve and blue striped wooden structure, with a false front, carried her still further into the nightmare. She paid her bill beside a stolid, plain-featured Englishwoman, who, hearing her inquire about the train to Hagenzeele, volunteered to come with her.

'I'm going to Hagenzeele myself,' she explained .'Not to Hagenzeele Third; mine is Sugar Factory, but they call it La Rosière now. It's just south of Hagenzeele Three. Have you got your room at the hotel there!'

'Oh yes, thank you. I've wired.'

'That's better. Sometimes the place is quite full, and at others there's hardly a soul. But they've put bathrooms into the old Lion d'Or—that's the hotel on the west side of Sugar Factory—and it draws off a lot of people, luckily.'

'It's all new to me. This is the first time I've been over.'

'Indeed! This is my ninth time since the Armistice. Not on my own ac-count. *I* haven't lost any one, thank God—but, like every one else, I've a lot of friends at home who have. Coming over as often as I do, I find it helps them to have some one just look at the—the place and tell them about it afterwards. And one can take photos for them, too. I get quite a list of commissions to execute.' She laughed nervously and tapped her slung Kodak. 'There are two or three to see at Sugar Factory this time, and plenty of others in the cemeteries all about. My system is to save them up, and arrange them, you know. And when I've got enough com-missions for one area to make it worth while, I pop over and execute them. It *does* comfort people.'

'I suppose so,' Helen answered, shivering as they entered the little train.

'Of course it does. (Isn't it lucky we've got window-seats!) It must do or they wouldn't ask one to do it, would they! I've a list of quite twelve or fifteen commissions here'—she tapped the Kodak again—'I must sort them out tonight. Oh, I forgot to ask you. What's yours!'

'My nephew,' said Helen. 'But I was very fond of him.'

'Ah, yes! I sometimes wonder whether *they* know after death! What do you think?'

'Oh, I don't—I haven't dared to think much about that sort of thing,' said Helen, almost lifting her hands to keep her off.

'Perhaps that's better,' the woman answered. 'The sense of loss must be enough, I expect. Well, I won't worry you any more.'

Helen was grateful, but when they reached the hotel Mrs Scarsworth (they had exchanged names) insisted on dining at the same table with her, and after the meal, in the little, hideous salon full of low-voiced relatives, took Helen through her 'commissions' with biographies of the dead, where she happened to know them, and sketches of their next of kin. Helen endured till nearly half-past nine, ere she fled to her room.

Almost at once there was a knock at her door and Mrs Scarsworth entered; her hands, holding the dreadful list, clasped before her.

'Yes—yes—*I* know,' she began. 'You're sick of me, but I want to tell you something. You—you aren't married, are you? Then perhaps you won't ... But it doesn't matter. I've *got* to tell some one. I can't go on any longer like this.'

'But please—' Mrs Scarsworth had backed against the shut door, and her mouth worked dryly.

In a minute,' she said. 'You—you know about these graves of mine I was telling you about downstairs, just now! They really *are* commissions. At least several of them are.' Her eye wandered round the room. 'What extraordinary wall-papers they have in Belgium, don't you think? ...Yes. I swear they are commissions. But there's *one*, d'you see, and—and he was more to me than anything else in the world. Do you understand?'

Helen nodded.

'More than any one else. And, of course, he oughtn't to have been. He ought to have been nothing to me. But he *was*. He *is*. That's why I do the commissions, you see. That's all.'

'But why do you tell me!' Helen asked desperately.

'Because I'm *so* tired of lying. Tired of lying—always lying—year in and year out. When I don't tell lies I've got to act 'em and I've got to think 'em, always. *You* don't know what that means. He was everything to me that he oughtn't to have been—the one real thing—the only thing that ever happened to me in all my life; and I've had to pretend he wasn't. I've had to watch every word I said, and think out what lie I'd tell next, for years and years!'

'How many years?' Helen asked.

'Six years and four months before, and two and three-quarters after. I've gone to him eight times, since. Tomorrow'll make the ninth, and—and I can't—I *can't* go to him again with nobody in the world knowing. I want to be honest with some one before I go. Do you understand! It doesn't matter about *me*. I was never truthful, even as a girl. But it isn't worthy of *him*. So I—I had to tell you. I can't keep it up any longer. Oh, I can't.'

She lifted her joined hands almost to the level of her mouth and brought them down sharply, still joined, to full arms' length below her waist. Helen reached forward, caught them, bowed her head over them, and murmured: 'Oh, my dear! My—' Mrs Scarsworth stepped back, her face all mottled.

'My God!' said she. 'Is *that* how you take it!'

Helen could not speak, and the woman went out; but it a long while before Helen was able to sleep.

Next morning Mrs Scarsworth left early on her round of commissions, and Helen walked alone to Hagenzeele Third. The place was still in the making, and stood some five or six feet above the metalled road, which it flanked for hundred yards. Culverts across a deep ditch served for entrances through the unfinished boundary wall. She climbed a few wooden-faced earthen steps and then met the entire crowded level of the thing in one held breath. She did not know Hagenzeele Third counted twenty-one thousand dead already. All she saw was a merciless sea of black crosses, bearing little strips of stamped tin at all angles across their faces. She could distinguish no order or arrangement in their mass; nothing but a waist-high wilderness as of weeds stricken dead, rushing at her. She went forward, moved to the left and the right hopelessly, wondering by what guidance she should ever come to her own. A great distance away there was a line of whiteness. It proved to be a block of some two or three hundred graves whose headstones had already been set, whose flowers planted out, and whose new-sown grass showed green. Here she could see clear-cut letters at the ends of the rows, referring to her slip, realized that it was not here she must look.

A man knelt behind a line of headstones—evidently a gardener, for he was firming a young plant in the soft earth. She went towards him, her paper in her hand. He rose at her approach and without prelude or salutation asked: 'Who are you looking for?'

'Lieutenant Michael Turrell—my nephew,' said Helen slowly and word for word, as she had many thousands of times in her life.

The man lifted his eyes and looked at her with infinite compassion before he turned from the fresh-sown grass toward the naked black crosses.

'Come with me,' he said, 'and I will show you where your son lies.'

When Helen left the Cemetery she turned for a last look. In the distance she saw the man bending over his young plants; and she went away, supposing him to be the gardener.

The Burden

One grief on me is laid
Each day of every year,
Wherein no soul can aid,
Whereof no soul can hear:
Whereto no end is seen
Except to grieve again--
Ah, Mary Magdalene,
Where is there greater pain?

To dream on dear disgrace
Each hour of every day--
To bring no honest face
To aught I do or say:

To lie from morn till e'en--
To know my lies are vain--
Ah, Mary Magdalene,
Where can be greater pain?

To watch my steadfast fear
Attend mine every way
Each day of every year--
Each hour of every day:
To burn, and chill between--
To quake and rage again--
Ah, Mary Magdalene,
Where shall be greater pain:

One grave to me was given--
To guard till Judgment Day--
But God looked down from Heaven
And rolled the Stone away!
One day of all my years--
One hour of that one day--
His Angel saw my tears
And rolled the Stone away!

Thoughts on The Gardener

When this story was written, only seven years after the armistice of 1918, grieving mothers and fathers, sisters and brothers were still visiting the last resting places of the British war dead, as many were to do for decades after. Kipling visited the grave that bore his son's name, but whether it contained the right body or not has since become a matter of dispute. As a member of the Imperial (subsequently Commonwealth) War Graves Commission Kipling became acquainted with many such cemeteries, no doubt lending authenticity to this, one of his most densely written and compassionate stories. Its style is markedly more restrained than anything in his earlier works.

Another short story writer has commented, 'The final effect of "The Gardener" is like a blow but hinges on a single word of dialogue that can easily be missed; by this time Kipling's style is pared down beyond ellipsis to the point of ambiguity. Patriotism is not the issue here, let alone jingoism. This is a tale told in the whispering voice of a man who knows loss in his bones, burns with rage, but still feels the impulse towards reticence. The emotion could scarcely feel more contemporary.' (Richard Rayner, LA Review of Books. 27 August, 2011.)

'The Gardener' is full of enigmas, but the two main ones concern the parentage of Michael and the significance of the gardener figure.

Clues to Michael's parentage abound, but can be misleading. By the second page it is clear that, rather than picking up the child of her late 'discreditable' brother and an Indian woman, as she had told the village, Helen had gone abroad to have her own child before returning home 'thin and worn but triumphant'. She encouraged the little boy to call her Auntie, until at the age of six she allowed him to call her 'Mummy' at bedtime. At the age of ten the bright young lad realized that 'his civil status was not quite regular'. He agreed not to speak of it, but the knowledge hurt him deeply, and Helen was troubled by her own deceit.

It is difficult in light of 'the gardener's' awareness of Helen's parentage, to believe, as some have suggested, that he was meant to be no more than a mortal man who simply displayed Christ-like compassion. The obvious reading of 'The Gardener' is to be found in the Fourth Gospel in which Mary Magdalene is afforded a vision of the Risen Christ. We are told that she addressed him, 'supposing him to be the gardener'. Sometimes the obvious is the correct interpretation. Those who doubt it should consider the epigraph, in particular its second stanza.

Helen's lie concerned Michael's parentage. Her burden, like the stone outside the tabernacle, was removed by the gardener's disclosure of her true relationship with the boy.

After the encounter between Helen and the gardener no further words are exchanged between them and we must assume either that she did not hear his reference to 'her' son or, as I suspect was the author's intention, chose to ignore it. (By contrast, the Biblical Mary had no qualms in addressing the gardener as 'rabboni', or Master.)

'The Gardener' offers further nuances for the careful reader. Helen, no saint, seems more concerned with the views of her neighbours than with her moral duty, commenting, 'how little it interfered with life's affairs to go and see one's grave'. In this, she compares unfavourably with that 'stolid, plain featured Englishwoman', Mrs Scarsworth who is so tired of lying about her son's origins that she chooses to unburden herself to a complete stranger.

I doubt if 'The Gardener' will ever be fully 'explained' to everyone's complete satisfaction. Those wishing to delve more deeply into this complex and infinitely moving tale are recommended to read Joyce Tompkinson's brilliant study of it in 'The Art of Rudyard Kipling', 1959.

The cemetery that Kipling used as a model for the fictional 'Hagenzeele Third' was outside the village of Bois Guillaume near Rouen. He visited it on 14 March 1925 and later described to his friend, H. Rider Haggard how he had 'collogued' with the gardener there.

THE WISH HOUSE

Late Came the God

Late came the God, having sent his forerunners who were not regarded—
Late, but in wrath;
Saying: 'The wrong shall be paid, the contempt be rewarded
On all that she hath.'
He poisoned the blade and struck home, the full bosom receiving
The wound and the venom in one, past cure or relieving.

He made treaty with Time to stand still that the grief might be fresh—
Daily renewed and nightly pursued through her soul to her flesh—
Mornings of memory, noontides of agony, midnights unslaked for her,
Till the stones of the streets of her Hells and her Paradise ached for her.

So she lived while her body corrupted upon her.
And she called on the Night for a sign, and a Sign was allowed,
And she builded an Altar and served by the light of her Vision—
Alone, without hope of regard or reward, but uncowed,
Resolute, selfless, divine.
These things she did in Love's honour . . .
What is a God beside Woman? Dust and derision!

The new Church Visitor had just left after a twenty minutes' call. During that time, Mrs. Ashcroft had used such English as an elderly, experienced, and pensioned cook should, who had seen life in London. She was the readier, therefore, to slip back into easy, ancient Sussex (Ts softening to 'd's as one warmed) when the 'bus brought Mrs. Fettley from thirty miles away for a visit, that pleasant March Saturday. The two had been friends since childhood; but, of late, destiny had separated their meetings by long intervals.

Much was to be said, and many ends, loose since last time, to be ravelled up on both sides, before Mrs. Fettley, with her bag of quilt-patches, took the couch beneath the window commanding the garden, and the football-ground in the valley below.

'Most folk got out at Bush Tye for the match there,' she explained, 'so there weren't no one for me to cushion agin, the last five mile. An' she *do* just-about bounce ye.'

'You've took no hurt,' said her hostess. 'You don't brittle by agein', Liz.'

Mrs. Fettley chuckled and made to match a couple of patches to her liking. 'No, or I'd ha' broke twenty year back. You can't ever mind when I was so's to be called round, can ye? '

Mrs. Ashcroft shook her head slowly—she never hurried—and went on stitching a sack-cloth lining into a list-bound rush tool-basket. Mrs. Fettley laid out more patches in the Spring light through the geraniums on the window-sill, and they were silent awhile.

'What like's this new Visitor o' yourn?' Mrs. Fettley inquired, with a nod towards the door. Being very short-sighted, she had, on her entrance, almost bumped into the lady.

Mrs. Ashcroft suspended the big packing-needle judicially on high, ere she stabbed home. 'Settin' aside she don't bring much news with her yet, I dunno as I've anythin' special agin her.'

'Ourn, at Keyneslade,' said Mrs. Fettley, 'she's full o' words an' pity, but she don't stay for answers. Ye can get on with your thoughts while she clacks.'

'This 'un don't clack. She's aimin' to be one o' those High Church nuns, like.'

'Ourn's married, but, by what they say, she've made no great gains of it . . .' Mrs. Fettley threw up her sharp chin. 'Lord! How they dam' cherubim do shake the very bones o' the place! '

The tile-sided cottage trembled at the passage of two specially chartered forty-seat charabancs on their way to the Bush Tye match; a regular Saturday' shopping' 'bus, for the county's capital, fumed behind them; while, from one of the crowded inns, a fourth car backed out to join the procession, and held up the stream of through pleasure-traffic.

'You're as free-tongued as ever, Liz,' Mrs. Ashcroft observed.

'Only when I'm with you. Otherwhiles, I'm Granny—three times over. I lay that basket's for one o' your gran'chiller—ain't it? '

''Tis for Arthur—my Jane's eldest.'

'But he ain't workin' nowheres, is he? '

'No. 'Tis a picnic-basket.'

'You're let off light. My Willie, he's allus at me for money for them aireated wash-poles folk puts up in their gardens to draw the music from Lunnon, like. An' I give it 'im—pore fool me! '

'An' he forgets to give you the promise-kiss after, don't he?' Mrs. Ashcroft's heavy smile seemed to strike inwards.

'He do. 'No odds 'twixt boys now an' forty year back. ''Take all an' give naught-an' we to put up with it! Pore fool we! Three shillin' at a time Willie'll ask me for!'

'They don't make nothin' o' money these days,' Mrs. Ashcroft said.

'An' on'y last week,' the other went on, 'me daughter, she ordered a quarter pound suet at the butchers's; an' she sent it back to 'im to be chopped. She said she couldn't bother with choppin' it.'

'I lay he charged her, then.'

'I lay he did. She told me there was a whisk-drive that afternoon at the Institute, an' she couldn't bother to do the choppin'.'

'Tck!'

Mrs. Ashcroft put the last firm touches to the basket-lining. She had scarcely finished when her sixteen-year-old grandson, a maiden of the moment in attendance, hurried up the garden-path shouting to know if the thing were ready, snatched it, and made off without acknowledgment. Mrs. Fettley peered at him closely.

'They're goin' picnickin' somewheres,' Mrs. Ashcroft explained.

'Ah,' said the other, with narrowed eyes. 'I lay *he* won't show much mercy to any he comes across, either. Now 'oo the dooce do he remind me of, all of a sudden? '

'They must look arter theirselves—'same as we did.' Mrs. Ashcroft began to set out the tea.

'No denyin' *you* could, Gracie,' said Mrs. Fettley.

'What's in your head now?'

'Dunno . . . But it come over me, sudden-like—about dat woman from Rye—I've slipped the name—Barnsley, wadn't it? '

'Batten—Polly Batten, you're thinkin' of.'

'That's it—Polly Batten. That day she had it in for you with a hay-fork—'time we was all hayin' at Smalldene—for stealin' her man.'

'But you heered me tell her she had my leave to keep him?' Mrs. Ashcroft's voice and smile were smoother than ever.

'I did—an' we was all looking that she'd prod the fork spang through your breastes when you said it.'

'No-oo. She'd never go beyond bounds—Polly. She shruck too much for reel doin's.'

'Allus seems to *me*,' Mrs. Fettley said after a pause, 'that a man 'twixt two fightin' women is the foolishest thing on earth. 'Like a dog bein' called two ways.'

'Mebbe. But what set ye off on those times, Liz? '

'That boy's fashion o' carryin' his head an' arms. I haven't rightly looked at him since he's growed. Your Jane never showed it, but—*him*! Why, 'tis Jim Batten and his tricks come to life again! . . . Eh?'

'Mebbe. There's some that would ha' made it out so—bein' barren-like, themselves.'

'Oho! Ah well! Dearie, dearie me, now! . . . An' Jim Batten's been dead this——'

'Seven and twenty year,' Mrs. Ashcroft answered briefly. 'Won't ye draw up, Liz?'

Mrs. Fettley drew up to buttered toast, currant bread, stewed tea, bitter as leather, some home-preserved pears, and a cold boiled pig's tail to help down the muffins. She paid all the proper compliments.

'Yes. I dunno as I've ever owed me belly much,' said Mrs. Ashcroft thoughtfully. 'We only go through this world once.'

'But don't it lay heavy on ye, sometimes?' her guest suggested.

'Nurse says I'm a sight liker to die o' me indigestion than me leg.' For Mrs. Ashcroft had a long-standing ulcer on her shin, which needed regular care from the Village Nurse, who boasted (or others did, for her) that she had dressed it one hundred and three times already during her term of office.

'An' you that *was* so able, too! It's all come on ye before your full time, like. *I*'ve watched ye goin'.' Mrs. Fettley spoke with real affection.

'Somethin's bound to find ye sometime. I've me 'eart left me still,' Mrs. Ashcroft returned.

'You was always big-hearted enough for three. That's somethin' to look back on at the day's eend.'

'I reckon you've *your* back-lookin's, too,' was Mrs. Ashcroft's answer.

'You know it. But I don't think much regardin' such matters excep' when I'm along with you, Gra'. 'Takes two sticks to make a fire.'

Mrs. Fettley stared, with jaw half-dropped, at the grocer's bright calendar on the wall. The cottage shook again to the roar of the motortraffic, and the crowded football-ground below the garden roared almost as loudly; for the village was well set to its Saturday leisure.

***

Mrs. Fettley had spoken very precisely for some time without interruption, before she wiped her eyes. 'And,' she concluded, 'they read 'is death-notice to me, out o' the paper last month. O' course it wadn't any o' *my* becomin' concerns—let be I 'adn't set eyes on him for so long. O' course *I* couldn't say nor show nothin'. Nor I've no rightful call to go to Eastbourne to see 'is grave, either. I've been schemin' to slip over there by the 'bus some day; but they'd ask questions at 'ome past endurance. So I 'aven't even *that* to stay me.'

'But you've 'ad your satisfactions?'

'Godd! Yess! Those four years 'e was workin' on the rail near us. An' the other drivers they gave him a brave funeral, too.'

'Then you've naught to cast-up about. 'Nother cup o' tea?'

***

The light and air had changed a little with the sun's descent, and the two elderly ladies closed the kitchen-door against chill. A couple of jays squealed and skirmished through the undraped apple-trees in the garden. This time, the word was with Mrs. Ashcroft, her elbows on the teatable, and her sick leg propped on a stool . . . .

'Well I never! But what did your 'usband say to that?' Mrs. Fettley asked, when the deep-toned recital halted.

"'E said I might go where I pleased for all of 'im. But seein' 'e was bed-rid, I said I'd 'tend 'im out. 'E knowed I wouldn't take no advantage of 'im in that state. 'E lasted eight or nine week. Then he was took with a seizure-like; an' laid stone-still for days. Then 'e propped 'imself up abed an' says: "You pray no man'll ever deal with you like you've dealed with some." "An' you?" I says, for *you* know, Liz, what a rover 'e was. "It cuts both ways," says 'e, "but *I'm* death-wise, an' I can see what's comin' to you." He died a-Sunday an' was buried a-Thursday . . . An' yet I'd set a heap by him—one time or—did I ever? '

'You never told me that before,' Mrs. Fettley ventured.

'I'm payin' ye for what ye told me just now. Him bein' dead, I wrote up, sayin' I was free for good, to that Mrs. Marshall in Lunnon—which gave me my first place as kitchen-maid—Lord, how long ago! She was well pleased, for they two was both gettin' on, an' I knowed their ways. You remember, Liz, I used to go to 'em in service between whiles, for years—when we wanted money, or − or my 'usband was away − on occasion.'

"E *did* get that six months at Chichester, didn't 'e?' Mrs. Fettley whispered. 'We never rightly won to the bottom of it.'

"E'd ha' got more, but the man didn't die.'

"None o' your doin's, was it, Gra'?'

'No! 'Twas the woman's husband this time. An' so, my man bein' dead, I went back to them Marshall's, as cook, to get me legs under a gentleman's table again, and be called with a handle to me name. That was the year you shifted to Portsmouth.'

'Cosham,' Mrs. Fettley corrected. 'There was a middlin' lot o' new buildin' bein' done there. My man went first, an' got the room, an' I follered.'

'Well, then, I was a year—abouts in Lunnon, all at a breath, like, four meals a day an' livin' easy. Then, 'long towards autumn, they two went travellin', like, to France; keepin' me on, for they couldn't do without me. I put the house to rights for the caretaker, an' then I slipped down 'ere to me sister Bessie—me wages in me pockets, an' all 'ands glad to be'old of me.'

'That would be when I was at Cosham,' said Mrs. Fettley.

'*You* know, Liz, there wasn't no cheap-dog pride to folk, those days, no more than there was cinemas nor whisk-drives. Man or woman 'ud lay hold o' any job that promised a shillin' to the backside of it, didn't they? I was all peaked up after Lunnon, an' I thought the fresh airs 'ud serve me. So I took on at Smalldene, obligin' with a hand at the early potato-liftin, stubbin' hens, an' such-like. They'd ha' mocked me sore in my kitchen in Lunnon, to see me in men's boots, an me petticoats all shorted.'

'Did it bring ye any good?' Mrs. Fettley asked.

"Twadn't for that I went. You know, 's'well's me, that na'un happens to ye till it 'as 'appened. Your mind don't warn ye before'and of the road ye've took, till you're at the far eend of it. We've only a backwent view of our proceedin's.'

''Oo was it? '

''Arry Mockler.' Mrs. Ashcroft's face puckered to the pain of her sick leg.

Mrs. Fettley gasped. ''Arry? Bert Mockler's son! An' *I* never guessed! '

Mrs. Ashcroft nodded. 'An' I told myself—*an*' I beleft it—that I wanted field-work.'

'What did ye get out of it? '

'The usuals. Everythin' at first—worse than naught after. I had signs an' warnings a-plenty, but I took no heed of 'em. For we was burnin' rubbish one day, just when we'd come to know how 'twas with—with both of us. 'Twas early in the year for burnin', an' I said so. "No!" says he. " The sooner dat old stuff's off an' done with," 'e says, "the better." 'Is face was harder'n rocks when he spoke. Then it come over me that I'd found me master, which I 'adn't ever before. I'd allus owned 'em, like.'

'Yes ! Yes ! They're yourn or you're theirn,' the other sighed. 'I like the right way best.'

'I didn't. But 'Arry did . . . 'Long then, it come time for me to go back to Lunnon. I couldn't. I clean couldn't! So, I took an' tipped a dollop o' scaldin' water out o' the copper one Monday mornin' over me left 'and and arm. Dat stayed me where I was for another fortnight.'

'Was it worth it?' said Mrs. Fettley, looking at the silvery scar on the wrinkled fore-arm.

Mrs. Ashcroft nodded. 'An' after that, we two made it up 'twixt us so's 'e could come to Lunnon for a job in a liv'rystable not far from me. 'E got it. *I*'tended to that. There wadn't no talk nowhere. His own mother never suspicioned how 'twas. He just slipped up to Lunnon, an' there we abode that winter, not 'alf a mile 'tother from each.'

'Ye paid 'is fare an' all, though'; Mrs. Fettley spoke convincedly.

Again Mrs. Ashcroft nodded. 'Dere wadn't much I didn't do for him. 'E was me master, an'—O God, help us!—we'd laugh over it walkin' together after dark in them paved streets, an' me corns fair wrenchin' in me boots! I'd never been like that before. Ner he! Ner he!'

Mrs. Fettley clucked sympathetically.

'An' when did ye come to the eend?' she asked.

'When 'e paid it all back again, every penny. Then I knowed, but I wouldn't *suffer* meself to know. "You've been mortal kind to me," he says. "Kind!" I said. "'Twixt *us*?" But 'e kep' all on tellin' me 'ow kind I'd been an' 'e'd never forget it all his days. I held it from off o' me for three evenin's, because I would *not* believe. Then 'e talked about not bein' satisfied with 'is job in the stables, an' the men there puttin' tricks on 'im, an' all they lies which a man tells when 'e's leavin' ye. I heard 'im out, neither 'elpin' nor 'inderin'. At the last, I took off a fiddle brooch which he'd give me an' I says: "Dat'll do. *I* ain't askin' na'un'." An' I turned me round an' walked off to me own sufferin's. 'E didn't make 'em worse. 'E didn't come nor write after that. 'E slipped off 'ere back 'ome to 'is mother again.'

'An' 'ow often did ye look for 'en to come back?' Mrs. Fettley demanded mercilessly.

'More'n once—more'n once! Goin' over the streets we'd used, I thought de very pave-stones 'ud shruck out under me feet.'

'Yes,' said Mrs. Fettley. 'I dunno but dat don't 'urt as much as aught else. An' dat was all ye got? '

'No. 'Twadn't. That's the curious part, if you'll believe it, Liz.'

'I do. I lay you're further off lyin' now than in all your life, Gra'.'

'I am . . . An' I suffered, like I'd not wish my most arrantest enemies to. God's Own Name! I went through the hoop that spring! One part of it was 'eddicks which I'd never known all me days before. Think o' *me* with an 'eddick! But I come to be grateful for 'em. They kep' me from thinkin' . . .'

''Tis like a tooth,' Mrs. Fettley commented. 'It must rage an' rugg till it tortures itself quiet on ye; an' then—then there's na'un left.'

'*I* got enough lef' to last me all my days on earth. It come about through our charwoman's fiddle girl—Sophy Ellis was 'er name—all eyes an' elbers an' hunger. I used to give 'er vittles. Otherwhiles, I took no special notice of 'er, an' a sight less, o' course, when me trouble about 'Arry was on me. But—you know how fiddle maids first feel it sometimes— she come to be crazy-fond o' me, pawin' an' cuddlin' all whiles; an' I 'adn't the 'eart to beat 'er off . . . One afternoon, early in spring 'twas, 'er mother 'ad sent 'er round to scutchel up what vittles she could off of us. I was settin' by the fire, me apern over me head, halfmad with the 'eddick, when she slips in. I reckon I was middlin' short with 'er. "Lor'!" she says. "Is *that* all? I'll take it off you in two-twos! " I told her not to lay a finger on me, for I thought she'd want to stroke my forehead; an'—I ain't that make. "*I* won't tech ye," she says, an' slips out again. She 'adn't been gone ten minutes 'fore me old 'eddick took off quick as bein' kicked. So I went about my work. Prasin'ly, Sophy comes back, an' creeps into my chair quiet as a mouse. 'Er eyes was deep in 'er 'ead an' 'er face all drawed. I asked 'er what 'ad 'appened. "Nothin'," she says. "On'y *I've* got it now." "Got what?" I says. " Your 'eddick," she says, all hoarse an' sticky-tipped. "I've took it on me." "Nonsense," I says, "it went of itself when you was out. Lay still an' I'll make ye a cup o' tea." "'Twon't do no good," she says, "till your time's up. 'Ow long do *your* 'eddicks last?" "Don't talk silly," I says, "or I'll send for the Doctor." It looked to me like she might be hatchin' de measles. "Oh, Mrs. Ashcroft," she says, stretchin' out 'er fiddle thin arms. "I do love ye." There wasn't any holdin' agin that. I took 'er into me lap an' made much of 'er. "Is it truly gone?" she says. "Yes," I says, "an' if 'twas you took it away, I'm truly grateful." "'*Twas* me," she says, layin' 'er cheek to mine. "No one but me knows how." An' then she said she'd changed me 'eddick for me at a Wish 'Ouse.'

'Whatt?' Mrs. Fettley spoke sharply.

'A Wish House. No! *I*'adn't 'eard o' such things, either. I couldn't get it straight at first, but, puttin' all together, I made out that a Wish 'Ouse 'ad to be a house which 'ad stood unlet an' empty long enough for Some One, like, to come an' in'abit there. She said a fiddle girl that she'd played with in the livery-stables where 'Arty worked 'ad told 'er so. She said the girl 'ad belonged in a caravan that laid up, o' winters, in Lunnon. Gipsy, I judge.'

'Ooh! There's no sayin' what Gippos know, but *I*'ve never 'eard of a Wish 'Ouse, an' I know—some things,' said Mrs. Fettley.

'Sophy said there was a Wish 'Ouse in Wadloes Road just a few streets off, on the way to our green-grocer's. All you 'ad to do, she said, was to ring the bell an' wish your wish through the slit o' the letter-box. I asked 'er if the fairies give it 'er? "Don't ye know," she says, "there's no fairies in a Wish 'Ouse? There's on'y a Token."'

'Goo' Lord A'mighty! Where did she come by *that* word?' cried Mrs. Fettley; for a Token is a wraith of the dead or, worse still, of the living.

'The caravan-girl 'ad told 'er, she said. Well, Liz, it troubled me to 'ear 'er, an' lyin' in me arms she must ha' felt it. "That's very kind o' you," I says, holdin' 'er tight, "to wish me 'eddick away. But why didn't ye ask somethin' nice for yourself?" "You can't do that," she says. "All you'll get at a Wish 'Ouse is leave to take some one else's trouble. I've took Ma's 'eddicks, when she's been kind to me; but this is the first time I've been able to do aught for you. Oh, Mrs. Ashcroft, I *do* just—about love you." An' she goes on all like that. Liz, I tell you my 'air e'en a'most stood on end to 'ear 'er. I asked 'er what like a Token was. "I dunno," she says, "but after you've ringed the bell, you'll 'ear it run up from the basement, to the front door. Then say your wish," she says, "an'

go away." "The Token don't open de door to ye, then?" I says. "Oh no,"
she says. "You on'y 'ear gigglin', like, be'ind the front door. Then you
say you'll take the trouble off of 'oo ever 'tis you've chose for your
love; an' yell get it," she says. I didn't ask no more—she was too 'ot an'
fevered. I made much of 'er till it come time to light de gas, an' a fiddle
after that, 'er 'eddick—mine, I suppose—took off, an' she got down an'
played with the cat.'

'Well, I never!' said Mrs. Fettley. 'Did—did ye foller it up, anyways?'

'She askt me to, but I wouldn't 'ave no such dealin's with a child.'

'What *did* ye do, then?'

"Sat in me own room 'stid o' the kitchen when me 'eddicks come on. But
it lay at de back o' me mind.'

"Twould. Did she tell ye more, ever?'

'No. Besides what the Gippo girl 'ad told 'er, she knew naught, 'cept that
the charm worked. An', next after that—in May 'twas—I suffered the
summer out in Lunnon. 'Twas hot an' windy for weeks, an' the streets
stinkin' o' dried 'orsedung blowin' from side to side an' lyin' level with
the kerb. We don't get that nowadays. I 'ad my 'ol'day just before hoppin', an' come down 'ere to stay with Bessie again. She noticed I'd lost
flesh, an' was all poochy under the eyes.'

'Did ye see 'Arry?"

Mrs. Ashcroft nodded. 'The fourth—no, the fifth day. Wednesday 'twas.
I knowed 'e was workin' at Smalldene again. I asked 'is mother in the
street, bold as brass. She 'adn't room to say much, for Bessie—you know
'er tongue—was talkin' full-clack. But that Wednesday, I was walkin'
with one o' Bessie's chillern hangin' on me skirts, at de back o' Chanter's
Tot. Prasin'ly, I felt 'e was be'ind me on the footpath, an' I knowed by
'is tread 'e'd changed 'is nature. I slowed, an' I heard 'im slow. Then
I fussed a piece with the child, to force him past me, like. So 'e *'ad* to

come past. 'E just says "Good-evenin'," and goes on, tryin' to pull 'isself together.'

'Drunk, was he?' Mrs. Fettley asked.

'Never! S'runk an' wizen; 'is clothes 'angin' on 'im like bags, an' the back of 'is neck whiter'n chalk. 'Twas all I could do not to oppen my arms an' cry after him. But I swallered me spittle till I was back 'ome again an' the chillern abed. Then I says to Bessie, after supper, "What in de world's come to 'Arry Mockler?" Bessie told me 'e'd been a-Hospital for two months, 'long o' cuttin' 'is foot wid a spade, muckin' out the old pond at Smalldene. There was poison in de dirt, an' it rooshed up 'is leg, like, an' come out all over him. 'E 'adn't been back to 'is job—carterin' at Smalldene—more'n a fortnight. She told me the Doctor said he'd go off, likely, with the November frostes; an' 'is mother 'ad told 'er that 'e didn't rightly eat nor sleep, an' sweated 'imself into pools, no odds 'ow chill 'e lay. An' spit terrible o' mornin's. "Dearie me," I says. "But, mebbe, hoppin' 'll set 'im right again," an' I licked me thread-point an' I fetched me needle's eye up to it an' I threads me needle under de lamp, steady as rocks. An' dat night (me bed was in de wash-house) I cried an' I cried. An' *you* know, Liz—for you've been with me in my throes—it takes summat to make me cry.'

'Yes; but Chile-bearin' is on'y just pain,' said Mrs. Fettley.

'I come round by cock-crow, an' dabbed cold tea on me eyes to take away the signs. Long towards nex' evenin'—I was settin' out to lay some flowers on me 'usband's grave, for the look o' the thing—I met 'Arry over against where the War Memorial is now. 'E was comin' back from 'is 'orses, so 'e couldn't *not* see me. I looked 'im all over, an' "'Arry," I says twix' me teeth, "come back an' rest-up in Lunnon." "I won't take it," he says, "for I can give ye naught." "I don't ask it," I says. "By God's Own Name, I don't ask na'un ! On'y come up an' see a Lunnon doctor." 'E lifts 'is two 'eavy eyes at me: "'Tis past that, Gra'," 'e says. "I've but a few months left." "'Arry!" I says. "*My* man!" I says. I couldn't say no more. 'Twas all up in me throat. "Thank ye kindly, Gra'," 'e says (but 'e never says "my woman"), an' 'e went on upstreet an' 'is mother—Oh, damn 'er!—she was watchin' for 'im, an' she shut de door be'ind 'im.'

Mrs. Fettley stretched an arm across the table, and made to finger Mrs. Ashcroft's sleeve at the wrist, but the other moved it out of reach.

'So I went on to the churchyard with my flowers, an' I remembered my 'usband's warnin' that night he spoke. 'E *was* death-wise, an' it '*ad* 'appened as 'e said. But as I was settin' down de jam-pot on the grave-mound, it come over me there was one thing I *could* do for 'Arry. Doctor or no Doctor, I thought I'd make a trial of it. So I did. Nex' mornin', a bill came down from our Lunnon green-grocer. Mrs. Marshall, she'd lef' me petty cash for suchlike—o' course—but I tole Bess 'twas for me to come an' open the 'ouse. So I went up, afternoon train.'

'An'—but I know you 'adn't—'adn't you no fear? '

'What for? There was nothin' front o' me but my own shame an' God's croolty. I couldn't ever get 'Arry—'ow *could* I? I knowed it must go on burnin' till it burned me out.'

'Aie!' said Mrs. Fettley, reaching for the wrist again, and this time Mrs. Ashcroft permitted it.

'Yit 'twas a comfort to know I could try *this* for 'im. So I went an' I paid the green-grocer's bill, an' put 'is receipt in me hand-bag, an' then I stepped round to Mrs. Ellis—our char-an' got the 'ouse-keys an' opened the 'ouse. First, I made me bed to come back to (God's Own Name! Me bed to lie upon!). Nex' I made me a cup o' tea an' sat down in the kitchen thinkin', till 'long towards dusk. Terrible close, 'twas. Then I dressed me an' went out with the receipt in me 'and-bag, feignin' to study it for an address, like. Fourteen, Wadloes Road, was the place—a liddle basement-kitchen 'ouse, m a row of twenty-thirty such, an' tiddy strips o' walled garden in front—the paint off the front doors, an' na'un done to na'un since ever so long. There wasn't 'ardly no one in the streets 'cept the cats. *'Twas* 'ot, too! I turned into the gate bold as brass; up de steps I went an' I ringed the front-door bell. She pealed loud, like it do in an empty house. When she'd all ceased, I 'eard a cheer, like, pushed back on de floor o' the kitchen. Then I 'eard feet on de kitchen-stairs, like it might ha' been a heavy woman in slippers.

They come up to de stairhead, acrost the hall—I 'eard the bare boards creak under 'em—an' at de front door dey stopped. I stooped me to the letter-box slit, an' I says: "Let me take everythin' bad that's in store for my man, 'Arry Mockler, for love's sake." Then, whatever it was 'tother side de door let its breath out, like, as if it 'ad been holdin' it for to 'ear better.'

'Nothin' was *said* to ye?' Mrs. Fettley demanded.

'Na'un. She just breathed out—a sort of *A-ah*, like. Then the steps went back an' downstairs to the kitchen—all draggy—an' I heard the cheer drawed up again.'

'An' you abode on de doorstep, throughout all, Gra'? '

Mrs. Ashcroft nodded.

'Then I went away, an' a man passin' says to me: "Didn't you know that house was empty?" "No," I says. "I must ha' been give the wrong number." An' I went back to our 'ouse, an' I went to bed; for I was fair flogged out. 'Twas too 'ot to sleep more'n snatches, so I walked me about, lyin' down betweens, till crack o' dawn. Then I went to the kitchen to make me a cup o' tea, an' I hitted meself just above the ankle on an old roastin' jack o' mine that Mrs. Ellis had moved out from the corner, her last cleanin'. An' so—nex' after that—I waited till the Marshalls come back o' their holiday.'

'Alone there? I'd ha' thought you'd 'ad enough of empty houses,' said Mrs. Fettley, horrified.

'Oh, Mrs. Ellis an' Sophy was runnin' in an' out soon's I was back, an' 'twixt us we cleaned de house again top-to-bottom. There's allus a hand's turn more to do in every house. An' that's 'ow 'twas with me that autumn an' winter, in Lunnon.'

'Then na'un hap—overtook ye for your doin's? '

Mrs. Ashcroft smiled. 'No. Not then. 'Long in November I sent Bessie ten shillin's.'

'You was allus free-'anded,' Mrs. Fettley interrupted.

'An' I got what I paid for, with the rest o' the news. She said the hop-pin' 'ad set 'im up wonderful. 'E'd 'ad six weeks of it, and now 'e was back again carterin' at Smalldene. No odds to me 'ow it 'ad 'appened— 'slong's it *ad*. But I dunno as my ten shillin's eased me much. 'Arry bein' dead, like, 'e'd ha' been mine, till Judgment. 'Arry bein' alive, 'e'd like as not pick up with some woman middlin' quick. I raged over that. Come spring, I 'ad somethin' else to rage for. I'd growed a nasty little weep-in' boil, like, on me shin, just above the boot-top, that wouldn't heal no shape. It made me sick to look at it, for I'm clean-fleshed by nature. Chop me all over with a spade, an' I'd heal like turf. Then Mrs. Marshall she set 'er own doctor at me. 'E said I ought to ha' come to him at first go-off, 'stead o' drawn' all manner o' dyed stockm's over it for months. 'E said I'd stood up too much to me work, for it was settin' very close atop of a big swelled vein, like, behither the small o' me ankle. "Slow come, slow go," 'e says. "Lay your leg up on high an' rest it," he says, "an' 'twill ease off. Don't let it close up too soon. You've got a very fine leg, Mrs. Ashcroft," 'e says. An' he put wet dressin's on it.'

''E done right.' Mrs. Fettley spoke firmly. 'Wet dressin's to wet wounds. They draw de humours, same's a lamp-wick draws de oil.'

'That's true. An' Mrs. Marshall was allus at me to make me set down more, an' dat nigh healed it up. An' then after a while they packed me off down to Bessie's to finish the cure; for I ain't the sort to sit down when I ought to stand up. You was back in the village then, Liz.'

'I was. I was, but—never did I guess!'

'I didn't desire ye to.' Mrs. Ashcroft smiled. 'I saw 'Arry once or twice in de street, wonnerful fleshed up an' restored back. Then, one day I didn't see 'im, an' 'is mother told me one of 'is 'orses 'ad lashed out an' caught 'im on the 'ip. So 'e was abed an' middlin' painful. An' Bessie, she says to his mother, 'twas a pity 'Arry 'adn't a woman of 'is own to take the nursin' off 'er. And the old lady *was* mad! She told us that 'Arry 'ad never looked after any woman in 'is born days, an' as long as she was atop the mowlds, she'd contrive for 'im till 'er two 'ands dropped off. So I knowed she'd do watch-dog for me, 'thout askin' for bones.'

Mrs. Fettley rocked with small laughter.

'That day,' Mrs. Ashcroft went on, 'I'd stood on me feet nigh all the time, watchin' the doctor go in an' out; for they thought it might be 'is ribs, too. That made my boil break again, issuin' an' weepin'. But it turned out 'twadn't ribs at all, an' 'Arry 'ad a good night. When I heard that, nex' mornin', I says to meself, "I won't lay two an' two together *yit*. I'll keep me leg down a week, an' see what comes of it." It didn't hurt me that day, to speak of—'seemed more to draw the strength out o' me like—an' 'Arry 'ad another good night. That made me persevere; but I didn't dare lay two an' two together till the week-end, an' then, 'Arry come forth e'en a'most 'imself again—na'un hurt outside ner in of him. I nigh fell on me knees in de washhouse when Bessie was up-street. "I've got ye now, my man," I says. "You'll take your good from me 'thout knowin' it till my life's end. O God, send me long to live for 'Arry's sake!" I says. An' I dunno that didn't still my ragin's.'

'For good?' Mrs. Fettley asked.

'They come back, plenty times, but, let be how 'twould, I knowed I was doin' for 'im. I *knowed* it. I took an' worked me pains on an' off, like regulatin' my own range, till I learned to 'ave 'em at my command-ments. An' that was funny, too. There was times, Liz, when my trouble 'ud all s'rink an' dry up, like. First, I used to try an' fetch it on again; bein' fearful to leave 'Arry alone too long for anythin' to lay 'old of. Prasin'ly I come to see that was a sign he'd do all right awhile, an' so I saved myself'

''Ow long for?' Mrs. Fettley asked, with deepest interest.

'I've gone de better part of a year onct or twice with na'un more to show than the liddle weepin' core of it, like. *All* s'rinked up an' dried off. Then he'd inflame up—for a warnin'—an' I'd suffer it. When I couldn't no more—an' I *'ad* to keep on goin' with my Lunnon work—I'd lay me leg high on a cheer till it eased. Not too quick. I knowed by the feel of it, those times, dat 'Arry was in need. Then I'd send another five shillin's to Bess, or somethin' for the chillern, to find out if, mebbe, 'e'd took any hurt through my neglects. 'Twas *so*! Year in, year out, I worked it dat way, Liz, an' 'e got 'is good from me 'thout knowin'—for years and years.'

'But what did *you* get out of it, Gra'?' Mrs. Fettley almost wailed. 'Did ye see 'im reg'lar? '

'Times—when I was 'ere on me 'ol'days. An' more, now that I'm 'ere for good. But 'e's never looked at me, ner any other woman 'cept 'is mother. *'Ow* I used to watch an' listen! So did she.'

'Years an' years!' Mrs. Fettley repeated. 'An' where's 'e workin' at now?'

'Oh, 'e's give up carterin' quite a while. He's workin' for one o' them big tractorisin' firms—plowin' sometimes, an' sometimes off with lorries—fur as Wales, I've 'eard. He comes 'ome to 'is mother 'tween whiles; but I don't set eyes on him now, fer weeks on end. No odds! 'Is job keeps 'im from continuin' in one stay anywheres.'

'But just for de sake o' sayin' somethin'—s'pose 'Arry *did* get married?' said Mrs. Fettley.

Mrs. Ashcroft drew her breath sharply between her still even and natural teeth. 'Dat ain't been required of me,' she answered. 'I reckon my pains 'ull be counted agin that. Don't *you*, Liz?'

'It ought to be, dearie. It ought to be.'

'It *do* 'urt sometimes. You shall see it when Nurse comes. She thinks I don't know it's turned.'

Mrs. Fettley understood. Human nature seldom walks up to the word 'cancer.'

'Be ye certain sure, Gra'?' she asked.

'I was sure of it when old Mr. Marshall 'ad me up to 'is study an' spoke a long piece about my faithful service. I've obliged 'em on an' off for a goodish time, but not enough for a pension. But they give me a weekly 'lowance for life. I knew what *that* sinnified—as long as three years ago.

'Dat don't *prove* it, Gra'.'

'To give fifteen bob a week to a woman 'oo'd live twenty year in the course o' nature? It *do*!'

'You're mistook! You're mistook!' Mrs. Fettley insisted.

'Liz, there's *no* mistakin' when the edges are all heaped up, like—same as a collar. You'll see it. An' I laid out Dora Wickwood, too. *She* 'ad it under the arm-pit, like.'

Mrs. Fettley considered awhile, and bowed her head in finality.

''Ow long d'you reckon 'twill allow ye, countin' from now, dearie?'

'Slow come, slow go. But if I don't set eyes on ye 'fore next hoppin', this'll be good-bye, Liz.'

'Dunno as I'll be able to manage by then—not 'thout I have a liddle dog to lead me. For de chillern, dey won't be troubled, an'—O Gra'! I'm blindin' up—I'm blindin' up!'

'Oh, *dat* was why you didn't more'n finger with your quilt-patches all this while! I was wonderin' . . . But the pain *do* count, don't ye think, Liz? The pain *do* count to keep 'Arry where I want 'im. Say it can't be wasted, like.'

'I'm sure of it—sure of it, dearie. You'll 'ave your reward.'

'I don't want no more'n this—*if* de pain is taken into de reckonin'.'

''Twill be—'twill be, Gra'.'

There was a knock on the door.

'That's Nurse. She's before 'er time,' said Mrs. Ashcroft. 'Open to 'er.'

The young lady entered briskly, all the bottles in her bag clicking. 'Evenin', Mrs. Ashcroft,' she began. 'I've come raound a little earlier than usual because of the Institute dance to-na-ite. You won't ma-ind, will you?,

'Oh, no. Me dancin' days are over.' Mrs. Ashcroft was the self-contained domestic at once.

'My old friend, Mrs. Fettley 'ere, has been settin' talkin' with me a while.'

'I hope she 'asn't been fatiguing you?' said the Nurse a little frostily.

'Quite the contrary. It 'as been a pleasure. Only—only—just at the end I felt a bit—a bit flogged out like.'

'Yes, yes.' The Nurse was on her knees already, with the washes to hand. 'When old ladies get together they talk a deal too much, I've noticed.'

'Mebbe we do,' said Mrs. Fettley, rising. 'So now I'll make myself scarce.'

'Look at it first, though,' said Mrs. Ashcroft feebly. 'I'd like ye to look at it.'

Mrs. Fettley looked, and shivered. Then she leaned over, and kissed Mrs. Ashcroft once on the waxy yellow forehead, and again on the faded grey eyes.

'It *do* count, don't it—de pain?' The lips that still kept trace of their original moulding hardly more than breathed the words.

Mrs. Fettley kissed them and moved towards the door.

Rahere

King Henry's jester, feared by all the Norman Lords
For his eye that pierced their bosoms, for his tongue that shamed their swords;
Fed and flattered by the Churchmen - well they knew how deep he stood
In dark Henry's crooked counsels - fell upon an evil mood.

Suddenly, his days before him and behind him seemed to stand
Stripped and barren, fixed and fruitless as those leagues of naked sand
When St. Michael's ebb slinks outward to the bleak horizon-bound,
And the trampling wide-mouthed waters are withdrawn from sight and sound.

Then a Horror of Great Darkness sunk his spirit and anon,
(Who had seen him wince and whiten as he turned to walk alone)
Followed Gilbert the Physician, and muttered in his ear,
"Thou hast it, O my brother?" "Yea, I have it," said Rahere.

"So it comes," said Gilbert smoothly, "man's most immanent distress.
'Tis a humour of the Spirit which abhorreth all excess;
And, whatever breed the surfeit - Wealth, or Wit, or Power, or Fame
(And thou hast each) the Spirit laboureth to expel the same.

"Hence the dulled eye's deep self-loathing - hence the loaded leaden brow;
Hence the burden of Wanhope that aches thy soul and body now.
Ay, the merriest fool must face it, and the wisest Doctor learn;
For it comes - it comes," said Gilbert, " as it passes - to return."

But Rahere was in his torment, and he wandered, dumb and far,
Till he came to reeking Smithfield where the crowded gallows are..
(Followed Gilbert the Physician) and beneath the wrynecked dead,
Sat a leper and his woman, very merry, breaking bread.

He was cloaked from chin to ankle - faceless, fingerless, obscene
Mere corruption swaddled man-wise, but the woman whole and clean;

And she waited on him crooning, and Rahere beheld the twain,
Each delighting in the other, and he checked and groaned again.

So it comes, - it comes," said Gilbert, "as it came when Life began.
'Tis a motion of the Spirit that revealeth God to man.
In the shape of Love exceeding, which regards not taint or fall,
Since in perfect Love, saith Scripture, can be no excess at all.

Hence the eye that sees no blemish - hence the hour that holds no shame.
Hence the Soul assured the Essence and the Substance are the same.
Nay, the meanest need not miss it, though the mightier pass it by;
For it comes - it comes," said Gilbert, "and, thou seest, it does not die!"

Thoughts on The Wish House

Kipling brought off a literary coup by setting this tale of the (apparently) supernatural in such mundane settings: 'The tile-sided cottage trembled at the passage of two specially chartered forty-seat charabancs on their way to the Bush Tye match; a regular Saturday 'shopping' 'bus, for the county's capital, fumed behind them; while, from one of the crowded inns, a fourth car backed out to join the procession, and held up the stream of through pleasure-traffic.' No less plausible a location for a Wish House can be imagined than 14 Wadloes Road, a terrace house with peeling paint, nor such a Token as the unseen 'heavy woman with slippers', yet their combined effect is horrifying.

The desire to take on the suffering of a loved one is at least as old as the crucifixion. It ties in well with the widespread suspicion that love can heal the body and the mind. When someone desperate to secure her loved one's health discovers that her friend has recovered she may come to believe that it was as a result of her own actions. It seems unlikely that Kipling intended us to believe that the Wish House had any real powers; it is what Grace herself believed that matters.

At the beginning of the story it seems that we are overhearing nothing more than two old women gossiping about their ailments; gradually, however, the tale turns darker as we realize that one of them is dying of cancer, and that this may be the pair's last meeting. Kipling's mastery of motivations is demonstrated in part by the fact that he paints Grace as fundamentally selfish: she wants her man to love her and her alone. The author plays his 'grace' note at the end of the tale when Grace reveals to her friend her doubts about the reality of the whole superstitious procedure. ('It do count, don't it - de pain?')

The reference to 'hoppin'' is to the former East End practice of working families going to Kent to pick the hops.

Angus Wilson described 'The Wish House' as 'probably Kipling's most successful single story.'

As to the epilogue poem, Rahere was the jester to King Henry I and is supposed to have founded St Bartholomew's hospital with his own money. His tomb is in the Priory church near the hospital, but little else is known about him. Kipling's attribution of depression to him is inspired. Gilbert the physician lived in another age entirely. The description of the 'love exceeding' between the leper and his woman is impossibly moving, which alone justified appending the poem to the story.

A MADONNA OF THE TRENCHES

'Whatever a man of the sons of men
Shall say to his heart of the lords above,
They have shown man, verily, once and again,
Marvellous mercies and infinite love.

***

'O sweet one love, O my life's delight,
Dear, though the days have divided us,
Lost beyond hope, taken far out of sight,
Not twice in the world shall the Gods do thus.'
Swinburne, 'Les Noyades'

Seeing how many unstable ex-soldiers came to the Lodge of Instruction (attached to Faith and Works E.C. 5837) in the years after the war, the wonder is there was not more trouble from Brethren whom sudden meetings with old comrades jerked back into their still raw past. But our round, torpedo-bearded local Doctor—Brother Keede, Senior Warden— always stood ready to deal with hysteria before it got out of hand; and when I examined Brethren unknown or imperfectly vouched for on the Masonic side, I passed on to him anything that seemed doubtful. He had had his experience as medical officer of a South London Battalion, during the last two years of the war; and, naturally, often found friends and acquaintances among the visitors.

Brother C. Strangwick, a young, tallish, new-made Brother, hailed from some South London Lodge. His papers and his answers were above suspicion, but his red-rimmed eyes had a puzzled glare that might mean nerves. So I introduced him particularly to Keede, who discovered in him a Headquarters Orderly of his old Battalion, congratulated him on his return to fitness—he had been discharged for some infirmity or other—and plunged at once into Somme memories.

'I hope I did right, Keede,' I said when we were robing before Lodge.

'Oh, quite. He reminded me that I had him under my hands at Sampoux in 'Eighteen, when he went to bits. He was a Runner.'

'Was it shock?' I asked.

'Of sorts—but not what he wanted me to think it was. No, he wasn't shamming. He had jumps to the limit—but he played up to mislead me about the reason of 'em . . . . Well, if we could stop patients from lying, medicine would be too easy, I suppose.'

I noticed that, after Lodge-working, Keede gave him a seat a couple of rows in front of us, that he might enjoy a lecture on the Orientation of King Solomon's Temple, which an earnest Brother thought would be a nice interlude between Labour and the high tea that we called our 'Banquet.' Even helped by tobacco it was a dreary performance. About half-way through, Strangwick, who had been fidgeting and twitching for some minutes, rose, drove back his chair grinding across the tesselated floor, and yelped 'Oh, My Aunt! I can't stand this any longer.' Under cover of a general laugh of assent he brushed past us and stumbled towards the door.

'I thought so!' Keede whispered to me. 'Come along!' We overtook him in the passage, crowing hysterically and wringing his hands. Keede led him into the Tyler's Room, a small office where we stored odds and ends of regalia and furniture, and locked the door.

'I'm—I'm all right,' the boy began, piteously.

''Course you are.' Keede opened a small cupboard which I had seen called upon before, mixed sal volatile and water in a graduated glass, and, as Strangwick drank, pushed him gently on to an old sofa. 'There,' he went on. 'It's nothing to write home about. I've seen you ten times worse. I expect our talk has brought things back.'

He hooked up a chair behind him with one foot, held the patient's hands in his own, and sat down. The chair creaked.

'Don't!' Strangwick squealed. 'I can't stand it! There's nothing on earth creaks like they do! And—and when it thaws we—we've got to slap 'em back with a spa-ade ! 'Remember those Frenchmen's little boots under the duckboards? . . . What'll I do? What'll I do about it?'

Some one knocked at the door, to know if all were well.

'Oh, quite, thanks!' said Keede over his shoulder. 'But I shall need this room awhile. Draw the curtains, please.'

We heard the rings of the hangings that drape the passage from Lodge to Banquet Room click along their poles, and what sound there had been, of feet and voices, was shut off.

Strangwick, retching impotently, complained of the frozen dead who creak in the frost.

'He's playing up still,' Keede whispered. '*That's* not his real trouble—any more than 'twas last time.'

'But surely,' I replied, 'men get those things on the brain pretty badly. 'Remember in October——'

'This chap hasn't, though. I wonder what's really helling him. What are you thinking of?' said Keede peremptorily.

'French End an' Butcher's Row,' Strangwick muttered.

'Yes, there were a few there. But suppose we face Bogey instead of giving him best every time.' Keede turned towards me with a hint in his eye that I was to play up to his leads.

'What was the trouble with French End?' I opened at a venture.

'It was a bit by Sampoux, that we had taken over from the French. They're tough, but you wouldn't call 'em tidy as a nation. They had faced both sides of it with dead to keep the mud back. All those trenches were like gruel in a thaw. Our people had to do the same sort of thing—elsewhere; but Butcher's Row in French End was the—er—show-piece. Luckily, we pinched a salient from Jerry just then, an' straightened things out—so we didn't need to use the Row after November. You remember, Strangwick?'

'My God, yes! When the Buckboard-slats were missin' you'd tread on 'em, an' they'd creak.'

'They're bound to. Like leather,' said Keede. 'It gets on one's nerves a bit, but—'

'Nerves? It's real! It's real!' Strangwick gulped.

'But at your time of life, it'll all fall behind you in a year or so. I'll give you another sip of—paregoric, an' we'll face it quietly. Shall we?'

Keede opened his cupboard again and administered a carefully dropped dark dose of something that was not sal volatile. 'This'll settle you in a few minutes,' he explained. 'Lie still, an' don't talk unless you feel like it.'

He faced me, fingering his beard.

'Ye-es. Butcher's Row wasn't pretty,' he volunteered. 'Seeing Strangwick here, has brought it all back to me again. 'Funny thing! We had a Platoon Sergeant of Number Two—what the deuce was his name?—an elderly bird who must have lied like a patriot to get out to the front at his age; but he was a first-class Non-Com., and the last person, you'd think, to make mistakes. Well, he was due for a fortnight's home leave in January, 'Eighteen. You were at B.H.Q. then, Strangwick, weren't you?'

'Yes. I was Orderly. It was January twenty-first'; Strangwick spoke with a thickish tongue, and his eyes burned. Whatever drug it was, had taken hold.

'About then,' Keede said. 'Well, this Sergeant, instead of coming down from the trenches the regular way an' joinin' Battalion Details after dark, an' takin' that funny little train for Arras, thinks he'll warm himself first. So he gets into a dug-out, in Butcher's Row, that used to be an old French dressing-station, and fugs up between a couple of braziers of pure charcoal! As luck 'ud have it, that was the only dug-out with an inside door opening inwards—some French anti-gas fitting, I expect—and, by what we could make out, the door must have swung to while he was warming. Anyhow, he didn't turn up at the train. There was a search at once. We couldn't afford to waste Platoon Sergeants. We found him in the morning. He'd got his gas all right. A machine-gunner reported him, didn't he, Strangwick?'

'No, Sir. Corporal Grant—o' the Trench Mortars.'

'So it was. Yes, Grant—the man with that little wen on his neck. 'Nothing wrong with your memory, at any rate. What was the Sergeant's name?'

'Godsoe—John Godsoe,' Strangwick answered.

'Yes, that was it. I had to see him next mornin'—frozen stiff between the two braziers—and not a scrap of private papers on him. *That* was the only thing that made me think it mightn't have been—quite an accident.'

Strangwick's relaxing face set, and he threw back at once to the Orderly Room manner.

'I give my evidence—at the time—to you, sir. He passed—overtook me, I should say—comin' down from supports, after I'd warned him for leaf. I thought he was goin' through Parrot Trench as usual; but 'e must 'ave turned off into French End where the old bombed barricade was.'

'Yes. I remember now. You were the last man to see him alive. That was on the twenty-first of January, you say? Now, *when* was it that Dearlove and Billings brought you to me—clean out of your head?' . . . Keede dropped his hand, in the style of magazine detectives, on Strangwick's shoulder. The boy looked at him with cloudy wonder, and muttered: 'I was took to you on the evenin' of the twenty-fourth of January. But you don't think I did him in, do you?'

I could not help smiling at Keede's discomfiture; but he recovered himself. 'Then what the dickens *was* on your mind that evening—before I gave you the hypodermic?'

'The—the things in Butcher's Row. They kept on comin' over me. You've seen me like this before, sir.'

'But I knew that it was a lie. You'd no more got stiffs on the brain then than you have now. You've got something, but you're hiding it.'

''Ow do *you* know, Doctor?' Strangwick whimpered.

'D'you remember what you said to me, when Dearlove and Billings were holding you down that evening?'

'About the things in Butcher's Row?'

'Oh, no! You spun me a lot of stuff about corpses creaking; but you let yourself go in the middle of it—when you pushed that telegram at me. What did you mean, f'rinstance, by asking what advantage it was for you to fight beasts of officers if the dead didn't rise?'

'Did I say "Beasts of Officers"?'

'You did. It's out of the Burial Service.'

'I suppose, then, I must have heard it. As a matter of fact, I 'ave.' Strangwick shuddered extravagantly.

'Probably. And there's another thing—that hymn you were shouting till I put you under. It was something about Mercy and Love. 'Remember it?'

'I'll try,' said the boy obediently, and began to paraphrase, as nearly as possible thus: '"Whatever a man may say in his heart unto the Lord, yea, verily I say unto you—Gawd hath shown man, again and again, marvellous mercy an'—an' somethin' or other love."' He screwed up his eyes and shook.

'Now where did you get *that* from?' Keede insisted.

'From Godsoe—on the twenty-first Jan . . . . 'Ow could I tell what 'e meant to do?' he burst out in a high, unnatural key—'Any more than I knew *she* was dead.'

'Who was dead?' said Keede.

'Me Auntie Armine.'

'The one the telegram came to you about, at Sampoux, that you wanted me to explain—the one that you were talking of in the passage out here just now when you began: "O Auntie," and changed it to "O Gawd," when I collared you?'

'That's her! I haven't a chance with you, Doctor. *I* didn't know there was anything wrong with those braziers. How could I? We're always usin' 'em. Honest to God, I thought at first go-off he might wish to warm himself before the leaf-train. I—I didn't know Uncle John meant to start—'ouse-keepin'.' He laughed horribly, and then the dry tears came.

Keede waited for them to pass in sobs and hiccoughs before he continued: 'Why? Was Godsoe your Uncle?'

'No,' said Strangwick, his head between his hands. 'Only we'd known him ever since we were born. Dad 'ad known him before that. He lived almost next street to us. Him an' Dad an' Ma an'—an' the rest had always been friends. So we called him Uncle—like children do.'

'What sort of man was he?'

'One o' *the* best, sir. 'Pensioned Sergeant with a little money left him—quite independent—and very superior. They had a sittin'-room full o' Indian curios that him and his wife used to let sister an' me see when we'd been good.'

'Wasn't he rather old to join up?'

'That made no odds to him. He joined up as Sergeant Instructor at the first go-off, an' when the Battalion was ready he got 'imself sent along. He wangled me into 'is Platoon when I went out—early in 'Seventeen. Because Ma wanted it, I suppose.'

'I'd no notion you knew him that well,' was Keede's comment.

'Oh, it made no odds to him. He 'ad no pets in the Platoon, but 'e'd write 'ome to Ma about me an' all the doin's. You see'—Strangwick stirred uneasily on the sofa—'we'd known him all our lives—lived in the next street an' all . . . . An' him well over fifty. Oh dear me! *Oh* dear me! What a bloody mix-up things are, when one's as young as me!' he wailed of a sudden.

But Keede held him to the point. 'He wrote to your Mother about you?'

'Yes. Ma's eyes had gone bad followin' on air-raids. 'Blood-vessels broke behind 'em from sittin' in cellars an' bein' sick. She had to 'ave 'er letters read to her by Auntie. Now I think of it, that was the only thing that you might have called anything at all—'

'Was that the Aunt that died, and that you got the wire about?' Keede drove on.

'Yes—Auntie Armine—Ma's younger sister, an' she nearer fifty than forty. What a mix-up! An' if I'd been asked any time about it, I'd 'ave sworn there wasn't a single sol'tary item concernin' her that everybody didn't know an' hadn't known all along. No more conceal to her doin's than—than so much shop-front. She'd looked after sister an' me, when needful—whoopin' cough an' measles just the same as Ma. We was in an' out of her house like rabbits. You see, Uncle Armine is a cabinet-maker, an' second-'and furniture, an' we liked playin' with the things. She 'ad no children, and when the war came, she said she was glad of it. But she never talked much of her feelin's. She kept herself to herself, you understand.' He stared most earnestly at us to help out our understandings.

'What was she like?' Keede inquired.

'A biggish woman, an' had been 'andsome, I believe, but, bein' used to her, we two didn't notice much—except, per'aps, for one thing. Ma called her 'er proper name, which was Bella; but Sis an' me always called 'er Auntie Armine. See?'

'What for?'

'We thought it sounded more like her—like somethin' movin' slow, in armour.'

'Oh! And she read your letters to your mother, did she?'

'Every time the post came in she'd slip across the road from opposite an' read 'em. An'—an' I'll go bail for it that that was all there was to it for as far back as I remember. Was I to swing to-morrow, I'd go bail for *that*! 'Tisn't fair of 'em to 'ave unloaded it all on me, because—because—if the dead *do* rise, why, what in 'ell becomes of me an' all I've believed all me life? I want to know *that*! I—I——'

But Keede would not be put off. 'Did the Sergeant give you away at all in his letters?' he demanded, very quietly.

'There was nothin' to give away—we was too busy—but his letters about me were a great comfort to Ma. I'm no good at writin'. I saved it all up for my leafs. I got me fourteen days every six months an' one over . . . . I was luckier than most, that way.'

'And when you came home, used you to bring 'em news about the Sergeant?' said Keede.

'I expect I must have; but I didn't think much of it at the time. I was took up with me own affairs—naturally. Uncle John always wrote to me once each leaf, tellin' me what was doin' an' what I was li'ble to expect on return, an' Ma 'ud 'ave that read to her. Then o' course I had to slip over to his wife an' pass her the news. An' then there was the young lady that I'd thought of marryin' if I came through. We'd got as far as pricin' things in the windows together.'

'And you didn't marry her—after all?'

Another tremor shook the boy. '*No!*' he cried. ''Fore it ended, I knew what reel things reelly mean! I—I never dreamed such things could be! . . . An' she nearer fifty than forty an' me own Aunt! . . . But there wasn't a sign nor a hint from first to last, so 'ow *could* I tell? Don't you *see* it? All she said to me after me Christmas leaf in' '18, when I come to say good-bye—all Auntie Armine said to me was: "You'll be seein' Mister Godsoe soon?" "Too soon for my likings," I says. " Well then, tell 'im from me," she says, " that I expect to be through with my little trouble by the twenty-first of next month, an' I'm dyin' to see him as soon as possible after that date."'

'What sort of trouble was it?' Keede turned professional at once.

'She'd 'ad a bit of a gatherin' in 'er breast, I believe. But she never talked of 'er body much to any one.'

'' see,' said Keede. 'And she said to you?'

Strangwick repeated: '"Tell Uncle John I hope to be finished of my drawback by the twenty-first, an' I'm dying to see 'im as soon as 'e can after that date." An' then she says, laughin': "But you've a head like a sieve. I'll write it down, an' you can give it him when you see 'im." So she wrote it on a bit o' paper an' I kissed 'er good-bye—I was always her favourite, you see—an' I went back to Sampoux. The thing hardly stayed in my mind at all, d'you see. But the next time I was up in the front line—I was a Runner, d'ye see—our platoon was in North Bay Trench an' I was up with a message to the Trench Mortar there that Corporal Grant was in charge of. Followin' on receipt of it, he borrowed a couple of men off the platoon, to slue 'er round or somethin'. I give Uncle John Auntie Armine's paper, an' I give Grant a fag, an' we warmed up a bit over a brazier. Then Grant says to me: "I don't like it"; an' he jerks 'is thumb at Uncle John in the bay studyin' Auntie's message. Well, *you* know, sir, you had to speak to Grant about 'is way of prophesyin' things—after Rankine shot himself with the Very light.'

'I did,' said Keede, and he explained to me 'Grant had the Second Sight—confound him! It upset the men. I was glad when he got pipped. What happened after that, Strangwick?'

'Grant whispers to me: "Look, you damned Englishman. 'E's for it." Uncle John was leanin' up against the bay, an' hummin' that hymn I was tryin' to tell you just now. He looked different all of a sudden—as if 'e'd got shaved. *I* don't know anything of these things, but I cautioned Grant as to his style of speakin', if an officer 'ad 'eard him, an' I went on. Passin' Uncle John in the bay, 'e nods an' smiles, which he didn't often, an' he says, pocketin' the paper "This suits *me*. I'm for leaf on the twenty-first, too."'

'He said that to you, did he?' said Keede.

'*Pre*cisely the same as passin' the time o' day. O' course I returned the agreeable about hopin' he'd get it, an' in due course I returned to 'Eadquarters. The thing 'ardly stayed in my mind a minute. That was the eleventh January—three days after I'd come back from leaf. You remember, sir, there wasn't anythin' doin' either side round Sampoux the first part o' the month. Jerry was gettin' ready for his March Push, an' as long as he kept quiet, we didn't want to poke 'im up.'

357

'I remember that,' said Keede. 'But what about the Sergeant?'

'I must have met him, on an' off, I expect, goin' up an' down, through the ensuin' days, but it didn't stay in me mind. Why needed it? And on the twenty-first Jan., his name was on the leaf-paper when I went up to warn the leaf-men. I noticed *that*, o' course. Now that very afternoon Jerry 'ad been tryin' a new trench-mortar, an' before our 'Eavies could out it, he'd got a stinker into a bay an' mopped up 'alf a dozen. They were bringin' 'em down when I went up to the supports, an' that blocked Little Parrot, same as it always did. *You* remember, sir?'

'Rather! And there was that big machine-gun behind the Half-House waiting for you if you got out,' said Keede.

'I remembered that too. But it was just on dark an' the fog was comin' off the Canal, so I hopped out of Little Parrot an' cut across the open to where those four dead Warwicks are heaped up. But the fog turned me round, an' the next thing I knew I was knee-over in that old 'alf-trench that runs west o' Little Parrot into French End. I dropped into it—almost atop o' the machine-gun platform by the side o' the old sugar boiler an' the two Zoo-ave skel'tons. That gave me my bearin's, an' so I went through French End, all up those missin' Buckboards, into Butcher's Row where the *poy-looz* was laid in six deep each side, an' stuffed under the Buckboards. It had froze tight, an' the drippin's had stopped, an' the creakin's had begun.'

'Did that really worry you at the time?' Keede asked.

'No,' said the boy with professional scorn. 'If a Runner starts noticin' such things he'd better chuck. In the middle of the Row, just before the old dressin'-station you referred to, sir, it come over me that somethin' ahead on the Buckboards was just like Auntie Armine, waitin' beside the door; an' I thought to meself 'ow truly comic it would be if she could be dumped where I was then. In 'alf a second I saw it was only the dark an' some rags o' gas-screen, 'angin' on a bit of board, 'ad played me the trick. So I went on up to the supports an' warned the leaf-men there, includin' Uncle John. Then I went up Rake Alley to warn 'em in the front line. I didn't hurry because I didn't want to get there till Jerry 'ad quieted down a bit. Well, then a Company Relief dropped in—an' the officer got the wind up over some lights on the flank, an' tied 'em into knots, an' I 'ad to hunt up me leaf-men all over the blinkin' shop. What with one thing an' another, it must 'ave been 'alf-past eight before I got back to the supports. There I run across Uncle John, scrapm' mud off himself, havin' shaved—quite the dandy. He asked about the Arras train, an' I said, if Jerry was quiet, it might be ten o'clock. "Good!" says 'e. "I'll come with you." So we started back down the old trench that used to run across Halnaker, back of the support dug-outs. *You* know, sir.'

Keede nodded.

'Then Uncle John says something to me about seein' Ma an' the rest of 'em in a few days, an' had I any messages for 'em? Gawd knows what made me do it, but I told 'im to tell Auntie Armine I never expected to see anything like *her* up in our part of the world. And while I told him I laughed. That's the last time I 'ave laughed." Oh—you've seen 'er, 'ave you? says he, quite natural-like. Then I told 'im about the sand-bags an' rags in the dark, playin' the trick. "Very likely," says he, brushin' the mud off his putties. By this time, we'd got to the corner where the old barricade into French End was—before they bombed it down, sir. He turns right an' climbs across it. "No, thanks," says I. "I've been there once this evenin'." But he wasn't attendin' to me. He felt behind the rubbish an' bones just inside the barricade, an' when he straightened up, he had a full brazier in each hand.

'"Come on, Clem," he says, an' he very rarely give me me own name. "You aren't afraid, are you?" he says. "It's just as short, an' if Jerry starts up again he won't waste stuff here. He knows it's abandoned." "Who's afraid now?" I says. "Me for one," says he. "I don't want *my* leaf spoiled at the last minute." Then 'e wheels round an' speaks that bit you said come out o' the Burial Service.'

For some reason Keede repeated it in full, slowly: 'If after the manner of men I have fought with beasts at Ephesus, what advantageth it me, if the dead rise not?'

'That's it,' said Strangwick. 'So we went down French End together—everything froze up an' quiet, except for their creakin's. I remember thinkin'——' his eyes began to flicker.

'Don't think. Tell what happened,' Keede ordered.

'Oh! Beg y' pardon! He went on with his braziers, hummin' his hymn, down Butcher's Row. Just before we got to the old dressin'station he stops and sets 'em down an' says "Where did you say she was, Clem? Me eyes ain't as good as they used to be."

'"In 'er bed at 'ome," I says. "Come on down. It's perishin' cold, an' *I'm* not due for leaf."

'"Well, I am," 'e says. "*I* am. . . ." An' then—'give you me word I didn't recognise the voice—he stretches out 'is neck a bit, in a way 'e 'ad, an' he says: "Why, Bella!" 'e says. "Oh, Bella!" 'e says. "Thank Gawd!" 'e says. Just like that! An' then I saw—I tell you I saw—Auntie Armine herself standin' by the old dressin'station door where first I'd thought I'd seen her. He was lookin' at 'er an' she was lookin' at him. I saw it, an' me soul turned over inside me because—because it knocked out everything I'd believed in. I 'ad nothin' to lay 'old of, d'ye see? An' 'e was lookin' at 'er as though he could 'ave et 'er, an' she was lookin' at 'im the same way, out of 'er eyes. Then he says: "Why, Bella," 'e says, "this must be only the second time we've been alone together in all these years." An' I saw 'er half hold out her arms to 'im in that perishin' cold. An' she nearer fifty than forty an' me own Aunt! You can shop me for a lunatic to-morrow, but I saw it—I *saw* 'er answerin' to his spoken word . . . Then 'e made a snatch to unsling 'is rifle. Then 'e cuts 'is hand away saying: "No! Don't tempt me, Bella. We've all Eternity ahead of us. An hour or two won't make any odds." Then he picks up the braziers an' goes on to the dug-out door. He'd finished with me. He pours petrol on 'em, an' lights it with a match, an' carries 'em inside, flarin'. All that time Auntie Armine stood with 'er arms out—an' a look in 'er face! *I* didn't know such things was or could be! Then he comes out an' says: "Come in, my dear"; an' she stoops an' goes into the dug-out with that look on her face—that look on her face! An' then 'e shuts the door from inside an' starts wedgin' it up. So 'elp me Gawd, I saw an' 'eard all these things with my own eyes an' ears!'

He repeated his oath several times. After a long pause Keede asked him if he recalled what happened next.

'It was a bit of a mix-up, for me, from then on. I must have carried on—they told me I did, but—but I was—I felt a—a long way inside of meself, like—if you've ever had that feelin'. I wasn't rightly on the spot at all. They woke me up sometime next morning, because 'e 'adn't showed up at the train; an' some one had seen him with me. I wasn't 'alf cross-examined by all an' sundry till dinner-time.

'Then, I think, I volunteered for Dearlove, who 'ad a sore toe, for a front-line message. I had to keep movin', you see, because I hadn't anything to hold *on* to. Whilst up there, Grant informed me how he'd found Uncle John with the door wedged an' sand-bags stuffed in the cracks. I hadn't waited for that. The knockin' when 'e wedged up was enough for me. 'Like Dad's coffin.'

'No one told *me* the door had been wedged.' Keede spoke severely.

'No need to black a dead man's name, sir.'

'What made Grant go to Butcher's Row?'

'Because he'd noticed Uncle John had been pinchin' charcoal for a week past an' layin' it up behind the old barricade there. So when the 'unt began, he went that way straight as a string, an' when he saw the door shut, he knew. He told me he picked the sand-bags out of the cracks an' shoved 'is hand through and shifted the wedges before any one come along. It looked all right. You said yourself, sir, the door must 'ave blown to.'

'Grant knew what Godsoe meant, then?' Keede snapped.

'Grant knew Godsoe was for it; an' nothin' earthly could 'elp or 'inder. He told me so.'

'And then what did you do?'

'I expect I must 'ave kept on carryin' on, till Headquarters give me that wire from Ma—about Auntie Armine dyin'.'

'When had your Aunt died?'

'On the mornin' of the twenty-first. The mornin' of the 21st! That tore it, d'ye see? As long as I could think, I had kep' tellin' myself it was like those things you lectured about at Arras when we was billeted in the cellars—the Angels of Mons, and so on. But that wire tore it.'

'Oh! Hallucinations! I remember. And that wire tore it?' said Keede.

'Yes! You see'—he half lifted himself off the sofa—'there wasn't a single gor-dam thing left abidin' for me to take hold of, here or hereafter. If the dead *do* rise—and I saw 'em—why—why, *anything* can 'appen. Don't you understand?'

He was on his feet now, gesticulating stiffly.

'For I saw 'er,' he repeated. 'I saw 'im an' 'er—she dead since mornin' time, an' he killin' 'imself before my livin' eyes so's to carry on with 'er for all Eternity—an' she 'oldin' out 'er arms for it! I want to know where I'm *at*! Look 'ere, you two—why stand *we* in jeopardy every hour?'

'God knows,' said Keede to himself.

'Hadn't we better ring for some one?' I suggested. 'He'll go off the handle in a second.'

'No, he won't. It's the last kick-up before it takes hold. I know how the stuff works. Hul-lo!'

Strangwick, his hands behind his back and his eyes set, gave tongue in the strained, cracked voice of a boy reciting. 'Not twice in the world shall the Gods do thus,' he cried again and again.

'And I'm damned if it's goin' to be even once for me!' he went on with sudden insane fury. '*I* don't care whether we '*ave* been pricin' things in the windows . . . . *Let* 'er sue if she likes! She don't know what reel things mean. *I* do—I've 'ad occasion to notice 'em . . . . *No*, I tell you! I'll 'ave 'em when I want 'em, an' be done with 'em; but not till I see that look on a face . . . that look. . . . I'm not takin' any. The reel thing's life an' death. It *begins* at death, d'ye see. *She* can't understand . . . . Oh, go on an' push off to Hell, you an' your lawyers. I'm fed up with it—fed up!'

He stopped as abruptly as he had started, and the drawn face broke back to its natural irresolute lines. Keede, holding both his hands, led him back to the sofa, where he dropped like a wet towel, took out some flamboyant robe from a press, and drew it neatly over him.

'Ye-es. *That's* the real thing at last,' said Keede. 'Now he's got it off his mind he'll sleep. By the way, who introduced him?'

'Shall I go and find out?' I suggested.

'Yes; and you might ask him to come here. There's no need for us to stand to all night.'

So I went to the Banquet, which was in full swing, and was seized by an elderly, precise Brother from a South London Lodge, who followed me, concerned and apologetic. Keede soon put him at his ease.

'The boy's had trouble,' our visitor explained. 'I'm most mortified he should have performed his bad turn here. I thought he'd put it be'ind him.'

'I expect talking about old days with me brought it all back,' said Keede. 'It does sometimes.'

'Maybe! Maybe! But over and above that, Clem's had post-war trouble, too.'

'Can't he get a job? He oughtn't to let that weigh on him, at his time of life,' said Keede cheerily.

"'Tisn't that—he's provided for—but'—he coughed confidentially behind his dry hand—'as a matter of fact, Worshipful Sir, he's—he's implicated for the present in a little breach of promise action.'

'Ah! That's a different thing,' said Keede.

'Yes. That's his reel trouble. No reason given, you understand. The young lady in every way suitable, an' she'd make him a good little wife too, if I'm any judge. But he says she ain't his ideel or something. 'No getting at what's in young people's minds these days, is there?'

'I'm afraid there isn't,' said Keede. 'But he's all right now. He'll sleep. You sit by him, and when he wakes, take him home quietly . . . . Oh, we're used to men getting a little upset here. You've nothing to thank us for, Brother—Brother——'

'Armine,' said the old gentleman. 'He's my nephew by marriage.'

'That's all that's wanted!' said Keede.

Brother Armine looked a little puzzled. Keede hastened to explain. 'As I was saying, all he wants now is to be kept quiet till he wakes.'

Thoughts on A Madonna of the Trenches

Kipling tells this extraordinary tale without making clear whether the reader is intended to believe Bella's ghost to have been actually present with her lover at the time of his death in the dug-out. But there are clues.

The only fact of which we can be certain is that Godsoe, the dependable platoon sergeant, deliberately killed himself. As Strangwick tells it, his uncle first considered shooting himself, but abandoned the attempt before it got anywhere. We know that Aunt Bella, dying of what must have been breast cancer, had told her nephew that she expected 'to be through with my little trouble by the twenty-first of next month, an' I'm dyin' to see him [Godsoe] as soon as possible after that date.' Prior to her 'ghost' being seen in the trench a telegram was received that presumably reported her death - which is about as strong a confirmation of Strangwick's interpretation of events as we can hope for. The extract from Swinburne quoted at the head of the story tends to confirm the hypothesis that, just for once, Kipling contemplated a situation where love impelled the supernatural to take precedence over reality.

But why should his 'uncle's' death have disturbed Strangwick so much? He had, it is true, discovered the Sergeant's adultery with a married woman, but he seemed more concerned with the fact that his aunt, whom he believed to love him before all others, preferred someone else. ('An' she nearer fifty than forty an' me own aunt.')

Strangwick's statement that, 'if the dead do rise - and I saw 'em - why - why anything can 'appen' was a powerful confirmation of conventional Christian morality and enough to shake any doubter. (See 1 Corinthians 16: 'if the dead rise not, then is not Christ raised'.)

But why should Strangwick have broken off his engagement? The answer is to be found in his incoherent rant which makes clear that a conventional marriage could never satisfy someone who had witnessed such passionate love as that between Godsoe and Bella, another confirmation of the 'reality' of the dead Bella's appearance.

'A Madonna of the Trenches' is a masterpiece of the author's art, built up, in Philip Mason's words, in little dabs of paint and spurts of light – filled in with reminiscent detail. Strangwick's report of how in parts of the line the corpses of men were buried in the trenches they had manned is well authenticated. His description of how 'the frozen dead ... creak in the frost' (mirrored in the story by the creaking of a chair) is enough to freeze the blood. Joyce Tompkins described how 'the uncompromising challenge of the enclosed narrative is set at a distance, we see it through a lattice of criss-cross suggestions ... The stories of the war require this modesty of method, since they handle real and recent wounds and the healer dare not claim too much.'

It should be noticed that the date of Godsoe's death, 21 January, was the feast of St Agnes, the day before that on which young girls who invoked the Saint were supposed to be able to see their future beloved, as recounted in Keats' great poem 'St Agnes Eve'.

The Kipling Society points out that the name Bella Armine is reminiscent of a Cardinal of the church, Robert Bellarmine. One of the works of this brilliant man was a hymn to Mary Magdalene who was the first to recognize the risen Christ after the rock had been rolled back. Such subtleties of association were certainly not beyond Kipling.

The Masonic Lodge Faith and Works 5837 is fictional, but in its partculars Kipling must have drawn on the many lodges he belonged to or visited, in particular the Lodge of Hope and Perseverance no. 782 in Lahore EC, of which for some years he was secretary.

DAYSPRING MISHANDLED

C'est moi, c'est moi, c'est moi!
Je suis la Mandragore!
La fille des beaux jours qui s'éveille à l'aurore—
Et qui chante pour toi!

C. Nodier.

In the days beyond compare and before the Judgments, a genius called Graydon foresaw that the advance of education and the standard of living would submerge all mind-marks in one mudrush of standardised reading-matter, and so created the Fictional Supply Syndicate to meet the demand.

Since a few days' work for him brought them more money than a week's elsewhere, he drew many young men—some now eminent—into his employ. He bade them keep their eyes on the Sixpenny Dream Book, the Army and Navy Stores Catalogue (this for backgrounds and furniture as they changed), and *The Hearthstone Friend*, a weekly publication which specialised unrivalledly in the domestic emotions. Yet, even so, youth would not be denied, and some of the collaborated love-talk in 'Passion Hath Peril,' and 'Ena's Lost Lovers,' and the account of the murder of the Earl in 'The Wickwire Tragedies'—to name but a few masterpieces now never mentioned for fear of blackmail—was as good as anything to which their authors signed their real names in more distinguished years.

Among the young ravens driven to roost awhile on Graydon's ark was James Andrew Manallace—a darkish, slow northerner of the type that does not ignite, but must be detonated. Given written or verbal outlines of a plot, he was useless; but, with a half-dozen pictures round which to write his tale, he could astonish.

And he adored that woman who afterwards became the mother of Vidal Benzaquen,1 and who suffered and died because she loved one unworthy. There was, also, among the company a mannered, bellied person called Alured Castorley, who talked and wrote about 'Bohemia,' but was always afraid of being 'compromised' by the weekly suppers at Neminaka's Cafes in Hestern Square, where the Syndicate work was apportioned, and where everyone looked out for himself. He, too, for a time, had loved Vidal's mother, in his own way.

Now, one Saturday at Neminaka's, Graydon, who had given Manallace a sheaf of prints—torn from an extinct children's book called *Philippa's Queen*—on which to improvise, asked for results. Manallace went down into his ulster-pocket, hesitated a moment, and said the stuff had turned into poetry on his hands.

'Bosh!'

'That's what it isn't,' the boy retorted. 'It's rather good.'

'Then it's no use to us.' Graydon laughed. 'Have you brought back the cuts?'

Manallace handed them over. There was a castle in the series; a knight or so in armour; an old lady in a horned head-dress; a young ditto; a very obvious Hebrew; a clerk, with pen and inkhorn, checking wine-barrels on a wharf; and a Crusader. On the back of one of the prints was a note, 'If he doesn't want to go, why can't he be captured and held to ransom?' Graydon asked what it all meant.

'I don't know yet. A comic opera, perhaps,' said Manallace.

Graydon, who seldom wasted time, passed the cuts on to someone else, and advanced Manallace a couple of sovereigns to carry on with, as usual; at which Castorley was angry and would have said something unpleasant but was suppressed. Half-way through supper, Castorley told the company that a relative had died and left him an independence; and that he now withdrew from 'hackwork' to follow 'Literature.' Generally, the Syndicate rejoiced in a comrade's good fortune, but Castorley had gifts of waking dislike. So the news was received with a vote of thanks, and he went out before the end, and, it was said, proposed to 'Dal Benzaquen's mother, who refused him. He did not come back. Manallace, who had arrived a little exalted, got so drunk before midnight that a man had to stay and see him home. But liquor never touched him above the belt, and when he had slept awhile, he recited to the gas-chandelier the poetry he had made out of the pictures; said that, on second thoughts, he would convert it into comic opera; deplored the Upas-tree influence of Gilbert and Sullivan; sang somewhat to illustrate his point; and—after words, by the way, with a negress in yellow satin— was steered to his rooms.

In the course of a few years, Graydon's foresight and genius were rewarded. The public began to read and reason upon higher planes, and the Syndicate grew rich. Later still, people demanded of their printed matter what they expected in their clothing and furniture. So, precisely as the three guinea hand-bag is followed in three weeks by its thirteen and sevenpence ha'penny, indistinguishable sister, they enjoyed perfect synthetic substitutes for Plot, Sentiment, and Emotion. Graydon died before the Cinemacaption school came in, but he left his widow twenty-seven thousand pounds.

Manallace made a reputation, and, more important, money for Vidal's mother when her husband ran away and the first symptoms of her paralysis showed. His line was the jocundly-sentimental Wardour Street brand of adventure, told in a style that exactly met, but never exceeded, every expectation.

As he once said when urged to 'write a real book': 'I've got my label, and I'm not going to chew it off. If you save people thinking, you can do anything with 'em.' His output apart, he was genuinely a man of letters. He rented a small cottage in the country and economised on everything, except the care and charges of Vidal's mother.

Castorley flew higher. When his legacy freed him from 'hackwork,' he became first a critic—in which calling he loyally scalped all his old associates as they came up—and then looked for some speciality. Having found it (Chaucer was the prey), he consolidated his position before he occupied it, by his careful speech, his cultivated bearing, and the whispered words of his friends whom he, too, had saved the trouble of thinking. It followed that, when he published his first serious articles on Chaucer, all the world which is interested in Chaucer said: 'This is an authority.' But he was no impostor. He learned and knew his poet and his age; and in a month-long dogfight in an austere literary weekly, met and mangled a recognised Chaucer expert of the day. He also, 'for old sake's sake,' as he wrote to a friend, went out of his way to review one of Manallace's books with an intimacy of unclean deduction (this was before the days of Freud) which long stood as a record. Some member of the extinct Syndicate took occasion to ask him if he would—for old sake's sake—help Vidal's mother to a new treatment. He answered that he had 'known the lady very slightly and the calls on his purse were so heavy that,' etc. The writer showed the letter to Manallace, who said he was glad Castorley hadn't interfered. Vidal's mother was then wholly paralysed. Only her eyes could move, and those always looked for the husband who had left her. She died thus in Manallace's arms in April of the first year of the War.

During the War he and Castorley worked as some sort of departmental dishwashers in the Office of Co-ordinated Supervisals. Here Manallace came to know Castorley again. Castorley, having a sweet tooth, cadged lumps of sugar for his tea from a typist, and when she took to giving them to a younger man, arranged that she should be reported for smoking in unauthorised apartments. Manallace possessed himself of every detail of the affair, as compensation for the review of his book. Then there came a night when, waiting for a big air-raid, the two men had talked humanly, and Manallace spoke of Vidal's mother. Castorley said something in reply, and from that hour—as was learned several years later—Manallace's real life-work and interests began.

The War over, Castorley set about to make himself Supreme Pontiff on Chaucer by methods not far removed from the employment of poison-gas. The English Pope was silent, through private griefs, and influenza had carried off the learned Hun who claimed continental allegiance. Thus Castorley crowed unchallenged from Upsala to Seville, while Manallace went back to his cottage with the photo of Vidal's mother over the mantelpiece. She seemed to have emptied out his life, and left him only fleeting interests in trifles. His private diversions were experiments of uncertain outcome, which, he said, rested him after a day's gadzooking and vitalstapping. I found him, for instance, one weekend, in his toolshed-scullery, boiling a brew of slimy barks which were, if mixed with oak-galls, vitriol and wine, to become an ink-powder. We boiled it till the Monday, and it turned into an adhesive stronger than birdlime, and entangled us both.

At other times, he would carry me off, once in a few weeks, to sit at Castorley's feet, and hear him talk about Chaucer. Castorley's voice, bad enough in youth, when it could be shouted down, had, with culture and tact, grown almost insupportable. His mannerisms, too, had multiplied and set. He minced and mouthed, postured and chewed his words throughout those terrible evenings; and poisoned not only Chaucer, but every shred of English literature which he used to embellish him. He was shameless, too, as regarded self-advertisement and 'recognition'—weaving elaborate intrigues; forming petty friendships and confederacies, to be dissolved next week in favour of more promising alliances; fawning, snubbing, lecturing, organising and lying as unrestingly as a politician, in chase of the Knighthood due not to him (he always called on his Maker to forbid such a thought) but as tribute to Chaucer. Yet, sometimes, he could break from his obsession and prove how a man's work will try to save the soul of him. He would tell us charmingly of copyists of the fifteenth century in England and the Low Countries, who had multiplied the Chaucer MSS., of which there remained—he gave us the exact number—and how each scribe could by him (and, he implied, by him alone) be distinguished from every other by some peculiarity of letter-formation, spacing or like trick of pen-work; and how he could fix the dates of their work within five years. Sometimes he would give us an hour of really interesting stuff and then return to his overdue 'recognition.' The changes sickened me, but Manallace defended him, as a master in his own line who had revealed Chaucer to at least one grateful soul.

This, as far as I remembered, was the autumn when Manallace holi-
dayed in the Shetlands or the Faroes, and came back with a stone
'quern'—a hand corn-grinder. He said it interested him from the ethno-
logical standpoint. His whim lasted till next harvest, and was followed
by a religious spasm which, naturally, translated itself into literature.
He showed me a battered and mutilated Vulgate of 1485, patched up the
back with bits of legal parchments, which he had bought for thirty-five
shillings. Some monk's attempt to rubricate chapter-initials had caught,
it seemed, his forlorn fancy, and he dabbled in shells of gold and silver
paint for weeks.

That also faded out, and he went to the Continent to get local colour
for a love-story, about Alva and the Dutch, and the next year I saw
practically nothing of him. This released me from seeing much of
Castorley, but, at intervals, I would go there to dine with him, when his
wife—an unappetising, ash-coloured woman—made no secret that his
friends wearied her almost as much as he did. But at a later meeting,
not long after Manallace had finished his Low Countries' novel, I found
Castorley charged to bursting-point with triumph and high information hardly withheld. He confided to me that a time was at hand when
great matters would be made plain, and 'recognition' would be inevitable. I assumed, naturally, that there was fresh scandal or heresy afoot in
Chaucer circles, and kept my curiosity within bounds.

In time, New York cabled that a fragment of a hitherto unknown
Canterbury Tale lay safe in the steel-walled vaults of the seven-million-
dollar Sunnapia Collection. It was news on an international scale—the
New World exultant—the Old deploring the 'burden of British taxation
which drove such treasures, etc.,' and the lighterminded journals dis-
porting themselves according to their publics; for 'our Dan,' as one earnest Sunday editor observed, 'lies closer to the national heart than we
wot of.' Common decency made me call on Castorley, who, to my surprise, had not yet descended into the arena. I found him, made young
again by joy, deep in just-passed proofs.

Yes, he said, it was all true. He had, of course, been in it from the first.
There had been found one hundred and seven new lines of Chaucer

tacked on to an abridged end of *The Persone's Tale,* the whole the work of Abraham Mentzius, better known as Mentzel of Antwerp (1388 - 1438/9)—I might remember he had talked about him—whose distinguishing peculiarities were a certain Byzantine formation of his g's, the use of a 'sickle-slanted' reed-pen, which cut into the vellum at certain letters; and, above all, a tendency to spell English words on Dutch lines, whereof the manuscript carried one convincing proof. For instance (he wrote it out for me), a girl praying against an undesired marriage, says:—

'Ah Jesu-Moder, pitie my oe peyne.
Daiespringe mishandeelt cometh nat agayne.'

Would I, please, note the spelling of 'mishandeelt'? Stark Dutch and Mentzel's besetting sin! But in *his* position one took nothing for granted. The page had been part of the stiffening of the side of an old Bible, bought in a parcel by Dredd, the big dealer, because it had some rubricated chapter-initials, and by Dredd shipped, with a consignment of similar odds and ends, to the Sunnapia Collection, where they were making a glass-cased exhibit of the whole history of illumination and did not care how many books they gutted for that purpose. There, someone who noticed a crack in the back of the volume had unearthed it. He went on: 'They didn't know what to make of the thing at first. But they knew about *me*! They kept quiet till I'd been consulted. You might have noticed I was out of England for three months.

'I was over there, of course. It was what is called a "spoil"—a page Mentzel had spoiled with his Dutch spelling—I expect he had had the English dictated to him—then had evidently used the vellum for trying out his reeds; and then, I suppose, had put it away. The "spoil" had been doubled, pasted together, and slipped in as stiffening to the old book-cover. I had it steamed open, and analysed the wash. It gave the flour-grains in the paste-coarse, because of the old millstone—and there were traces of the grit itself. What? Oh, possibly a handmill of Mentzel's own time. He may have doubled the spoilt page and used it for part of a pad to steady wood-cuts on. It may have knocked about his workshop for years. That, indeed, is practically certain because a beginner from the Low Countries has tried his reed on a few lines of some monkish hymn—not a bad lilt tho'—which must have been common form. Oh yes, the page may have been used in other books before it was used for the Vulgate. That doesn't matter, but *this* does. Listen! I took a wash, for analysis, from a blot in one corner—that would be after Mentzel had given up trying to make a possible page of it, and had grown care-less—and I got the actual *ink* of the period! It's a practically eternal stuff compounded on—I've forgotten his name for the minute—the scribe at Bury St. Edmunds, of course—hawthorn bark and wine. Anyhow, on *his* formula. *That* wouldn't interest you either, but, taken with all the other testimony, it clinches the thing. (You'll see it all in my Statement to the Press on Monday.) Overwhelming, isn't it?'

'Overwhelming,' I said, with sincerity. 'Tell me what the tale was about, though. That's more in my line.'

'I know it; but *I* have to be equipped on all sides. The verses are rela-tively easy for one to pronounce on. The freshness, the fun, the human-ity, the fragrance of it all, cries—no, shouts—itself as Dan's work. Why "Daiespringe mishandled" alone stamps it from Dan's mint. Plangent as doom, my dear boy—plangent as doom! It's all in my Statement. Well, substantially, the fragment deals with a girl whose parents wish her to marry an elderly suitor. The mother isn't so keen on it, but the father, an old Knight, is. The girl, of course, is in love with a younger and a poorer man. Common form? Granted. Then the father, who doesn't in the least want to, is ordered off to a Crusade and, by way of passing on the kick, as we used to say during the War, orders the girl to be kept in duresse till his return or her consent to the old suitor. Common form, again? Quite so. That's too much for her mother. She reminds the old Knight of his age and infirmities, and the discomforts of Crusading. Are you sure I'm not boring you?'

'Not at all,' I said, though time had begun to whirl backward through my brain to a red-velvet, pomatum-scented side-room at Neminaka's and Manallace's set face intoning to the gas.

'You'll read it all in my Statement next week. The sum is that the old lady tells him of a certain Knight-adventurer on the French coast, who, for a consideration, waylays Knights who don't relish crusading and holds them to impossible ransoms till the trooping-season is over, or they are returned sick. He keeps a ship in the Channel to pick 'em up and transfers his birds to his castle ashore, where he has a reputation for doing 'em well. As the old lady points out:

'And if perchance thou fall into his honde

By God how canstow ride to Holilonde?'

'You see? Modern in essence as Gilbert and Sullivan, but handled as only Dan could! And she reminds him that "Honour and olde bones" parted company long ago. He makes one splendid appeal for the spirit of chivalry:

> Lat all men change as Fortune may send,
> But Knighthood beareth service to the end,

and *then*, of course, he gives in

> For what his woman willeth to be don
> Her manne must or wauken Hell anon.

'Then she hints that the daughter's young lover, who is in the Bordeaux wine-trade, could open negotiations for a kidnapping without compromising him. And then that careless brute Mentzel spoils his page and chucks it! But there's enough to show what's going to happen. You'll see it all in my Statement. Was there ever anything in literary finds to hold a candle to it? … And they give grocers Knighthoods for selling cheese!'

I went away before he could get into his stride on that course. I wanted to think, and to see Manallace. But I waited till Castorley's Statement came out. He had left himself no loophole. And when, a little later, his (nominally the Sunnapia people's) 'scientific' account of their analyses and tests appeared, criticism ceased, and some journals began to demand 'public recognition.' Manallace wrote me on this subject, and I went down to his cottage, where he at once asked me to sign a Memorial on Castorley's behalf. With luck, he said, we might get him a K.B.E. in the next Honours List. Had I read the Statement?

'I have,' I replied. 'But I want to ask you something first. Do you remember the night you got drunk at Neminaka's, and I stayed behind to look after you?'

'Oh, *that* time,' said he, pondering. 'Wait a minute! I remember Graydon advancing me two quid. He was a generous paymaster. And I remember—now, who the devil rolled me under the sofa—and what for?'

'We all did,' I replied. 'You wanted to read us what you'd written to those Chaucer cuts.'

'I don't remember that. No! I don't remember anything after the sofa-episode.... *You* always said that you took me home—didn't you?'

'I did, and you told Kentucky Kate outside the old Empire that you had been faithful, Cynara, in your fashion.'

'Did I?' said he. 'My God! Well, I suppose I have.' He stared into the fire. 'What else?'

'Before we left Neminaka's you recited me what you had made out of the cuts—the whole tale! So—you see?'

'Ye-es.' He nodded. 'What are you going to do about it?'

'What are *you*?'

'I'm going to help him get his Knighthood—first.'

'Why?'

'I'll tell you what he said about 'Dal's mother—the night there was that air-raid on the offices.'

He told it.

'That's why,' he said. 'Am I justified?'

He seemed to me entirely so.

'But after he gets his Knighthood?' I went on.

'That depends. There are several things I can think of. It interests me.'

'Good Heavens! I've always imagined you a man without interests.'

'So I was. I owe my interests to Castorley. He gave me every one of 'em except the tale itself.'

'How did *that* come?'

'Something in those ghastly cuts touched off something in me—a sort of possession, I suppose. I was in love too. No wonder I got drunk that night. I'd *been* Chaucer for a week! Then I thought the notion might make a comic opera. But Gilbert and Sullivan were too strong.'

'So I remember you told me at the time.'

'I kept it by me, and it made me interested in Chaucer—philologically and so on. I worked on it on those lines for years. There wasn't a flaw in the wording even in '14. I hardly had to touch it after that.'

'Did you ever tell it to anyone except me?'

'No, only 'Dal's mother—when she could listen to anything—to put her to sleep. But when Castorley said—what he did about her, I thought I might use it. 'Twasn't difficult. *He* taught me. D'you remember my bird-lime experiments, and the stuff on our hands? I'd been trying to get that ink for more than a year. Castorley told me where I'd find the formula. And your falling over the quern, too?'

'That accounted for the stone-dust under the microscope?'

'Yes. I grew the wheat in the garden here, and ground it myself. Castorley gave me Mentzel complete. He put me on to an MS. in the British Museum which he said was the finest sample of his work. I copied his "Byzantine *g*'s" for months.'

'And what's a "sickle-slanted" pen?' I asked.

'You nick one edge of your reed till it drags and scratches on the curves of the letters. Castorley told me about Mentzel's spacing and margining. I only had to get the hang of his script.'

'How long did that take you?'

'On and off—some years. I was too ambitious at first—I wanted to give the whole poem. That would have been risky. Then Castorley told me about spoiled pages and I took the hint. I spelt "Dayspring mishandeelt" Mentzel's way—to make sure of him. It's not a bad couplet in itself. Did you see how he admires the "plangency" of it?'

'Never mind him. Go on!' I said.

He did. Castorley had been his unfailing guide throughout, specifying in minutest detail every trap to be set later for his own feet. The actual vellum was an Antwerp find, and its introduction into the cover of the Vulgate was begun after a long course of amateur bookbinding. At last, he bedded it under pieces of an old deed, and a printed page (1686) of Horace's *Odes*, legitimately used for repairs by different owners in the seventeenth and eighteenth centuries; and at the last moment, to meet Castorley's theory that spoiled pages were used in workshops by beginners, he had written a few Latin words in fifteenth century script the Statement gave the exact date—across an open part of the fragment. The thing ran: *'Illa alma Mater ecca, secum afferens me acceptum. Nicolaus Atrib.'* The disposal of the thing was easiest of all. He had merely hung about Dredd's dark bookshop of fifteen rooms, where he was well known, occasionally buying but generally browsing, till, one day, Dredd Senior showed him a case of cheap black-letter stuff, English and Continental—being packed for the Sunnapia people—into which Manallace tucked his contribution, taking care to wrench the back enough to give a lead to an earnest seeker.

'And then?' I demanded.

'After six months or so Castorley sent for me. Sunnapia had found it, and as Dredd had missed it, and there was no money-motive sticking out, they were half convinced it was genuine from the start. But they invited him over. He conferred with their experts, and suggested the scientific tests. *I* put that into his head, before he sailed. That's all. And now, will you sign our Memorial?'

I signed. Before we had finished hawking it round there was a host of influential names to help us, as well as the impetus of all the literary discussion which arose over every detail of the glorious trove. The upshot was a K.B.E.2 for Castorley in the next Honours List; and Lady Castorley, her cards duly printed, called on friends that same afternoon.

Manallace invited me to come with him, a day or so later, to convey our pleasure and satisfaction to them both. We were rewarded by the sight of a man relaxed and ungirt—not to say wallowing naked—on the crest of Success. He assured us that 'The Title' should not make any difference to our future relations, seeing it was in no sense personal, but, as he had often said, a tribute to Chaucer; 'and, after all,' he pointed out, with a glance at the mirror over the mantelpiece, 'Chaucer was the prototype of the "veray parfit gentil Knight" of the British Empire so far as that then existed.'

On the way back, Manallace told me he was considering either an unheralded revelation in the baser Press which should bring Castorley's reputation about his own ears some breakfast-time, or a private conversation, when he would make clear to Castorley that he must now back the forgery as long as he lived, under threat of Manallace's betraying it if he flinched.

He favoured the second plan. 'If I pull the string of the shower-bath in the papers,' he said, 'Castorley might go off his veray parfit gentil nut. I want to keep his intellect.'

'What about your own position? The forgery doesn't matter so much. But if you tell this you'll kill him,' I said.

'I intend that. Oh—my position? I've been dead since—April, Fourteen, it was. But there's no hurry. What was it *she* was saying to you just as we left?'

'She told me how much your sympathy and understanding had meant to him. She said she thought that even Sir Alured did not realise the full extent of his obligations to you.'

'She's right, but I don't like her putting it that way.'

'It's only common form—as Castorley's always saying.'

'Not with *her*. She can hear a man think.'

'She never struck me in that light.'

'*You* aren't playing against her.'

"Guilty conscience, Manallace?"

'H'm! I wonder. Mine or hers? I *wish* she hadn't said that. "More even than *he* realises it." I won't call again for awhile.'

He kept away till we read that Sir Alured, owing to slight indisposition, had been unable to attend a dinner given in his honour.

Inquiries brought word that it was but natural reaction, after strain, which, for the moment, took the form of nervous dyspepsia, and he would be glad to see Manallace at any time. Manallace reported him as rather pulled and drawn, but full of his new life and position, and proud that his efforts should have martyred him so much. He was going to collect, collate, and expand all his pronouncements and inferences into one authoritative volume.

'I must make an effort of my own,' said Manallace. 'I've collected nearly all his stuff about the Find that has appeared in the papers, and he's promised me everything that's missing. I'm going to help him. It will be a new interest.'

'How will you treat it?' I asked.

'I expect I shall quote his deductions on the evidence, and parallel 'em with my experiments—the ink and the paste and the rest of it. It ought to be rather interesting.'

'But even then there will only be your word. It's hard to catch up with an established lie,' I said. 'Especially when you've started it yourself.'

He laughed. 'I've arranged for *that*—in case anything happens to me. Do you remember the "Monkish Hymn"?'

'Oh yes! There's quite a literature about it already.'

'Well, you write those ten words above each other, and read down the first and second letters of 'em; and see what you get.1 My Bank has the formula.'

He wrapped himself lovingly and leisurely round his new task, and Castorley was as good as his word in giving him help. The two practically collaborated, for Manallace suggested that all Castorley's strictly scientific evidence should be in one place, with his deductions and dithyrambs as appendices. He assured him that the public would prefer this arrangement, and, after grave consideration, Castorley agreed.

'That's better,' said Manallace to me. 'Now I sha'n't have so many hiatuses in my extracts. Dots always give the reader the idea you aren't dealing fairly with your man. I shall merely quote him solid, and rip him up, proof for proof, and date for date, in parallel columns. His book's taking more out of him than I like, though. He's been doubled up twice with tummy attacks since I've worked with him. And he's just the sort of flatulent beast who may go down with appendicitis.'

We learned before long that the attacks were due to gall-stones, which would necessitate an operation. Castorley bore the blow very well. He had full confidence in his surgeon, an old friend of theirs; great faith in his own constitution; a strong conviction that nothing would happen to him till the book was finished, and, above all, the Will to Live.

He dwelt on these assets with a voice at times a little out of pitch and eyes brighter than usual beside a slightly-sharpening nose.

I had only met Gleeag, the surgeon, once or twice at Castorley's house, but had always heard him spoken of as a most capable man. He told Castorley that his trouble was the price exacted, in some shape or other, from all who had served their country; and that, measured in units of strain, Castorley had practically been at the front through those three years he had served in the Office of Co-ordinated Supervisals. However, the thing had been taken betimes, and in a few weeks he would worry no more about it.

'But suppose he dies?' I suggested to Manallace.

'He won't. I've been talking to Gleeag. He says he's all right.'

'Wouldn't Gleeag's talk be common form?'

'I *wish* you hadn't said that. But, surely, Gleeag wouldn't have the face to play with me—or her.'

'Why not? I expect it's been done before.' But Manallace insisted that, in this case, it would be impossible.

The operation was a success and, some weeks later, Castorley began to recast the arrangement and most of the material of his book. 'Let me have my way,' he said, when Manallace protested. 'They are making too much of a baby of me. I really don't need Gleeag looking in every day now.' But Lady Castorley told us that he required careful watching. His heart had felt the strain, and fret or disappointment of any kind must be avoided. 'Even,' she turned to Manallace, 'though you know ever so much better how his book should be arranged than he does himself.'

'But really,' Manallace began. 'I'm very careful not to fuss——'

She shook her finger at him playfully. 'You don't think you do; but, remember, he tells me everything that you tell him, just the same as he told me everything that he used to tell *you*. Oh, I don't mean the things that men talk about. I mean about his Chaucer.'

'I didn't realise that,' said Manallace, weakly.

'I thought you didn't. He never spares me anything; but *I* don't mind,' she replied with a laugh, and went off to Gleeag, who was paying his daily visit. Gleeag said he had no objection to Manallace working with Castorley on the book for a given time—say, twice a week—but supported Lady Castorley's demand that he should not be over-taxed in what she called 'the sacred hours.' The man grew more and more difficult to work with, and the little check he had heretofore set on his self-praise went altogether.

'He says there has never been anything in the History of Letters to compare with it,' Manallace groaned. 'He wants now to inscribe—he never dedicates, you know—inscribe it to me, as his "most valued assistant." The devil of it is that *she* backs him up in getting it out soon. Why? How much do you think she knows?'

'Why should she know anything at all?'

'You heard her say he had told her everything that he had told me about Chaucer? (I *wish* she hadn't said that!) If she puts two and two together, she can't help seeing that every one of his notions and theories has been played up to. But then—but then . . . Why is she trying to hurry publication? She talks about me fretting him. *She's* at him, all the time, to be quick.'

Castorley must have over-worked, for, after a couple of months, he complained of a stitch in his right side, which Gleeag said was a slight sequel, a little incident of the operation. It threw him back awhile, but he returned to his work undefeated.

The book was due in the autumn. Summer was passing, and his publisher urgent, and—he said to me, when after a longish interval I called—Manallace had chosen this time, of all, to take a holiday. He was not pleased with Manallace, once his indefatigable *aide*, but now dilatory, and full of time-wasting objections. Lady Castorley had noticed it, too.

Meantime, with Lady Castorley's help, he himself was doing the best he could to expedite the book; but Manallace had mislaid (did I think through jealousy?) some essential stuff which had been dictated to him. And Lady Castorley wrote Manallace, who had been delayed by a slight motor accident abroad, that the fret of waiting was prejudicial to her husband's health. Manallace, on his return from the Continent, showed me that letter.

'He has fretted a little, I believe,' I said.

Manallace shuddered. 'If I stay abroad, I'm helping to kill him. If I help him to hurry up the book, I'm expected to kill him. *She* knows,' he said.

'You're mad. You've got this thing on the brain.'

'I have not! Look here! You remember that Gleeag gave me from four to six, twice a week, to work with him. She called them the "sacred hours." You heard her? Well, they *are*! They are Gleeag's and hers. But she's so infernally plain, and I'm such a fool, it took me weeks to find it out.'

'That's their affair,' I answered. 'It doesn't prove she knows anything about the Chaucer.'

'She *does*! He told her everything that he had told me when I was pumping him, all those years. She put two and two together when the thing came out. She saw exactly how I had set my traps. I know it! She's been trying to make me admit it.'

'What did you do?'

''Didn't understand what she was driving at, of course. And then she asked Gleeag, before me, if he didn't think the delay over the book was fretting Sir Alured. He didn't think so. He said getting it out might deprive him of an interest. He had that much decency. *She's* the devil!'

'What do you suppose is her game, then?'

'If Castorley knows he's been had, it'll kill him. She's at me all the time, indirectly, to let it out. I've told you she wants to make it a sort of joke between us. Gleeag's willing to wait. He knows Castorley's a dead man. It slips out when they talk. They say "He was," not "He is." Both of 'em know it. But *she* wants him finished sooner.'

'I don't believe it. What are you going to do?'

'What can I? I'm not going to have him killed, though.'

Manlike, he invented compromises whereby Castorley might be lured up by-paths of interest, to delay publication. This was not a success. As autumn advanced Castorley fretted more, and suffered from returns of his distressing colics. At last, Gleeag told him that he thought they might be due to an overlooked gallstone working down. A second comparatively trivial operation would eliminate the bother once and for all. If Castorley cared for another opinion, Gleeag named a surgeon of eminence. 'And then,' said he, cheerily, 'the two of us can talk you over.' Castorley did not want to be talked over. He was oppressed by pains in his side, which, at first, had yielded to the liver-tonics Gleeag prescribed; but now they stayed—like a toothache—behind everything. He felt most at ease in his bedroom-study, with his proofs round him. If he had more pain than he could stand, he would consider the second operation. Meantime Manallace—'the meticulous Manallace,' he called him—agreed with him in thinking that the Mentzel page-facsimile, done by the Sunnapia Library, was not quite good enough for the great book, and the Sunnapia people were, very decently, having it re-processed. This would hold things back till early spring, which had its advantages, for he could run a fresh eye over all in the interval.

One gathered these news in the course of stray visits as the days shortened. He insisted on Manallace keeping to the 'sacred hours,' and Manallace insisted on my accompanying him when possible. On these occasions he and Castorley would confer apart for half an hour or so, while I listened to an unendurable clock in the drawing-room. Then I would join them and help wear out the rest of the time, while Castorley rambled. His speech, now, was often clouded and uncertain—the result of the 'liver-tonics'; and his face came to look like old vellum.

It was a few days after Christmas—the operation had been postponed till the following Friday—that we called together. She met us with word that Sir Alured had picked up an irritating little winter cough, due to a cold wave, but we were not, therefore, to abridge our visit. We found him in steam perfumed with Friar's Balsam. He waved the old Sunnapia facsimile at us. We agreed that it ought to have been more worthy. He took a dose of his mixture, lay back and asked us to lock the door. There was, he whispered, something wrong somewhere. He could not lay his finger on it, but it was in the air. He felt he was being played with. He did not like it. There was something wrong all round him. Had we noticed it? Manallace and I severally and slowly denied that we had noticed anything of the sort.

With no longer break than a light fit of coughing, he fell into the hideous, helpless panic of the sick—those worse than captives who lie at the judgment and mercy of the hale for every office and hope. He wanted to go away. Would we help him to pack his Gladstone? Or, if that would attract too much attention in certain quarters, help him to dress and go out? There was an urgent matter to be set right, and now that he had The Title and knew his own mind it would all end happily and he would be well again. *Please* would we let him go out, just to speak to—he named her; he named her by her 'little' name out of the old Neminaka days? Manallace quite agreed, and recommended a pull at the 'liver-tonic' to brace him after so long in the house. He took it, and Manallace suggested that it would be better if, after his walk, he came down to the cottage for a week-end and brought the revise with him. They could then re-touch the last chapter. He answered to that drug and to some praise of his work, and presently simpered drowsily. Yes, it *was* good—though he said it who should not. He praised himself awhile till, with a puzzled forehead and shut eyes, he told us that *she* had been saying lately that it was too good—the whole thing, if we understood, was *too* good. He wished us to get the exact shade of her meaning. She had suggested, or rather implied, this doubt. She had said—he would let us draw our own inferences—that the Chaucer find had 'anticipated the wants of humanity.' Johnson, of course. No need to tell *him* that. But what the hell was her implication? Oh God! Life had always been one long innuendo! *And* she had said that a man could do anything with anyone if he saved him the trouble of thinking. What did she mean by that? *He* had never shirked thought. He had thought sustainedly all his life. It *wasn't* too good, was it? Manallace didn't think it was too good—did he? But this pick-pick-picking at a man's brain and work was too bad, wasn't it? *What* did she mean? Why did she always bring in Manallace, who was only a friend—no scholar, but a lover of the game—Eh?—Manallace could confirm this if he were here, instead of loafing on the Continent just when he was most needed.

'I've come back,' Manallace interrupted, unsteadily. 'I can confirm every word you've said. You've nothing to worry about. It's *your* find—*your* credit—*your* glory and—all the rest of it.'

'Swear you'll tell her so then,' said Castorley. 'She doesn't believe a word I say. She told me she never has since before we were married. Promise!'

Manallace promised, and Castorley added that he had named him his literary executor, the proceeds of the book to go to his wife. 'All profits without deduction,' he gasped. 'Big sales if it's properly handled. *You* don't need money . . . . Graydon'll trust *you* to any extent. It 'ud be a long . . .'

He coughed, and, as he caught breath, his pain broke through all the drugs, and the outcry filled the room. Manallace rose to fetch Gleeag, when a full, high, affected voice, unheard for a generation, accompanied, as it seemed, the clamour of a beast in agony, saying: 'I wish to God someone would stop that old swine howling down there! *I* can't . . . I was going to tell you fellows that it would be a dam' long time before Graydon advanced *me* two quid.'

We escaped together, and found Gleeag waiting, with Lady Castorley, on the landing. He telephoned me, next morning, that Castorley had died of bronchitis, which his weak state made it impossible for him to throw off. 'Perhaps it's just as well,' he added, in reply to the condolences I asked him to convey to the widow. 'We might have come across something we couldn't have coped with.'

Distance from that house made me bold.

'You knew all along, I suppose? What was it, really?'

'Malignant kidney-trouble—generalised at the end. 'No use worrying him about it. We let him through as easily as possible. Yes! A happy release. . What? . . . Oh! Cremation. Friday, at eleven.'

There, then, Manallace and I met. He told me that she had asked him whether the book need now be published; and he had told her this was more than ever necessary, in her interests as well as Castorley's.

'She is going to be known as his widow—for a while, at any rate. Did I perjure myself much with him?'

'Not explicitly,' I answered.

'Well, I have now—with *her*—explicitly,' said he, and took out his black gloves. . . .

As, on the appointed words, the coffin crawled sideways through the noiselessly-closing doorflaps, I saw Lady Castorley's eyes turn towards Gleeag.

1 'The Village that voted the Earth was Flat'. A Diversity of Creatures.

2 Officially it was on account of his good work in the Departmental of Co-ordinated Supervisals, but all true lovers of literature knew the real reason, and told the papers so.

3 Illa alma Mater ecca secum afferens me acceptum Nicolaus Atrib.

Gertrude's Prayer

(Modernized from the 'Chaucer' of Manallace)

That which is marred at birth Time shall not mend,
Nor water out of bitter well make clean;
All evil thing returneth at the end,
Or elseway walketh in our blood unseen.
Whereby the more is sorrow in certaine--
Dayspring mishandled cometh not agen.

To-bruized be that slender, sterting spray
Out of the oake's rind that should betide
A branch of girt and goodliness, straightway
Her spring is turned on herself, and wried
And knotted like some gall or veiney wen.--
Dayspring mishandled cometh not againe.

Noontide repayeth never morning-bliss--
Sith noon to morn is incomparable;
And, so it be our dawning goth amiss,
None other after-hour serveth well.
Ah! Jesu-Moder, pitie my oe paine--
Dayspring mishandled cometh not againe!

Thoughts on Dayspring Mishandled

Departing radically from Kipling's usual handling of revenge stories, 'Dayspring Mishandled' examines what happens when revenge has to be withheld, even turned on its head, with the person wronged finding himself sympathizing with, even assisting the wrong-doer. Despite the simplicity of this central theme the story has multiple elements resembling nothing so much as a cabinet of secrets.

Some commentators have seriously misjudged this tale. Lord Birkenhead, for example, described it as 'a gloomy labyrinth of treachery, disease and death' and Kingsley Amis thought it, 'a squalid revenge tragedy'. It is in fact, one of the author's most subtle and complex pieces of work, replete with as much humour as horror, social commentary and surprise. It is difficult to believe that this tale, the plot of which stretches over some thirty years, was written in only a fortnight.

Part of the story's subtlety lies in not portraying Castorley as a villain or even a fake scholar, but merely a greedy and ambitious man who in the course of a long life betrayed a woman. Manallace, the 'darkish, slow northerner of the type that does not ignite, but must be detonated, knows all about his rival's mistreatment of their mutual friend, but it takes an insult to light his fuse. The reader is not made aware at the time of the nature of the insult, and when it is finally revealed, the disclosure is to the narrator only, a notable coup de théâtre. Similarly, Manallace, however, is no plaster saint; his work 'exactly met but never exceeded every expectation'.

As with the epigraph, 'Gertrude's Prayer' the 'villain's' end lies in his beginnings. Castorley dies messily with 'malignant kidney trouble', while the once vengeful Manallace compassionately seeks to relieve his last moments ('Your find, your credit, your glory'). His long fashioned but abortive revenge has resulted only in the waste of his own life. It is the poisonous Lady Castorly who has the last laugh as her 'eyes turn towards' her next victim.

Tompkins summed the story up with her usual economy: 'The tale is very tightly written. There are no flourishes in it; every sentence tells and matters. The writing is of that 'infolded' sort which, at first reading, may seem to present a crumpled mass, but which gradually fills and spreads and tightens with the fullness and tension of its meanings, until it is a House of Life itself, a tent covering the erring and suffering spirit of man. The title offers us two handles. It is a phrase from the Chaucerian fragment that Manallace forges, as an instrument of his revenge on Castorley, the Chaucer specialist; it is also the condition of Manallace which has nourished that revenge.'

Now for some points of detail.

To understand the origin of Vidal Benzaguen one must turn to another of the author's revenge stories, 'The Village that Voted the Earth was Flat' in which a character of that name appears, a young star of the music hall; hence our character's appearance as 'Vidal's mother'.

The Mandragora mentioned in Nodier's poem quoted at the beginning of the story is another name for the mandrake, a plant that can bear a vague resemblance to the shape of a man and was said to shriek when uprooted. It was also regarded as a love philter. The relevance of these lines is discussed at length by Philip Mason.

The Kipling Society web site contains an enlightening but complex explanation of the Latin cipher mentioned in the story.

THE CHURCH THAT
WAS AT ANTIOCH

'But when Peter was come to Antioch, I withstood him to the face, because he was to be blamed.'—St. Paul's Epistle to the Galatians, ii. II.

His mother, a devout and well-born Roman widow, decided that he was doing himself no good in an Eastern Legion so near to free-thinking Constantinople, and got him seconded for civil duty in Antioch, where his uncle, Lucius Sergius, was head of the urban Police. Valens obeyed as a son and as a young man keen to see life, and, presently, cast up at his uncle's door.

'That sister-in-law of mine,' said the elder, 'never remembers me till she wants something. What have you been doing?'

'Nothing, Uncle.'

'Meaning everything?'

'That's what mother thinks. But I haven't.'

'We shall see. Your quarters are across the inner courtyard. Your—er—baggage is there already. . . . Oh, I shan't interfere with your private arrangements! I'm not the uncle with the rough tongue. Get your bath. We'll talk at supper.'

But before that hour 'Father Serga,' as the Prefect of Police was called, learned from the Treasury that his nephew had marched overland from

Constantinople in charge of a treasure-convoy which, after a brush with brigands in the pass outside Tarsus, he had duly delivered.

'Why didn't you tell me about it?' his uncle asked at the meal.

'I had to report to the Treasury first,' was the answer.

Serga looked at him. 'Gods! You *are* like your father,' said he. 'Cilicia is scandalously policed.'

'So I noticed. They ambushed us not five miles from Tarsus town. Are we given to that sort of thing here?'

'You make yourself at home early. No. *We* are not, but Syria is a Non-regulation Province—under the Emperor—not the Senate. We've the entire unaccountable East to one side; the scum of the Mediterranean on the other; and all hellicat Judaea southward. Anything can happen in Syria. D'you like the prospect?'

'I shall—under you.'

'It's in the blood. The same with men as horses. Now what have you done that distresses your mother so?'

'She's a little behind the times, sir. She follows the old school, of course— the home-worships, and the strict Latin Trinity. I don't think she recognises any Gods outside Jupiter, Juno, and Minerva.'

'I don't either—officially.'

'Nor I, as an officer, sir. But one wants more than that, and—and—what I learned in Byzant squared with what I saw with the Fifteenth.'

'You needn't go on. All Eastern Legions are alike. You mean you follow Mithras—eh?'

The young man bowed his head slightly.

'No harm, boy. It's a soldier's religion, even if it comes from outside.'

'So I thought. But Mother heard of it. She didn't approve and—I suppose that's why I'm here.'

'Off the trident and into the net! Just like a woman! All Syria is stuffed with Mithraism. *My* objection to fancy religions is that they mostly meet after dark, and that means more work for the Police. We've a College here of stiff-necked Hebrews who call themselves Christians.'

'I've heard of them,' said Valens. 'There isn't a ceremony or symbol they haven't stolen from the Mithras ritual.'

"No news to *me!* Religions are part of my office-work; and they'll be part of yours. Our Synagogue Jews are fighting like Scythians over this new faith.'

'Does that matter much?'

'So long as they fight each other, we've only to keep the ring. Divide and rule—especially with Hebrews. Even these Christians are divided now. You see—one part of their worship is to eat together.'

'Another theft! The Supper is the essential Symbol with us,' Valens interrupted.

'With *us*, it's the essential symbol of trouble for your uncle, my dear. Anyone can become a Christian. A Jew may; but he still lives by his Law of Moses (I've had to master that cursed code, too), and it regulates all his doings. Then he sits down at a Christian love-feast beside a Greek or Westerner, who doesn't kill mutton or pig—No! No! Jews don't touch pork—as the Jewish Law lays down. Then the tables are broken up—but not by laughter—No! No! Riot!'

'That's childish,' said Valens.

"Wish it were. But my lictors are called in to keep order, and I have to take the depositions of Synagogue Jews, denouncing Christians as traitors to Caesar. If I chose to act on half the stuff their Rabbis swear to, I'd have respectable little Jew shop-keepers up every week for conspiracy. *Never* decide on the evidence, when you're dealing with Hebrews! Oh, you'll get your bellyful of it! You're for Market-duty to-morrow in the Little Circus ward, all among 'em. And now, sleep you well! I've been on this frontier as far back. as anyone remembers—that's why they call me the Father of Syria—and oh—it's good to see a sample of the old stock again!'

Next morning, and for many weeks after, Valens found himself on Market-inspection duty with a fat Aedile, who flew into rages because the stalls were not flushed down at the proper hour. A couple of his uncle's men were told off to him, and, of course, introduced him to the thieves' and prostitutes' quarters, to the leading gladiators, and so forth.

One day, behind the Little Circus, near Singon Street, he ran into a mob, where a race-course gang were trying to collect, or evade, some bets on recent chariot-races. The Aedile said it was none of his affair and turned back. The lictors closed up behind Valens, but left the situation in his charge. Then a small hard man with eyebrows was punted on to his chest, amid howls from all around that he was the ringleader of a conspiracy. 'Yes,' said Valens, 'that was an old trick in Byzant; but I think we'll take *you*, my friend.' Turning the small man loose, he gathered in the loudest of his accusers to appear before his uncle.

'You were quite right,' said Serga next day.

'That gentleman was put up to the job—by someone else. I ordered him one Roman dozen. Did you get the name of the man they were trying to push off on you?'

'Yes. Gaius Julius Paulus. Why?'

'I guessed as much. He's an old acquaintance of mine, a Cilician from Tarsus. Well-born—a citizen by descent, and well-educated, but his people have disowned him. So he works for his living.'

'He spoke like a well-born. He's in splendid training, too. 'Felt him. All muscle.'

'Small wonder. He can outmarch a camel. He is really the Prefect of this new sect. He travels all over our Eastern Provinces starting their Colleges and keeping them up to the mark. That's why the Synagogue Jews are hunting him. If they could run him in on the political charge, it would finish him.'

'Is he seditious, then?'

'Not in the least. Even if he were, I wouldn't feed him to the Jews just because they wanted it. One of our Governors tried that game down-coast—for the sake of peace—some years ago. He didn't get it. Do you like your Market-work, my boy?'

'It's interesting. D'you know, uncle, I think the Synagogue Jews are better at their slaughter-house arrangements than we.'

'They are. That's what makes 'em so tough. A dozen stripes are nothing to Apella, though he'll howl the yard down while he's getting 'em. You've the Christians' College in your quarter. How do they strike you?'

''Quiet enough. They're worrying a bit over what they ought to eat at their love-feasts.'

'I know it. Oh, I meant to tell you—we mustn't try 'em too high just now, Valens. My office reports that Paulus, your small friend, is going down-country for a few days to meet another priest of the College, and bring him back to help smooth over their difficulties about their victuals. That means their congregation will be at loose ends till they return. Mass without mind always comes a cropper. So, *now* is when the Synagogue Jews will try to compromise them. I don't want the poor devils stampeded into what can be made to look like political crime. ''Understand?'

Valens nodded. Between his uncle's discursive evening talks, studded with kitchen-Greek and out-of-date Roman society-verses; his morning tours with the puffing Aedile; and the confidences of his lictors at all hours; he fancied he understood Antioch.

So he kept an eye on the rooms in the colonnade behind the Little Circus, where the new faith gathered. One of the many Jew butchers told him that Paulus had left affairs in the hands of some man called Barnabas, but that he would come back with one, Petrus—evidently a well-known character—who would settle all the food-differences between Greek and Hebrew Christians. The butcher had no spite against Greek Christians as such, if they would only kill their meat like decent Jews.

Serga laughed at this talk, but lent Valens an extra man or two, and said that this lion would be his to tackle, before long.

The boy found himself rushed into the arena one hot dusk, when word had come that this was to be a night of trouble. He posted his lictors in an alley within signal, and entered the common-room of the College, where the love-feasts were held. Everyone seemed as friendly as a Christian—to use the slang of the quarter—and Barnabas, a smiling, stately man by the door, specially so.

'I am glad to meet you,' he said. 'You helped our Paulus in that scuffle the other day. We can't afford to lose *him*. I wish he were back!'

He looked nervously down the hall, as it filled with people, of middle and low degree, setting out their evening meal on the bare tables, and greeting each other with a special gesture.

'I assure you,' he went on, his eyes still astray, '*we've* no intention of offending any of the brethren. Our differences can be settled if only—'

As though on a signal, clamour rose from half a dozen tables at once, with cries of 'Pollution! Defilement! Heathen! The Law! The Law! Let Caesar know!' As Valens backed against the wall, the crowd pelted each other with broken meats and crockery, till at last stones appeared from nowhere.

'It's a put-up affair,' said Valens to Barnabas.

'Yes. They come in with stones in their breasts. Be careful! They're throwing your way,' Barnabas replied. The crowd was well-embroiled now. A section of it bore down to where they stood, yelling for the justice of Rome. His two lictors slid in behind Valens, and a man leaped at him with a knife.

Valens struck up the hand, and the lictors had the man helpless as the weapon fell on the floor. The clash of it stilled the tumult a little. Valens caught the lull, speaking slowly: 'Oh, citizens,' he called, '*must* you begin your love-feasts with battle? Our tripe-sellers' burial-club has better manners.'

A little laughter relieved the tension.

'The Synagogue has arranged this,' Barnabas muttered. 'The responsibility will be laid on me.'

'Who is the Head of your College?' Valens called to the crowd.

The cries rose against each other.

'Paulus! Saul! *He* knows the world — No! No! Petrus! Our Rock! He won't betray us. Petrus, the Living Rock.'

'When do they come back?' Valens asked. Several dates were given, sworn to, and denied.

'Wait to fight till they return. I'm not a priest; but if you don't tidy up these rooms, our Aedile (Valens gave him his gross nick-name in the quarter) will fine the sandals off your feet. And you mustn't trample good food either. When you've finished, I'll lock up after you. Be quick. *I* know our Prefect if you don't.'

They toiled, like children rebuked. As they passed out with baskets of rubbish, Valens smiled. The matter would not be pressed further.

'Here is our key,' said Barnabas at the end. 'The Synagogue will swear I hired this man to kill you.'

'Will they? Let's look at him.'

The lictors pushed their prisoner forward.

'Ill-fortune!' said the man. 'I owed you for my brother's death in Tarsus Pass.'

'Your brother tried to kill me,' Valens retorted.

The fellow nodded.

'Then we'll call it even-throws,' Valens signed to the lictors, who loosed hold. 'Unless you *really* want to see my uncle?'

The man vanished like a trout in the dusk. Valens returned the key to Barnabas, and said:

'If I were you, I shouldn't let your people in again till your leaders come back. You don't know Antioch as I do.'

He went home, the grinning lictors behind him, and they told his uncle, who grinned also, but said that he had done the right thing—even to patronising Barnabas.

'Of course, *I* don't know Antioch as you do; but, seriously, my dear, I think you've saved their Church for the Christians this time. I've had three depositions already that your Cilician friend was a Christian hired by Barnabas. 'Just as well for Barnabas that you let the brute go.'

'You told me you didn't want them stampeded into trouble. Besides, it was fair-throws. I may have killed his brother after all. We had to kill two of 'em.'

'Good! You keep a level head in a tight corner. You'll need it. There's no lying about in secluded parks for *us*! I've got to see Paulus and Petrus when they come back, and find out what they've decided about their infernal feasts. Why can't they all get decently drunk and be done with it?'

'They talk of them both down-town as though they were Gods. By the way, uncle, all the riot was worked up by Synagogue Jews sent from Jerusalem—not by our lot at all.'

'You *don't* say so? Now, perhaps, you understand why I put you on market-duty with old Sow-Belly! You'll make a Police-officer yet.'

Valens met the scared, mixed congregation round the fountains and stalls as he went about his quarter. They were rather relieved at being locked out of their rooms for the time; as well as by the news that Paulus and Petrus would report to the Prefect of Police before addressing them on the great food-question.

Valens was not present at the first part of that interview, which was official. The second, in the cool, awning-covered courtyard, with drinks and *hors-d'œuvre*, all set out beneath the vast lemon and lavender sunset, was much less formal.

'You have met, I think,' said Serga to the little lean Paulus as Valens entered.

'Indeed, yes. Under God, we are twice your debtors,' was the quick reply.

'Oh, that was part of my duty. I hope you found our roads good on your journey,' said Valens.

'Why, yes. I think they were.' Paulus spoke as if he had not noticed them.

'We should have done better to come by boat,' said his companion, Petrus, a large fleshy man, with eyes that seemed to see nothing, and a half-palsied right hand that lay idle in his lap.

'Valens came overland from Byzant,' said his uncle. 'He rather fancies his legs.'

'He ought to at his age. What was your best day's march on the Via Sebaste?' Paulus asked interestedly, and, before he knew, Valens was reeling off his mileage on mountain-roads every step of which Paulus seemed to have trod.

'That's good,' was the comment. 'And I expect you march in heavier order than I.'

'What would you call your best day's work? ' Valens asked in turn.

'I have covered . . .' Paulus checked himself. 'And yet not I but the God,' he muttered. 'It's hard to cure oneself of boasting.'

A spasm wrenched Petrus' face.

'Hard indeed,' said he. Then he addressed himself to Paulus as though none other were present. 'It is true I have eaten with Gentiles and as the Gentiles ate. Yet, at the time, I doubted if it were wise.'

'That is behind us now,' said Paulus gently.

'The decision has been taken for the Church—that little Church which you saved, my son.' He turned on Valens with a smile that half-captured the boy's heart. 'Now—as a Roman and a Police-officer—what think you of us Christians?'

'That I have to keep order in my own ward.'

'Good! Caesar must be served. But—as a servant of Mithras, shall we say—how think you about our food-disputes?'

Valens hesitated. His uncle encouraged him with a nod. 'As a servant of Mithras I eat with any initiate, so long as the food is clean,' said Valens.

'But,' said Petrus, '*that* is the crux.'

'Mithras also tells us,' Valens went on, 'to share a bone covered with dirt, if better cannot be found.'

'You observe no difference, then, between peoples at your feasts?' Paulus demanded.

'How dare we? We are all His children. Men make laws. Not Gods,' Valens quoted from the old Ritual.

'Say that again, child!'

'Gods do not make laws. They change men's hearts. The rest is the Spirit.'

'You heard it, Petrus? You heard that? It is the utter Doctrine itself!' Paulus insisted to his dumb companion.

Valens, a little ashamed of having spoken of his faith, went on:

'They tell me the Jew butchers here want the monopoly of killing for your people. Trade feeling's at the bottom of most of it.'

'A little more than that perhaps,' said Paulus. 'Listen a minute.' He threw himself into a curious tale about the God of the Christians, Who, he said, had taken the shape of a Man, and Whom the Jerusalem Jews, years ago, had got the authorities to deal with as a conspirator. He said that he himself, at that time a right Jew, quite agreed with the sentence, and had denounced all who followed the new God. But one day the Light and the

Voice of the God broke over him, and he experienced a rending change of heart—precisely as in the Mithras creed. Then he met, and had been initiated by, some men who had walked and talked and, more particularly, had eaten, with the new God before He was killed, and who had seen Him after, like Mithras, He had risen from His grave. Paulus and those others—Petrus was one of them—had next tried to preach Him to the Jews, but that was no success; and, one thing leading to another, Paulus had gone back to his home at Tarsus, where his people disowned him for a renegade. There he had broken down with overwork and despair. Till then, he said, it had never occurred to any of them to show the new religion to any except right Jews; for their God had been born in the shape of a Jew. Paulus himself only came to realise the possibilities of outside work, little by little. He said he had all the foreign preaching in his charge now, and was going to change the whole world by it.

Then he made Petrus finish the tale, who explained, speaking very slowly, that he had, some years ago, received orders from the God to preach to a Roman officer of Irregulars down-country; after which that officer and most of his people wanted to become Christians. So Petrus had initiated them the same night, although none of them were Hebrews. 'And,' Petrus ended, 'I saw there is nothing under heaven that we dare call unclean.'

Paulus turned on him like a flash and cried 'You admit it! Out of your own mouth it is evident.' Petrus shook like a leaf and his right hand almost lifted.

'Do *you* too twit me with my accent?' he began, but his face worked and he choked.

'Nay! God forbid! And God once more forgive *me*!' Paulus seemed as distressed as he, while Valens stared at the extraordinary outbreak.

'Talking of clean and unclean,' his uncle said tactfully, 'there's that ugly song come up again in the City. They were singing it on the city-front yesterday, Valens. Did you notice?'

He looked at his nephew, who took the hint.

'If it was "Pickled Fish," sir, they were. Will it make trouble?'

'As surely as these fish'—-a jar of them stood on the table—'make one thirsty. How does it go? Oh yes.' Serga hummed

He twanged it off to the proper gutter-drawl.

> Oie-eaah!
> 'From the Shark and the Sardine—the clean and the unclean—
> To the Pickled Fish of Galilee, said Petrus, shall be mine.
> (Ha-ow?)
> In the nets or on the line,
> Till the Gods Themselves decline.
> (Whe-en?)
> When the Pickled Fish of Galilee ascend the Esquiline!

That'll be something of a flood—worse than live fish in trees! Hey?'

'It will happen one day,' said Paulus.

He turned from Petrus, whom he had been soothing tenderly, and resumed in his natural, hardish voice:

'Yes. We owe a good deal to that Centurion being converted when he was. It taught us that the whole world could receive the God; and it showed *me* my next work. I came over from Tarsus to teach here for a while. And I shan't forget how good the Prefect of Police was to us then.'

'For one thing, Cornelius was an early colleague,' Serga smiled largely above his strong cup. '"Prime companion"—how does it go?—"we drank the long, long Eastern day out together," and so on. For another, I know a good workman when I see him. That camel-kit you made for my desert-tours, Paul, is as sound as ever. And for a third—which to a man of my habits is most important—that Greek doctor you recommended me is the only one who understands my tumid liver.'

He passed a cup of all but unmixed wine, which Paulus handed to Petrus, whose lips were flaky white at the corners.

'But your trouble,' the Prefect went on, 'will come from your own people. Jerusalem never forgives. They'll get you run in on the charge of *laesa majestatis* soon or late.'

'Who knows better than I?' said Petrus. 'And the decision we *all* have taken about our love-feasts may unite Hebrew and Greek against us. As I told you, Prefect, we are asking Christian Greeks not to make the feasts difficult for Christian Hebrews by eating meat that has not been lawfully killed. (Our way is much more wholesome, anyhow.) Still, we may get round that. But there's *one* vital point. Some of our Greek Christians bring food to the love-feasts that they've bought from your priests, after your sacrifices have been offered. That we can't allow.'

Paulus turned to Valens imperiously.

'You mean they buy Altar-scraps,' the boy said. 'But only the very poor do it; and it's chiefly block-trimmings. The sale's a perquisite of the Altar-butchers. They wouldn't like its being stopped.'

'Permit separate tables for Hebrew and Greek, as I once said,' Petrus spoke suddenly.

'That would end in separate churches. There shall be but *one* Church,' Paulus spoke over his shoulder, and the words fell like rods. 'You think there may be trouble, Valens?'

'My uncle——' Valens began.

'No, no!' the Prefect laughed. 'Singon Street Markets are your Syria. Let's hear what our Legate thinks of his Province.'

Valens flushed and tried to pull his wits together.

'Primarily,' he said, 'it's pig, I suppose. Hebrews hate pork.'

'Quite right, too. Catch *me* eating pig east the Adriatic! *I* don't want to die of worms. Give me a young Sabine tush-ripe boar! I have spoken!'

Serga mixed himself another raw cup and took some pickled Lake fish to bring out the flavour.

'But, still,' Petrus leaned forward like a deaf man, 'if we admitted Hebrew and Greek Christians to separate tables we should escape——'

'Nothing, except salvation,' said Paulus. 'We have broken with the whole Law of Moses. We live in and through and by our God only. Else we are nothing. What is the sense of harking back to the Law at meal-times? Whom do we deceive? Jerusalem? Rome? The God? You yourself have eaten with Gentiles! You yourself have said——'

'One says more than one means when one is carried away,' Petrus answered, and his face worked again.

'This time you will say precisely what is meant,' Paulus spoke between his teeth. 'We will keep the Churches *one*—in and through the Lord. You dare not deny this?'

'I dare nothing—the God knows! But I have denied Him. . . . I denied Him. . . . And He said—He said I was the Rock on which His Church should stand.'

'*I* will see that it stands, and yet not I——' Paulus' voice dropped again. 'To-morrow you will speak to the one Church of the one Table the world over.'

'That's *your* business,' said the Prefect. 'But I warn you again, it's your own people who will make you trouble.'

Paulus rose to say farewell, but in the act he staggered, put his hand to his forehead and, as Valens steered him to a divan, collapsed in the grip of that deadly Syrian malaria which strikes like a snake. Valens, having suffered, called to his rooms for his heavy travelling-fur. His girl, whom he had bought in Constantinople a few months before, fetched it. Petrus tucked it awkwardly round the shivering little figure; the Prefect ordered lime juice and hot water, and Paulus thanked them and apologised, while his teeth rattled on the cup.

'Better to-day than to-morrow,' said the Prefect. 'Drink—sweat—and sleep here the night. Shall I send for my doctor?'

But Paulus said that the fit would pass naturally, and as soon as he could stand he insisted on going away with Petrus, late though it was, to prepare their announcement to the Church.

'Who was that big, clumsy man?' his girl asked Valens as she took up the fur. 'He made more noise than the small one, who was really suffering.'

'He's a priest of the new College by the Little Circus, dear. He believes, uncle told me, that he once denied his God, Who, he says, died for him.'

She halted in the moonlight, the glossy jackal skins over her arm.

'Does he? *My* God bought me from the dealers like a horse. Too much, too, he paid. Didn't he? 'Fess, thou?'

'No, thee!' emphatically.

'But I wouldn't deny *my* God—living or dead! ... Oh—but *not* dead! My God's going to live—for me. Live—live Thou, my heart's blood, for ever!'

It would have been better had Paulus and Petrus not left the Prefect's house so late; for the rumour in the city, as the Prefect knew, and as the long conference seemed to confirm, was that Caesar's own Secretary of State in Rome was, through Paulus, arranging for a general defilement of the Hebrew with the Greek Christians, and that after this had been effected, by promiscuous eating of unlawful foods, all Jews would be lumped together as Christians—members, that is, of a mere free-thinking sect instead of the very particular and trouble-some 'Nation of Jews within the Empire.' Eventually, the story went, they would lose their rights as Roman citizens, and could then be sold on any slave-stand.

'Of course,' Serga explained to Valens next day, 'that has been put about by the Jerusalem Synagogue. Our Antioch Jews aren't clever enough. Do you see their game? Petrus is a defiler of the Hebrew nation. If he is cut down to-night by some properly primed young zealot so much the better.'

'He won't be,' said Valens. 'I'm looking after him.'

"Hope so. But, if he isn't knifed,' Serga went on, 'they'll try to work up city riots on the grounds that, when all the Jews have lost their civil rights, he'll set up as a sort of King of the Christians.'

'At Antioch? In the present year of Rome? That's crazy, Uncle.'

'*Every* crowd is crazy. What else do we draw pay for? But, listen. Post a Mounted Police patrol at the back of the Little Circus. Use 'em to keep the people moving when the congregation comes out. Post two of your men in the Porch of their College itself. Tell Paulus and Petrus to wait there with them, till the streets are clear. Then fetch 'em both over here. Don't hit till you have to. Hit hard *before* the stones fly. Don't get my little horses knocked about more than you can help, and—look out for "Pickled Fish"!'

Knowing his own quarter, it seemed to Valens as he went on duty that evening, that his uncle's precautions had been excessive. The Christian Church, of course, was full, and a large crowd waited outside for word of the decision about the feasts. Most of them seemed to be Christians of sorts, but there was an element of gesticulating Antiochene loafers, and like all crowds they amused themselves with popular songs while they waited. Things went smoothly, till a group of Christians raised a rather explosive hymn, which ran

'Enthroned above Caesar and Judge of the Earth!
We wait on Thy coming—oh tarry not long!
As the Kings of the Sunrise
Drew sword at Thy Birth,
So we arm in this midnight of insult and wrong!'

'Yes—and if one of their fish-stalls is bumped over by a camel—it's *my* fault!' said Valens. 'Now they've started it!'

Sure enough, voices on the outskirts broke into 'Pickled Fish,' but before Valens could speak, they were suppressed by someone crying:

'Quiet there, or you'll get your pickle before your fish.'

It was close on twilight when a cry rose from within the packed Church, and its congregation breasted out into the crowd. They all talked about the new orders for their love-feasts, most of them agreeing that they were sensible and easy. They agreed, too, that Petrus (Paulus did not seem to have taken much part in the debate) had spoken like one inspired, and they were all extremely proud of being Christians. Some of them began to link arms across the alley, and strike into the 'Enthroned above Caesar' chorus.

'And *this*, I think,' Valens called to the young Commandant of the Mounted Patrol, 'is where we'll begin to steer 'em home. Oh! And "Let night also have her well-earned hymn," as Uncle 'ud say.'

There filed out from behind the Little Circus four blaring trumpets, a standard, and a dozen Mounted Police. Their wise little grey Arabs sidled, passaged, shouldered, and nosed softly into the mob, as though they wanted petting, while the trumpets deafened the narrow street. An open square, near by, eased the pressure before long. Here the Patrol broke into fours, and gridironed it, saluting the images of the Gods at each corner and in the centre. People stopped, as usual, to watch how cleverly the incense was cast down over the withers into the spouting cressets; children reached up to pat horses which they said they knew; family groups re-found each other in the smoky dusk; hawkers offered cooked suppers; and soon the crowd melted into the main traffic avenues. Valens went over to the Church porch, where Petrus and Paulus waited between his lictors.

'That was well done,' Paulus began.

'How's the fever?' Valens asked.

'I was spared for to-day. I think, too, that by The Blessing we have carried our point.'

'Good hearing! My uncle bids me say you are welcome at his house.'

'That is always a command,' said Paulus, with a quick down-country gesture. 'Now that this day's burden is lifted, it will be a delight.'

Petrus joined up like a weary ox. Valens greeted him, but he did not answer.

'Leave him alone,' Paulus whispered. 'The virtue has gone out of me— him—for the while.' His own face looked pale and drawn.

The street was empty, and Valens took a short cut through an alley, where light ladies leaned out of windows and laughed. The three strolled easily together, the lictors behind them, and far off they heard the trumpets of the Night Horse saluting some statue of a Caesar, which marked the end of their round. Paulus was telling Valens how the whole Roman Empire would be changed by what the Christians had agreed to about their love-feasts, when an impudent little Jew boy stole up behind them, playing 'Pickled Fish' on some sort of desert bag-pipe.

'Can't you stop that young pest, one of you?' Valens asked laughing. 'You shan't be mocked on this great night of yours, Paulus.'

The lictors turned back a few paces, and shook a torch at the brat, but he retreated and drew them on. Then they heard Paulus shout, and when they hurried back, found Valens prostrate and coughing—his blood on the fringe of the kneeling Paul's robe. Petrus stooped, waving a helpless hand above them.

'Someone ran out from behind that well-head. He stabbed him as he ran, and ran on. Listen!' said Paulus.

But there was not even the echo of a footfall for clue, and the Jew boy had vanished like a bat. Said Valens from the ground

'Home! Quick! I have it!'

They tore a shutter out of a shop-front, lifted and carried him, while Paulus walked beside. They set him down in the lighted inner courtyard of the Prefect's house, and a lictor hurried for the Prefect's physician.

Paulus watched the boy's face, and, as Valens shivered a little, called to the girl to fetch last night's fur rug. She brought it, laid the head on her breast, and cast herself beside Valens.

'It isn't bad. It doesn't bleed much. So it *can't* be bad—can it?' she repeated. Valens' smile reassured her, till the Prefect came and recognised the deadly upward thrust under the ribs. He turned on the Hebrews.

'To-morrow you will look for where your Church stood,' said he.

Valens lifted the hand that the girl was not kissing.

'No—no!' he gasped. 'The Cilician did it! For his brother! He said it.'

'The Cilician you let go to save these Christians because I——?' Valens signed to his uncle that it was so, while the girl begged him to steal strength from her till the doctor should come.

'Forgive me,' said Serga to Paulus. 'None the less I wish your God in Hades once for all. . . . But what am I to write his mother? Can't either of you two talking creatures tell me what I'm to tell his mother?'

'What has *she* to do with him?' the slave-girl cried. 'He is mine—mine! I testify before all Gods that he bought me! I am his. He is mine.'

'We can deal with the Cilician and his friends later,' said one of the lictors. ' But what now?'

For some reason, the man, though used to butcher-work, looked at Petrus.

'Give him drink and wait,' said Petrus. 'I have—seen such a wound.' Valens drank and a shade of colour came to him. He motioned the Prefect to stoop.

'What is it? Dearest of lives, what troubles?'

'The Cilician and his friends. . . . Don't be hard on them. . . . They get worked up. . . . They don't know what they are doing. . . . Promise!'

'This is not I, child. It is the Law.'

''No odds. You're Father's brother. . . . Men make laws—not Gods. . . . Promise! . . . It's finished with me.'

Valens' head eased back on its yearning pillow.

Petrus stood like one in a trance. The tremor left his face as he repeated

'"Forgive them, for they know not what they do." Heard you *that*, Paulus? He, a heathen and an idolator, said it!'

'I heard. What hinders now that we should baptize him?' Paulus answered promptly.

Petrus stared at him as though he had come up out of the sea.

'Yes,' he said at last. 'It is the little maker of tents. . . . And what does he *now*—command?'

Paulus repeated the suggestion.

Painfully, that other raised the palsied hand that he had once held up in a hall to deny a charge.

'Quiet!' said he. 'Think you that one who has spoken Those Words needs such as *we* are to certify him to any God?'

Paulus cowered before the unknown colleague, vast and commanding, revealed after all these years.

'As you please—as you please,' he stammered, overlooking the blasphemy. 'Moreover there is the concubine.'

The girl did not heed, for the brow beneath her lips was chilling, even as she called on her God who had bought her at a price that he should not die but live.

The Disciple

He that hath a Gospel,
To loose upon Mankind,
Though he serve it utterly—
Body, soul, and mind—
Though he go to Calvary
Daily for its gain—
It is His Disciple
Shall make his labour vain.

He that bath a Gospel,
For all earth to own—
Though he etch it on the steel,
Or carve it on the stone—
Not to be misdoubted
Through the after-days—
It is His Disciple
Shall read it many ways.

It is His Disciple
(Ere Those Bones are dust)
Who shall change the Charter
Who shall split the Trust—
Amplify distinctions,
Rationalise the Claim,
Preaching that the Master
Would have done the same.

It is His Disciple
Who shall tell us how
Much the Master would have scrapped
Had he lived till now—
What he would have modified
Of what he said before— It is His Disciple
Shall do this and more. . . .

He that hath a Gospel
Whereby Heaven is won
(Carpenter, or Cameleer,
Or Maya's dreaming son),
Many swords shall pierce Him,
Mingling blood with gall;
But His Own Disciple
Shall wound Him worst of all!

Thoughts on The Church that was at Antioch.

It is sometimes difficult to know which to admire most about a Kipling story, the plot, the style, or the emotions and thoughts to which they give rise. 'The Church that was at Antioch' is a prime example.

The Biblical Antioch, now Antakya in Turkey on the border with Syria, was the city from which Paul and Barnabas, his deputy, left on their travels throughout the Mediterranean. And it was the place where the term, 'Christians' was first used to describe Christ's disciples. (Acts, 11.26.) The action takes place around the year 50 A.D. when the emperor Claudius was on the throne. Shortly after that time the Roman historian Suetonius recorded that, 'Since the Jews constantly made disturbances at the instigation of Chrestus, he expelled them from Rome.' Historians cannot agree on the meaning of this statement, but it was certainly not good news for the Jews.

Ricketts suggested that this story was 'at heart deeply anti-Semitic', but this probably reflects no more than Kipling's attitude to the Zionist problems then being faced by Britain in the Mandated territory of Palestine.

Commentators have been quick to point out the resemblance between the young roman officer (whose name,' Valens', translates as strong or capable) and the ideal British subaltern of the type the author so much admired. Valens' religion, the Eastern cult of Mithras, was on its way to replacing the primitive pantheism or emperor worship that were then the only options for a Roman soldier.

Chief among the Christians who figure in this story are Peter and Paul, or Saul to give him his Roman name. (The presence of the historical Peter at Antioch is not mentioned in Acts, though it is in Galatians.) Kipling had always been fascinated by the quick witted Paul who, as pointed out in the accompanying poem,' The Disciple', goes on to convert an obscure Jewish sect into a world church. But, in this tale the simpler, more emotionally profound Peter is the greater man.

The crux of the plot is the assassination of Valens – at the hand, be it noted, of a man he had already forgiven for an earlier attempt on his life. The dying officer implores his uncle, the Prefect, 'Don't be hard on [the assassin and his friends]...They don't know what they are doing.' Hearing this, Paul at once proposes that Valens should be baptized, only to be stopped by Peter's thunderous intervention, 'Think you that one who has spoken Those Words needs such as we are to certify him to any God?' This is Kipling's clearest statement of the transcendence of common humanity over dogma, just as elsewhere throughout the story he makes plain his view that virtue is not the sole prerogative of any particular faith.

The author characteristically reserved the last words for the story's least regarded character, the slave girl whom Valens had bought as a mere concubine, but who had come to love him. Her plea that her god (and saviour?) 'should not die, but live' is ignored by all the 'important' men present, but the strength of her passion shines out from the page. Was she intended to be the Mary Magdalene to Valens' Christ?

The definitive commentary on this wonderful story is Dr David Sergeant's article in the March 2009 edition of the Kipling Journal, which deserves to be read in full.

Kipling may have written tales technically superior to this ('The Eye of Allah' and 'The Wish House', for example), and as profound ('The Gardener'), but there is none that touches the present editor more deeply.

SELECT BIBLIOGRAPHY

Allen, Charles. *Kipling Sahib. India and the Making of Rudyard Kipling.* 2008.

Birkenhead, Lord. *Rudyard Kipling.* 1978.

Bodelson, Carl. *'Aspects of Kipling's Art'.* 1964.

Carrington, Charles. *Rudyard Kipling, his Life and Work.* 1955.

Cornell. *Kipling in India.* 1966.

Dobrée, Bonamy. *Rudyard Kipling. Realist and Fabulist.* 1967.

Eliot, T.S., *A Choice of Kipling's Verse.* 1942.

Gilmour, David. *The Long Recessional. The Imperial Life of Rudyard Kipling.* 2002.

Kipling, Rudyard, *Something of Myself.* 1937.

Lycett, Andrew. *Rudyard Kipling.* 1999.

Mason, Philip. *Kipling, The Glass, the Shadow and the Fire.* 1975.

Maugham, W. Somerset. *A Choice of Kipling's Prose.* 1952.

Page, Norman. *A Kipling Companion.* 1984.

Pinney, Thomas. *Rudyard Kipling. Something of Myself and other Autobiographical Writings.* 2013.

Ricketts, Harry. *The Unforgiving Minute: A life of Rudyard Kipling.* 1999.

Tompkins, J.M.S. *The Art of Rudyard Kipling.* 1959.

Wilson, Angus. *The Strange Ride of Rudyard Kipling.* 1977.

Wilson, Edmund. *The Kipling that Nobody Read.* 1941.

Printed in Great Britain
by Amazon.co.uk, Ltd.,
Marston Gate.